LEGENDARY HEROES OF AN ENCHANTED PAST

QUEEN MEAVE—the flaming-haired warrior queen of Eire. She was beloved by all who beheld her until her bright dreams of conquest turned into black visions conjured up by an evil enchanter.

FERGUS MACROGH—a mighty eviled Chieftain. His love pledged him forever to Queen Meave . . . but an old blood oath bound him to the enemy.

CALATIN—the Queen's High Druid adviser. He was a magician who had her trust and who could unleash unknown terrors against the armies of Ulster.

CUCULAIN—Ireland's greatest hero, descended from a mysterious Celtic race. Superhuman strength spurred him to challenge an army single-handedly.

A STORM
UPON ULSTER

Kenneth C. Flint

BANTAM BOOKS
TORONTO · NEW YORK · LONDON · SYDNEY · AUCKLAND

A STORM UPON ULSTER
A Bantam Book / April 1981
2nd printing . . . March 1985

Map by David Perry.

ISBN 0-553-24710-7

Published simultaneously in the United States and Canada

PRINTED IN THE UNITED STATES OF AMERICA

H   11 10 9 8 7 6 5 4 3 2

For Judy and Devin

ACKNOWLEDGEMENTS

The legend of the war for the bull of Cuailgne is drawn from *Cuchulain of Muirthemne* by Lady Gregory, first published in 1902 by John Murray; and from the *History of Ireland* by Standish James O'Grady, first published in London, 1878-80.

The author also gratefully acknowledges the assistance of Mark Lampe, whose research and editing skills made this work possible.

CONTENTS

BOOK THREE:
THE WALL OF BRASS

BOOK FOUR:
PATH OF DESTRUCTION

BOOK FIVE:
THE COMING OF ULSTER

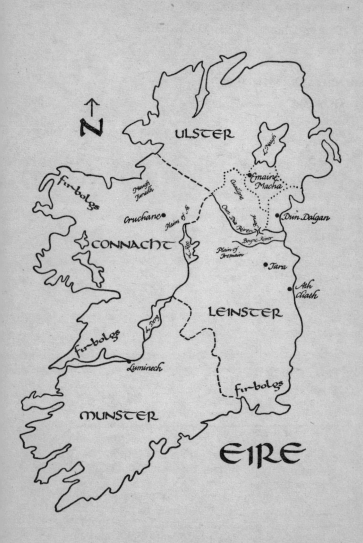

PROLOGUE

"Cuculain!"

The voice called to him, forcing its way into his uneasy sleep.

He dreamed of a tree whose leaves glittered silver in the bright sunlight as it grew and spread and bore strange fruit. But the calling of his name seemed to blight it, for the fruit rotted on the tree and fell, and the leaves tarnished to black and fluttered down to leave only bare, gnarled branches.

"Cuculain!" said the voice again, soft and bright as a child's laugh, sorrowful and insistent as death. This time it awoke him fully and he sat up in the bed to peer around him at the room. The full moon threw a shaft of light through the single window and lit even the chamber's corners. They were empty.

The voice seemed to have come from the window. He lifted the cover and climbed carefully out of the bed, not wishing to disturb his wife who slept peacefully on. The sharp chill of the air tingled against his skin as he crossed the room to the window and looked out.

Below him the Dun Dalgan cliffs dropped sheer away to the sea. At their base the great waves of the Eastern Ocean crashed against the rocks with an endless rhythm. The moon's brilliance struck the sea spray and made the rising peaks of water titanic blossoms of light that bloomed only an instant before exploding into fragments on the cliff face.

It was only the sound of the waves he heard, he told himself sleepily, and moved back to the bed. He sat down upon it, but looked up in alarm as something caused the light from the window to suddenly flicker and dim.

A tall, slender woman in a long, gray cloak stood in the

shaft of moonlight. She seemed barely past childhood, her face smooth, her hair a flow of white-gold. Her skin glowed with a subtle inward illumination as a banked fire glows with the deep-buried embers. She seemed even to emanate a warmth that drove the chill of the sea from the room.

In confusion, Cuculain looked from her to the still form of his wife.

"It is all right," the woman assured him in a voice as fine as a strand of thinly drawn silver wire. "Your wife will not awaken. It was only you I came to see."

"And who are you?" he asked.

"Faythleen, I am. Prophetess of Tara."

He understood, then. She was of the Sidhe, that ancient race who seemed more of the air than of the earth. But the realization only deepened his confusion. The Sidhe seldom came out from their hidden places to speak directly with men.

"What is it you want?"

"You must go out of the Province of Ulster for a time," she answered. "You must leave your home."

The words of the Prophetess were without tone, but still they carried some deeper meaning to him. Some hidden fear, it was, that chilled him more than the sea air.

"Is something to happen here?" he asked on impulse. "If so, I'll not be leaving. I am a warrior of the Red Branch."

"Be easy in your mind. Nothing which you can help will be happening here." She spoke with quiet assurance and he did not doubt her. The Sidhe did not lie.

"Then what is it I am to do?" he asked.

"I wish you only to come to Tara. A small enough thing for you. I must see you there in a fortnight's time. When you come, you will understand the reasons why."

His mind was still hazy with sleep and unable to clear itself. He could find no will to argue her strange request.

"I will come," he agreed.

She leaned toward him, bringing a scent of warm spring with her. A hand slid forward out of the folds of the cloak and gripped his lower arm. It was a long, slim hand, but it gripped him with a strength that surprised him, the delicate fingers pressing deeply into his flesh.

"You will remember?" she said.

"I will remember," he replied.

A sudden, overwhelming weariness seized him, then, and when she released his arm, he lay back on his bed and closed his eyes.

"Remember," said the voice again, drifting away to be lost in the thunder of the waves.

When he awoke again, the dawn sun lit the room. He felt he had dreamed a strange dream that had faded almost away. But something drew him to look down at his arm, and there he found five marks where a hand whose strength no mortal knew had gripped him.

He remembered.

Book One

THE BULL OF CUAILGNE

Chapter One
MEAVE

The broad Plains of Ai shimmered with a green glory beneath the clear sun of early spring. The wealth of Eire lay openly revealed in them. It thrust itself up from the earth in the lush grasses, thick with new growth, that covered all the fields. It wandered freely in the cattle herds, swelled with spring calves, that fed on those grasses and filled the plains to the distant hills.

Two chariots sat in the heart of those plains, amidst the richness. Their horses grazed quietly while the man and woman who were their drivers examined the cattle about them.

"They are a fine spring herd," said Queen Meave with satisfaction.

"They are that," said the young man beside her, "and I've seen few finer springs in all my life."

His pleasure fairly beamed from him as he spoke, and Meave could not help but smile broadly in return. His open exuberance seemed a natural response to the grand day, and she was feeling the lift of it herself.

Hard it was to be a queen when the air was fresh with the scent of new grass and the sky was the cloudless blue so rare in Eire but in its brief spring. Not so many years before she would have played in the fields on such a day, chasing the long-legged calves and climbing the low hills as the energy pent in by the cold rains of winter was released.

Indeed, she seemed far from a queen now as she stood in her chariot, her lithe form relaxed, her head tilted back to feel the sun's heat. Though past her thirtieth year, the vigor and freshness of youth were with her yet. The lines of her face were clean and bold, and the brilliant sunlight struck flickering sparks in her flaming red-gold hair as the gentle breezes stirred and lifted it.

"It is a mighty job you've done with the herds," the young man remarked.

His words recalled her. She was no longer a girl of the forths and fens. She was a queen, and her pleasures in life were of a different kind. The pull of spring and of the past was brought firmly to heel.

"The work here is your own, Fardia, not mine," she told the chieftain honestly. "Your Firbolgs have worked magic with these beasts."

"There's many would say the reason for that lies in our being beasts ourselves," he replied. He spoke with a smile, but his words were tinged with bitter truth, as both of them well knew.

Still, Fardia himself would have provided little evidence for such reasoning. The young warrior was not a common man of his race. The Firbolg warriors were heavy of body and coarse featured, given to thick beards and long hair that went unfastened and unkempt. In contrast, Fardia's clean-shaven face revealed quite pleasant features, while his dark hair was combed back and caught in a golden brooch. He was well proportioned in shape and smooth limbed, carrying himself casually erect with a warrior's unconscious pride in his own power.

Very young he was, even for a warrior of Connacht, being barely past twenty years in age. But he had fought for many of those years, gaining renown in Eire and in Espan across the Southern Sea. Now he was a chieftain of the Firbolgs and a swiftly growing influence among all their tribes.

It was because of this last fact that Meave's voice was grave when she spoke to him again. She needed this man and his savage people. She needed to keep his loyalty.

"Fardia, you must believe there's no ill feeling in me for your people. There is much you know that we would benefit in learning."

"Aye," he said, smiling, "that's true enough. But you'll have need of many years to learn what we know. It was the land itself taught us . . . and our blood is in the very stones and trees of it!"

"I understand. Your people held the land for a long time before we came."

"No one can hold it," he corrected. "We wandered it, yes. We lived with it and learned some of its secrets. Yet, Eire is a fierce and a lonely mistress that always holds danger for its lover. The land made wanderers of us, divided our tribes and left us unable to stand against the strength of you Milesians when you came. It was only that made us your subjects."

She heard a colder tone in this. A hint of something deeper.

"Would you wish to change that?"

"The druids say my people labored as slaves before they came to Eire. We've a hatred of bondage that lies deep in the heart. We would be free. . . ."

He said this last reflectively, then stopped abruptly and looked toward the queen, as if suddenly remembering her presence.

"Ah, Queen, I meant nothing serious by my words," he assured her with obvious embarrassment. "Our freedom would never be at your own cost. There's much you've done for us already. No, we'll earn our rights . . . and slowly, if we must."

She smiled. "It won't be slow with such as you about."

The praise only deepened the young warrior's sense of modesty, and he hastened to shift the subject from himself.

"Well, tell me now, have you seen enough of cattle for one day? Would you be wishing to return to the dun?"

"Yes, I think so," she answered, looking about once more on the quiet scene. "I can't be forever riding the plains and breathing this spring air like some unburdened child."

But even as she said this, the spirit of the day assailed her senses once again and, this time, as if to counter the solemn nature of their talk, she let the spirit win. It was intoxication of a kind, a dropping of the sobering limits of her station. Suddenly she felt only the need to do something, to find some way of saluting the spring.

"Fardia," she said, "I'll wager you can't make it back to the dun before I do!"

He was startled by the challenge, and by the note of

youthful caprice in her voice. He was uncertain how to react until he saw the glowing of her face and the sparkling in her eye as she lifted the horses' reins in anticipation. For that moment they were but two young people, matched well in daring and in skill, and so he accepted it.

"I'll race you," he responded boldly, "but it will be no easy run you get from me!"

"Then be about it!" she cried.

Together the two chariots leaped forward as the teams obeyed their drivers' commands. The vehicles were for pleasure only and lightly built, and the powerful animals pulled them along as if nothing at all held them back. The racers flew over the broad plains. They met and vaulted low walls and narrow ravines. They skirted rocks and wheeled about alarmed cattle by a reckless margin, and still the drivers urged their steeds to even greater efforts.

Fardia laughed aloud at the pace, so exhilarating it was, but his sideways glance at Meave showed him an opponent grimly intent, crouched low over her reins, calling commands to her team in a clear, hard voice.

Ahead of the racing chariots, against the distant gray-green hills, a darker mound began to show. As they moved toward it, it seemed to rise and swell rapidly until its presence dominated the Plains of Ai and structures became visible upon its flattened crest.

The hill was Dun Cruchane, chief city of Connacht, raised years before by Meave's husband, King Aileel. Then it had been but a simple fortress, an artificially built mound whose brow was crowned by a round, timber palace surrounded by a high palisade. Now Connacht's rise in power was reflected in the new buildings within the fortress walls and the growing town which clustered close without.

Meave and Fardia sped toward this goal without a slowing in the pace. For long no watcher could have called a leader. The four animals ran as if harnessed side by side in the same traces, their chariots almost touching hubs. But soon a change was evident. The steady run began to tell on the horses of the queen, while Fardia's, bred and trained by Firbolg masters, went on untiring. Slowly he began to pull ahead.

While caught up in the race, Meave could not ignore

the wearing of her team and was quick enough to judge her chances lost. With a sign to Fardia she reined in, still a good distance from the limits of the town.

Fardia circled and pulled up beside her, his expression purposely neutral as he tried to judge how she had taken the loss.

"A fair win, Fardia," she said simply.

"Thank you, my Queen," he answered with relief. "I think that now we'd best walk them in to cool them."

They drove on slowly and in silence for a time. Then Meave smiled ruefully at him and shook her head.

"You know, it seems to me it was the horses and not our skill that decided this. My team was no match for yours."

"And glad I am of that!" said Fardia. "For had your animals been as good as mine, I'd likely be the one left behind."

"Ah, but then nothing is solved. We might never know which driver is the better."

"But we may," he said knowingly. "My Queen, you've many fine animals for your chariots of war, but they're bred to size, not speed. No driver with your skill should be without racing horses, and my people have animals the like of which can be found nowhere else. Let me give you a pair I have in mind, both tall and proud and with a fire blazing in their black eyes. They'd suit you well."

"I'm certain now your people will achieve success with a poet's tongue like yours to speak for them. I'll accept your offer gladly."

Again Fardia flushed with pleasure and embarrassment, and for a moment his youthfulness was very evident in him.

"Good, my Queen. Tomorrow you will have a team like no one in Connacht . . ." he paused and smiled ". . . except, perhaps, for me. The next time we race, we will be matched for certain!"

"A bond I'll hold you to," she said. "But there must be no gifts. These horses must be bought."

He tried to protest, but she stopped him.

"No, Fardia. Some token amount at least must change hands, or else I'll not feel the animals are truly mine."

He nodded. "All right, my Queen. I understand."

By this time they had entered the town about the dun's base and they drove up its broad street toward the fortress gates. At the town's outer edge they passed only the small, stone huts of the many workers who provided service to the dun, but nearer the palisades these huts were replaced by the larger roundhouses of higher ranks. As Connacht had grown in influence, so had the number of these residences grown, for more and more people of means sought to be near this seat of rule. Now land near to the walls was very dear, and the structures had begun to crowd upon one another, seeming to shoulder each other away as did their owners when seeking an audience with the king and queen.

The two passed many people as they drove, but these only waved or nodded as Meave passed. There was no riotous celebration at her every appearance, for she was often about in the town and well known to everyone. So, thus unhindered, they passed on through the gates of the dun, left always open in daylight, and entered the Royal Enclosure itself. There they pulled up before low stables built against the inside of the walls. Attendants moved to hold Meave's steeds while she climbed from the chariot.

"Take special care with the horses," she told a gray-bearded overseer. "They've been well run today." She noted, then, that Fardia still stood in his vehicle.

"What are you doing there?" she asked. "Climb down. Here, someone, take his horses."

None of the attendants moved. They only looked uncertainly toward the gray-bearded man.

"The Firbolg's, my Queen?" the overseer asked, distaste evident in his words.

Meave flared. "Yes, the Firbolg's! And now! Take his horses and give them the same care you give mine."

There was no threat. She needed to make none. It was in the very tone of her voice. Five men leaped at once to take the Firbolg's horses.

But still Fardia hesitated.

"My Queen, perhaps I should not go. . . ."

"Fardia," she said firmly, "I've business with you. Come along."

With great reluctance the young warrior climbed from his chariot and released it into the attendants' care. He and Meave then started up the slope toward the Tec Meadcuarta, the immense gathering hall of the dun and the center of its life.

At its wide doors Fardia paused once again, and Meave looked quizzically at him.

"For one so quick to race not long ago, you've certainly a slowness on you now."

"My Queen, you're not meaning for me to go in?"

"And why not?" she demanded. "Are you afraid of my company?"

"The opposite was more in my mind, my Queen. Few of the Milesians share your friendship with the Firbolgs. We've just seen the evidence of that."

"More reason, then, for me to welcome you," she said with decisiveness. "Come, let's go in."

Though as a warrior Fardia had faced many terrors unafraid, he felt a strange kind of apprehension when he passed the threshold and entered the cavernous space beyond. The Firbolgs were a subject race and had no part in the running of the province. Even Fardia, a chieftan, had been but twice within the dun and never in the great hall. As it opened before him, he was awed by its size.

From the top of an outer wall of thick logs set upright to form a wide circle, roof timbers rose toward a central pillar. Much of the vast area thus enclosed was filled with rows of low tables; enough to easily serve hundreds of the warriors of Connacht. At this hour of the day, however, the hall was empty save for a few servants at work sweeping the stone floor, and a few sleeping dogs who impeded their moving brooms.

Meave and Fardia started toward the room's farther end, stepping over a massive wolfhound who merely opened one incurious eye to note their passing. Beyond the middle of the tec and its immense, central pillar, they reached and circled a broad fire-pit of stone, deeply sunken in the floor. Here, and for more days of the year than not, a fire blazed of such size as to warm the entire hall. Today, for the first time since late fall, the warmth of the weather allowed that fire to be put out, and several men labored to clear the pit of the ashes that had filled it to its edge.

The fire-pit formed a barrier of sorts between the rulers

and those ruled. Once past it, they left the section devoted
to the warriors and entered the domain of the sovereigns.
There the dais of the king and queen rose waist-high
above the floor and, from the couches of state that sat
upon it, those two could see about the entire room and be
heard by all if they should speak aloud.

"We'll talk in the sunroom," Meave told Fardia. "Today we'll have a fine view of the plains."

She led the way toward a wooden staircase on one side
of the dais that mounted to a balcony along the outer
wall. As she went up, the warrior followed her at once.
He made no further protests, for a boyish curiosity had
fully seized him, and he could only look about in wonder
at this edifice of power.

When they reached the balcony, he found that behind
it was a high room running across the upper-rear portion
of the tec. At least, Fardia assumed it did. At the moment
they entered it he found he could really see very little, for
the room was dark and quite filled with smoke. The young
warrior could scarcely breathe without coughing.

"What is happening?" said Meave and moved away
from him to disappear into the gray cloud.

In a moment there was a rattle of metal against wood,
and light appeared as she thrust open broad shutters to
let in the day.

"It is too fine outside to be shut up here," Meave said
chidingly.

Her tone confused Fardia, for he certainly agreed with
her. But, before he could reply, another voice spoke up
from the smoke.

"Fine for you, perhaps," it said in a thin, complaining
tone.

As the smoke began to clear from the room, Fardia
could dimly see the speaker, crouched by a small peat fire
that was vented, but only in part, through a brass-edged
leather chimney hung above.

Meave moved along the outer wall, throwing open all
the windows to air the room and bring in the sunshine.
Finally Fardia was able to see the figure clearly, and
barely managed to suppress an exclamation of surprise. It
was Aileel himself, High-King of all Connacht, who
squatted on a tiny stool and shivered before a tiny fire.

"The day is a fine one for us all," Meave insisted with good cheer. "It is bright and warm."

"No more for me," Aileel replied. "The light is only a dim one to my eyes, and the sun cannot drive out the winter cold that has settled itself in my bones."

"That I'll not believe," Meave said quickly, glancing toward the young Firbolg. But there was no hiding the truth in the king's words, and she could read the shock in Fardia's eyes.

He had never seen the Ard-Rie closely. Those recent times Aileel had shown himself outside the dun, he had been but a distant fluttering of cloth and flash of jewels. Now, divested of the trappings of a king, he was but a wasted, shriveled old man whose near end was prophesized in the death's head he already wore.

Fardia looked from the king to Meave and assayed her with new eyes. So now he knew all the stories were true! She it was who ruled Connacht, and she it was who in these past few years had extended its powers across Eire from the Southern Sea to the very borders of Ulster.

And this same woman he had raced today with the reckless abandon of a child!

Meave met Fardia's gaze, then, and he saw in her expression a plea for support. He recognized her need to comfort this failing man, and he hastened to give her his aid.

"My King," he began, trying to assume a hearty tone, "you look to me now as you did when I saw you as a boy. A fine, proud warrior you seemed, striding through our village in victory."

Meave nodded and smiled gratefully, but the words had a different effect on Aileel. He started violently and swiveled himself on the stool to face the young warrior. As he did so Fardia realized the reason for his astonishment, for the deeply sunken eyes which peered toward him were only a faint glitter dimly visible in the black sockets.

"Who is that there with you, Meave?" the king demanded querulously. He pulled himself upright and tugged his cloak about him to hide his frail limbs. "You should have told me you were not alone."

"It is young Fardia," she replied.

"What, the Firbolg?" he said.

Fardia feared some hostility from the king but, once more, he was surprised. Aileel relaxed and smiled with real pleasure.

"Glad I am to see you here. Many a Firbolg warrior did I fight when I first came to Connacht, and never have I fought better."

"I have heard the same praise given you by my tribe," Fardia told him truthfully.

At that the king laughed, and a ring of youthful vigor could be heard in it.

"Meave tells no tales when she speaks of you," he said. "She has told me what work your people are doing with our herds."

"They are, indeed," said Meave with satisfaction. She went to a window and gazed out across the plains below. "And, Aileel, it is a fine thing to look out from here and see broad Ai so filled with our herds."

"That's your doing as much as ours, my Queen," said Fardia. "It was you who asked our help, and you who had the white bull brought from Alban. He's the cause for many of those strong, healthy calves."

From where she stood, Meave could see the giant animal Fardia had mentioned in its stable close within the palisade. A powerful bull he was, but Meave noted with amusement that today he must have felt the pleasure of the spring as did she, for he stood quiet and content beneath the stroking brushes of his attendants.

"He is a fine bull," she told her husband.

"I believe what you say," Aileel answered with good humor. "There's little else you've talked about since his arrival. I am glad you find him worth the price."

"It is far more than just his value in new blood for our herds," she explained, trying to help him see the reasons for her pleasure. "He is a symbol of our new power . . . of the new strength we will bring to all of Eire."

"Then, a poor enough symbol he is, my Queen," said a quiet voice.

Meave turned from the window and found that a man had entered the sunroom. She had not heard him come, but there he was, standing at the top of the main stairway. At his sudden appearance she shivered slightly, as from an unexpected draught of chill air.

Chapter Two
THE ENCHANTER

"Calatin," said Meave. "You frightened me."

"That is often my purpose, my Queen," said the man in a voice soft and slow and filled with mild amusement, "but . . . only with others. Never with you."

Meave wondered at the truth of that. Her high-druid had never failed to serve her well, but she had more than once sensed a pressure, a force that seemed to demand acceptance of his advice. She knew others who claimed to have felt this force more directly, for he had worked his way to his position in a few years and was said to make use of many kinds of power. She had even heard many strong, fearless warriors confess to feeling that Calatin wore horror about him like a cloak.

Still there was nothing visible about him to explain the feeling. In appearance he was a broad, strong man with coarse but not unpleasant features. His only blemish was in a spot of baldness high on his head, partially concealed by the long, dark hair which he combed back across it. In dress he was modest, avoiding the extravagance in clothing many of his station displayed. His only marks of office were the multi-hued cloak on his shoulders and the golden torc about his neck.

"What is it you want here?" Aileel asked irritably, for the old king disliked this man and made no attempt to hide it.

"I only came to see if there was anything you might be desiring," Calatin explained graciously. It was an effort for him to speak so, to tolerate this attitude from the king. From any lesser man such a tone would have drawn a swift and venomous reply.

17

"We desire only to be left without interruption," Aileel said.

"Well enough," the ard-druid replied and turned to go, but Meave stopped him.

"Wait, Calatin! What did you mean about our bull? Is there something wrong?"

Calatin had expected that and he smiled inwardly. He knew he had managed to pique her curiosity with his first remark.

"There is nothing wrong," he said with elaborate casualness. He stepped to the window beside her and looked down into the bull's enclosure. "Nothing . . . if you are satisfied with this animal."

"Satisfied?" Meave looked at him closely. She knew his methods. He was building toward something, but she would have to draw it from him. "And isn't this the finest bull in all of Eire?"

"There is one other," he said as if it were a fact of small importance. "He has only a score of attendants to brush his great hide and bring fresh grass to him. And he is entertained merely by harpers and bards who play soothing tunes and recite noble tales for him."

"That talk is foolish," Aileel said with harshness.

"Is it so?" Calatin responded evenly. He did not look toward the old man but only toward Meave. "My Queen, many of your own chieftains can support what I say. They have seen this bull themselves, in Ulster."

"What is it you are speaking about?" Meave asked impatiently, already weary of trying to play this game with her druid. "Tell me now, Calatin."

Her advisor hesitated. To this point he had ignored Fardia's presence, but now he cast a contemptuous look toward the young warrior.

"Send out the Firbolg," he said with undisguised arrogance.

Meave was surprised. "And why might I do that?"

"These are important matters," Calatin explained. "They're not to be discussed before thralls."

"Fardia is no thrall to us," Meave told him coldly. "It is my invitation which brings him here, and he may stay by his own choice."

"No, my Queen, it is all right," the young warrior said quickly, unable to hide his anger and chagrin. "I've no place here. I'll be going."

But, as he turned to leave, Meave stepped forward, smiling warmly to counter the druid's insulting attitude.

"Wait, Fardia," she said soothingly. "We've a matter yet to settle between us. Please, go to the hall below. Refresh yourself. We'll talk later."

The Firbolg nodded stiffly and left the room. Meave watched him start down the stairs, then turned her gaze back upon her advisor.

"Now, Calatin, what of this bull?" she asked him curtly, annoyed by his harsh treatment of Fardia. "Why is it I've heard nothing of it before?"

He shrugged. "That is simple enough. Since word has come into the southern provinces about this animal, many a chieftain of Eire has gone to Ulster to try to purchase it. It would be a prize indeed to have such a bull . . ." he paused, then added slowly ". . . a prize to make its winner the rival of Meave herself."

"Your foolish talk grows worse, Enchanter," said the king. "Madness it is, now."

"Maybe not mad," Meave told him thoughtfully. "Aileel, you cannot deny that many of our chieftains are capable of this."

"A few," he conceded unwillingly. "But, for such men, would ownership of this bull make a difference?"

"Not in fact, perhaps," said Calatin, "but, in the minds of some of your subjects . . ."

He left the implication of this for Meave to grasp. He had no fear that she would fail to do so. The queen was shrewder in dealings than any man he had ever met. Honed by the constant challenge of equaling men in strength, her wits were sharply attuned to even subtle threats to her carefully built authority.

He saw the idea working on her as she moved back to the window to stand, looking out without seeing now, lost in the twists and turnings of the problem.

Aileel had understood none of it. He shook his head angrily.

"The minds . . . the minds," he said. "What matter are

they? The arm and the sword it is that makes the difference. What does it mean to own a bull? Either we have the power or we do not. What good is this plotting?"

Calatin looked with disdain at the king. To him the weak, aging man was something to be pitied. Aileel would never understand that there were better ways to power, that it was no longer a matter of mindless bravery and bloody combat. The world was not that simple anymore. But the druid felt no unhappiness that the king and the other warriors of Eire seemed incapable of understanding this. Their single-minded honor and casually ordered society often made things much easier for him.

"My King," said Meave, "I've no liking for plots myself, but if this bull is what Calatin says, then we have little choice! We cannot afford anyone in our provinces of Eire to own it but ourselves."

"No one in Eire will have it." The king had become insistent now. "Ulster is no friend to us. It has never been one. And now that we control the other provinces, it has become the more arrogant about its freedom. King Conchobar and his Red Branch warriors suspect everything we do. They'd not sell even a dry milk-cow to us."

Meave nodded. "My husband speaks the truth. If this bull is Ulster's, what can we do?"

"There are ways of gaining things, even from Ulster," said Calatin, speaking slowly as if picking each word with a mind to its effect. "I have talked with many who went to the North and have found out much more with . . . other methods. I think there is a way."

This drew jeering laughter from Aileel.

"And what would that be, Enchanter? Are you thinking to cast your spells on the warriors of Ulster, and walk the bull away while they're asleep?"

The druid's calm remained. His reply was smooth and softly spoken. "There are means more direct."

"But not more honest," the king shot back. "Certain I am of that!"

"Please, my King," said Meave soothingly. "I must have the knowledge my advisor has."

At that the king turned away on the stool and began poking angrily at the glowing peat with an iron rod. Freed of his harassment, Calatin turned his full attention on the queen.

"It is Dary, King of Cuailgne, who is custodian of the bull," he said. "I see hope in that for two reasons. The first is that the tuath of Cuailgne is in the south of Ulster, on its borders with the rest of Eire. It is a great way from Ulster's capital of Emain Macha and from the power of Conchobar."

"Loyalty to Conchobar does not depend on distance in Ulster," Meave noted, "and his chieftains control the duns to the very borders of the province."

"You'll have no argument on that," the druid agreed. "Still, there's another thing in our favor. Dary is a proud man. He has ruled Cuailgne since long before Conchobar was high-king of Ulster. He is independent. The proper offer made to him might. . . ."

"Might do nothing," Aileel grumbled, looking down at the fire as if addressing it. "Dary may be an independent man, but he is not a foolish one. He'd never risk all Ulster's wrath by selling something put into his trust."

"Perhaps so," said Calatin with a smile, "but if the price we offered was not to buy?"

"There it is, now!" The king was triumphant. "The Enchanter plans to bribe the bull from them!"

"I have in mind to borrow it," the druid replied calmly. "It might be that the bull could be brought from Ulster to Connacht for a season, to strengthen only the blood of our herds."

"Very dear would be the price for that," Aileel complained.

"There the king is right," Calatin grudgingly admitted to Meave. "You must be prepared to pay a great deal."

"What is this talk of paying?" Aileel looked up toward Calatin, the light in his dim eyes flaring brightly with anger now. "We've made our herds fat with the taking of animals in raids on others. It was the strength of arms did it, not bargaining like the old women at market."

"Things change," Meave told him brusquely, as a tutor might address a troublesome child. "We can't fight battles over a few cows. We're no longer small tribes. We're a vast nation. It would be too costly."

Aileel's anger died at that. The pride in his warrior past that had brought him erect left him, and he seemed to shrink back.

"It may be you are right," he said wearily. "I am an old man now. Then our tribes were small and so were our battles. We fought one another to survive. I am sorry. I've lived no other way."

At once Meave regretted her words. His years of fighting had brought them much, and she had made it sound as nothing. She moved to him and placed a hand upon his shoulder.

"My King, I've been a warrior at my heart since I was wed to you. It was you taught me the pleasures of hostings and war, the feel of a true spear, the biting weight of a good sword. A child of the Morrigu I am, and as far from understanding these new methods as yourself. Still, our power is now great enough to show itself in other ways. We'll build with it. We'll create a stronger Eire."

Her words seemed to cheer Aileel. He lifted his head and smiled at her.

"Ah, thank you, my wife. No better partner could a man have to cover his back in a fight. You've made right choices for us this far, and all my trust lies with you."

"Then we'll have this bull of Ulster's," she said and met the druid's eyes levelly. "But understand, Calatin: we want the bull only to strengthen our herds, and not because of any fear that others might have it."

"Why, of course, my Queen," Calatin assured her solemnly, bowing his head in compliance. As he did, the hint of a smile tugged upward at his lips. He knew she would never voice any fear of threat or challenge, for that would be a show of weakness. Yet he knew well enough it was the real reason she would have to act, and he was satisfied.

"We should move swiftly," Meave said decisively. "We'll decide upon a generous offer and carry it to King Dary at once."

The druid nodded. "Well said. I will make preparations to leave for Cuailgne."

"You?" Meave was surprised by this. "I have never

known you to go on such missions. My thought was to send a messenger."

"This is a task which needs some care," he told her. "It would interest me to undertake it."

Aileel roused himself again. "Meave, you can't be sending this one. He's despised by every real warrior who sees him. Their very spirits are repulsed by the presence of him . . ."

"Aileel," Meave said sharply to cut the flow of words. "You'll not be speaking so of my advisor." She turned to the druid. "Calatin, I am sorry . . ."

"Do not apologize for me," the king said fiercely. He was angered by his wife's patronizing tone and refused to be silenced. "If you will not heed my warnings about the enchanter, then at least think of this: you will have trouble enough in Ulster trying to secure the bull without sending any outsider there. Calatin admits himself how much care is needed. Be sending someone who has a chance of getting the animal!"

There was much sense in that, and Meave considered it.

"But who could do it?" she asked. "Who might you be thinking of?"

"Fergus MacRogh," Aileel stated with simple finality.

For a moment Calatin's face went rigid with astonishment, but then he exploded with laughter.

"Fergus!" he said. "You pick the one man in Eire who would never go! Fergus is an exile from Ulster, a man who went to war against his own king and was expelled by force for it."

"To become the commander of our armies," Aileel added stubbornly. "The best I have ever known."

"Only more reason he would never be tolerated in Ulster." The druid argued forcefully now, amusement gone from him as he realized the king's sincerity.

"He is right, Aileel," Meave agreed. "How is it Fergus could help? His own son was killed by Conchobar in a dispute. Fergus and all his tribe swore vengeance for it. They are the enemies of Ulster."

"Not of all Ulster," Aileel persisted. "There's many a warrior who sympathized with Fergus for Conchobar's wrong to him. Many chose to be exiled with him, including the king's own son, young Conlingas. But for loyalty to the king, all of Ulster would have joined the revolt. To most, MacRogh still carries the fame he earned as a right arm to Conchobar. Very little would be denied him in his old homeland, and never would his word be doubted."

"That's true enough," said Meave thoughtfully. "Any offer he might give would be believed. If Dary was certain he could trust our offer, he might lend the bull."

Calatin shrugged. "Ah, it is possible, but Fergus would never go back to Ulster. You may ask him, but he would refuse."

"If I ask him, Calatin, he cannot refuse," Meave answered pointedly.

Inwardly the druid cursed his ill-chosen words. To suggest that MacRogh's power might allow him to defy the queen only challenged her to prove that he could not. The commander was too popular with her people and too outspoken to let even a minor dispute be won by him.

Calatin had judged her reaction correctly, for those same thoughts were in Meave's mind as she walked to the balcony overlooking the main hall.

Below her, alone at a table, Fardia still waited patiently, sipping at a mug of heavy ale.

"Fardia!" she called to him, and he looked up toward her.

"Yes, my Queen?"

"Could you find Fergus MacRogh for me? I've need of him here."

"He's at the training ground, teaching chariot-fighting to the young warriors," the Firbolg called back. "He'll not like to come away from it."

This second suggestion of her commander's independence brought all Meave's sense of outraged authority to the fore and Fardia, unknowing of his sin, caught its full force.

"It is very little I care about him liking it or not," she said, commanding and cold as the full moon on a clear winter's night. "Tell him to come . . . now!"

"Yes, my Queen," the Firbolg said, bewildered by this change in Meave's demeanor. He rose at once and all but ran from the hall in his haste to do her bidding.

Chapter Three
FERGUS MACROGH

Fardia went down from the Tec Meadcuarta on foot, passing out of the main gates and turning to circle the dun to the broad field beside it.

The training ground was little more than a wide square of dirt, grassless and beaten to smooth hardness by years of wheels and hooves. It was filled now with warriors at their chariot drills.

To one untrained in the subtleties of warfare, the drills might have seemed little more than a confused and dangerous milling of vehicles, horses and men. But to Fardia, the chariots sweeping dangerously close to one another with warriors climbing precariously about in them were being precisely choreographed to perform with lethal purpose.

Many different activities were underway on the field. On one side lads of fourteen or fifteen years, paired with veteran drivers, learned to cast their spears from moving chariots or to swing the longswords swiftly from side to side to hold a circle of enemies away. Most of the young warrior's normal fighting position. One hand held a drawn finer points of this hard, fast method of fighting.

Fardia walked about the field, seeking Fergus Mac-Rogh in each group of men. Then he saw a familiar face lifted above the center of a crowd and went toward it. It was Cormac Conlingas, son of King Conchobar, second in importance among the ex-Ulstermen. He was standing in a war chariot and speaking with savage intensity as he explained the proper working of chariot scythes to the surrounding youths.

"You've got to swing them out at the last moment," he

said. He turned to stand directly behind the driver in the
warriors were clumsy, but they were quickly learning the
sword while the other gripped a metal rail which ran
about the top of the large chariot's bulwark.

"Now, lads, keep a close watch here," he continued.
"Ride straight in toward the enemy ranks as if you're
bound to go at them iron to iron. Wait as long as you're
able. Then, at the last moment, throw them out!"

At this he sheathed the sword to take hold of the rail
with both hands. He pressed upward to lift his feet from
the chariot floor and swung his legs forward together.

On either side his leather-armored shins struck curved
handles set in the chariot walls. In one, smooth movement
they pivoted forward, and wide blades of almost two
arms' length swung out from the vehicle's sides, locking
open, cutting edges toward the front.

"You must be quick," he told his rapt audience emphatically. "Before they see what's coming, you'll take
them off at their knees. But remember: if they see it,
they'll move out of the way. Then you may have them in
behind you, and you'll be caught with your great, metal
wings only slowing you."

He looked about him closely at the group to discover
any signs of even slight doubt. Seeing none, he nodded
with satisfaction.

"All right, young warriors, let's see if you can do what
you've watched."

As he climbed down and the boys lined up to practice,
Fardia approached the Ulsterman. Their greeting was a
warm one, for Cormac, like most of the Exiles, felt a
kinship with this other people whose own land had been
torn from them. To him, Fardia was no member of a
servile race, but a warrior equal in prowess and to be
treated so.

"What is it you're doing here?" he asked the Firbolg.
"Come for some practice?"

"I wouldn't mind that," Fardia said, "but I've come
from the queen. She's wishing to talk with Fergus. Have
you seen him?"

"Seen him?" Cormac laughed. "Can't you hear him
now, bellowing with the voice of two mad bulls?"

Fardia laughed too, for he could indeed hear the commander's voice. He and Cormac had no difficulty in directing themselves toward it.

They came upon Fergus MacRogh supervising a drill in fighting from the chariot-pole. Skilled drivers took the vehicles up an avenue formed by two rows of stakes, man-height and topped by wooden heads. The young warriors' precarious task was to climb over the front bulwark and walk out the pole between the animals, striking to left and right with their swords at the "enemies" as they sped past. It was a valuable technique for protecting the vulnerable horses in a crush of men, but a hard one to learn. The mistakes made by the lads kept Fergus shouting constantly at them.

Even in repose the commander was a figure to inspire fear or awe and now, heated as he was by the frustrating work, he seemed terrible indeed. He was an enormous man, made giantlike in contrast to the striplings about him. His size came both in height and girth, nowhere showing signs of excess weight, for years of combat had kept him solid and hard of body.

The fire of his present mood was echoed in the heavy beard curling from his broad face like deep-red flames. He wore his hair unbound, and it formed a thick mass, mingling with the beard and framing his whole head with the blaze of it.

It amused Fardia to think that this Milesian looked more a Firbolg than many of his own tribe. He shared some kinships in spirit, too, seeing life with their harsh practicality and simple honesty and, for that, they respected him.

Still, there was much more to the Exile. Like many of the Milesians, Fergus was something beyond merely a warrior, for he was a product of a culture which saw a person as mind and body both, and his teaching came as much from the druids as from the champions. That he was a warrior was clear in him, but it might have startled someone not of Eire to discover how much of the philosopher lay in him too.

Today that philosopher was fully hidden as he roared his instructions. When he saw Cormac and Fardia approaching, he paused in the tirade to greet them. But, before they could speak, his attention was called back to the field by a crisis.

A young warrior had missed a stake in passing and his wasted swing had struck the driver a glancing blow, not dangerous but painful. The chariot had slewed about and stopped, almost throwing the youth out. Now he, angry and embarrassed, was railing at the still-dazed charioteer.

"Hold on, there," Fergus cried, and started toward them.

The youth looked up toward him.

"This fool could have killed me," he whined. "Can't servants be trained . . ."

Fergus came up to the chariot and, without pausing, took hold of the young warrior's tunic and threw him heavily upon the ground.

"You should be dead, and little enough loss it would be . . . no . . . don't get up . . ." he planted a wide foot on the fallen youth's chest and pushed him back ". . . lie there and listen." He raised his voice. "Listen, all of you!"

The noise about him died away at once. The other warriors moved to form a circle around the commander.

"Now, I am going to make this clear one time to you, for I'll not stand this happening again. This 'servant,' as you call him, is worth your life; worth two of you, in truth. He's skilled and tested by war and proven. That he wears pants makes him no less than you. There are no stations when the fighting's joined. Remember, lads, driver and warrior are fused by blood, by their very need to live. Each needs the other's skill as a single man needs two arms, or a chariot two wheels. One animal, one machine you are. Respect that, and him, and you'll live to become gray."

He gazed about him, searching the youthful faces for any uncertainty of expression. Assured by their direct return gazes that they understood, he let up the chastized youth.

"All of you need far more work in this," he announced and turned toward where the young Firbolg stood. "Fardia, you are the foremost chariot-fighter in all Connacht. Show these whelps the proper way."

"Aye, Fergus," the warrior replied. He climbed into the chariot the young novice had so quickly exited.

"Are you feeling able to do this with me?" Fardia asked the driver.

"My head's clear, right enough," the man answered, then smiled broadly at the Firbolg. "Besides, I'd not be missing a chance to show these awkward babes some skillful work. I've had to put up with them this whole, long day."

"All right, then," said Fardia, drawing his sword, "go in at your best speed, charioteer!"

The driver wheeled the chariot about and brought it back toward the avenue of heads again. Fardia vaulted across the vehicle's front with agility and walked out the pole with the ease of one treading a broad highway.

Between the heads of the plunging steeds he stood, at ease, the sword held down next to him until the first of the poles was almost alongside. Then, with sudden speed, the sword came up. In a shining blur it flashed from side to side, and from each stake the wooden head was cut, severed by a single, well-aimed stroke. Back and forth, so close above the horses it seemed it must strike them, the sword whirled, and each time a head flew on either side, until the last fell and the driver pulled up again.

A cheer rose from the awestruck boys who watched. Fardia, made self-conscious by this honoring of his skill, only nodded to them and climbed from the car, thanking the charioteer.

"Now you see the talent that few of you will survive long enough to learn," said Fergus. "But, if you do, you will insure a full and healthy life. Try this again yourselves . . . and tie back your hair while you are working! Let it hang about your shoulders and you'll be catching it in the wheels or the harness surely. Be about it, then!"

He rejoined his two comrades, shaking his head.

"I've not seen poorer lads in all my life," he complained. "Look at them. They wear a warrior's trappings and walk about as if they were champions of Eire, and without the skill among them to defeat an unarmed crone."

"Go easy, Fergus," said Fardia. "On such a day I'd find it hard myself to work at this."

"Then why is it that you're here with us now?" Fergus asked with curiosity.

"By the Dagda, I've forgotten," said Fardia in consternation. "I've come for you to see the queen at once, and here I've delayed."

"At once?" said Fergus. "Does she know my work here?"

"She knows," the Firbolg assured him, "and she does not care. A strange temper was on her when she sent me."

"What kind of temper?"

"There's no way of telling. It was a sudden change. She was in high spirits before Calatin came . . ."

"Calatin?" Fergus broke in. "Is that Enchanter with her?"

"Aye. Come on some matter which seemed important."

"I'd best be going then," said Fergus, his words suddenly tinged with anxiousness. "That man brings some scheme with him every time he sees the queen. Cormac, can you take charge of the drills?"

"I can," said Conlingas.

"I'll stay to help him," Fardia offered.

"Good. I'll be returning . . . and soon."

MacRogh followed the way back up toward the tec with long strides, frowning deeply as he tried to guess what trouble the ard-druid was brewing now. He entered the hall, spied Meave watching from the balcony above and went up the stairs, stopping in the center of the room to face her.

"You seem not happy, Fergus," said Meave. "I am sorry to pull you away from your work."

Fergus did not reply to that. "Well, what is it you wish me for?" he bluntly asked instead, and eyed the druid coldly. "I have men waiting."

"Better that they should wait than I," the queen said loftily. "You have something to do here."

Fergus sighed. "And what is it?"

"It is a mission, for me and for Connacht," she said. "I would like you to go to Ulster and barter for a great bull owned by Dary."

"What?" he said, clearly disconcerted. "Why?"

Calatin spoke up at that. "You know the what and the why of this. You have heard about the bull."

"I have, of course," said Fergus. "I do not understand why you'd be wishing it."

"Fergus, if the tales of it are true, it would be a great value to our herds."

"I agree," he conceded slowly. His eyes were narrowed and he thought carefully as he spoke, trying to puzzle out the forces here, and what they required of him. "The bull I have heard rumor of might be of some value."

"Good. Then you must also agree that if anyone is to have this bull, it must be Connacht."

"I agree only that it could be of value. I do not see my purpose in this. If you mean to have the bull, send a messenger north to barter for it. It's little chance I'll give him, but he may try."

"Ulster might not give it to me, Fergus," said Meave, "but, for your friendship, and the proper gifts . . ."

"It would take half a province to tempt Dary to give up a possession of Ulster!" Fergus said this with some anger in his voice. He knew the honorable King of Cuailgne well and was outraged by any suggestion that he might be bribed.

"Wait, Fergus, you move too fast," said Meave, and her tones became a soothing, cooling sound, like that of a soft, spring shower. "I only wish it brought here for a time, to breed in our herds and strengthen them."

Fergus considered. "A time? How long would it be?"

"A season only. I would make any offer you see as fair."

"It is possible," he agreed reluctantly, "but, I cannot return to Ulster now. I warred against them. I was exiled."

"I have heard you still have friends there, and you would go back as my ambassador. This Dary, would he see you?"

"Yes," said Fergus, thoughtfully. For a moment his mind turned inward to past times and comrades. "Yes . . . he was a friend." Then he shook himself mentally. "Still, that was all five years past. I am of Connacht now. I've no wish to go back."

"Fergus," Aileel said, "Calatin has offered to go."

"Oh?" said the commander, and threw the druid a piercing look. He did not trust Calatin's offer and sensed the same mistrust was in Aileel. The man could not be allowed to go.

"All right, then," he agreed. "I will go north. But I'll make no promise. I'll present your offer and nothing more."

"Do your best, Fergus," said Meave. "What will you need?"

"A small escort only, my Queen. We will travel fastest that way."

"And I will accompany you," Calatin added.

"You?" said Fergus. "Why?"

"I might offer assistance, should problems arise."

"I want none of your kind of help, Enchanter," Fergus told him bluntly.

"No, Fergus," Meave said warningly. These two had been at odds before. She could not understand the common dislike they felt and was constantly distressed by the division.

"I think you both should go," she went on. "My two advisors must get along. Perhaps this venture will have you working together."

"Yes, my Queen," said Fergus, darkly.

Calatin only smiled.

The balance of the day was busy for Fergus after that. He sent word to Cormac and Fardia to finish out the chariot-training, himself remaining at the dun to see to preparations for the trip and find the proper men to accompany him.

These arrangements, though simple, took much time, and the sun was long since down when finally he returned to his own quarters in the tec.

The room was lit by a faint yellow light cast by a single taper, and seemed filled with black shadows lying like deep pools beneath stools and tables and making the corners into endless voids. On entering, Fergus removed his cloak and turned to hang it from a hook beside the door, but some small noise alarmed him, and he whirled to face the corner from where the sound had come, his hand dropping to his sword.

"I've waited long enough for you to expect a better welcome," a softly chiding voice said from the shadows.

At once Fergus relaxed, but a grimness remained in his expression.

"If you've had to wait, it was no other's fault but your own," he answered, unclasping his sword-belt and hanging the weapon beside his cloak.

There was a movement in the darkness of the corner and a tall, slender figure arose, gliding forward into the soft circle of the light.

"Fergus," the voice said gently, "you cannot be angry with me for that!"

He turned again to face a graceful form, clad in a long tunic of white linen. In the pale light it glowed a mellow gold while the hair which flowed about its shoulders flickered with the colors of a fire.

He wanted to reply in anger, but as he looked upon the appealing figure before him, the harshness faded in him.

"Ah, Meave. My trouble is a strange one, but I'll not hold you to blame for it." He said this quietly, but with a note of despair he could not hide.

Concerned, Meave crossed to him and placed a hand on each of his arms.

"No more of that. We've made our bond to put aside that life when we're alone. It's the proud queen and her fine champion who play their games of power. Here stand only two simple human beings, stripped of their offices along with their weapons and their crowns."

He shook his head. "You've no need of them. Your power is here . . ." he lifted a hand to lightly touch her temple, then moved it to caress the thickly curling flow of hair ". . . and the only ornament you'll ever need will always crown you."

She smiled and gently rubbed her cheek against the hand, but he only pulled it down and stood, impassive, meeting her searching gaze.

Disconcerted by his strange coldness, she moved away and sat down on the mound of rugs and furs which served him as a bed.

"Come, now. Sit here by me."

He complied, lying down beside her on the rugs, looking up silently to the rafters where the fluttering candle-light caused a maze of shadows to shift constantly.

His continued brooding disturbed her, for she had grown to understand his nature and knew that, removed from the demands of leadership, he was a man of cheer-fulness and warmth.

"Why is it so hard for you to put off our public life?" she asked him archly. "It was not hard for Fardia to do so today."

He raised himself and looked at her. "Fardia?" he said with suspicion. "What of him?"

"Ah, so there is some fire in you," she said, laughing. "I hoped I could rake up the flames with that." She leaned close and her voice dropped low in earnestness. "Fergus, I only rode with him. Since my marriage to Aileel, there's been only one other who has shared my love and been a match to me in spirit."

"Meave, you are too clever for your good," he said, at last smiling in return. He reached up and pulled her down and held her, looking closely into her gray eyes.

"You've eyes like the cloudy skies of Eire," he said, "and as changeable; from soft mist to threatening storm. Are you so unpredictable as they? How often do you use your wiles on me without my ever knowing it?"

"Fergus, that I would never do," she told him as one arm went about his neck and pulled him down to her.

Late in the night a dream brought restlessness to Mac-Rogh. He saw again a bond broken by Conchobar of Ulster. He watched men under his vow of protection killed by the jealous king, trapped in a burning house and dying valiantly, and the son of Fergus with them. The flames of it rose up and threatened to engulf him, and he cried out in his sleep.

Meave woke with alarm and found him thrashing wild-ly about. Her alarm was heightened by that, for never had she known him to spend an uneasy night. She felt some deep distress must surely grip him now.

"Wake up!" she called, shaking him. "Fergus, what is wrong?"

He awoke and stared up unseeing at her, the naked

fear and anger revealed in his eyes. Then he recognized her and shook his head.

"Oh . . . Meave," he breathed, raising a hand to wipe his sweating brow. "It . . . it was a dream. It was a fire, the Sons of Usna and my own son killed and Conchobar grinning in the red glare. . . ."

"Fergus, I am sorry," she told him. She laid her head upon his chest and held him tightly. "I did not realize how much the memory of that still haunted you. You've hidden it too well. I'd never have made you go if I had known."

"It is all right," he said, stroking her arm with a reassuring gentleness. "I'll be far enough from Emain Macha and from Conchobar." But then, he thought grimly, to himself: "Yet the gods help us both if ever he comes within my sword's reach again!"

Chapter Four
THE BARTER

It was three days later that seven chariots crossed the Oun Dia river, which marked the southern boundary of Ulster.

The chariots had come swiftly up out of the heart of Eire, and they continued on into the north with unslackened speed, their drivers urging them ahead. Behind the charioteers, the warriors hung on stoically, bouncing with the vehicles and trying to ignore their boredom for, at the rapid pace, they could not even converse with their fellows.

Leading them was the chariot of Fergus MacRogh, half-again larger than the rest and simply adorned, much like its occupant. Calm and quiet the commander stood by his driver, lightly gripping the handrail to steady himself without a conscious effort, gazing out upon the passing countryside with an expression both thoughtful and sad.

The expression seemed especially worthy of notice, for it was so out of place in this man. But, to come back to a place he felt he would never see again, and to come back as an alien, was a hard thing for him.

Behind and around Fergus rode the rest of the small troop. They were all armored and heavily armed with sword and ax and spears, as was their leader. Like him as well, all were exiles from Conchobar's Ulster, trusted men chosen by Fergus to make this strange journey with him.

Only the chariot of the druid Calatin seemed out of place in the company. Large and richly ornamented it was and driven by a thin, yellow man who kept it in a place behind the others at a little distance.

Darkness was coming on them when, ahead, amidst the landscape of soft, green hills, one prominence less natural could be distinguished. The sky behind it to the east was growing dark, but the late sun illuminated the hilltop with warm, golden light, showing clearly the ramparts and walls which circled it, and the large, low structures that filled its top.

The chariots moved up toward the drawbridge in the outer palisades of the fortress, where massive gates were flanked by two, high towers. They halted there at the edge of a wide, deep foss, for the bridge had been drawn up for the night, closing the entrance in the wall.

Fergus directed his charioteer to rein in at the very brink of the ditch where a round, bronze gong hung suspended between two posts. Drawing out his great-sword, he leaned forward over the vehicle's side and struck the metal circle a solid blow. The gong resounded with a deep, echoing clang that hung shaking in the air for several moments. The sound had not even died away before lights appeared on the top of the palisades, and a voice called down to them.

"Who is it who visits Dun Cuailgne in the darkness?"

"It is Fergus MacRogh," the large man bellowed, "ambassador to Queen Meave of Connacht. We have come a great way to visit King Dary."

"Fergus!" the voice returned, astonishment clear in the single word. "We are glad to know who visits. Welcome you are here."

At this the bridge over the foss was lowered and the troop passed across the wooden span into the enclosure.

Before the dun's main hall the chariots halted again. The yard was brightly lit by many flaring torches in the hands of a company of household troops who met them. Fergus and his companions climbed from their vehicles, gave them into the care of their drivers, and approached the knot of men. As they did, a stooped, gray-haired man in servant's dress stepped forward and held up a hand in greeting.

"So, it is you, Fergus MacRogh," he said in a voice
that quavered with age.

"And good it is to see you," Fergus replied with cheer.
He knew well this ancient servant, for he was Feogh,
steward to King Dary and to Dary's father before that.
"How is Dary?"

"Dary is well . . . very well," Feogh answered, head
bobbing on the scrawny neck making him seem like some
time-worn and battered crow. "Come into our tec now.
Waitin' there himself, he is, to give you proper greeting."

The small company of visitors followed their guide
through the main entrance into the hall, finding it lit dimly
by a few candles set in sconces along the walls. The room
was empty save for a handful of men, sitting at the tables,
talking or playing chess. But the entrance of the newcomers brought these activities to a halt, and the men at the
tables watched with curiosity as Fergus and his party
passed along the side of the hall toward its far end, taking
care not to trip over one or another of the inevitable
complement of sleeping hounds in the darkness.

In the round, central hearth a great fire burned, sending its heat and smoke up through the roofholes. The
spring wood was damp and smoking a great deal and,
because of its curtain and the dim light, Fergus could not
see the royal dais or those upon it until his party had
circled the broad pit and reached the open space before
the low platform.

The old man who occupied the couch upon it did not
wait for ceremony. On seeing Fergus he rose at once and
moved to greet the commander.

"Fergus!" he cried. "Never did I think I would see you
again in Ulster."

A shadow of sadness passed once more across the
other's face. "And never again did I think to see Ulster,"
he agreed. "It is not an easy thing to come back to these
green lands."

The time had been good to Dary, Fergus saw. Though
signs of age had appeared in him since their last meeting,
the King of Cuailgne seemed no less powerful and had
lost none of the proud air of authority that had made him
one of Conchobar's most assertive and self-reliant chieftains.

"Proper honor must be done you," Dary told his visitor, and raised his voice to address the hall. "We will feast tonight in honor of Fergus, son of Rogh," he announced, and the few warriors in the room exchanged wondering looks at the mention of the name. "Feogh, light all the candles now. Have food and drink prepared. Call the entertainers."

It was suddenly a room of activity as the men rushed to their tasks. The king paid little mind to it, himself directing the men of Fergus to seat themselves at a table nearby while he brought Fergus to sit in the champion's seat, near his own, that they might talk.

In the great hall, men went about lighting the tall candles, forcing out the shadows and enabling those on the dais to see clearly the entire room. Bards and jugglers appeared and began to wander along the rows of tables, stopping here and there to entertain groups of warriors with their skills. More warriors began to come into the hall, eager to see this famous visitor, and very soon the tec was crowded with men, lively with talk and music, fragrant with the odor of cooking food.

A satisfied man was Dary as he looked out over the gathering. It had been long since he had found a reason for feasting as excellent as this visit from a friend of past days.

"Look, there, at the young ones," he said with enjoyment, pointing toward the warriors who craned their necks above their fellows to catch a glimpse of Fergus. "It is just a name you've been to most of them. Just an image they've built of you in their minds as they learned the proper way to swing an ax or balance themselves on a chariot-pole. Many were boys when you were at Conchobar's right hand."

"They are still boys ... unbloodied and soft," Fergus replied. "It is surprised I am to find they do not see me as some black spirit ... some bitter enemy to their king."

At that Dary grew solemn. He leaned close to Fergus and his voice dropped low. "You had good reason for turning against him. Understand, Fergus, you never were an enemy to some of us. Many in Ulster felt the king was wrong." Then, more heartily, he added, "You are a champion here, Fergus, as you always were."

"It is all past now, Dary," Fergus reminded him. "Better it would be for you to think of me as a man of Connacht, commander of its battalions and ambassador of its Queen Meave."

"As you wish," said Dary thoughtfully. "Then, what is it this great queen could wish in Ulster, in my poor tuath?"

Fergus had determined he would not delay in his mission but make it known at the first opportunity. Now Dary had provided the chance and the Exile went ahead, telling the story as directly as he knew. When he had finished, Dary's air of thoughtfulness had deepened and he sat quiet a moment before he finally spoke.

"So, it is the Black Bull Meave wants from us. I should have known it would be that."

"You have such a bull, then? The rumors heard of it in Connacht are true?"

"They're true enough. It's great packs of crying, begging men I've had to deal with here, coming to offer their daughters, their lands, even their cattle for this beast. One and all I've sent away, some kindly, some with the flat of a sword stinging their arrogant backside." He grinned broadly. "I've found it all to be great sport."

Fergus nodded. "I knew that would be the way of it. It was a foolish offer and a wasted trip, but it's been made and done and my task is ended. Now it may be forgotten."

"No, Fergus," Dary said with caution. "I have not yet heard what offer you bring from Meave. I would hear it all."

Fergus shrugged. "It is your choice. The offer is a simple one: a hundred picked calves of our own herds in exchange for a season's service from your bull."

"A season only? And the animal to be returned after?" Dary looked please. "Now, Fergus, that is a better offer than any I've yet heard. It is a proud thing to have so fair an offer from such a source as Meave. But, we'll talk no more of it now. Look, the food is coming. We'll talk further of it after eating."

When the food arrived, Dary insisted that Fergus carve the roasted haunch of beef and take the champion's portion for himself; an act that brought a cheer of agreement from the assembled men. When the banquet had concluded, the food was removed and drinking began in earnest. Servants moved along the tables, collecting the plates and the remains of dinner, and bringing full pitchers of wine.

As Dary poured some of the liquor out, he nodded toward the table where the rest of the men of Fergus were seated.

"I've been eying those men of yours while we ate," he said. "It's a fine, strong lot you've brought with you, but for those two."

Fergus was filling his own cup and did not even bother to look up.

"Do they sit apart from the others?" he asked.

"They do. One seems a noble man, but there is an atmosphere about him I do not like."

"Calatin it is," Fergus said. "He is advisor to the queen."

"A druid?"

"He calls himself that, but it is said he learned their arts in his homeland of Espan. He makes use of their knowledge, but there are rumors he makes use of darker powers the druids of Eire would shun."

"I'd not have such as my advisor. I would not trust him to guard my back in a fight," said Dary with a smile. "And, who is that bleached stick of a man with him?"

Fergus smiled, too. "That is one of his sons. You know, he has twenty-six of them, each as pale and unfit to be a warrior as this one. I have been told he had them by as many wives, but it seems he could not find a good match. Perhaps his own part was too flawed."

The king laughed at this, but Fergus became sober. It was easy to laugh at the Enchanter, but there was no way to deny the power he had with Meave. And, for the commander, there was no humor in that.

"It was he who suggested this bartering," Fergus went on, "and it was a senseless thing. I told Meave that Ulster would never let the bull go."

"Hold on, Fergus, you presume too much." Dary spoke as if affronted by these words. "Why do you say 'Ulster'? The men of Ulster do not dictate to me. I am custodian of the bull, and I alone am the one responsible for it. I am king of Cuailgne and subject to the ard-rie of Ulster only by my own will." He clapped a hand upon the shoulder of his guest. "Fergus, I have decided. Conchobar MacNessa may make me an Exile too, but I will send the bull to Queen Meave!"

"Dary, are you certain of this? Do not make a mistake."

"No mistakes, Fergus. You have promised to take the bull only one season and offered ample reward. And who can doubt that Fergus MacRogh would go to war to defend his bond?"

"It is your choice," said Fergus, carefully keeping all feeling from his voice.

"Then, let us drink to our bargain," Dary said and filled both their cups. "In the morning you will have the bull."

Reluctantly, Fergus lifted his cup and drank with the king.

Dary then called for his ard-ollaf and asked the bard to relate the poem he had composed about the Black Bull of Cuailgne as an appropriate entertainment for that evening. The lay went on at great length, detailing every event of the animal's life since its birth. By its end, many had fallen asleep at the tables while others had quietly withdrawn. The great quantities of wine and the tedium of the tale had wearied even the king and he was forced to say goodnight to his guests and retire.

The rest of the company dispersed, leaving Fergus and his group alone with a few servants. They did not stay up long after the others. Soon, Fergus asked that he and his men be shown to their sleeping quarters. As the servant led them out to their rooms, Fergus looked back and noted that one of their party had stayed behind. It was Calatin, and he was deep in conversation with Feogh, the king's steward.

Idly, Fergus wondered what two such men would have of any mutual concern.

King Dary had little sleep that night. Not long after retiring, he was awakened by a knock at his chamber door and Feogh came in.

"King Dary," he said hesitantly, "I must talk with you. It is strange words I've heard tonight."

"Strange words?" repeated Dary, his mind still clouded with sleep. "What is it, Feogh?"

"Well, sir, it is hard to tell . . ."

"Feogh, I am trying to get my rest. What is it, and what makes you so afraid?"

"All right, sir, if you're wishin' to know. I served the Connacht-men after your warriors had gone. Fair drinkin' they did, then, and their tongues loosened in their heads."

"Their tongues?" said Dary, fully awake now. "What are you about, man? Tell it out!"

"Yes sir, I'm tellin' as well as I can. You see, they got to talkin' and one says how fine a king you are to be lettin' the bull go from Ulster."

"Fair enough praise, Feogh," said Dary irritably.

"To start, surely. But then another replies, 'You need not be a praisin' of him. It's well he let the bull go, else Meave would have come and taken it from him!' "

Dary was stunned by this. Then, with a move as swift as that of any young man, he leaped to his feet and seized the ancient steward by either shoulder with a hard grip.

"By my fathers and by yours, Feogh," he said fiercely, "is it the truth you tell me now, or was it only mad voices come from too much wine that you heard?"

Wounded by the accusation, the old servant drew himself up straight.

"I've had no drink tonight, my King, in order to better serve your honored guests."

"My honored guests!" Dary repeated bitterly. He dropped his arms back limply to his sides as a great weariness flowed over him. "Aye, that they were, by me given food and drink and shelter and the very bull entrusted me by all of Ulster. And for that my honored guests dishonor me . . . at my own table!"

He turned and walked away, but stopped to look back toward the steward.

"And Fergus . . . was he a part of this?"

"That I cannot tell you. He was there with them. Remember, Dary, Fergus is now a man of Connacht."

"I live too much in the old days," Dary said. "Too certain I was that things were still as they were."

As anger filled him his weariness dropped away. He knew what had to be done.

"Feogh, call my chieftains," he commanded. Then, to himself, he said: "I've no wish to kill him, but I cannot trust him any longer."

When Fergus had roused his warriors next morning, he found one of Dary's lieutenants waiting. The young man told him that he would find the black bull in an enclosure outside the dun, just to the west, and that Dary was waiting there for him. Fergus and his party entered their chariots and rumbled across the drawbridge and down the hill to the plain below.

But the land to the west was empty. They found no enclosures and no one awaited them.

"I don't understand," said Fergus, looking back up the hill toward the dun. As he did, the bridge over the foss began to lift.

"By the gods . . . come on!" Fergus cried. He pulled the reins from his driver and, with a shout, he urged the horses back up toward the gates.

He reached the foss ahead of the others, but not before the bridge had been raised too far to allow passage. In frustration he brought the chariot to a halt beside the bronze gong, pulled out his heavy mace, and began to beat upon the metal circle like a madman.

The sound rang through the countryside, booming back from the surrounding hills for miles around, falling back upon itself in a confused, deafening reverberation that continued long after he had stopped.

"Dary, show yourself to me," Fergus bellowed. "What is happening here?"

For moments there was no response, but then the king appeared atop the wall by the gates.

"You'll not give insult to us, Fergus MacRogh," he cried. "Go back to your queen, now, with empty hands."

"Insult?" Fergus said. "Tell me what has happened."

"Well enough you know. You'll not be taking the Black Bull of Cuailgne from this place. And, one thing more I'll say: if Meave, Queen of Connacht, wishes the bull now, she herself will have to come and take it!"

Chapter Five
THE JUDGMENT

Fergus and his companions returned to Cruchane and were greeted by the cheers of its populace.

Their return had been reported to Queen Meave long before their arrival, and she had taken this time to arrange a proper welcome. The feat was not difficult in Cruchane, a city of several thousands. It needed only an announcement from Meave to bring most of them out to honor the popular chieftain. So, as MacRogh and his small troop wound up the main avenue to the entrance of the fortress, they found the entire way lined with crowds of joyous citizens.

Fergus led his men, his face as hard as if the cold marble of Connemara were carved in his guise. Close behind him rode Calatin, his own, calm look concealing his satisfaction at seeing the mighty warrior so discomfited. The Enchanter knew well that Fergus, already confused and angered by the actions of Dary, must be further thrown aback by this unexpected embarrassment. He laughed inwardly to think how such a dreadful error had been made.

Within Cruchane's main gates the party dismounted and entered the Tec Meadcuarta. Inside they found the walls hung with the shields and banners of the subject tribes and the long tables filled with scores of warriors who stood and raised a cheer as Fergus appeared.

But the cheering died almost at once, silence rolling back through the gathering as a ripple rushes away from a stone dropped in a pond. Fergus took on the nature of such a stone in his advance across the floor, for all in the room knew the commander's moods, and his dark, un-smiling countenance told them there was no reason to rejoice.

At the far end of the hall Meave waited before the royal couch with Aileel at her side. Proud and tall she stood to receive her champion, smiling with welcome. Then that smile faded as she watched Fergus striding through the now quiet men toward her.

He stopped before the dais, standing with his legs set solidly apart as if to brace himself for battle. Behind him his party stopped and clustered, all apprehensive save for the seemingly impassive druid.

Fergus had planned on a simple statement to the queen, but this misunderstanding of his mission's outcome had fully bewildered him. Now he struggled to find some way of beginning that might soften the blunt truth, though it came hard to one used to directness.

But his first words were forestalled by a grim irony. Aileel, unable to see the reactions of those around him, had remained caught up with the spirit of celebration. Now he stepped forward and clasped Fergus heartily on the shoulder.

"Full honors to you, Fergus MacRogh," he said resoundingly. "We welcome you and the great bull of Cuailgne."

The words hung mockingly in the silent room. For a moment they turned every man to stone. In shock and agony, Fergus could only look from Aileel to Meave, for he had no way to respond to this.

The queen reacted swiftly and simply. She lifted a hand to her husband's arm.

"Aileel," she said gently, "I am afraid our welcome's come a bit too soon."

"Oh?" said the king uncertainly and peered into the commander's face. Then his other senses closed the gap. He became aware of the silence, of the tenseness about him. He felt, rather than saw, the dismay in MacRogh, and full understanding came home.

"I . . . I am sorry, Fergus," Aileel told him in a faltering voice and stepped back. "What has happened?"

"It is I who should be sorry, my King," Fergus replied. "I got no animal, though I had no thought you would be so certain I could. I said before I left that Ulster would never agree."

In the quiet hall a faint murmuring was heard as Fergus's words were passed back through the crowd.

"We meant only to honor you in this," Meave assured him. "We had some mistaken word that you had won the bull. Why did you fail to get it? Was the wealth I offered in exchange too little for it?"

"It could be that, my Queen," Fergus answered. "And it could be that the pride of Ulster would not let it go."

While these words were being exchanged, Calatin moved from the group behind Fergus to stand at one side, closer to the queen. As Fergus concluded, the ard-druid spoke for the first time.

"Your offer was not turned down, my Queen. At first, Dary accepted it!"

"And he had a free will to change his mind as well," Fergus shot toward him tersely.

"But why did their minds change?" Meave asked, perplexed.

"I have no certain reason," Fergus responded truthfully.

"Yet, Dary did agree," Calatin said again.

"No final settlement was made, Enchanter," Fergus said slowly. "He was not bound. The freedom to withdraw was clear."

"I will not abide this longer, Queen," said Calatin. "Fergus does not tell you all."

With the swiftness of a bull tormented beyond its short patience, Fergus wheeled angrily on the druid.

"Watch yourself, Calatin. It's I who tell this."

Calatin coolly ignored the threat. "My Queen, Fergus finds it difficult to speak, perhaps from his old feelings of loyalty to . . ."

A hand smashed the druid back against a roof pillar and a sword point touched his belly. It needed only a push from Fergus to pin the man to the wood.

"If you question my loyalty here . . . I'll kill you," the commander grated.

There were some murmurs in the assembly at this sudden action, but no one lifted a voice in protest, except for Meave.

"Fergus, wait!" she cried.

"Yes, wait," said Calatin, unruffled, amused by his ability to arouse the Exile's wrath. "You are too sensitive about your loyalty, MacRogh. You have a right to be. I meant no disrespect. I can understand you wishing to avoid casting dishonor on your own homeland."

"What are you speaking of, Calatin?" Meave asked, bewildered by this exchange. "Fergus, let him speak."

Reluctantly, Fergus released the man and moved back, but his sword stayed out, glittering in his hand as he shifted it angrily.

"I would not speak," said Calatin, pushing past the weapon nonchalantly, "but this outrage cannot be ignored. The bull may not have been brought back, but Dary had agreed to give it to us. Then, for no reason, he turned us out by trickery."

"He may have had reasons," said Fergus. "He made mention of an insult. It might be there was some misunderstanding . . ."

"Fergus may struggle to find excuses if he likes," Calatin interrupted, and raised his voice so those around could clearly hear, "but there is something else he cannot excuse. King Dary has challenged Meave and all of Eire!"

Now the whole assembly did respond, with cries of anger and astonishment.

"Challenged?" Meave repeated. "How?"

Calatin turned to face the crowd and spoke directly to them. "His last words to us were: 'Let Meave take the bull!' "

The murmur of the crowd grew in volume at that, the anger in it assuming a harder, more strident note.

"I said it would be so," Aileel said harshly. "Our herds were made vast with swords, not words. We offer words and they laugh and cast us out like so many poor beggars."

"Be easy, my King," Meave cautioned. She knew the mood of her men was dark and unsettled, and she wanted no chance of losing full control of this situation. In a carefully neutral voice she added: "Perhaps there were reasons for this unfortunate happening."

Aileel was uncompromising. "There are no reasons that can lessen such a challenge."

"Perhaps," she told him, soothingly, "but we must know all the facts."

"And know them honestly, my Queen," Fergus said. "The druid is trying to stir the crowd to follow him . . ."

"I speak nothing but the truth in this . . ." Calatin protested.

"Silence, all of you!" the Queen said in an even, quiet voice which could not be ignored. All conversation stopped. "We will go up to my quarters to discuss it. Fergus, Calatin and you other chieftains, come with me." She raised her voice to address the assembly. "You warriors stay and drink and talk, and you will hear my decision in good time. But, speak no more upon the matter now before me until I have heard it all!"

With that warning she turned and left the dais. Arm in arm with Aileel, she led the way up the stairs to the sunroom, followed by a score of chieftains and advisors. She crossed the room and turned to face the men who formed a half-circle about her and the king. In the open space between, Calatin and Fergus stood facing one another with the wariness of a wolf and a wolfhound, each trying to estimate the other's strength.

"Now, MacRogh," said Meave, "you mentioned reasons Dary may have had. And, what would they be?"

"I say he may have had reasons, but I've no way of knowing what it was," Fergus admitted.

"Just say there was," Meave asked. "Only tell me what this reason might have been."

Though her voice was still even, still carefully neutral, yet did Fergus feel the plea in it. She asked him for some fact, some object to grasp, some excuse to neutralize the horrifying implications of this insult before it was too late.

"Fergus," she prompted again, "tell me, or I will have no more a free hand in this."

He searched his memory for some clue, some shred of fact to explain Dary's actions, but there was nothing. Save falsehood, there was no way to give Meave any reasons. He shook his great head in despair.

"I cannot lie, my Queen. Dary is an old man, and a proud one . . . but he would never act without cause. Still, I cannot explain."

Meave shook her head. "I am sorry, Fergus, but we must conclude that this challenge is unjust. If it is, it cannot be ignored. Do you understand that?"

He nodded. He knew that to let such an insult go would mean dishonor to Connacht and death to her power.

"Why so reluctant, Fergus?" asked the druid. "Was it the war which exiled you that so destroyed your taste for again meeting Ulster in battle?"

Fergus turned a gaze of cold rage on Calatin. "Twice today you have given me fair cause to claim that head you're wearing, Enchanter. Take care not to make it a third."

"Fergus is not the only one who might have doubts in this," said Cormac Conlingas, stepping out from the circle of chiefs.

"Another Exile speaks to echo the first," the druid said.

Meave ignored him. "What are your doubts, Cormac?" she asked.

"My Queen, regardless of your worthy advisor's subtle insinuations . . ." several laughed openly at that ". . . you must know none of the Exiles hesitates because our home was Ulster. We are with Fergus. We'll war against Conchobar gladly . . . for a reason. But, the price of a bull seems a poor reason for men to die!"

"It is much more than that, now," said Calatin.

"Aye, it is!" a voice boomed, and a square giant of a man, topping Fergus himself by nearly a head, shouldered his way to the front of the group.

"Lok MacFavash," said Meave. "Surprised I am to hear such a lengthy speech from the chieftain of Lath Moah."

"That's true enough," he answered fiercely. "I'm not given much to talk, save when I'm angered to it. And, no anger has ever raged as hot in me as that caused by this insult from Ulster. Too many years have they kept separate from the rest of Eire and held themselves better. This is not our only insult from them. It is only the last!"

A sword flashed into his hand, the great blade fragile-seeming in his giant grip.

"Make them swallow iron and see how well they speak of us," he said. "Eire has waited years to do that."

"Not so fast, my bloodthirsty comrade," cautioned Lewy MacNeesh, the young and thoughtful leader of the Clan Falva. "Ulster may brag, I'll not deny it, but there's more than a little truth behind the words. No one here could easily deny that Ulster would be a fair opponent ... even against all the other four provinces of Eire."

"You stand with Cormac, then?" asked Meave.

"That's a hard thing to say, my Queen. I'd not like to cross my sword with the likes of Ulster, but I'd like to see her united with Eire at last."

"And under Queen Meave and King Aileel," Calatin added emphatically, drawing enthusiastic agreement from the chieftains.

"Still, still ..." Lewy went on reflectively, "it is a weighty judgment. Perhaps ..." he looked at Calatin appraisingly "... perhaps we should consult our other druids."

"There is no need," Meave said decisively. "This matter has gone beyond advice. The challenge has been made. The reasons for it and the results it will have take no part in our decision. Let us leave it to our warriors, now."

She walked to the balcony and looked down into the hall.

"Men of Eire," she called, and the eyes of all turned up to her. "What do you say? Do we go to Ulster?"

From the throat and heart of every man a single answer came at once.

"To Ulster!"

Book Two

THE HOSTING
OF MEAVE

Chapter Six
PROPHECY

Meave rode out alone from Cruchane, far to the north of Ai. Near by the Plains of Maugh Turiedh she halted her light chariot at the foot of a small, round hill.

Leaving her vehicle, she climbed a narrow path to the top where sat a tiny stone hut surrounded by a low wall of rocks, both laid together without mortar. An old, old man sat before the hut, basking in the rare sun. He seemed asleep, but at her approach he opened his eyes and looked toward her without sign of surprise.

"You have come a long way," he stated. "Would you have something to refresh yourself?"

"I'm comfortable enough, thank you," she told him.

Her manner was reserved, and the man's countenance darkened.

"What is it you've come to me for, my Queen?" he asked. "Before, you've never been so formal and so grim. I feel the portent of terrible things in you this day."

"Terrible they may be," she said. "I have sent messengers through the provinces of Eire, to all who give me allegiance or fear my power or owe me a debt.

"Now all the land shakes and from every rath and cathir and dun come the warlike children of Milith to join me. They gather now upon the Plains of Ai to war against Ulster."

"Ulster?" The old man seemed appalled by this news. "What has brought such a thing about?"

"Their own arrogance has brought it on them. Too long has that single province defied the rest of Eire."

"Can there be a no mistake?" he asked. "Can you not wait . . ."

"There is not time for waiting," she interrupted. "Spring and its sun are with us now, and now is our best chance to move against them. Soon enough will the summer rains begin. But, why all these questions? I've come to ask you of this, not tell."

"I know nothing," he said, shaking his head sadly. "This future is all closed to me."

"How can that be?" Meave asked. "Always we have come to you, and never have you failed to favor us."

"Forces far beyond my poor abilities are set in motion here. I cannot help you. There is only one thing I can tell you: the plains here were once the ground for a battle between the Firbolgs and the Riders of the Sidhe. No bloodier conflict has Eire seen since then. But listen, Meave, if the four provinces of Eire war against Ulster, that battle's match in death may yet be made."

"You are too old," Meave said angrily. "You have forgotten the glory of war. Sit on your hill, sheltered from the world, separate from men and from men's hopes and desires."

"We all grow old, Queen, unless we are taken to Tir-na-nog by the de Dannan," he reminded her sharply, "and all wars do not end in glory. You may lose this one."

Meave wished no further argument with him. She left the old man, then, and returned to her chariot, frustrated and disturbed by his inability to help her. But as she entered her vehicle and prepared to drive away, a voice behind her spoke in tones as light as soaring birds upon the air.

"The future is not closed to me, Meave."

She whirled about and found a figure had suddenly appeared on the road. It was a woman, tall and slender and pale, clad in a shimmering cloak of silver-gray.

"Who are you?" asked the queen.

"Faythleen, I am, the Prophetess of Tara. I've come to you now, hearing that you wish to know what will happen."

Meave did not question this. She accepted the existence of the Sidhe with their strange powers, as did all those of Eire.

"My army lies south, on the Plains of Ai," she said.

"Soon they will go to war against Ulster. Tell me, how do you see them faring?"

The prophetess closed her eyes. For a moment she was still, as if in thought, and then she spoke:

"Bloodied, I see them all, and crimson."

"And the Red Branch?" Meave asked quickly. "What of Ulster's warriors?"

"Bloodied all, and crimson," the prophetess intoned. "But a great hound I see, rending the host of Eire with its iron claws."

This dark vision concerned Meave, for it seemed to suggest that the old man's warning could not be ignored. The prophecy of wounds and deaths brought another urgent question to her mind, but a dread of the answer made her hesitate before she spoke.

"And what of me? How do you see me in this?"

Faythleen seemed troubled by the question. For the first time the finely drawn lines of her face hardened in concentration. When finally she replied it was with a faint reluctance, as if the words were pulled from her against her will.

"You will survive, O Queen."

"Ah," breathed Meave, released from her alarm. "For a moment I envisioned black defeat and all of us destroyed. But, if I do survive, why that must be in part a prophecy of our victory, bloody though you see it. The warriors of Eire expect some death in war."

The prophetess opened her eyes. The soft lights shining there had hardened to become the icy chill of a winter sun flashing sharply from the frozen snow.

"See the portents as you wish, Meave," she said, "but beware. It is not an easy way you choose. Any advice you hear, judge carefully, for any bargains you make you may regret."

With that, waiting no reply, Faythleen turned and was gone, flitting away like the shadow of a leaf blown across the plain by an autumn wind.

The prophetess left Meave deeply distressed of mind and heart. She felt an immense weariness sweep over her and impatiently urged her horses ahead, suddenly anxious to return to the comforting fastness of Dun Cruchane.

The way had been short to her before, but now there

seemed no ending to it. As she drove on and on through a countryside of barren, rocky hills, her thoughts were plagued with shadowed images of strange, savage beasts and of men deeply torn by ragged wounds.

Even the day seemed bent toward weighing upon her humor, for gray clouds were drawn over the sun, and cold mists gathered to clutch at the hilltops and fill the valleys with their clinging dampness.

Still, the journey finally reached its end, and as abruptly as did the barony of hills. Meave crossed a final rise and the Plains of Ai opened before her, with such a fair sight as to drive the dark spirits from her mind. For there, about the royal dun, the plains were filled with a vast army of men.

From tribes and tuaths throughout the four provinces, thousands of warriors had already gathered. The colored cloaks and shields and banners of them made a bright, shifting pattern against the green fields. And in the air, too, was another splendid mixture, but of sound. A great cacophony it was, of clanging weapons, neighing steeds, the creak of harness and chariot wheels, the shouts of officers and the cheers of men that spoke out brazenly of power and might and roused the spirit with a martial exhilaration.

And more men were coming constantly. Even as she approached, the gray-cloaked battalions of Lewy Mac-Neesh appeared on the opposite horizon, and within the army the newly arrived tribes of Firbolgs were being assigned their sites for camp.

Those units which had arrived before were already engaged in various tasks. Some were involved in the construction of the vast encampment, some ordered the formation of the many battalions of infantry while, on the training fields, Cormac Conlingas directed squadrons of attack-chariots in maneuvers, their extended scythes glinting wickedly as they swept about to cut down imaginary enemies.

Through the center of this maelstrom of warriors, Fergus MacRogh seemed to sail in his chariot, as serene and sure as a great ship upon a quiet sea. Meave noted with admiration that under his skillful direction things about

her commander were already taking on a greater degree
of calm.

She would have ridden directly to the dun, but this
view of her hosting army had restored some of her confidence, and she wished to inhale the rich atmosphere of
war more fully now. She wanted the might of Eire about
her, to banish all the images of defeat.

Meave reached the outer fringes of the force and
stopped, throwing back the hood of her cloak. No sign of
authority was needed to signal her presence. Even the
faint sunlight caused her hair to glow with an aura more
brilliant than that of any red-gold crown. At once the
men of Eire turned and began to cry out her name.

"Meave! Meave!" The shout went up and grew and
grew with swiftness as it carried through the army. Men
stopped their work and moved toward her, forming a
dense mass about her chariot a hundred deep, all chanting her name.

The noise of it was deafening, but that she did not
mind. The cheers were an intoxicant like the finest ale, to
be consumed in great draughts and let to course warmly
through the blood. She smiled proudly and raised one of
her battle spears to salute the warriors, and they cried out
the louder in reply. She asked herself how she could
doubt the invincibility of such men.

Then Meave saw Fergus across the mass of warriors,
pushing his chariot toward her through the press. He saw
her watching him and held her eye, his look hard with his
displeasure.

He felt there was good cause for anger. His long efforts
at order had been swept away by this single display of
egotism on her part. How was he to shape her army in
only a few days if he was not left alone to do so?

Meave read this in his look and, at first affronted by it,
tried to return his glare with bold command. But her
fairness of mind told her this act had been no help to him.
So she waved a parting to the men, drove out of the
crowd and up the hill to the dun.

In front of the main gates of the fortress she found
Aileel seated on a couch. Before him was spread a view
of the host of Eire and, because he could see little of it, a

young bard stood beside him to describe the scene in colorful detail. To this he listened, and to the sounds of the army itself, and was soothed by them, for to him these were more beautiful than the playing of any harp or the lay of any fili.

Meave paused upon the bridge to watch him, grateful to see him so at ease.

"You are happy, husband?" she called to him.

He looked toward her when he heard her voice.

"Meave! You are quickly returned. Aye, wife, it is happy I am. One, final hosting this may be for me, and I am glad to know what I can of it."

"Talk no such foolishness," she told him sternly, but the fatalistic words had done their work on her. As she parted from him and drove into the dun, a sense of doubt once more assailed her.

She climbed from her chariot before the stables and gave the horses over to the attendants' care. She walked up to the Tec Meadcuarta and at its door she found Calatin waiting.

"I've been watching for your return from the parapet walk," he explained. "How are the signs?"

"There are none from the prophet," she answered him as they entered the hall, "but a young woman causes me some fears."

At first Calatin only seemed amused by this. "Some fears? What, did she foretell doom?"

Meave's reply was grave. "Not in plain words, but I feel there is some threat from Ulster."

The ard-druid sensed the seriousness in her and was sobered at once.

"This was no mere woman to bring such a cloud over you."

"No mere woman," Meave agreed. "One of the Sidhe it was."

"Aye, I thought it might have been," he said, but then his voice assumed a hearty and persuasive tone, "yet, remember my Queen, the powers of the Sidhe are not so great. It is not they who rule our fate, but each of us. You've powers at your own command to rival theirs."

She would have protested that, so much despondency she felt, but she saw the look in his face and it made her

pause. She met his eyes and recognized there an overwhelming confidence. It seemed to flow into her as their
gazes locked, flooding her with new strength greater than
any she had known.

"My powers are vast, Meave," he said. "They tell me
more than anyone, mortal or Sidhe. I tell you that no one
will withstand us."

He spoke and she believed. The words of the prophetess were swept away and only his assurances remained.

"I rely on you, Calatin," she said. "I hold you to be
one of my strongest supporters."

"Some day I hope to be the strongest," he replied.

After Meave and Aileel and the rest of the dun had
gone to sleep, after the army on the plains had rolled
itself into its cloaks for the night, then did the druid
Calatin begin to act.

He called his many sons to him and, together, they
took chariots and rode stealthily away from Cruchane.

For a great distance at a great speed they rode until, at
last, in the dark time just past the night's heart, they
reached the Moher Cliffs that rose steeply above the
Western Sea.

At once the sons of Calatin fell to work. From the
chariots they unloaded large quantities of wood, of yew
and mountain ash and other druidic trees. A giant pyre
was built of it and set alight. Carefully was the fire fed
and strengthened until its flames seemed as a red shining
forest of strange trees.

While the sons labored, Calatin went onto the very
edge of the high cliffs. Far below, their face dropped
straight away to the ocean. Black and smooth the water
lay beneath the thin curve of the aging moon; a sea with
no limit, but at the very edge of all.

The druid raised his arms and spoke aloud to the
spirits there, the spirits he commanded. Soon the waters
out before him began to roll and seethe like the waters of
a cauldron heated by a fire of its own. Upon the surface a
haze collected and began to writhe as if blown by disor-
dering winds. A heavy fog, gray-black and odorous, rose
out of the deepest realms of the ocean where lived things
ancient, cold, and alien to man. Soon it covered miles of

sea and it grew more and more, rolling up ever thicker from beneath.

When it had covered the night sky above the cliffs, Calatin returned to the fire, now sending its flames so high they colored the hanging belly of the clouds with a tinge of blood. From one of his sons the druid took a large, round object, a ball made up of many elements culled from the sea and sky and air. He lifted the ball and cast it into the heart of the blaze. It flared at once with a bright light and the fire began to send up a column of smoke, black and oily and smelling as from burning pitch.

As the viscous smoke billowed up to mate unnaturally with the clouds, Calatin and his sons linked arms about the pyre. The flames glinted redly in the circle of eyes and raised a florid glow in the pale faces that shifted and changed eerily as the clan moved about. While the sons chanted a nameless incantation, the father spoke aloud to the roiling fog.

"Now, go north into Ulster," he commanded. "Roll over the lands of the Red Branch and take my poisoned seeds to the gates of Emain Macha itself. Bring madness and confusion on all who breathe your vapors."

As if in answer to his orders, a wind rose from the west. It sent the long, dark banks of clouds over the heads of the Clan Calatin and on toward the north.

The ard-druid watched it move away, then turned and looked about him at his sons. As he did, their chanting died and they stood silent, waiting, meeting his appraising eye.

"And for you," he said to them, "it is a sorry, misshapen lot of men you are, unfit for war or love or nobility. But you're clever and you're hard, each one of you, and you've been taught by me to make your talents work. They laugh at you, but now you'll wield more power with my ways than any of those strutting fools with their absurd weapons and useless honor.

"The mist will bring a weakness on Ulster's minds, but that is all. It is you who will use that weakness against them. You must go now, disperse and enter Ulster ahead of Meave's army. You must visit every dun and every liss. Spread confusion with wild rumors and tales of horror and woe. Many will believe you, more will be thrown into disorder, but all must be led astray. There's not a man of Ulster who can know of our attack or move to stop it until it is too late!"

Chapter Seven
THE APPOINTMENT

In the fortress of Dun Dalgan, atop the cliffs on Eire's Eastern Sea, Cuculain awoke early to find his wife, Emer, had already risen. He dressed himself in the warrior's loose linen tunic and went out of the sleeping quarters into the central hall. There Emer was at work directing servants in the laying out of breakfast.

"Is it guests we are having this morning?" he asked with curiosity.

"Good day, husband," Emer greeted him. "Are you well?"

"Well I am, and hungry. But, what is all of this?"

"This is a morning meal, and for you. We dine alone."

"I said that I was hungry, but I have the hunger of only one man," he said with amusement. He sat down at the table and looked over plates of meat and cakes and fresh picked watercresses without enthusiasm, for he was not given to such hearty meals.

"You should fill yourself properly today," she told him firmly, seating herself across from him. "No man should travel with a hunger in him."

He looked at her in surprise. "Travel? And what would make you think I had that in my mind?"

"It's been nearly a fortnight since your visit from the prophetess. You must start today to reach Tara in time to meet with her."

"You've a great deal of certainty in something I've not spoken much about."

"Not spoken of, no . . . not in words. But last night I woke with that thought in my mind, and there you were, rolling about and muttering in your own sleep. We've not been married but two years, but I know your moods well enough to understand what such uneasiness might mean."

"Ah, beautiful Emer," he said with sadness, for it pained him to think of leaving his fair-haired young wife. "Little enough time I've had to be with you, and now my leave from Conchobar and Emain Macha is to be broken. Perhaps I should not go."

"You must go," she answered simply. "The Sidhe cannot be denied."

He looked at her appraisingly and smiled. "You know my very mind. There's no need for talk with the two of us."

"That's as it should be. But why is there this doubt in you?"

"There's something in this that I've no liking for. I'm asked to do a thing I do not understand, Emer."

"The Sidhe have chosen you to help them in some way, Cuculain. You are needed by them."

"But why? I've not asked for it."

She looked down at her plate, and her voice dropped. "You know why that may be."

"I know nothing of why," he replied hotly. "I am the son of Sualtim . . . that is all!"

Her voice remained soft. "And yet, you are not like other men." She raised her eyes to him and smiled gently. "Oh, husband, I could wish you were, but what other boy of barely eighteen years could have carried me away from my father with a whole army so set against him?"

His anger left him, and he took her hand.

"Emer," he said, "what man would not have tried?"

At that she blushed with pleasure and modesty, but she would not be diverted from her way.

"Enough now," she told him with mock sternness. She took his hand from hers and placed a knife in it. "Get to your eating and leave none of this food."

"What?" he cried. "Then I'd best wait until tomorrow to make my start. I'll be needing today to finish breakfasting."

"Enough of your attempts at humor, too. It's poor enough without you trying it so early in the day!"

He put on a thoroughly abashed expression at that. "As you command, my lady," he said submissively, "but first let me see to my going. I must give orders to have a chariot made ready."

"That has been done. Laeg is making ready my own chariot and horses for your traveling."

"Your own? I'll not take them," he protested. "This is an easy journey. Any animals of ours could make it."

"No arguments. It has been done. Now, please eat."

After they had dined, Cuculain returned to his quarters to ready himself while Emer went about gathering supplies for his trip. His preparation was a simple one. About the waist of the knee-length shirt he buckled a light, cloth belt with a finely wrought silver buckle, wondering as he did if he could fasten it after the meal his wife had forced upon him. Over this he strapped on a heavier belt that supported the scabbard of his long sword. About his shoulders he threw a long, wool cloak of deep crimson, securing it across his chest by a silver clasp. A similar clasp held his long hair behind his shoulders.

He returned again to the central hall and, seeing no one there but the servants cleaning, went to the main doors. Here he encountered another man who was about to enter.

In appearance and stature this man and Cuculain were much alike; both tall and fair, both with a confidence and grace of movement that belied their youthful looks and the good-natured glint in their eyes. Chariot driver and companion they were, but the only difference in them was in the pants worn by the newcomer, a sign of the serving classes. In all ways they were equals to each other, each skilled in his own profession, each respectful and proud of the other's skill.

"Laeg!" said Cuculain with good cheer. "Is Emer's chariot ready?"

"It is, Cu," the other replied. "When is it we'll be starting?"

"We two will not start at all. I'll be going alone, my friend. There's not much reason for us both to ride to Tara."

"You'd not take your driver? How can you go alone?"

Cuculain laughed. "I can drive myself, Laeg, even though I know you doubt any warrior capable of it."

Laeg nodded. "Aye, most of your noble class are a helpless lot when it comes to the animals. Still," he added grudgingly, "you've skill enough to manage it, after your poor fashion. Even so, I'd like to go with you. You might be needing the companionship."

"No, I can go alone and . . ." Cuculain frowned as he tried to strengthen a vague impression that had entered his mind, ". . . and I've a feeling that it ought to be that way."

At that a look of disappointment filled the driver's face, and as Cuculain noted it, he smiled in understanding.

"Poor Laeg. It's bored you are with this simple, quiet life we country people lead. You've need of some adventure." He put an arm about his friend and spoke in confidence to him. "I know what you should do: return to Emain Macha! There are happenings enough there to amuse even so worldly a man as you."

Laeg eyed him without conviction.

"Oh, that's just fine, that is. And what about you, roving the country alone with your spirited team?"

"You've too much worry in you," Cuculain said casually. "It is a simple journey I'm going on. When I return, I'll come to meet you in the capital."

They went out of the tec into the courtyard enclosed by the fortress walls. There the pleasure-chariot of Emer was drawn up, its two splendid chestnut horses standing calmly while Emer, with a servant's help, loaded baskets into it.

Curious, the two men stopped and stood in rapt observation of her labors. With her brow furrowed in concentration, she worked with care to arrange the containers within the confined space, then shook her head and had them pulled out to begin the painstaking process all again. Laeg and Cuculain were immensely intrigued by this strange activity, exchanging bemused looks and puzzled shrugs. After they had watched for some time, Cuculain was moved to make inquiry of her.

"My dear wife, what is it you're doing here? I'm to be gone a few days only. I've little need of such a quantity of supplies as you are loading . . . unless you've been thinking I'm to take half the garrison in my one vehicle!"

"You may have need of this," she answered with determination, arranging another basket precisely. Then, turning to him, concern came into her eyes. "But, what of you, husband? Why is it you're dressed so? Where is your armor and your other weapons?"

Cuculain's look of puzzlement grew. "Why, Emer, my armor is in the armories of Emain Macha, as is my chariot-of-war and horses. Have you known me yet to bring them home with me? They are weapons of battle and I'm at rest here."

"You are right," she said with disappointment. "I only hoped . . . I thought you might need them on the journey."

"I have my sword," he clasped the inlaid hilts, "and I have my hunting spears and my clog to cut kindling for my fires. There's no more that I need."

She was not satisfied. "Very well, if you go so unarmed, then take the food I've brought."

"Gladly I will, but not so much of it!"

"Let me be humored in this," she entreated, moving to him and laying a hand on his arm. "Take the food, for it will ease your way and the worry in my heart."

"What is this worry you're speaking of? You it was who told me to go!"

"You must go, but I've some feelings in this that have me wishing to see you go prepared."

So earnest was she that Cuculain could not refuse her.

"All right," he agreed, trying to match her seriousness with his own. "I'll take your food if I can get into the chariot with it."

"Sentanta," said a voice, addressing Cuculain by his boyhood name, "please let me go with you."

Those around the chariot turned to find an older man standing in the doorway to the hall.

He was a stooped and bony figure, face heavily lined and twisted with emotions openly displayed as in the face of a small child. Visitors to Dun Dalgan assumed him to be one weakened in mind and body by age and were amazed to find he was Cuculain's father, Sualtim, a man still in his middle years.

Not so long before, when Cuculain had been a boy in the military school of Emain Macha, Sualtim had ruled the tuath of Muirthemne with skill and wisdom. But then, it seemed, the pressures of his trust had brought a weakness on his mind. His rule, his very life had grown too complex for him. A madman he had become, flying into rages at the most innocent words, trusting no one, shrinking into himself until he could no longer be reached.

It was the Fool-of-the-Forth had touched him, many said, and even the physicians and the druids of Ulster could do little for his ills. Finally his family, fearful and uncertain, had locked him away for his own safety.

But when Cuculain had attained his warrior status and returned to rule Muirthemne, he had found no value to Sualtim's imprisonment. He had seen that his father was harmless to all and had ordered him released. That had been a cure of sorts, for the man had recovered a partial sanity, recognizing his friends and his surroundings once again. Still, a vagueness remained, a reluctance to commit himself to act, to be responsible, as if the mind knew what had hurt it before and sought to avoid that pain again at any cost. So, Sualtim wandered about the fortress and the countryside, enjoying his freedom but remaining close to Cuculain, the way a starved hound remains close to one who feeds him.

For his part, Cuculain tried to help his father and was a patient and loving attendant to him. In most things he allowed Sualtim to go along, but for his present mission he wanted no company. Gently but firmly he told the man that he must remain behind and Sualtim, disappointment clear in his openly expressive face, turned and moved away.

"It's sorry I am," Cuculain explained, looking after his father, "but I'll travel faster alone and return the sooner."

"That you hope," Laeg remarked with the easy directness which marked the close nature of their relationship. "I'm still thinking it's the errand of a fool to meet with one of the Sidhe."

"The Sidhe do not lie," Cuculain reminded his driver, "and they're not given to coming on false missions."

"Maybe," Laeg conceded, "yet, who can say why they act? They've reasons in what they do that are far removed from ours."

"They know more of the weave of things than we. Our ends may be the same, though we often seem to move at cross purposes. Still, understanding it or not, I am bound by my word to see what Faythleen has to say."

"Well, be wary of her movements, my lad," warned Laeg who, for all his cleverness, still felt the serving classes' fear of these beings. "If not, you'll find yourself entangled in some otherworldly quest of hers before you can blink. I've an uncle went away with them for a year . . . no laughing, now, from you . . . and he had to serve them and milk their cows. A fine life that would be for the Champion of Ulster."

"I'm glad to hear you agree he should be wary," Emer declared before her husband could reply to Laeg. "I've no feeling we should fear the Sidhe, but some danger may yet lie in this for him."

Cuculain looked from one to the other and shrugged. "You've trapped me well between. I'll be crushed by so much logic, even if it is logic a little twisted to your own minds. Let me be going now, and I promise you I'll return in a few days."

"Take care, husband," Emer told him, wholly sober now. "Don't be taking my feelings lightly, for it's said that Eire's women may know of things long before they are begun!"

"I will take care," he assured her in like soberness, and then embraced her tightly for a moment.

A warrior of Eire was not much given to display affection in public beyond words, and this simple sign meant much for these two. When Cuculain released her, he turned to Laeg and clasped his shoulder.

"Take your own care in Emain Macha. It's you, I think, who go into most danger with sports and ale and too many . . . other pleasures."

At that the boyish driver colored with embarrassment. He lifted a light, red-painted shield with Cuculain's black boar's head device from the ground beside the chariot and handed it to his companion.

"Get on with you now," he said, "and return quickly or I'll not be saving any ale for you."

"That had best be all you save," Emer told Laeg in a voice at once chiding and full of merriment.

For a moment more the three young people stood there, silently. Then Cuculain swung himself into the chariot and lifted the reins.

"Good-bye," he said, but then he paused. "Where is my father gone?"

The others looked about, but the man had vanished.

"Ah, well, he's doubtless off on some errand of his own," said Cuculain. "Just as well, for it is as hard to take leave of him as of a small boy. Good-bye once more. I'll see you in a few days' time."

With that he urged the horses on and rode out through the outer wall. Down the rocky pathway from the cliffs he went, finally into the greener lands that made up the rich heart of the tuath of Muirthemne. He saw no one for some time as he rode until, on crossing a wide plain, he chanced to look behind and spied a small moving shape far to his rear.

Curious, he pulled his horses up and waited, watching as the tiny point grew larger and resolved itself into a chariot like his own occupied by one rider who he was finally able to recognize.

"Father!" he cried sternly as the other vehicle reached him. "You were to stay in Dun Dalgan."

Sualtim looked about with nervous eyes as does a child caught in a mischievous act. It pained Cuculain greatly to see this once strong man so reduced in mind, and he had no heart to be so harsh with him.

"Please, go back," he said more gently. "This trip will not be pleasant."

"I have convinced myself I can drive again," Sualtim pleaded. "I have not ridden out in years. Let me try."

The plea was not lost on Cuculain. The idea that here lay hope for his father's improvement worked on him. The trip might be a good one for such a trial.

"And, do you harness the animals yourself?" he asked, for he knew this job must be handled by his father or he would be too great a burden.

"I do that," Sualtim said, smiling with pleasure at his accomplishment.

"All right then. I think Emer has provided us with just sufficient for two." He looked down at the baskets crowded in around him and grinned at the understatement. "There's nothing to stop our journeying to Tara together."

They moved on toward the south, keeping their chariots close beside one another and conversing cheerfully on the beauty of the spring countryside as they went. It was a glorious day, the air sharp with the sea breezes, the sky a cloudless blue and the sun warm. By late afternoon they had reached the main ford of the Oun Dia river which served as Ulster's southern border. As they crossed it and headed on, Cuculain looked back, then stopped, wonder filling his expression.

"Look, Father," he said, pointing.

Dark clouds, thick and low to the ground, were rolling along the northern horizon, blotting out both sky and earth as they went.

"Ah, we've luck with us," said Sualtim. "We've just missed some bad weather. It looks as if a storm is moving across all Ulster!"

Chapter Eight
ENCOUNTER

While Cuculain and his father were setting out for Tara, the army of Meave was beginning its own march.

The thousands awoke in the fresh, bright morning, alive with expectation, vigorous, impatient, ready to move. The many tribes and province armies were a single force, now, welded together by Fergus in the past few days. Their sounds of preparation filled a morning made for peace with the clamor of war as the host gathered itself and set out.

The preparation and the march were a simple thing, even for a body so large. By nature the Milesians were a mobile people; the result of a long nomadic existence. Always had their lives depended on the cattle and, from earliest times, they had moved from pasture to pasture with the grazing animals. As a result, the force was geared to travel, with its battalions of chariots pulled by strong, tireless horses and its companies of infantry well trained to swift, steady marches.

They moved in a spearhead, with the bulk of the force grouped in a broad wedge that protected the horse and cattle herds between its outstretched arms. Behind the head a spear-tree made up of supply carts followed, making the role of support a literal as well as figurative one. The cutting edge of this great weapon was formed of the Exiles, while at the killing-point rode Fergus himself with Cormac Conlingas beside him.

For two days the force advanced toward Ulster. They circled the long, narrow Lough Ree to cross the Shannon River, then turned toward the northwest. As they moved closer to Ulster's borders, they prepared for a first en-

counter with opposing forces, but they saw no sign of
Ulstermen and met no hostile force of any kind. The
march was smooth and pleasant under the clear, spring
skies, and the spirits of the men were high. Some sang as
they marched, and their rolling tunes drifted through the
army.

Fergus was pleased with the fine mood of the men, but
he was taking no risks and he wanted no surprises. In
advance of the army he sent two scouts to keep him
informed of any dangers that might lie before them.

Two men might have seemed little enough to guard the
march of an army so mighty, but the two who Fergus
chose were more than sufficient for the task. The Neara
brothers they were, the finest trackers and scouts in
all of Eire and among the fiercest of its warriors as
well.

Back and forth in front of that army's line of march
they ranged, to keep sharp watch for anything of question. They rode together in one chariot, taking turns at
the driving, for no driver in all of Eire could follow their
orders, so often did they change speed and direction in
their search.

It was on the third morning of the host's journey, only
a long day's ride from the Oun Dia river, that these two
scouts found the remains of a camp in a forest.

In a small clearing, some distance ahead of the army,
two chariots coming from the south had stopped. By the
signs a fire had been lighted there and food eaten. Then
the chariots had divided. One had headed on to the north
while the other had turned off toward the west.

Though it was the first such sign the two brothers had
seen, they thought little of it. The tracks of the chariots
showed them to be light, pleasure vehicles, not heavy
chariots-of-war. So the Nearas went on, seeing nothing
else until, nearing midday, they came upon tracks again,
this time coming from the east.

"Look here, Sheeling." One of the two pointed at the
ground ahead. "That's surely one of those that camped in
the clearing. I know its wheel marks."

"You're right, Angus," the other replied. "The one that
turned west it is. But it's coming now from the opposite
way! Could it have circled our army so quickly?"

"With good horses. But, why?"

Sheeling had no need to give answer. Both knew there was only one reason for such a ride: to investigate their forces.

"It seems to be running right ahead of us now," said Angus. "Let's follow it."

The track was a straight one that went on before them, making no turns and leaving clear marks. It was too much as if those who left it meant it to be seen, and the Nearas followed slowly and warily.

"Are those in this chariot fools or are they asking to be found?" Sheeling asked.

The answer to this came very soon. They went on only a little farther and then were stopped by a new discovery.

Near the trail ahead they saw a tall, stone pillar, a monument to mark the resting place of some forgotten warrior. Circling its thin spire of stone near the top was a hoop of wood, formed of a thick branch cut, bent onto itself and tied with strips of leather.

The brothers rode up to the stone and examined the hoop carefully.

"It's been freshly cut," said Angus. "See, the sap's still running in it. It must have been done by those we're following."

"It has ogham writing on it," said Sheeling, lifting the ring off to examine the evenly spaced slashes of the Celtic writing. "But, we've no skill to read it."

"If it is a message left for us, it's best we have it read at once!" Angus told him.

Sheeling agreed, turning their chariot and urging the horses back toward the army.

Meave turned the strange device in her hands, examining the marks carefully. The queen and the small group of ollafs and druids who traveled with her had pulled up in a small circle to examine the Nearas' find. The march of the rest of the host continued, and it surged about them, breaking to move around both sides of the circle as a flowing stream parts at a protruding rock. Beside Meave stood Calatin in his chariot while, in front of her, the Nearas waited in patient silence.

After a moment's scrutiny of the wooden hoop, she passed it to her ard-druid.

"Does this strange writing have any meaning for you?"

Calatin briefly examined the script, shook his head, and handed it on. The other druids did the same, passing it from one to another as they tried in vain to decipher it.

"It is strange writing to us," the last one said as he returned the hoop to her. "It is druid ogham, but of a type we do not know."

It was then that the chariot of Fergus, pushing back through the host from its position at the point, reached the knot of the chariots around Meave. He had seen the two scouts arrive and had followed them at once, impatient to know what had brought them in. His attention was immediately drawn to the object Meave held.

"What is this thing?"

"Merely a crude marker." Calatin spoke contemptuously, taking the hoop and holding it out to the chieftain. "It is something we cannot read. Perhaps it is some barbaric language of Ulster." He smiled. "Could you read it for us, Fergus?"

The commander ignored this remark, but snatched the wooden marker from the druid's hand.

"Why, this is the language of the high-druids of Ulster, taught to our warriors in the schools," said Fergus. Glancing toward Calatin, he added coldly, "It is hardly barbaric. The students of the ard-druid Cathbad learned this. . . ."

He stopped suddenly. He had turned the hoop as he spoke, reading the inscription along its side.

Meave saw the concern cloud his features. "What is it, Fergus?" she demanded anxiously. "What does it say?"

"It is only a name," he replied, his voice at once devoid of all expression. "It says 'Cuculain.' "

"Cuculain?" Meave repeated. "The Hound of Culain? What animal is that?"

"No animal, but a man. A warrior of the Red Branch of Ulster and one of King Conchobar's youngest champions."

"What does this warrior here, in the south?"

"I've no way of knowing that. His home is in Dun

Dalgan, more than two days distant from here. But, there is no doubt that he has somehow found us." Fergus looked toward the two brothers. "Did you find any sign of those who left this? How many were there?"

"There were the marks of only one, light chariot by the place where we found the sign," said Angus, "but we know there was another chariot with that one earlier."

Fergus showed interest in that. "A second chariot? Where was it? When?"

"Some way back we came upon the tracks of this chariot in company with those of another," Sheeling explained. "The second chariot turned north while this one made a circuit of our host."

"Then we are revealed," Fergus said with grim resignation. "Cuculain had stayed to watch our movements and some other has gone to warn Ulster. The Red Branch will gather against us."

Calatin remained unperturbed. "You are too fearful, MacRogh. We need not worry about them."

Fergus eyed the druid narrowly. The confidence with which this statement was made puzzled him.

"What is it you're saying, Enchanter? You think the men of Ulster will not come?"

The druid shrugged. "Perhaps they are afraid of so mighty a force."

Fergus only laughed at that. "Not ten times this force would frighten them."

"I'd not be as sure of that as you seem to be, Mac-Rogh. But, even if they do decide to come against us, it will be days before they can act. Long before that we will be in control of the whole south of Ulster and have the bull."

"I agree," Meave said decisively. "This changes nothing. We go on as before. You . . ." she looked to the Nearas, "return to your scouting."

"Wait," said Fergus. "We must make provisions for Cuculain. He is out before us somewhere."

"Provisions?" Meave laughed. "Against one man? Perhaps you are too cautious, Fergus."

"Or something else," Calatin added with an easy recklessness.

Fergus turned toward the man, his temper hot, but the

queen moved again to head off the collision of these two antagonistic wills.

"Fergus, this Cuculain is only one man. What can he do? Since he has warned us of his presence, he cannot even fall on us by surprise."

"Perhaps he does not mean to," Fergus said darkly.

Cuculain and his father had come upon the army of Eire by simple chance.

They had made the journey to Tara without incident and had waited for the prophetess, Faythleen, but she had never come. They had stayed two days, for at first Cuculain feared he had mistaken the time of the appointment. But by the second day puzzlement and anger began to grow in him, for the Sidhe were not given to idle pranks, and Cuculain could see no reason why he had been brought on this useless venture. Finally, his patience at an end, he had given up and started back toward home with his father.

That first night of their return journey they had made camp in a thick wood and Cuculain had proudly watched his father unhitch and feed the horses, set up the camp, and make an evening fire. If nothing else, he mused, the trip had been good for Sualtim. The man's self-confidence was vastly improved, as was his health. He seemed more erect, stronger, more like the man Cuculain remembered from his childhood.

They ate a simple meal and sat near the fire, talking to ward off the loneliness that came on one in the wild, sheoguy places of Eire, where the most ancient spirits, the oldest gods of the world had once held sway and still made their power felt. Then, tired by their travel, they rolled in their cloaks and slept in a forest that, itself, slept silently around them.

At first sun, Cuculain suddenly awoke, tense and alert. He was certain something had awakened him ... some alien sound.

He listened for a time, but the forest was still silent except for the movements of animals and the rasping cries of great blackbirds that circled above. Stretching himself and inhaling the fresh, dawn air, Cuculain arose and walked about, moving quietly to allow his father more sleep. Strolling to a low rise that gave some view of the country beyond, he looked about him at the land.

At first he only surveyed the rolling hills with a casual, appreciative eye but, suddenly, he stopped and gazed intently toward one spot. To the south he was certain he had seen glimmering points of light, so sharp and bright they could not be merely sunlight reflected from a pond or stream.

Alarmed, he found a tree he could easily climb and tall enough to give a vantage point. He pulled himself up into its branches until he had a clear view of the horizon.

Now the source of the lights was clear and his fears were made a certainty. Some few miles to the south a vast body of men was moving toward him, the morning sun flashing from their weapons and trappings as they marched. A gigantic force was marching toward Ulster out of Eire, and he had heard no hint of war.

He climbed down from the tree and returned swiftly to the camp, shaking his father awake.

"Father, please wake up. You must ride to Ulster."

"What . . . what is it?" Sualtim asked, the concern in his son's voice bringing him quickly to full consciousness.

"I've just seen an army moving north. It must be planning to invade our borders!"

"Invade?" repeated the old man, and a frightened look came into his eyes. "What can we do? We must flee!"

"No. We must give Ulster warning. You will have to do it, while I stay here and watch."

"I?" The man was suddenly uncertain. "I cannot do that. I am afraid."

"You must do it, Father. You can do it. You are well, now. Think that this mission will prove your health to you, and to all others."

Sualtim remained unconvinced. "I do not know. It is so much."

"No, it is simple." Cuculain told himself to keep his patience, though it was a hard task with an army fast approaching. But, his father had to be convinced that he could act. "Just ride to Emain Macha. Tell King Conchobar that an army comes. You must do it or Ulster will be taken unawares."

That seemed to bring assurance to the man. Still fearful, but now willing to try, he arose and harnessed his chariot. When he had finished, Cuculain supplied him with food and took his hand.

"Good luck, Father. Go like the wind, now. Only you can do it."

Sualtim summoned his courage. He stood erect, head up, and at that moment he again became more like the king he had been for so long.

"Take care, my son. I will warn Ulster."

With that he shook the reins and headed his chariot out of the clearing.

Cuculain watched him out of sight, then quickly loaded and harnessed his own chariot. Turning west, he went toward the army, riding in a wide circle around it, stopping here and there at well-hidden points to examine the host more closely.

What he saw only served to increase his alarm. All the fighting men of the four provinces seemed to be gathered there. A mighty force it was, well armed and well supplied as for a long campaign. Many old friends he saw amongst that host. Fergus MacRogh, once his trainer in Emain Macha, and Cormac Conlingas, his own king's son, were there. Even Lewy MacNeesh and Fardia, friends he had fought beside as a youth and had seen only months before, rode among them with their warriors beside them.

Cuculain did not understand. What reasons would take so mighty a force toward Ulster without warning? He could not guess, but he knew one brutal truth: they were invading. They were going to attack, and he was the only warrior of the Red Branch to know.

He made some rapid calculations as he rode on about the host. With luck, and with his father's continued courage, Sualtim might reach Emain Macha in two days. For Conchobar to raise an army would take perhaps two more, then three at least to return. But this force was two days or less from Ulster now. They would overrun half of it before anyone could act against them.

Unless they could be delayed.

Cuculain was not happy with this reasoning, but there was little choice. Somehow he, alone, would have to slow this awesome threat. Every hour, every moment he could make them slow would be more time for Ulster.

His face set itself in grim lines at the thought of the task before him. After completing his circuit of the army, he found the old, stone monument. He cut the branch, carved his ogham upon it, and left it there. He could have chosen to attack without forewarning, but he had no mind to fight that way, and too many friends rode with this host.

With the sign left to be found, he drove yet farther ahead, to await its discovery by the advancing army.

It was nearing mid-afternoon when he saw a chariot with two riders approaching him.

Chapter Nine
FIRST BLOOD

The chariot of the Neara brothers splashed across a narrow river ford and started into the woods on its far side.

Suddenly another chariot appeared on the path ahead.

The horses balked and turned their heads and the chariot came to a shuddering stop. The two men looked across to the sole occupant of the other vehicle who stood at ease, regarding them calmly. Startled by his abrupt appearance, they laid hands to their weapons, but a quick appraisal of the stranger they faced lessened their alarm.

He was little more than a boy in looks, his body lean and supple, his face smooth and beardless. He wore no armor and seemed unarmed but for a light shield and hunting spears racked harmlessly beside him. His chariot, too, was a light one, fit only for pleasure, not for war. To the brothers he was merely a lad on some casual enterprise.

"Good day," said Angus, cheerfully.

"Good day to you," the youth responded. "What do you on this road?"

"We go in advance of a force that means to enter Ulster. The army of Queen Meave is at our back. Best be away before you run onto it."

"An army?" the young man repeated with a tone of disbelief. "To invade Ulster? Why?"

He made no move to turn his chariot, and the Nearas grew impatient.

"We have no time to waste talking with you," said

Sheeling. "Now be off the path for we must be about our work."

"It is you who must be off," the young man said. "Go back with you, for I'll not let you go farther."

The brothers exchanged a puzzled glance.

"Might you be giving us challenge?" Angus asked.

"If that is your choice," the youth replied, his voice betraying nothing but a calm as strong as his demeanor.

Both the Neara brothers laughed.

"You are alone, without weapons, lad," Sheeling observed pointedly. "Leave off your foolish ideas."

"Foolishness is the invasion of Ulster," said the youth. "Now turn around, for I've no wish to kill you."

At that Angus leaned close to his brother and murmured: "I've no wish, myself, to kill this boy who only seems too brave for his own good. Let's charge at him. I judge he'll turn and run then."

"And, if he does not?"

"He is unarmed. What threat can he be? Without a driver, he'll not be trying to fight us both from his chariot."

Sheeling nodded and picked up the reins. "All right. Ready your spear."

He shouted loudly and urged the horses forward, hoping to frighten their opponent. But the youth stood quiet, holding back his own horses and waiting as the heavy war chariot plunged toward him.

Then, suddenly, the young man's arm whipped up. There was a crack and a whirring sound and Angus, his spear lifted to throw, jerked backward to fall from the chariot.

Sheeling reined to a sliding halt and looked back at his brother, crumpled motionless on the ground. He whirled toward the youth who was now calmly fitting a second pellet into his sling.

The sling was very new to Eire and Sheeling had never seen anyone so proficient with such a weapon. For a moment he hesitated, but then anger took him.

"A lucky throw to kill my brother, whelp," he said, pulling his own spear from its holder, "but you'll not be so lucky twice."

With that he urged the horses on again, directing them with his left hand and raising the spear to strike with his right.

The leading squadrons of the army of Meave approached the narrow ford, following the track laid by the Nearas to guide them.

The crossing point was no wider than three chariots hub-to-hub, and the wedge of the host had begun to close together in preparation for funneling through it. Then, abruptly and without warning, the first rank to reach the water's edge came to a complete halt.

The result was immediate and near calamitous.

Units moving forward came against those ahead and were stopped, too. In moments the army became a confused and tangled mass of close-packed animals, vehicles, and men, and the pressure continued to increase as more and more units, unaware of what had happened, collided with the jam from behind.

When Meave realized what had taken place, she shouted orders to the units in her rear to halt and bid her driver to press forward toward the point of stoppage.

The same actions were repeated by Fergus, who had been on the army's flank directing its movements. He forced his way across to encounter Meave and, together, their chariots crawled ahead through the dense crowds, surrounded by a roaring sea of angry shouts and neighing steeds and cries of pain as feet were trod on or sensitive points were poked by carelessly held weapons.

The horses of the two leaders shouldered their way through men who all but climbed upon their fellows to escape from hooves and wheels, while Meave and Fergus cried out commands in an attempt to still the arguments and bring some order to the chaotic mass. At last they reached the foremost units, lined in a solid rank along the river's edge.

The chariots of queen and commander broke through this final barrier to pull up in the shallow water beyond. Meave looked along the row of men and was startled, so changed was the mood here. In contrast with the angry host tangled behind them, these men were strangely silent and unmoving. They seemed more as a solid wall of colored stone built along the bank.

"What's happened here?" she demanded angrily. "This water is only a trickle. Why are you stopped?"

No one answered her, but a chieftain raised a hand and pointed across the ford. For the first time Meave turned her eyes toward the far bank and found them horribly met.

There, on the bare earth by the lapping flow, lay the bodies of the Neara brothers, neatly arranged. And, on a branched length of bleached driftwood stuck upright in the sand, two severed heads leered across at the men of Eire.

Fergus had seen the dead men before Meave had spoken, and she now realized that he had already started across toward them. Immediately she ordered her driver to follow, but Fergus, hearing this, pulled up and called back to her:

"Stay there, now. The one who did this may still be near."

"I'll not go back. If someone is around, you'll need a warrior to guard your back."

"A warrior you may be, but you are also the queen, and no skill at arms could save you if we were attacked. These men were killed by a sling."

Meave looked closely at the heads. It was true. The craterous wound of the iron pellet was clear on the foreheads of both. But this did not dissuade her. She would not go back and let her captain go on alone, and she could not go back at his order; not with her warriors watching.

She noted the arrival of Cormac Conlingas and ordered him to take the command.

"Fergus and I go to investigate," she said. "Sort out this tangle here and wait. When we signal that all is clear, start an advance party across."

"But, my Queen . . ." Cormac protested, not understanding why the two leaders of the army were going ahead alone.

"Be about it quickly, Cormac," Meave insisted, "or there may be many hurt in the press."

With that she turned away and ordered her driver to continue across, joining Fergus who had waited impatiently, his expression clearly revealing his displeasure.

"It was necessary for you to come, was it?" he asked her.

"As much as it was for you," she replied. "When my commanders feel they must ride into danger alone, I feel bound to give them my protection."

They crossed the ford and mounted the other bank, passing the dead men. They advanced cautiously until they reached an open spot and found the Nearas' chariot, its horses tethered and grazing peacefully. Here they halted and Fergus, with drawn sword, climbed from his vehicle and examined the ground intently. Near him Meave waited on guard, a spear poised to throw, her eyes searching the trees around for any movement.

"The Nearas came up here," said Fergus, indicating the tracks. "A single chariot met them. They attacked it and were both killed."

"What?" she said. "So easily? Were they taken in ambush?"

"No. A face-to-face fight it was. A skillful hand struck them both down, and I know only one sling so deadly in the throwing."

"You're speaking of your Cuculain, I suppose. Are you saying this lone warrior killed the Nearas? I'd heard it said ten men could not defeat them in a fight."

"Yet it was done," he assured her. "He is a warrior of many talents. He is here and he has left us a sign now that he means to slow us with any means he has. This is our last warning."

"Of what?" she demanded. "No matter what his skill, no single man can stop our whole army. He'll not delay us any longer." She gave orders to her driver and her chariot turned back toward the stream.

"Where are you going?" Fergus called after her.

"To send the first squadrons across," she answered simply.

"And our scouts?"

By now she was some distance away, and her terse reply was tossed back at him with seeming disregard:

"Next time, send four!"

Quickly Fergus mounted into his own chariot and followed. At the ford Meave issued commands for men to take down the heads and bury the Nearas at once. Then she started the army moving again. Fergus tried to argue further with her, but she would not listen. She splashed across the ford into the midst of the army and he was forced to abandon his attempt and set to work to organize the forces as they began to advance once more. He sent out another scouting party, but of Exiles this time, and ten in number, with orders to stay closely together.

The host of Eire headed on toward the north and west as before, but it took little time for Fergus to realize that the speed of the march was greatly reduced.

He knew, then, that the grinning heads planted at the ford had done their work. The brisk pace of the infantry had been replaced by one more cautious, and the minds of the chariot riders were less on the way ahead than on the trees about.

Through the army passed the rumor of the two men so easily killed and, as it passed, it grew in wildness. Not one man but a hundred men, skilled in the sling, had put the fierce Neara brothers to death. Each man listened to the tale, and each became alert for the whirr of a deadly missile sent from cover to strike them down too.

When Fergus saw what the spreading fear was doing, he knew it must be quickly put to rest. It was late afternoon and, though some time for march still remained, the slowness of their advance made it clear they would achieve very little distance more that day. He determined, instead, to call a halt and, as he passed orders for it, the army seemed visibly to relax. But they had barely halted when Meave descended in a fury upon her commander.

"What do you mean . . . to stop here?"

"It is necessary," he replied coldly.

"I ordered the advance to continue. Why have you ignored my command?"

"I am commander," Fergus reminded her. "Do you trust my feelings in this or not, my Queen?"

Meave met his eyes levelly. She saw the determination

in him and knew he was not to be challenged in this here and now.

"Very well, Fergus. We will camp. But we will meet once that is done, for I will know the why of this."

Chapter Ten
THE HOUND OF CULAIN

Once the preparations for the establishment of a camp had been completed, the perimeters laid out, and the sentries posted, Fergus and Cormac made their way toward the pavilion erected for the king and queen.

For an army of Eire, the making of a camp was not a thing simply or crudely done, though it was done quickly by those long used to it. Tents went up in the sectors alotted according to tribes and tuaths, with broad streets and open squares and even marketplaces where large, wooden stalls dispersed supplies in an atmosphere like that of a Tailteen fairday.

By the time the two Exiles left their men and started through the camp, they walked along the busy thoroughfare of a newly-made city. Around them the air was wonderfully odorous with the smell of vegetables and meat, cooking over numerous fires or baking in ovens made with heated stones. On all sides were the sounds of laughter and talk, of instruments and the songs of bards, and Fergus smiled in satisfaction as he heard these evidences of good spirits. They told him that making camp had, indeed, helped to drive away some of the vague fear that had gripped the host.

As they went, Fergus and Cormac encountered many tribal chieftains and tuath kings, also on their way to the meeting the queen had called. It was in a large group that they finally arrived at the tent of Aileel and Meave.

This royal pavilion was an immense affair, as suited the rank of those it quartered. Built after the manner of the great halls, it was an uncomplicated structure, with a high tent-pole in the center and low outer supports in a circle about it. Roof and sides were thatched with branches and covered with heavy cloth, oiled to keep out the rain. A vast space was thus enclosed, large enough to accommodate more than a hundred men.

Tonight, however, only two score of the highest ranks came through its doorway. Inside they found the queen, waiting on a platform at the far end with Calatin by her side.

"You know why you were called," she began, formally, as the men gathered before her. "Orders were given for an early stop. I want to know the reason for that!"

"Poor enough excuse for us to be called from our food," said Lewy MacNeesh. "Fergus gave the orders and we obeyed. What does all this mean?"

"Perhaps Fergus can explain," said Meave. "He refused to do so before."

"It is a simple matter," Fergus said patiently. "The army was unsettled by the deaths today. Fear was spreading and unfounded rumors growing. I thought it best to stop, let the fear pass, let the men regain their ease. I think it has worked."

There was a murmur of agreement at that, and even Meave, who had noticed the uneasiness of her host, was forced to concede the truth in his words.

"A reasonable enough explanation, Fergus," she said. "It is enough."

"No, my Queen," returned Fergus. "It is not enough. For today's events will only be repeated, with even more disastrous results."

"What do you mean?" she asked.

"I mean that Cuculain is about us, now, and any time he might strike at us!"

"And this, you think, should throw all the men of Eire into confusion?" observed Calatin, and laughed aloud. "One man alone? MacRogh, the only danger is that he might convince you to delay us and prevent us from conquering Ulster the sooner."

Fergus would have replied to that, but Cormac Conlingas stepped up beside him and spoke instead.

"I am with Fergus in this. Calatin treats Cuculain too

lightly. I know him, as do all the Exiles. He cannot be underestimated. Let Fergus tell you. He was a foster father to him in Ulster."

"Ah, is that so?" said Meave with interest. "You know him well?"

"I do," Fergus admitted. "Sentanta was his given name. He was the youngest to ever enter the king's service. At fourteen years he took arms and has done many deeds in the short time since."

"There have even been some tales that his true father is not Sualtim, but one of the Sidhe!" added Cormac.

This strange fact seemed to recall some vague image to Meave's mind. It was a memory of something she had been told, something she did not quite understand.

"Tell me, Fergus," she asked, "how comes he by that name, 'Hound of Culain'?"

"There is a tale to it," the chieftain explained. "At twelve years he came to Emain Macha from his home. He was accepted into the king's school to be trained as a warrior. I saw to his training as a fighter while Cathbad, the king's ard-druid, saw to his training in the mind. In both he excelled. Very early he was seen to be far beyond any lad of his age, and many who were older.

"Then, one night, the king and many of us were invited to feast at the house of Culain, Ulster's finest smith. Do you remember him, Cormac?"

"Ay, that I do," said Cormac, grinning. "As broad as he was tall, with an eternally blackened face and eyes glowing like two bright sparks in his own forge. Hard in spirit as in body, too, he was. He trusted no one. But he owed my father a meal, and Conchobar was bound to make the smith pay, mean though we knew the fare was bound to be."

"We went down to his home in a group," said Fergus, who took up the story with pleasure as the memory of it became clearer. "Young Sentanta was asked to come, but he was busy at playing hurley with the other lads and said he would come later. But in the time we took to make the journey he was forgotten."

"That was the reason for it all," Cormac put in. "Even after we arrived, and old Culain told us he left a guard dog to rove his compound after dark, no one remembered the boy. We watched the smith let the great wolfhound out to prowl between the house and the outer walls without so much as a thought to young Sentanta."

"At least, not until our meal was interrupted by a screaming howl from outside," said Fergus. "Fearing the animal had trapped some helpless servant, Culain ran from the house with us at his heels. We found the giant dog quite dead, and young Sentanta seated by him, unhurt save for a few scratches. He had followed after us, climbed the palisade, been attacked by the beast and killed it . . . and him unarmed but for his hurley stick and ball!"

Calatin shook his head. "That sounds a tale told by drunken warriors late in the night."

"We both saw it," Cormac returned defensively, "as did others here. But there is stranger yet. While we paid honor to Sentanta's victory, the smith only lamented the death of his hound. 'A year it took to train him from a pup!' he cried, 'and now it's dead, and for doing its proper work!'

"Sentanta was distressed by this. Without hesitation he offered to take the place of the beast for one year . . . until another could be trained. We tried to dissuade him, but he was certain, and bound to his honor. The smith took his word and, for a year, the boy served as the hound, guarding the herds, prowling the grounds, protecting the smith from predators—both human and animal alike! For that Cathbad gave him the name Cuculain, and so it has stayed."

"Well, thank you for your fine tale," the Enchanter told the two Exiles, sarcasm undisguised in his voice. "It was told with enough enjoyment to honor the work of a high-bard."

So much had Fergus and Cormac been caught up in their story, they had been drawn back to an Ulster of other times. Now the druid's words recalled them abruptly.

"It was at the queen's bidding we told it," Cormac answered coldly.

But Meave did not take note of this exchange. The end of the story had left her lost in thought, her smooth face deeply etched with lines of concentration.

"It is an interesting tale," she spoke slowly and reflectively, "and in some way it is disturbing to me. I do not doubt its truth but, what does it mean? What are you suggesting, Fergus?"

"I am suggesting strong scouting parties of ten all about the army, moving slowly and keeping constant watch."

"And slowing the whole force," Calatin added.

"It will be slowed more if Cuculain is allowed to strike," Fergus countered.

"MacRogh, your continued love of Ulster must make you speak this way," said the druid. "It is understandable that you might wish to . . . delay its invasion."

Fergus chose to ignore this clearly provocative remark, but Cormac exploded. Laying hand to his sword-hilt, he started forward, crying out:

"No man is more loyal here than Fergus, you . . ."

"Stop!" Meave commanded, standing up. "Fergus, I do agree that no threat is to be overlooked, and I believe your stories of this Cuculain, but he is only one man and he will not slow my army. Now, all of you listen: we advance tomorrow at a full march! Keep watch if you like, but do not delay. We will enter Ulster in one day more!"

Dismissed, the captains and chiefs left Meave's tent and returned to their units, but Fergus tarried behind. He told Cormac to go on without him and approached Meave's platform.

"May I speak with you . . ." he shot a glance toward Calatin, "and you alone?"

"I am advisor," the Enchanter replied. "What concerns the queen concerns me also."

"Fergus has a right to talk with me," said Meave. "Please leave us for a time."

With suspicion in his black eyes, the Enchanter left the platform and went out of the tent. Fergus watched until he had gone, then turned toward the queen, his face set in grim lines.

"Not many words ago I was accused by your 'advisor' of holding back the army to save Ulster. I ask you now, do you believe this to be true?"

"Why, Fergus," said Meave, surprised, "why did you not speak of this before?"

"I wanted no more public disputes with your sorcerer. I seem to lose such contests when you judge them."

"What means that, Fergus? Calatin is a good advisor and very . . ."

"I've no heart to argue his virtues," Fergus interrupted. "I am asking only one thing: do you suspect my loyalties in this campaign? For, if you do, I am no good to you as commander, since my motives for action will always be suspect."

"Fergus, I never meant to give you any cause to doubt my faith in you."

"Is that why I was called to give account of my orders before you and my subordinates like some servant who has forgotten to rub down your horses?"

"This was a natural thing," she contended. "Events happened too swiftly today. I wished to know what was going on about me, as did your fellow officers. It was not an inquest of your actions."

"You say not, and yet when the accusation was made you did not dispute it!"

"Only because it was passed over by you, Fergus. And, since you speak of accusations, speak of yourself. More than once you have accused me of siding with Calatin over you!"

"Simple fact, my Queen. It's often his advice is taken over mine . . . as in the matter of Cuculain."

"I saw no reason not to accept his viewpoint here."

Fergus moved closer to her, stepping up onto the platform.

"My Queen, I know Cuculain, but your Enchanter, for all his clever arts, does not. I know he will hang onto us with teeth and with claws. Like a hound with a bear he will hang on until he drags us down, until he stops us with fatigue and pain!"

"You are too in awe of this man," she said quickly, bothered by the image. "Do what he can, he cannot save Ulster."

"You are too in awe of yourself and Eire, Lady. Ulster can defend herself well enough."

"Oh?" said the queen, sitting back and looking at him appraisingly. "So, you see our campaign as a doomed one? Perhaps Calatin was right to question your motives after all."

Anger took Fergus at that. He stepped close to the queen and leaned forward, speaking with intensity.

"Fitter it would have been for you to stay in your dun and see to the running of Connacht than to march on this foray with your king, weak from age. And, better it would have been for you to remain at Cruchane, for here you are a disturbing influence, a second leader who seeks praise, constantly challenging my command, and weakening the careful authority I must maintain over this loose array of men from all Eire which you have gathered . . ."

At this Meave began to rise, flushed with a rage of her own, but Fergus pushed her back and she sat, shaking with emotion, as he went on:

"All these things are true, as you know they are, but never have I given cause not to be trusted, nor flinched, nor turned aside from a task. And I'll not turn aside from Ulster, nor fail in the fighting, if it be the death of all of us. If that is unacceptable to you, you must replace me."

With that he released her and turned away, starting back across the pavilion toward its doors. But he had not gone halfway when Meave, in her fury, lifted one of her war spears and made a cast.

Fergus heard the sound of its flight and wheeled about as it sank home, its iron head buried in the tent's center-pole only an arm's length from him.

He looked from the quivering tree to the tall, proud woman who stood on the platform, glaring at him.

Then he laughed. He knew the cast was made only as a sign of rage, for she could have as certainly made his back her target.

"Does the fact that I still live mean that I am to be retained?" he asked calmly.

"Curse you, Fergus," she said. "You know I cannot do without your Exiles . . . or you." She tried to speak in anger, but the throw had vented much of it and his change of humor had dispelled the rest. She sank back on the couch and smiled at him, but bewilderment showed in her gray eyes. "Oh, Fergus, you know you have my heart.

How can we argue? I ache for you each time I see you and know I cannot be with you . . ."

"No, Meave," Fergus cautioned. "Do not be doing that. We've vowed between us to set our own two lives apart while on this march. There is no place for it here."

She nodded. "Yes, Fergus, you are right. I must be queen and you commander." She drew herself proudly erect and in that act became the ruler of Connacht again. "Then, as your queen, I say you have my trust. You are the sole commander of the host."

"And Cuculain?" he asked.

"On your Cuculain I will not bend. I'll not be slowed in this advance."

Fergus's brow clouded again at that. "Then we are where we began, my Queen, for . . ."

But there was no chance for further words. A young warrior of the guards burst into the tent, fear and distress evident, breathless from great exertion.

"What is it?" said the queen, impatient at the interruption.

"My Queen," he said, "three perimeter guards, standing watch only a spear's throw from their fellows . . . they were killed . . . most horribly killed . . . and without a sound heard by anyone."

Fergus met the queen's astonished gaze.

"Now," he said, "do you understand what I've been fearing?"

Chapter Eleven
THE OUN DIA FORD

With Meave's consent, Fergus MacRogh labored throughout the night. The following morning, when the army moved again, it moved in a tighter formation. The barbs of the spearhead were pulled back into a narrower point and the supply carts, as well as the herds, were sheltered between them. The army had also developed an outer defense. At short intervals around the entire host heavily armed squadrons of chariots, ten in each, scoured the land ahead, behind, and to the sides of the line of march.

The movement of the army that day was greatly slowed, as Calatin had feared, but it was steady and uninterrupted by attacks. No sign of Cuculain or any other hostile force was seen that day, and the spirits of the army rose again.

By nightfall they had achieved almost the full distance Meave had hoped for. They fell just short of entering Ulster but, when they camped, they camped on the banks of the Oun Dia river and ahead, across a broad and shallow ford, the province lay open and undefended.

Meave all but gloated with triumph, her courage and her confidence completely renewed. She called a banquet in celebration that night and, several times, found excuse to point up to Fergus how unfounded his fears had seemed to be.

No Cuculain had appeared, she said, and nothing had stopped them. Now they had but to walk across the Oun Dia and Ulster was theirs. No other warrior of all that province had seen fit to even give them challenge.

Throughout it all, Fergus stayed quiet. Grave doubts assailed him, both because of Cuculain's failure to reappear and because of Ulster's failure to act. He was certain the province had been warned but, if so, why had they not come? He reasoned that perhaps they had not had time to act. It had been but two days since the Nearas had seen the tracks headed to the north.

Still, what of Cuculain? What had become of that young warrior while all Eire sat before the very gates of his country?

Unsettled in mind, Fergus left the banquet and went into the gray night, cloaked and cowled against the constant rain that turned the camp avenues into streams of mud. But rain and cold were facts of life to those of Eire, and they did nothing to detain him. He made a careful circuit of the camp's outer guards and only when it had been completed did the commander make his way back to his tent.

Because of the rain there were few men abroad, and Fergus was surprised when, on reaching his tent, he spied a close-wrapped figure approaching him.

"Fergus," a voice called.

"Meave!" he responded with astonishment. "What is it you're doing out tonight?"

"I've come to see you," was her simple answer.

"Meave, it's not good for us to be seeing each other this way."

She stood unmoving and her voice was firm: "I'll not leave here without speaking to you. Now, will you let me stand here in the rain, or will you invite me into your tent?"

She had left him no fair choice. He glared at her in angry frustration, but she only returned the look boldly.

Finally he shook his head. "All right, woman," he said, resigned. "I'll yet go mad from you. Come in, then, and quickly."

The tent of Fergus was a small one, sparsely furnished and empty, for he lived simply and wanted no servants to be in his way. As they entered, Meave removed her dripping cloak and handed it to him, as if to make firm her intention to stay.

Still reluctant, he hung it with his own close by the central fire. He stirred the embers, throwing on more fuel and, as he worked, he spoke to her without looking up.

"This was a dangerous thing. There's many who might think it strange for a queen to visit her commander in the dead of a stormy night."

She shrugged. "No one paid any mind to me. What few are still about are too absorbed in keeping dry to note the passing of another cloaked warrior."

"But why take such a chance?" he asked.

She came close to him, took one of his hands from the poker and held it in her own. "Fergus, I made sport of you tonight. It was unfair."

"It's of no matter," he said tonelessly, still avoiding her gaze.

"It is," she insisted. "I meant to get at you, to arouse your anger. Anything would be better than the wall of public performance we've built up between us!"

"It is necessary," he affirmed stolidly, but then he looked at her face, so intense, glowing softly in the fire's light, and he could no longer be cold with her.

"Meave, I understand your feelings. Why do you think I hold myself so aloof? The loneliness pulls hard at me, too."

"I'll not let this war drive us apart," she said fiercely. "It has been too long since we have been together as one, for ourselves alone."

He looked away. "And why should a war be any fairer to us? The other warriors are parted from those they love."

"The other warriors do not have to see their lovers every day and act as if there were nothing between them," she reasoned.

"I've little will to argue with you, Meave," he said, turning back to look at her again. "But, there is no way we can meet together in the midst of this entire host."

"Perhaps," she said, but then she smiled and lifted her arms. "Still, I am here now."

He smiled in return at that. There was nothing he could say to deny the truth of her words.

"You are, surely," he said.

While the careful guard kept up its watch about the camp, the others of the army went to sleep about fires piled high with fuel to keep back the dark and damp of the moonless night. Some hours of darkness later, when the rains had ceased and the fires had eaten themselves down to glowing remains, a warrior in the heart of the camp stirred, turned over restlessly and sat up.

He tried to peer into the hazy darkness beyond the pale circle of firelight. There was nothing there . . . and then there was. A man stood some feet away, a naked sword in his hand; a man the warrior had never seen before.

The man of Eire cried out and grabbed wildly for his own weapons. He died in that act. Others around him were aroused and tried to move, but were cut down too. Still, their shouts of warning aroused the camp.

Meave and Fergus awoke at once and rose quickly from the thick bed of furs. The commander donned his linen shirt and woolen cloak and left the tent, a war-ax swinging in his hand. Behind him Meave dressed also, armed herself with one of his spears and followed him.

As she left the tent she nearly collided with Calatin, who seemed somewhat surprised to find her there.

"What is happening?" he asked loudly, for a tumult of clanging weapons and confused shouts had risen about them. "Why are you here?"

She hesitated a moment. "I . . . I heard a cry and came to discover what was wrong."

"I see," the druid answered thoughtfully.

She had no more time for him.

"Get back out of this," she told him, brusquely. "I must catch up to Fergus."

She rushed on past the druid and after MacRogh, who was now moving through the tents, gathering men.

"What is it?" she asked her commander when she had reached his side.

"There is no way of knowing," he replied, and ordered men out in a broad fan around the area where the cries had originated.

"Some of you, move farther on," he commanded. "Circle beyond the fires and scout."

At this he saw many averted eyes and many hesitations. He knew that fear was at work and that he had to maintain an unquestioned control.

"Are you more afraid of what may be out there . . . or

of me?" he asked quietly, and lifted his ax in a meaning-ful way.

The warriors moved at once.

With Meave beside him he strode to the fire that was quickly becoming the center of a gathering of men. He found there what he had feared. Three men about the fire were dead. One had fallen across the embers and a strong odor of burning cloth and hair and flesh lay heavy in the still, humid night. The surrounding group stood frozen by horror, staring with a morbid fascination at the burning man. None of them moved to pull him away from the smoldering wood.

Fergus knew that the effect of this was worse than that of seeing the other dead. He strode into the circle and rolled the man off the fire with a push of his foot.

"Cover them all," he ordered, throwing his own cloak over the face still twisted by the warrior's dying scream.

Cormac appeared from the crowd nearby, accompa-nied by the chieftain Bras MacFirb.

"By the gods, he has done it again," MacFirb said, surveying the grim scene. "He walks into the middle of our camp as if we had no guards. He kills three men and walks away ... simply walks away ... and we cannot stop him!"

The man's voice rose sharply as he spoke. Meave recognized the signs of a nerve weakened to the point of breaking and acted quickly, for she, like Fergus, under-stood that fear openly displayed by a chieftain would sweep through the camp.

"Quiet!" she grated, stepping close to him. "Quiet, or I'll kill you now myself!"

The chieftain looked at her in surprise, not certain he had heard truly. But he read the truth of it in her eyes, and slunk wordlessly away.

Some of the men Fergus had sent out returned from searching the surrounding area then, and entered the circle at the fire.

"Any signs?" the commander asked.

"Nothing," said one, throwing a torch down by the fire. "We covered the ground from here to the river's edge. There was nothing. It might be he was never there ... or it might be he never left."

That caused some of the gathered men to grip their weapons more tightly and look about them with apprehension.

"No more of that," said Fergus, still trying to keep the fear in control. "He is just a man, and a sane enough one. He would not stay amongst us with the whole army alerted. Now, I want parties with torches out around the host all night. Cormac, go through the camp and be certain every leader is watchful. Each province is responsible for its own quadrant. He'll not be allowed to enter the camp again!"

"Aye, Fergus," Cormac agreed, "and the work will keep the men from thinking how frightened they are."

All the army was organized in heavy watches, but every man kept watch throughout that night, for no one slept.

The dawn was a cool and a cloudy one, deeply blanketed by a white mist that lay in the low ground along the river. Its first light saw Fergus circling the perimeter from guard to guard as he had done all night, and without a sign of weariness showing in him.

He entered the quadrant held by the warriors of Lewy MacNeesh and there he met the young chieftain, alert and watchful as himself.

"What signs?" he asked, as he had uncounted times before that night.

"We've seen nothing at all," Lewy replied, "though with this mist he could be a spear's throw away. Fergus, it gives me little cheer to guard for an attack by my own friend, and less to know what skill he has."

Fergus only nodded at that and peered out into the swirling clouds of white, where trees and rocks became gray patches without shape or name.

"Well, we can't be waiting any longer," he said finally. "Meave wants the host to enter Ulster now. Lewy, pass orders for camp to be broken, though there'll be no joy in anyone at hearing that!"

"My Chief," a guard exclaimed, his voice a hollow sound, "something is moving there!"

Fergus looked out again into the mists. There was a movement there, a large object, vague but becoming darker and more distinct as it came toward them at a rapid pace. At last it burst from the clinging mist, tearing away from the last fingers which clutched at it and revealing itself clearly to them.

A chariot of the flying squadrons of Connacht it was, with the forms of its two riders upright in it and its horses galloping madly toward the camp, foaming, wild of eye, as if a specter of their own deaths pursued them. It plunged through the outer ring of guards without a check and drove into the center of the camp, chased by Fergus and many other warriors who finally caught and stopped the terror-stricken animals.

The bits had been taken from the horses' mouths and the head-stalls from their heads. Behind them was one reason for their fear. It was a grim and a bloody cargo they brought as another message to the army of Meave.

Driver and warrior were dead, their chariot reins tied about them and the hand-rail, keeping them upright while their heads rolled back and they stared upward with sightless eyes.

As Fergus MacRogh looked on the men, only resignation showed in his expression.

"Now we'll not be wondering how our Hound came into camp," he said. "I set these men on guard myself. I hope we'll not be finding more of them like this."

Lewy looked about the crowd of warriors who surrounded them and saw the despairing faces and the fearful, sidelong glances.

"Fergus, you must hold off your orders to march," he said decisively. "I'm thinking the chieftains of Eire may wish to speak of this before we move again."

Lewy was right. This final horror, added to that of the long night, had taken a heavy toll. Weary and disturbed, the kings and chieftains gathered to demand another council with the high-queen. Meave saw that she must bow to their concern and, again, called them together in her pavilion.

"I am displeased by this show of fear and weakness in the men of Eire," she told them.

"The queen is unfair," Lok MacFavash retorted with anger, for his courage had never been doubted. "My warriors would not fear all of Ulster, were they to face them sword-to-sword. But this ... this killing from the darkness, this unstoppable slaughter they cannot understand."

"My own warriors now talk of a thousand men, not one, who lie in wait to attack from ambush once we cross the Oun Dia," said Ket, son of Magah. "Worse yet, some say the powers of the Sidhe are used by Cuculain, that he can appear and disappear before them and kill without a sound."

"I've heard like tales," Lok added. "They're speaking now of spirits who will destroy us certainly if we invade the sacred lands of Ulster."

"And when has Ulster become a sacred place?" Meave asked them harshly. "All this is foolish talk. We know it is just one man ... one mortal man!"

Lewy spoke up then in his quiet, reasonable way. "An easy thing to say, my Queen, but not an easy thing to make our warriors believe. The name 'Cuculain' now strikes more fear in them than the coming of a whole host, and I'm certain they'll not cross that river ford with the threat of this man over them. Each one sees himself killed while sleeping by his fire, struck down while on guard or even torn apart by some Sidhe-sent beast."

"We must do something," cried another of the chieftains in the group, and loud voices of assent were raised by all.

"Chieftains, wait!" Calatin asked them, stepping onto the royal platform. "Perhaps this Cuculain can be persuaded to foresake the Red Branch. Among us I do not doubt a large enough reward might be found."

"And who will offer this reward?" asked Bras Mac-Firb. "He'll not let any of us live if we come near to him."

"There are many in the camp to whom he would give ear," the ard-druid answered. "I've heard Lewy Mac-Neesh knew him some years. Cormac Conlingas and many of the Exiles were his friends in Ulster and, of course, Fergus was his foster-father." Calatin turned toward the commander who watched him narrowly, trying to determine the Enchanter's motives. "What of you, Fergus? You are the most likely of them all. It would seem your bond with Ulster was broken. Perhaps you can convince him to do the same."

"Aye, Fergus," Lok MacFavash agreed, "you are the one who can convince him."

Fergus shook his great head. "I know I'll not persuade him. When I rebelled against Conchobar MacNessa, a man not sent by me urged Cuculain to leave the school at Emain Macha and join my cause. But, though he sorrowed for me, he would not come. His bond is to King Conchobar and it is as strong as was his bond to the smith, or his bond to any man. While he lives he will remain a Red Branch warrior."

This argument did not sway the assembled chieftains. They saw no other, simpler way to quiet the fear that held their men so tightly. Finally Fergus consented to a compromise solution: he would seek out Cuculain and ask him if there were conditions he might accept.

"But I do not trust this plan," he said and looked at Calatin, "nor do I trust the one who suggests it. Even so, I am willing enough to go to Cuculain . . . if the assembled chiefs guarantee the performance of any conditions made and will take Cuculain under their protection should he strike a bargain with us."

"We do agree, Fergus," Lewy assured him, and those around him nodded in agreement.

"Such guarantees are an insult," cried Calatin with outrage. "Have you doubts that the queen would keep her word?"

"I am not thinking of the queen," Fergus replied.

Chapter Twelve
A BARGAIN

Fergus had his chariot readied and brought to him. Without good-byes he mounted and directed the driver toward the Oun Dia. The assembled chieftains followed him on foot through the camp to the river and watched as his chariot crossed the wide, shallow ford and disappeared into the trees on the far side.

Up into the low hills along the river's north bank rode the commander. Some way into their shelter he ordered the chariot halted. He bid the driver wait for his return and went on alone, climbing to the open top of a rounded eminence. From there he shouted out across the surrounding hills, calling for Cuculain by his boyhood name, Sentanta.

On his part, Cuculain had watched the chariot cross the Oun Dia from a careful distance and had seen Fergus climb the hill alone. Although he had wanted, then, to rush to greet his old friend, he had held back and waited to see what Fergus would do. Too many strange events had happened these past days to make him certain of anything. But, when he had heard the calling of his name, he had hesitated no longer. He moved from his concealment and made himself known to MacRogh.

The greeting of the two men, so close, so long parted, was warm but restrained, as befitted two warriors of Eire.

"It is happy I am to see you, Fergus," said Cuculain, clasping the man's arm tightly, "even if it must be as opponents."

"Aye, Cu, and even if my reasons for coming are not good ones."

"We'll speak of that soon enough," the young warrior promised. "Come, eat with me and talk with me as in the older days. For some time now I've lacked the comfort of another tongue. I welcome it, no matter for how long or for what purpose."

He led Fergus down from the hill and into an area densely overgrown with trees and underbrush. They pushed into a thicket that seemed quite solid, and Fergus was surprised to find its center hollow, forming a large clearing fully masked to any eyes without. There was enough room for Cuculain's chariot and gear, and grazing enough to satisfy the horses, which were hobbled and browsing at one side.

A perfect hiding place it was, thought Fergus, and no one could find it, for he himself had seen no track of chariot or man leading to it. But, still, something seemed wrong, and as he looked over Cuculain and his little camp again, he realized what it was.

"You have no armor with you," he observed with astonishment. "No chariot of war, no weapons. And where are your fine horses; the Gray of Macha and Black Shanglan?"

"All at Emain Macha, I'm afraid," Cuculain answered with a rueful smile. "I was on a short and peaceful journey when I came upon your army by strange chance."

"And you, alone, unarmed, plan to delay our army?"

"I have my sling and my good sword," Cuculain told him, "and I have succeeded so far. Sit down. I'll get us food."

He directed Fergus toward a small fire. Over it on spits he hung two cleaned salmon, freshly caught. He fetched ale and cups from the chariot and poured out a drink for them both.

"Now, Fergus," he said, sitting down cross-legged next to the doughty warrior, "before you tell me of your mission here, tell me something else. Why is this happening? Why does all of Eire turn itself suddenly toward Ulster?"

Fergus was momentarily taken aback by the question. "You do not know? How can you fight here and have no knowledge of the reason why?"

"I've had no way of knowing," was the young warrior's reply. "I heard no rumors of war before leaving Dun Dalgan and I've been here alone since I first saw your army."

"Of course," said Fergus. "All this has happened far too swiftly for even me to understand it fully. You see, it was less than a fortnight ago that I went into Ulster to attempt the barter for a bull . . ."

He related the story to the young man, who listened intently. When he had finished, Cuculain shook his head.

"It is hard to believe, Fergus. Ten men have I killed these past two days, and now you tell me this is all for a quarrel over a bull?"

"No, no, Cu, it is more than that, and you know the truth of it as well as I. For years now has the rivalry between Ulster and the rest of Eire grown. I argued against this war, but I knew it might come in its time. If it were not the bull, it would be something else."

"And you go with them, Fergus, against your own homeland?"

"Connacht is my homeland now," he said. "I go because of that new loyalty and, if possible, to reduce wanton destruction and keep violence in check."

"Yet, how can you fight for this woman against your cousins and your once-sworn king?"

At that the temper of Fergus flared. "I could ask how you fight for a king of treachery who makes bonds, breaks them, and kills others heedlessly for his own ends!" He caught himself, sighed, then laughed quietly. "I go too fast." He laid a hand on his ward's shoulder. "Let us not quarrel over this."

"Indeed we will not, Fergus," said Cuculain, feeling foolish for his remark. "I've not forgotten the wrong done you by Conchobar. Your son was my friend, too. But Conchobar is still my king, and I am still his subject. No, our fate is cast in this, without right or wrong. I am to one side, you to another . . . but an altogether bad and bloody circumstance it is."

"And yet," Fergus mused, "I've wondered if there might not be some good in it."

"How do you mean this?"

"Only that such a joining of Ulster and the other

provinces of Eire might be to the advantage of everyone. A united force under one strong ruler would see this a country of great strength and power."

"It might be, Fergus," said Cuculain doubtfully, "but the soul of Eire has never been so. No ruler can combine us all, or over-reach the many strong spirits that live here. And no war will do more than make the hatreds worse." He shrugged. "Ah, never mind. It's not our part to decide the politics of this. Leave that to druids and to kings. You've not yet told me why you come to seek me here."

"It is to bargain a way with you so we might go on, although I think you've given me an answer to that already."

"I have, Fergus. Still, your coming here tells me I've done some damage to your host."

"You have many shaking beneath their cloaks." Fergus smiled at the fear within Meave's army and wondered how foolish they would feel could they but see this innocent-looking young man who now grinned at him like a boy who had just won a victory in a hurley match. "The queen would offer you half her cattle, I'll wager, to let us pass."

"All the cattle in Eire would not buy that," the Hound replied, "for by now the men of Ulster must be hosting, or on their way. If I can hold them . . . hold you . . . for a little longer, I will have help enough."

"Without disloyalty to my queen, I hope you are right," Fergus told him earnestly. "Perhaps if Ulster arrives in strength before we can cross its border, the chieftains under Meave will see the folly of this campaign and the thing can be ended without blood. For, once we are in Ulster, it will not be stopped so easily."

"Only one matter continues to give me some sorrow, Fergus. To keep this fear upon the men of Eire, I must kill by stealth, at night, from cover or any other way which will create the most disquiet. That does not go well with me. I could wish to face my enemies openly."

"But then the fears of you would be dispelled," Fergus reminded him. "They would give you no chance and, though I know your strength and courage, you would not stand long against five thousand men."

"There's no denying that," said Cuculain unhappily. "But still I curse the ill-fate that brought me to this."

"Perhaps you'll not be needing to go on much longer. Already many of our warriors refuse to cross the river for their fear."

"Yet, that fear must be kept alive in them, and only constant attacks will do that."

Cuculain pulled the cooked fish from the spit and handed one to Fergus. For a time they ate in silence, considering the terrible impasse. Finally, Cuculain spoke again.

"Fergus, there is a way to end this nightly murdering, and keep the army below the Oun Dia, perhaps for days."

"A way?" said Fergus with interest. "What way?"

"I will issue a challenge to the army of Meave."

"What kind of madness do you bring us back, Fergus?" asked Queen Meave.

Fergus stood before the platform in the queen's pavilion. Around him were gathered the chieftains who had patiently awaited his return from the meeting with Cuculain.

"It is not madness," the commander told her stolidly. "It is an honest challenge from a warrior who only wishes to fight honorably."

"After killing our men from ambush every night?" This came from Calatin, who seemed to find the idea an ironic joke. "And just what is this 'honorable' challenge?"

"Cuculain agrees to meet one champion of our army at the ford each day. If we lose, we stay south of the Oun Dia. If we win, our path is clear."

Astonished cries and laughter forced out by surprise arose from the gathering.

"But, this isn't right," said Bras MacFirb. "Fergus told us that he was barely past boyhood."

"In age," responded Fergus, calmly. "I'll say no more about it. It is his offer."

"Well, I'll fight against no beardless lad," said the giant Lok MacFavash, a man long-famed as a warrior, "nor will any other champion of name. It would degrade him."

"This is a trick," Calatin announced with certainty. "No sane man would barter himself into his own death."

"You may not understand, Enchanter," said Fergus. "Cuculain is a warrior. He fights by a warrior's code. It needs only for us to accept or reject his offer. I guarantee it was made in good faith. Do any here challenge my guarantee?"

No one did.

The voice of Meave cut across the bickering of her men. "We must accept this offer," she said. When voices of dissent were heard in the gathering, she raised a hand to still them. "Think, my chieftains ... he gives us a simple way. We have a choice between an open battle and attempting to go on with this hound biting at our heels."

"She is right," said MacFirb. "We must take the fear from our men. It seems unfair but, if this Cuculain wishes to fight, we will do it!"

"You hear?" Meave said to all the crowd. "Now, do you all agree?"

Amidst the shouts of assent Fergus stood, arms crossed, face immobile and expressionless. Only one who knew him well might have seen the faint flicker of a smile pull at his lips.

Meave turned again to her commander. "Very well, Fergus, we are agreed. You will return to Cuculain with our acceptance. Tell him we will send our champion to meet him at dawn at the ford."

"You might tell him also that we thank him," Calatin added. "His foolish honor will make it easy for us."

"I will tell him what you say, Calatin," said Fergus with disdain. "We may all wish to remember who made such a prophecy."

He went out of the pavilion, walking back through the camp to where his chariot and driver awaited him.

"Harness fresh horses," Fergus commanded of his driver. "We'll be crossing the river once again today."

As he waited for this to be done, he observed another chariot in the process of preparation nearby. And, as he mounted into his own vehicle, he noted a young man climb into the other. He was a well-dressed warrior, in fine armor, with a brooch of gold fastening his rich cloak

and another golden ornament holding his long, carefully
groomed hair. Fergus did not know him, but had seen
him about the camp and had judged him as one too
worried about his appearance for a serious warrior. Now,
as Fergus ordered his driver to depart, this youth directed
his chariot alongside.

"Who are you, lad?" asked Fergus.

"Eiderkool, I am," he announced proudly, "of the Clan
Farna."

The name gave Fergus cause to revise his estimate
somewhat. He'd heard Eiderkool's name spoken with
renown as a young warrior. Still, the man's appearance
left a feeling in Fergus that renown meant much more to
the lad than simple skill.

"What is it you want, Eiderkool?" he demanded
brusquely. "I've little time for talk."

"Please, sir," the young man said, "I wish to go with
you to see this Cuculain who has such a fame in Ulster."

Fergus shook his head. "I'd not advise such a journey."

"And why not?"

"You are a proud man, I can see," he told the youth
bluntly. "If your pride and his met together, some misfor-
tune would surely happen."

Eiderkool smiled with assurance. "I will not anger him
in any way. I give my word to you on that. I mean only to
see him."

"Very well, then," Fergus agreed, seeing little more
than talk in the colorful youth. "But stay with me and
mind my orders, or I'll not be responsible."

The two chariots rode out, then, recrossing the Oun
Dia. But this time they did not go far into the hills for
Cuculain, seeing that Fergus was accompanied by another, came down to meet them in a clearing some distance below his hiding place.

When the chariots entered the clearing, and Fergus saw
Cuculain at its far side, he had his driver pull up.

"He is here," the commander told Eiderkool. "Now,
remember, stay behind me and do not speak."

The chariot of Fergus went on, that of the young

warrior falling in behind. When they reached Cuculain, Fergus climbed down and approached his old comrade while Eiderkool watched.

"Well, Fergus, you have brought a champion, I see."

"A curious peacock. He's come to see the infamous Hound of Ulster." Fergus said this with a smile, unable to conceal his amusement. "But, I've come to bring you word: the men of Eire accept your bargain. At dawn Meave will send a champion to fight, and you should know that the queen's ard-druid, Calatin, expects to see you dead before the sun has burned away the morning mist."

A light came into Cuculain's face at that and he smiled, grimly, in return.

"A great relief it is to hear that, Fergus, for now I can fight as I should. I'll no longer be having to kill in darkness."

"I'm hoping it is not for too long, my friend," said Fergus. "You have many hard fights ahead, but you may save many more lives . . . if you can win. Still, you are not fitted properly for a fight. You must take armor."

"No, Fergus. I can take nothing from you, for they will suspect treachery of you and break the bargain. For that same reason let's be parting now. Don't have fears for me; only hope this will be ended soon."

"That I will do," Fergus agreed. "Luck go with you!"

He climbed back into his chariot and had it turned about. As he passed the chariot of Eiderkool, it also turned and started after, but the young warrior looked back often to where Cuculain stood, watching them.

Eiderkool's mind had been racing since he had first seen Cuculain and realized his youth. Here was no mighty warrior, he thought, but a boy younger and no stronger in appearance than himself, and armed with only a sword on top of it! With those thoughts a bold decision came to him. It was true that no better way to win fame and become beloved of Meave existed than to finish this fool bargain now. He would kill Cuculain and reap the rewards promised!

And so he told his driver to slow and lag behind the chariot of Fergus which went ahead at a good pace back toward the river. The commander never looked about to see if his companion followed, sure of the word he had been given.

When Eiderkool saw Fergus was far enough ahead not to note him, he ordered the chariot around and back toward the clearing at a full gallop.

Cuculain, after watching the chariots drive away, was about to return to his own camp when he noticed one of them returning. He waited, curious to know what was wanted of him now. The vehicle came into the clearing and pulled up before him, and the young warrior looked down upon him with cold disdain.

"And what is it you are looking at?" said Cuculain.

"I am looking at yourself."

"Then take your eyes off me and go after Fergus, and you may think yourself as good a fighting man as the one on which you look."

"You look as good a fighter as I've seen . . . for one of your age," the other replied. "But you'd not be thought of as much amongst trained fighters or grown men."

Cuculain laughed at that.

"Go back, now, youth, unharmed to your camp, for you've come under the protection of Fergus, my friend and tutor."

That angered Eiderkool and, seeing that Cuculain made no warlike move, he began to be very brave. He climbed from his chariot and walked up to his rival.

"So you wish to give battle to the champions of Eire, and yet you are afraid to fight with me!"

"I will fight you. Accept my challenge to meet me at the ford at dawn and you will see me quick enough to fight."

"No. I will fight you now," Eiderkool demanded, pulling his sword from its sheath.

Cuculain's patience was rapidly ending. "I will not. You are under the protection of Fergus."

"I deny it," the other cried. "Now fight, or be seen as a coward!"

In a swift move, Cuculain's sword flashed out. With a dexterous hand he swung it in a finely executed stroke at the feet of Eiderkool, flipping a clod of turf against the other's breast before he could move his own weapon in reply.

"Go back now," said Cuculain, "for you have had warning."

Amazed as was the young warrior by the swiftness of this move, Eiderkool hung on to his courage. Alone, the speed meant nothing. He, too, had proven skill, and a veteran's stamina as well.

"I will not go back until I have fought with you," he insisted.

Again the sword of Cuculain flashed out. Before Eiderkool could lift his shield, the blade has passed behind it, to sheer away the knob of the golden brooch that held his hair.

"Now will you go back?" Cuculain asked. "Or, are you wishing to lose you fair tresses as well?"

But Eiderkool, though he would have been afraid of such a display, was angered by this insult to his pride. Mindless with rage, he moved on Cuculain, his weapon raised to strike.

"Now I'll make an end of you," he snarled.

By this time Fergus had almost reached the river and, looking about for the first time, realized his companion was gone. Fearing what had happened, he ordered the chariot back and his driver sent the horses racing toward the clearing.

They came into sight of the others just as Cuculain, still reluctant but having no more choice, parried the blow of Eiderkool and returned a hard stroke that killed the warrior instantly.

"Cuculain!" Fergus cried, riding up to them. "What is it you've done? He was under my protection!"

In sorrow Cuculain looked up from the dead man, into the shocked eyes of MacRogh. He knew what painful memories moved behind those eyes, what a dreadful specter he had raised with his act. Men under Fergus's protection had died once before at Conchobar's hand, died in a flaming house, and Fergus's son with them. Now this horror of betrayal seemed to be repeating itself.

"No, Fergus," Cuculain said quickly. "Ask his driver. He will tell you where blame lies for this."

Then Eiderkool's driver, frightened almost from his wits by his plight and by the sudden death of his master, told all that had happened. When Fergus heard it, his pain left him, to be replaced by cold anger.

"No blame falls on you, Cuculain," he said. "He was put up to this, I'm certain. He would never do it himself. If so, he has gotten his proper reward."

With that he climbed from his chariot and, with a leather thong, he lashed the hapless Eiderkool to the vehicle's back.

"I will return him to those who sent him," he said.

He rode back to Meave's camp, dragging the body behind him. The men of the army, seeing him come with his terrible load, followed through the camp in a great throng until he reached Meave's pavilion. In front of it the queen waited with Aileel and Calatin and others who had gathered hastily at the announcement of his return. He pulled up there and cut the thong holding the body behind, letting it fall limply in the grass.

"I return the young man you sent out," he told Meave. "His mission was a failure."

Meave was bewildered. "Fergus, I sent no one," she protested.

"If not you, then someone," said Fergus, looking about at the crowd. "He was not man enough to think of this himself."

"Eiderkool was a lad of promise," said Calatin. "We did not think he went under bad protection when he went with you."

"Ah, it is the one who sent him who's speaking now," said Fergus. "I should have known it would be you! Here, then . . ." He rolled the body over. The fine clothes were torn and soiled. The eyes, filmed with death, stared up at the crowd. "You bury him. And, know this: it is the treatment Cuculain will give any other fool like this you send out against him!"

Book Three

THE WALL OF BRASS

Chapter Thirteen
THE MADNESS OF ULSTER

In four days four champions of Eire went to the ford of the Oun Dia to give challenge to Cuculain.

In four days four men died.

While the army of Meave, thrown into confusion by this unexpected series of defeats, searched for some answer, the young warrior from Dun Dalgan waited in the hills and looked for Ulster's arrival.

Each evening he climbed to the highest hill nearby, which provided a vantage point to overlook the land to the north. He searched the horizon for some sign of a coming army, the flash of spearpoints in the late sun, the rising of dust from the churning wheels of a thousand chariots. But there was nothing, only an empty countryside before him, and a hostile army behind.

He could not understand why Ulster had not come. Had his father failed to reach Emain Macha? Had his message not been understood?

Then, on the evening of the fourth day, as Cuculain watched from his hill, he caught sight of movement far away. He gazed intently at it for some time until he saw it was but a single chariot, coming toward the river at full speed.

Hoping it was a messenger or an advance scout from King Conchobar, Cuculain moved to intercept the chariot, for it was moving to the ford as if to cross, not knowing what lay beyond.

He moved at right angles to the chariot's path, running

easily through the trees with a leaping stride, coming into the trail just ahead of the rushing vehicle.

Startled, the driver pulled up on the steeds and brought the chariot to a sliding halt. So covered with dirt and dust was the man that Cuculain did not recognize him, but he knew well enough the voice that spoke to him.

"Sentanta, thank the gods I've found you."

"Father!" said Cuculain. "What has happened? Where are the men of Ulster?"

"Oh, my son, I do not know how to tell it." Sualtim's voice was hoarse and he tightly clutched the handrail of the chariot as if to hold himself erect. "It's ill news that I've brought you. But I am tired . . . so tired."

Cuculain realized that the man, already weak from his long years of illness, was near the end of his strength after the hard journey. Asking no more questions, the young warrior vaulted into the chariot, took the reins from Sualtim, and directed the horses back toward his secret recess. There he unharnessed the steeds and, while he fed and watered them, his father bathed to clean and refresh himself. Only when the man had been made comfortable by a fire of turf and given some hot food from Cuculain's dwindling supplies did the young warrior feel he could ask Sualtim questions.

"Now, Father, I'm sorry to be wearying you further, but I must find out what has happened. Why have the men of Ulster not come?"

"All sorrow is with me, my son," said Sualtim. "I tried in every way I could. I tried many times."

He sounded so desolate that Cuculain hesitated to force him to recount his story; but he had to know.

"I believe you tried. Please, just tell me all of it."

Sualtim agreed. He sat a few moments in silence, carefully arranging all the facts of the journey in his mind. Then he began.

He told his son that, after leaving him, he rode straight north to Emain Macha. He was fearful about making the trip alone, but soon found the travel easy and was much buoyed in spirits. As he entered the capital city and rode up its broad avenue toward the high dun, he was prepared to make the announcement of the invasion strongly, proud of his success in completing his mission. But, as he rode along, crying the alarm as he went, only timorous citizens came out from their houses to flock after him.

As he approached the royal dun, he heard the war-steeds neighing in the stables by the fortress's outer walls. There he saw Laeg, leaning against the gate of the Chariot House in which the war chariots of Cuculain and the other warriors were stored.

"What? Laeg?" said Cuculain, interrupting his father's narrative. "Did he do nothing when he saw you?"

"I asked him what he was doing there," Sualtim replied, "while his master was contending alone against the four provinces of Eire."

"Yes? And he gave you no reply?"

Sualtim shook his head. "No, he only raised sorrowful eyes and gazed on me without speaking. I meant to talk further with him, but I heard a great clamor within the dun—the shouting of warriors and the clash of smitten shields—and I left him to see what was happening there."

In the Tec Meadcuarta, the immense central hall, he found assembled all the warriors of Conchobar MacNessa, and the chiefs of the permanent battalion of Emain Macha. And there, too, at the end of the chamber, King Conchobar himself harangued them. But he spoke in a strange and a rambling way that confused Sualtim. He mentioned vague, ancient prophecy and stories of the ancestors of the Red Branch and how the Milesians were one race of one tongue and destined to be combined in one, strong empire.

"It was foolish talk," Sualtim told his son. "The talk of a child. Still, the face of every warrior there was like a flame, and there was a huge uproar. Then the king said: 'Tomorrow will our empire be begun. We will go first to claim Manaan's Isle, once before subdued by my brave champion, Cuculain, but now in rebellion.'

"At that the warriors shouted again, but I, when I heard your name, sprang into the midst of the assembly and cried out: 'Cuculain is alone contending against the four provinces south of the Oun Dia!' "

"And then?" asked Cuculain with great intensity.

"Then Conchobar answered with a triumphant cry:

'It's good news you're bringing us, old man. Bid him be regent of the four provinces until the return of the Red Branch!'

"They'd listen no more to me, so I left the dun, and mounted my chariot, weeping in confusion, and around me crowded the citizens of the city, pale and afraid and asking me what was happening there . . . and I had nothing to tell them."

At this Cuculain shook his head in disbelief. What kind of emergency, what kind of horrible fear could draw away the king and all his men to a tiny isle and cloud their minds to the vast danger that came upon them out of all the rest of Eire? Unable to make any sense of this, he asked his father to continue.

Sualtim told him that he then drove toward the south of Emain Macha, seeking somewhere he might make his plea heard. He came to the dun of Leairey Bewda, the son of Iliach. Around the outer foss of that king's fortified hill, he found chariots and horsemen and many warriors assembled, for there was a great hosting of the chiefs and the warlike clans of his tuath. And, on the lawn before the dun, Sualtim saw a giant burial Cromlich, newly erected, with uprights of heavy boulders and a flat roof such as hundreds must have been needed to raise.

Curious as to what famous personage had died, Sualtim moved toward the entrance to the dun and there, by the main gates, he found King Leairey, clothed in robes of peace, as though prepared to travel.

"I went up close to him," Sualtim told his son, "pushing through the close ranks of men. He was speaking to his captains and saying that, now that the great son of Nessa had fallen, he, the new King of the Red Branch, would go without delay to Emain Macha to assume the Ard-Rieship of the province."

"Conchobar dead?" said Cuculain in confusion. "But, you saw him at the capital."

"I did that," Sualtim agreed, "but Leairey was certain he was gone and praised his name, noising along in that fashion for a time, while his warriors shouted approval.

"I began to fear he would never make an end, for his tongue never tired, and his eyes blazed beneath his white brows. Finally I rushed into the assembly, as I had done in Emain Macha, and cried out again that an army was invading Ulster. He paused and eyed me as if I were some strange sort of being who had interrupted him and asked that I be removed at once. But, when two strong warriors laid hands on me, a bard who was near said: 'Deal softly with him, for he is Cuculain's father.'

"At that the king seemed to know me, for he begged my forgiveness for his actions. 'It's glad I am to see you so well,' he said, 'for I had grieved, hearing of your affliction. Our own minds, too, the Sidhe may one day trouble and impair.' "

This seemed to bother Sualtim, for he hesitated as he said it and Cuculain, knowing his father's disquiet came from this reminder of his trouble, hastened to comfort him.

"Father, from what you have told me, the Sidhe may have done their work already. Of all Ulster, you seem the only sane one."

"Indeed?" Sualtim brightened, his confidence reinforced again. "Honestly, my son, many times these past days I've felt it must be me returned again to deepest madness, so strange was all about me."

"Do not be fearing that," Cuculain assured him. "Truly, Father, you have taken on a task most men in perfect health and filled with youth would have given up."

He did not lie as he spoke. He was amazed with his father's work and saw, besides, that the physical rigors of the journey, while tiring, had actually brought back much of the man's lost strength. Cuculain ceased to treat him as a child and talked with him as an equal in mind.

"Sentanta, I am glad to hear your words," said Sualtim, "for I had no more luck here than at Emain Macha. Even though I stayed all night with Leairey, and tried mightily to convince him of your plight, he took no heed. He talked as if he were already King of all Eire, and his own chiefs were ruling every dun within her borders. And, when I tried to tell him otherwise, he looked at me as if I were a madman, surely.

"In the morning, he had me conducted to the border of the territory by an escort and I saw no more of him."

"Father," said Cuculain in despair, "was there nowhere you found help?"

"I fear not, Sentanta, for things seemed worse wherever I went, with men confused or afraid or raging mad so that often I ran from them."

He went on to tell his son how he rode on, arriving next at the dun of Cethern, fiercest spirit of the Red Branch. There he came upon the strangest and most horrifying sight of all, for that brave chieftain in full armor and mounted in his great chariot of war pursued his own cattle through the pastures around his dun, screaming fearful oaths and shouting the high-king's name and the battle cry of his clan.

"Erect he stood in his great machine," said Sualtim, "and the charioteer, mad as he, urged the foaming steeds here and there across the plains, driving against the herds as if they were some fearsome enemy. And all his warriors joined him, now and again catching and felling some gentle beast, reddening their spears with the shameful blood, until all the plain was dotted with the dead and dying animals.

"I watched from some distance all the day but, finally, near nightfall, the evil mood seemed to burn out. Like men stricken with immense fatigue, the warriors dropped their weapons, left their slaughter, and returned to the dun to fall into a deep sleep.

"I approached the fortress, then, and found the women of the place had chosen this lull to act. Led by Iondan, Cethern's wife, they collected all the weapons and defensive armor into the armory and barred the entrance with strong bolts and locks.

"When Iondan saw me, she invited me in and, in great confusion and fear, asked me what was happening. I could neither tell her nor soothe her distress. When morning came the men, though now disarmed and unable to further destroy the herds, yet went out from the dun again and wandered the fields, or rode about in the chariots madly, like mindless beasts themselves."

"Your story takes more and more comfort from me as it goes," said Cuculain. "And what of Dun Cuailgne? I met with Fergus MacRogh and he told me that it was King Dary's insult to Meave that began this war with Ulster."

"It was the last place I visited," said Sualtim, "but no

sign of any distress did I find there. In fact, they seemed so strangely placid as not to be concerned about anything. King Dary met me politely and said there could be no war, for Fergus MacRogh had already taken the bull. He said this, though I could plainly hear the distant roaring of the great animal. After that I could do nothing more than return south, hoping to find you."

"I thank you, Father. You may have found no help, but you have done well."

"Then, let me stay with you now, for I feel my mind returned and my blood is young again. I would fight at your side."

Sualtim did, indeed, seem much stronger, and his eyes flashed with battle light. But, though Cuculain felt joy at this recovery, he had to disappoint his father.

"I would have you gladly," he said, "but you must go again into Ulster. You must find help somewhere for us. I cannot believe that all of Ulster lies under this madness."

"What could it be?"

"I cannot tell, but are you certain no one of Ulster played tricks with you?"

"To what end? To leave you to die and have our province overrun?"

"No, no. You are right. Something strange has happened, and you must find out what."

Unhappy, but realizing this thing must be done, Sualtim agreed. Then, weary and travel worn, he rolled himself amid his rugs and skins and slept.

But Cuculain slept not, pondering over the tale his father had brought.

In the camp of Meave, too, few slept that night. The whole host was troubled and, in the royal pavilion, the chieftains of the four provinces sat silent, while dark thoughts festered within them.

Many of those thoughts had been implanted by Calatin. The druid had been talking with the chieftains these past days, pushing them to act, and he had brought many to believe with him that something must be done. He had used many of his wiles to effect this, both his wealth and his powers of speech, and even the subtle influence of his black arts, for he did not know how long the spell put upon Ulster would last. Although his returning sons reported that confusion and madness reigned in the north, he feared that this effect would pass before the host of Meave could achieve the desired ends. And once the spell had gone and Ulster had been roused to war, no second spell by him would be strong enough to bring confusion upon them once again.

Now, through his labors, many at this gathering believed that they must act against Cuculain, but each desired that another would be the first to speak out openly.

At last Bras MacFirb, King of Osree, stood and addressed them in grim terms:

"Queen of Connacht and chieftains of Eire, we've gathered for a reason we all know clearly. How long will we sit here, idle, and delay in wasting the wealth of Ulster before the Red Branch can march against us? How long will we be making, of our own will, that dribbling stream of the Oun Dia into a barrier stronger than a wall of brass? Each day no army of Ulster comes, each day we face only one stripling youth, yet each day the sun sets on our mighty host sitting here as if enchanted, bound by a foolish compact. It's not for this we came together from the distant places in Eire. How can the warriors of all the provinces be held here on the borders of Ulster when we've come to trample and extinguish the deadly flame that's threatened to devour us all? Better it would be for us to break this bargain which we, ourselves, have made, than to have the Red Branch break us, and see the tributes and hostages of the rest of Eire go to Emain Macha."

When the King of Osree had finished, many in the assembly murmured agreement, but Queen Meave only looked sidelong toward Fergus where he sat on the left hand of Aileel.

Chapter Fourteen
PLOT

Before the murmuring ended, Fergus MacRogh stood up and looked about the room, and his fierceness of expression was matched by the thunder in his voice as he spoke.

"You, MacFirb, and many of you others, here, have become rotten and weak with fear from fearful talk. But I know well enough that the rest of the noble chieftains of Eire will not be persuaded to break our agreement with Cuculain. And, mark this: a warrior who would break his word is more loathsome than a night-stalking ghoul to me. If any of this host, I've no care who, crosses the Oun Dia before the Hound of Ulster is subdued, then my sword will drink his blood and the gray-necked crows will eat his body, unburied and unburned."

Many of the kings who had harbored such thoughts were shamed by the chieftain's words and sat quiet. Mac-Firb, himself, retreated into the assembly in a dazed way, like a young girl blinded by an unexpected flash of lightning striking too close.

Only Calatin dared Fergus's wrath, moving forward from the queen's side to address the warrior.

"It is well enough to throw up fairness and nobility to these men," he said, "but not at the cost of life." He paused to be certain this had its effect. While irritated at seeing his hard work ruined so easily, he had anticipated Fergus's opposition to simply breaking the oath with Cuculain and had devised an alternate scheme. Once assured of all attention, he continued:

"My chieftains, no warrior of Eire can easily compete with Cuculain, so skillful is he in the using of weapons, in spear and sword alike. From no teacher of this land did he learn those martial arts."

Cormac Conlingas spoke then, sarcasm unconcealed in his voice. "As always you are a great help to us, Enchanter. In your wisdom you've made it clear to us that there's not a man in the entire host who can go against the Hound and defeat him. Shall we all be going home?"

Calatin's reply was quick and biting. "As always, our friend Cormac's humor has overreached his sense. Many could try, and many might win, but it might take days to find one who could do so. There is a way to insure a better chance. You see, I've found that our Hound learned his feats of arms at the hands of Skaah, the warrior-queen who rules the ragged isle in the northern seas and teaches only select champions of the men of Eire and Alba. More, I have learned that, along with Cuculain, two warriors in our own army were trained with him. Lewy MacNeesh is one, the chief of the Clan Falva. The other is Fardia, son of Daman of the western Firbolgs."

"Firbolgs!" said Loc MacFavash with distaste. "We want no member of that filthy tribe to defend our honor here."

To this Fergus replied with heat. "It's foolishness you're speaking now! Though he's of a subject race, and not honored by you Milesian kings, yet he is to my mind the greatest warrior in all Eire."

"You have your own mind, Fergus," Lok returned, "but I'll not give honor or trust to backward thralls not fit to even raise their tents with the rest of us. Why, they only fight here because they owe us tribute. They are not even invited to our assemblies."

There was no disagreement from the other chieftains at that, and it was easily seen that no sympathy was held for the idea of letting this Fardia go against Cuculain.

"My chieftains," said Calatin soothingly, "there is no need for such discord. I mentioned the name of another among us who can slay the Hound of Ulster and remove the barrier: Lewy MacNeesh!"

A great roar of approval went up from the assembly, but that young warrior sprang forward and shouted over it.

"You'll not be choosing me to go against Cuculain, for my sword and his will never cross."

The crowd was quiet at once. Meave, in amazement, looked down at the stalwart warrior who now faced her, defiance flaring in his gray eyes.

"You'll not fight with him?" she asked. "What is it that keeps you, son of Neesh? Is it fear you're covering, or some strange loyalty? It cannot be the last, since I am sure this Hound would not hesitate in driving his spear through the likes of your very faithful breast."

"I've no fear of your charge of cowardice, Queen, nor is your judgment of Cuculain correct. It is more than brothers we are, bound in spirit and body by events no one here could understand, for we fought together when there was nothing to count on for life but the sword, the arm, and the eye of the other. No, my Queen, I'll not be fighting him, and he'll not fight me, if he has the choice."

Meave grew pale with anger at this, leaning forward on her couch and speaking with a cold determination.

"Remember, Lewy, your kingship is in my hands. Go out against Cuculain you will or be stripped of your sovereignty and driven from my realm."

No change of expression showed in the calm face of the warrior. Like a rock in a raging stream he faced the wrath of the queen, letting the torrent rush over and past him without being moved.

"You may take away what you have given," he said, "and you may have me taken beyond the Shannon, or beyond the sea. You may even have my life, should you choose to have it, but against my friend I'll not lift a spear."

Fergus felt some amusement at these words of bold challenge to the queen. He awaited her response, knowing that for her to really act against one of Eire's most powerful tribes would be a dangerous act, indeed.

Meave knew it too and, always subtle of mind, determined to change her direction. With the suddenness of sunshine appearing through a rent in heavy clouds, Meave smiled gently upon the young chieftain.

"It was in haste I spoke, Lewy, driven by a fear that grows within me as the days pass. MacFirb spoke truly when he warned against the coming of Ulster. Think, Lewy, on the shame for all of us should our great hosting of all Eire be brought to ruin by this simple bargain."

She stood, then, and walked down to the warrior. Lightly she took his right hand in hers, placing her other hand on his strong wrist. Deeply she looked into the cool, light eyes which met hers levelly.

"Come now, Lewy," she said cajolingly. "Kill this northern Hound whose claws have already torn many of our comrades. Save me and all of Eire from the shame which will fall on us, should we be trapped here."

She held his eyes as she spoke and, in her own, a glistening tear arose in evidence of the sorrow in her words. So confused and shamed was the young warrior by this plea that a tear rose in his eye, too. But then, behind the queen, he glimpsed the face of Fergus MacRogh, now grim and stony, and his powers of control and careful thought returned to him once more.

"My Queen," he said, "ask anything else in my poor power to give, but against Cuculain, who has my full heart's love, I will not go. Sooner would I draw my own life's blood with my own sword."

Suddenly tired and defeated by this wall of certainty, Meave dropped his hands and moved back toward the platform.

"I cannot force a man to go against his bond," she said. "Even if all Eire is the prize." She looked around at the room. "But, my chieftains, our problem is only the greater now. A champion must be found who can defeat Cuculain. Decide among you who it will be. Go out into your own battalions, talk among yourselves. Find someone . . . and soon!"

She and Aileel left the main tent, then, and went to their sleeping quarters. Aileel was tired, and Meave was also ready for rest, although it was yet early evening. She saw Aileel to his quarters and entered her own, only to find Calatin waiting for her there.

"Good evening, my Queen. May we talk?"

"I am tired, Calatin. The worry of this has been hard. Perhaps tomorrow."

The advisor persisted. "Your worry might be lessened, should we talk now."

"And how could that be?" she asked wearily, sitting down at her working table. "Your suggestion of Lewy gave me some hope, but now that is gone."

"That is my very reason for coming. Hope is not gone."

"Oh?" She looked at him with interest, some of her fatigue dropping away. "And what could be done to change this warrior's mind when he so easily puts aside my threats and promises?" She smiled with faint amusement. "Have you charms I lack?"

"Not charms, my Queen, but knowledge." He sat down at her table and leaned forward, speaking quietly but with intensity. "There is another man, a bright and charming young man named Fireaba Larna. He is a fine singer of songs and a fine player of the tiompan."

"You're wishing to send this bard against Cuculain? To sing him to sleep, perhaps?"

"He is an archer, too, my Queen, and a skilled one by all reports, although his skill until this campaign was directed to targets and small game."

Meave shook her head. "I do not understand you yet, Calatin. Do you suggest that this lad actually be our champion?"

"I do," he agreed.

"Then he will be killed," she said.

He shrugged his shoulders. "He may be. Or he may, with speed and accuracy, hit the Hound. Either way our purpose would be served, for he and Lewy are bound by a gesa to avenge one another's deaths."

"So now your direction is clear," said Meave. "If Fireaba is killed, then this bond will force Lewy to fight Cuculain."

"That is correct, my Queen," said Calatin with satisfaction.

Her face hardened. "It is the work of a deceiver," she said angrily. "You would send this young poet to his death to cause another to compromise his loyalty. That makes your plan doubly cursed. I would, myself, be dishonored to accept it."

Calatin did not waver. "I heard the Queen of Connacht say this night that shame would fall on all Eire were not the Hound destroyed. I would send one to his death and I

would force another to act in defense of his army against
an enemy. Does that make me dishonored or disloyal to
Eire?"

She shook her head as if to clear it of this obscuring
cloud of conflicting loyalties. She could not make this
decision so easily. She needed more advice than the druid
could give.

"I can make no judgment now, Calatin," she said.

He stepped toward her to protest, but she raised a
warning hand.

"No, Calatin. I must have more time to consider.
Leave me for a while. I promise you an answer soon."

"It must be soon, my Queen," he cautioned. "The
night goes fast."

After he had gone, Meave sat a while in thought. Then
she called a waiting messenger in to her.

"Find Fergus MacRogh," she told him, "and quickly,
now. Tell him I must see him at once."

The servant did his work swiftly, and Fergus did not
hesitate to respond. It was only moments later that the
commander appeared at the queen's tent door.

"Meave," he said, "your message seemed urgent. What
is wrong?"

She sat at her work table, a map of Ulster spread out
for her examination. She looked up from it to him and he
was startled by the fatigue that showed in her face.

"Fergus," she said slowly, "I have something to ask,
but I wish you to understand how and why I ask. I know
you are a friend to Cuculain, and my own heart is
troubled by what is happening here. But, as queen, I
must do what is best for all the host of Eire. I must ask
what can be done to free us of the Hound."

Fergus had no need to consider this question. He
answered immediately and his voice was sure.

"Nothing, my Queen."

"Are you certain?" Her voice was almost pleading
now.

"I do not understand. Our bargain is made. We can do
nothing else but honor it."

"I see," she said tonelessly. "I am sorry, Fergus. I
hoped you might think of some other way."

He sensed that there was something more in this,

something more that she wanted from him; but she seemed unable to put it into words. Such lack of certainty was unusual for her, and he traced the cause of it to the fatigue he saw in her.

"You're tired, Meave. You feel too much the disquiet in your men. Get some rest, now."

She nodded. "Perhaps you're right in what you say. Thank you for coming to me."

He wished he could do something more for her, but there seemed little else to say. He took his leave of her and left the tent.

When he had gone Meave stood and walked to the tent door. Outside the fires of the camp lit the ground with their uncountable, golden cones of light, and sent up spires of smoke that scented the night with the aroma of the burning peat. Thousands of men were gathered there, waiting only for the chance to act. The greatest army Eire had ever seen . . . and she had only to free them from the strange shackle that bound them, like a giant bound by a thread about one ankle.

When Calatin returned, he found her again at her table, head down, eyes upon the map before her. But, when she heard him enter, she lifted her head and fixed her gaze on him. In those gray eyes the druid saw the clear, cold light of her determination.

"Call Fireaba here to me," she said.

Chapter Fifteen
COUNTERPLOT

Lewy MacNeesh sat quiet in the darkness of his tent for some time after leaving the assembly. His heart was troubled by the queen's arguments, but he was slowly reassuring himself that he had made no mistake in refusing her.

Then his meditation was interrupted by the entrance of a guard who hesitated on the threshold, reluctant to disturb his commander.

"My chief. there is one here to see you. I did not know . . ."

"Who is it?" Lewy asked impatiently.

"Fireaba, it is."

"Well of course, then. Let him in," said Lewy. The young poet always brought laughter and brightness with him, and never had the youthful chieftain so much need of it as now.

Into his tent came as cheerful appearing a lad as might be found among the men of Eire. A different sort than the hardened warriors was he, without the grim set of face and heavy squareness of figure. He was slim and graceful and colorfully attired, his long, fair hair dressed and combed with meticulous care. But not a bard, either, was Larna, for that profession was only learned after hard years of study, and made too serious a business of songs and poetry for him.

Not too many years before, he and Lewy had wandered the country of Connacht and made fine songs after its beauties. When the assumption of the chieftainship had taken such youthful freedom from MacNeesh, he had asked the still unfettered Fireaba to stay with him as a reminder of the more carefree days.

Tonight, the chieftain noted, his friend seemed even more exuberant of spirit than usual.

"What is it that excites you so?" he asked with a smile. "For the night grows chill, and the wind might cool the blood of any man."

"This night even snow could not cool my blood," the other said. "And no music could bring me such joy. No, I've no time for music now. Lewy . . . I've been with the queen."

"The queen?" Lewy's smile disappeared as a vague apprehension began to stir in him. Fireaba was a harmless youth. Lewy could not believe that Meave would even know his name, much less invite him to speak alone with her. That she did was a cause for suspicion.

"What business had you with the queen?" he asked.

"That is what amazes me so," said Fireaba. "When I was summoned into her presence, I had no idea. My wit and my great eloquence, which few would deny I have in great abundance, left me completely." He laughed. "I faced the queen a tongue-tied fool. But she smiled on me, and placed me on a couch at her side, and told me what a fine man and a great poet I was. She is a beautiful woman, Lewy."

"She is the queen, Fireaba," Lewy reminded him harshly, fear taking him more and more. "What did she want?"

But the young man refused to be rushed, savoring every word of his story.

"Well, she told me that she had been brought close to disaster by this Cuculain. On account of him the narrow Oun Dia was like the lofty rampart of some great dun, protecting Ulster. She despaired of ever crossing until she heard the tales of my skill in archery."

"Your skill? Where could she hear of that?"

"I've done my feats of shooting at more than one fair," he said defensively. "My feats are well known."

"By the gods!" cried Lewy, suddenly understanding. "You did not agree to go against Cuculain!"

"I did," the young man coolly replied. "She promised

chieftainship of a goodly territory around Lough Oribsen and I have but to pierce this Ulsterman's heart with one arrow!"

"Oh, so simple a feat?" said Lewy mockingly. "You fool! Cuculain has killed four trained warriors in combat."

"With sword and spear," the other returned, "but his speed cannot match an arrow's flight." He plucked one from a quiver hung on the wall and looked along its shaft. "Not easily shall he escape a shower of such deadly rain. I must decide only whether to smite him to the heart through his shield and breast, or pierce the bone of his forehead between his bright eyes."

In despair, Lewy buried his face in his hands. "If you fight Cuculain, then your only decision will be whether you wish burial or cremation."

"Oh, come now," Larna said, hurt by his friend's reaction. "The wise Queen Meave would not choose a man she thought had no chance."

"Don't you see?" Lewy implored, meeting Fireaba's bewildered gaze. "She hopes to force me to a fight. Our gesa binds me to that." He shook his head. "So clever she is. She cannot lose. And I, who thought to protect you on your first hosting, now find you used against me."

"So, I've no value of myself," Fireaba said with pain. "I am merely a tool to get to you. I should have expected this attitude. It has been so since you became king. Once we were equals. Now you are sovereign and I your fool. It is for that reason I wished to come on this hosting . . . to prove my worth."

"I wanted that too, but not this way. I hoped to protect you."

"I want not your protection," Fireaba snapped angrily. "I will fight Cuculain. I will be a noble in my own right . . . a hero. I will fight Cuculain."

At that he whirled and dashed from the tent before Lewy could stop him.

For a moment the young chieftain looked after his friend with sorrow in his eyes. Then, with an effort, his strong spirit asserted itself again. He could not let this happen! He would not allow himself to be drawn into a battle against his will, and he would not stand by while his friend was killed. Somehow he had to stop Fireaba.

"Lamderg, come here!" he called aloud.

Across the tent a tall man of doleful looks was at work chinking cracks in the wattles that formed the tent sides with mud to keep out wind, and hanging thick rugs to further retain the heat within. At the call he stopped at once and moved to his master.

"Yes, Lewy?" Such familiarity would seem strange from a servant, but this was Lewy's charioteer; a close friend as well.

"Come with me now," the chieftain said. "We have work to do."

The two pulled heavy cloaks about them and left the tent, putting the cowls up over their heads as they walked, for the night was chill and damp and the wind was rising. The cold kept most of the army within their tents or clustered near their high-banked fires, and the streets of the camp were largely deserted as they made their way along. They went up the main avenue, past the market place and the royal pavilion, finally reaching the small, four-sided tent of Fergus MacRogh.

No guards watched the outside, so they pushed through its flaps to find Fergus and Cormac Conlingas, sitting at a table by the fire and drinking in grim silence. When the two entered, Fergus greeted them warmly and invited them to sit with him. Lamderg, as suited his place in such company, removed himself to a bench against the wall. Lewy took off his cloak and warmed himself by the fire while Cormac poured some ale for both newcomers.

"Well, well, come to keen with the rest of us?" Conlingas asked, his hearty tone belying his dark words. "Though, you've little reason to be despairing. You handled a difficult situation well tonight."

"But harder and harder it gets," Fergus put in. "Soon many of the army will side with that Enchanter."

"You've no reason to be so glum," said Cormac. "As long as stout hearts like Lewy, here, are with us, we can succeed in keeping the bond."

"That's why I am here now," said Lewy, now finding it

more difficult to begin. "I am afraid a way has been found to make me fight."

"What?" said Fergus. "What kind of means could be found?"

"Do you know Fireaba Larna?"

"What, that colorful poet who hangs about your battalions?" said Cormac, smiling. "Who could miss him?"

"That is the one. Well, he has been coerced by Meave into fighting, and I am bound by a gesa since our childhood to avenge him should he die."

"By the Dagda!" Fergus cried, striking the table a blow that bounced cups and flaggon high. "There is that cleverness at work again. I see Calatin's hand here."

Cormac laughed, but without humor now. "The scene is clear in my mind: the queen and your poet, her flattering him, playing on his weakness . . . as she does on others."

"Watch your words concerning the queen," said Fergus with a sharpness that surprised his comrade. "There is a dishonorable hand in this . . . but never hers. Only the Enchanter's. Lewy, has this friend any chance at all against Cuculain?"

Lewy shrugged. "He is swift with a bow, but no trained warrior."

"Then he is rotting meat now," said Cormac coldly. "No slight to your poet, but he is not the worry. It is his death that will cause us grief, for Lewy will then have to fight and I, for one, would not like to name the better warrior there."

"But, there is a way that I would not have to fight," said Lewy, whose cunning mind had been at work on the problem.

"How?" said Fergus, "unless your poet were to win."

"How if he were not to die?" Lewy suggested.

The other two were stricken for a moment. Then Fergus bellowed with excitement:

"Of course! If Cuculain could best him, but leave him alive, then you would be free."

"It is a great deal to ask of a man too sorely tried already," said Cormac.

"More sorely will he be tried if he and Lewy must

fight!" Fergus retorted. "He would accept our idea, I think."

"We must get word to him tonight, then," said Lewy. "It is why I came to you, knowing you knew where to find him."

"Aye, that I do, but none of us will go. Too many suspicions would be raised should one of us be seen leaving the camp."

"I've brought with me a man who can be trusted," said Lewy and, at that, Lamderg came forward, the fire lighting a rugged face, early worn by harsh experience. "He is my charioteer. He had a strange and a wild existence before I knew him. I saved him from certain death, and we've helped one another many times since. I'd trust him with my life . . . and yours. He will go."

"It will be a dangerous journey," Cormac warned.

"I will make it," Lamderg answered simply.

Fergus quickly gave the stolid man directions as to how to find Cuculain and, without a word, Lamderg went out into the night. With skill and ease he escaped the outer guards of the camp and went some distance upriver. He waded the flood and moved northwest into the hills, following unerringly the directions Fergus had given him.

At last he entered the dell where Fergus had last met with Cuculain. There he stood and called the name of Sentanta into the wind.

Suddenly, an opening appeared in the solid wall of foliage ahead. Against a red blaze of light a giant form, gaunt and terrible, was silhouetted.

For the first time in his life, Lamderg felt fear.

Chapter Sixteen
THE ARCHER

"Who is there?" came a cold and a deadly voice.

At the sound of it, Lamderg, at first frozen by his fear, was moved to speech.

"I am sent by Fergus MacRogh to bring you important word."

The challenge in the voice disappeared at that, to be replaced by gentle tones and gracious words.

"Then you are welcome here. Come, eat and drink and warm yourself from this night."

Lamderg took heart at this and moved forward past the tall figure, into the bower in the trees. There he found two chariots and a bright fire beside which a second man was sleeping.

"Go quietly," Cuculain whispered. "It is my father. He is weary from travel, but he must travel more tomorrow. Sit here, on the fire's far side."

They seated themselves on a rug Cuculain spread for them. The young warrior offered food and drink, but Lamderg refused.

"I must get back soon," he explained. "I will give you my message and be gone again."

"Very well. I know what danger it means to you and to Fergus to take such chances ... for one who opposes you."

"This concerns more than Fergus. Lewy MacNeesh is in it too. A plot has been laid to force your old comrade to fight you. Tomorrow you will go against one who Lewy has been bound to avenge, should he be killed."

"A plot?" said Cuculain. "This is ill news, indeed. For, were Lewy to put aside a gesa, his name and honor would be forever lost to him. But, this is not an act a man of Eire would put on another. How has this thing happened?"

"I do not know. I heard the name Calatin mentioned and know he is advisor to the queen, but what part he plays is unknown to me."

" 'Calatin.' The name echoes strangely in my mind, without my knowing why." He shook his head slowly, wearily, and Lamderg saw signs of great despair in him. "I tell you truly, this day has brought me more ill news than I can easily bear. Yet, what can be done? My bargain has bound me, and I've no choice. I must fight whoever is sent against me."

"But, if this man were not killed?"

"Not killed?" Cuculain repeated.

"If you can defeat this Fireaba Larna and not kill him, Lewy would not be bound to fight. He has no wish for it. Already he has defied Meave to avoid it."

"He is a true friend. But not to kill . . ." He considered this a moment, then asked: "What weapons does this Fireaba favor?"

"Bow, and good he is, but a stranger to war, and untrained as a combat warrior."

"Then there might be a way. There must be, for any chance would be better than to fight against Lewy. Too many battles we've fought together in years past. A sad day it would be were he and I to meet."

"In my time with Lewy, I have heard much of you. I know he feels the same. I'll carry your acceptance to him, then."

"Must you be away so soon? I've had no comfort to give you against the chill of the night."

"Comfort enough to be in our camp and wrapped in my own blanket," Lamderg told him. "Good fortune go with you tomorrow."

The first light of the morning found a crowd, the queen and her chieftains among its members, gathered before the tent of Fireaba Larna.

The numbers there were not nearly so large as in times past, however. So used had the army become to Cuculain's victories that many had lost interest in the daily combats. That was particularly true in this case, for word had passed through the camp of the young archer's lack of training in war, and the coming contest held less appeal in the chill, damp dawn than staying close beside a blazing fire.

When Fireaba appeared at the door of his tent, he seemed so full of pride and awareness of his honor that the thinness of his supporters' ranks went unnoticed by him. He was dressed for the coming battle in true, heroic fashion. On his thin shoulders hung a fine, if unserviceable, shield decorated with gold leaf, and in his hand he carried his bow of red yew inscribed with ogham verses and tipped with finely wrought walrus tooth.

When Fergus first saw him, he could not hold back an exclamation of surprise:

"Is that stripling our champion?" he asked Cormac.

"A poet if ever I saw one," his friend replied. He would have laughed openly had not the purpose behind this been so grim.

Fireaba paraded through the camp, leading the throng of anxious spectators. When he reached the ford, he walked to the edge of the water while the following company spread out along the banks. Halting on the first island of sand, he carefully fitted an arrow to his bow, tested the pull, and then stood easy, unafraid, waiting for Cuculain to appear.

"What calm he shows, standing there," said Meave. "A gallant youth for us to send to die." She looked at Calatin. "Perhaps, though, he has a chance to win."

"Of course, my Queen," Calatin responded with assurance. But, unnoticed by her, a faint sparkle of amusement flickered deep within the black pools of his eyes.

On the far side of the river, Cuculain suddenly came into view. He walked steadily toward the ford with long strides, but he seemed strangely unconcerned with the fight ahead. His left hand held his shield low, exposing a good portion of his chest, and his right hand carried his spears loosely, the hafts dragging upon the ground.

Now could Fireaba have killed Cuculain easily as the Hound came into the shallow water of the ford and started across. He raised the bow and took aim at the fair target of the broad chest. But he hesitated and lowered his bow. He could not understand Cuculain's attitude, the seeming lack of care to defend himself. He waited, expecting at any moment to see the sword come up and a position of attack or defense assumed. Still, nothing happened. Cuculain only came on and on in his steady way, not looking up.

"Shoot him!" Calatin cried. "Shoot him now . . . now!"

Again, indeed, had Fireaba listened to the voice of the Enchanter, could he have slain the Hound of Ulster. But still he hesitated longer in confusion, letting Cuculain close yet farther with him. And when, at last, he raised the bow again and took aim, he shouted a loud cry of challenge, as if in an attempt to bring his opponent out of his lethargy.

It worked with more effect than the archer had expected. Cuculain, now past midpoint of the ford, came to active life.

With a burst of energy the warrior leapt forward in a full run, bringing up his head and shield at once, charging directly toward his opponent.

The swift move startled Fireaba, but he was still expert enough archer to stand his ground and draw and loose his arrow.

His first shot struck the tough leather of Cuculain's light shield and stuck fast, but others followed, fired as fast as Fireaba could fit, pull and release. Cuculain closed the remaining distance quickly, but still the archer's skill was great for, though Cuculain caught most of the arrows on his shield, one penetrated, catching him in the back of his hand, and a second struck deeply into his thigh.

Then the Hound was on Fireaba and, before the youth could move, he swung a blow sideways with his shield, slamming it against the archer's side and head, knocking him breathless into the ford.

As Fireaba lay stunned in the shallow water, Cuculain stuck his spears into the sand, stooped over him, and lifted the exquisitely wrought bow. With a savage twist he snapped it in the middle and dropped it into the stream, pouring Fireaba's arrows after it. With the crowd watching, he pulled the arrows from his hand and leg, snapped them disdainfully and threw them away from him.

On the bank, Lewy MacNeesh felt relief wash over

him. He looked to Fergus and saw his feelings mirrored in the other's eyes and the two men exchanged a smile.

"I do not kill children who stand away and shoot at me with tiny barbs," Cuculain called to Meave. "Next time, send me a champion, or sit in your camp and tremble."

He turned, then, and walked away from them, fighting to keep from limping on his wounded leg. But he had taken only a few steps when a booming voice stopped him.

"Wait, Hound!"

Cuculain turned back and saw a man, giant in both girth and weight, pushing forward from the crowd.

"If you want a champion to fight . . . then you have one. I, Lok MacFavish, challenge you to fight. Sufficient now is the renown of Cuculain to render him a quarry worthy of my spear."

"And before I was but a youth, unworthy of notice?" said Cuculain with a humorless smile. "Very well. Tomorrow we will fight."

"Tomorrow," Lok agreed. "Now bind your wounds and rest, for I've no liking to fight any weakened man."

"My wounds are nothing, MacFavish," Cuculain retorted, unable to ignore this question of his strength. "If you've doubt of it, meet me today!"

"Tomorrow is time enough. You must be as strong an opponent as possible. Tomorrow we will meet."

"Why wait?" Cuculain asked, more insistently. "You have not met your bargain today. This one . . ." he nodded to the still dazed Fireaba who was being helped from the ford by two warriors, "he does not fill our agreement."

Now it was the courage of Lok that was under question and, like Cuculain, the giant warrior could not ignore that.

"Very well," he said. "I'll return to my tent and arm myself. Bind your wounds, rest, and meet me fresh."

"Done, Lok," said Cuculain. "I will return here when you do."

Without further words the young warrior turned and walked back across the ford into the woods. MacFavish watched him go, then started through the camp, the crowd now on his heels.

Queen Meave had looked in dark, unpleasant ways at Calatin as the archer and the ard-druid's plan had gone down in defeat. She had meant to have some words with him upon this failure, but the unexpected turn in events had stayed her tongue.

"What do you think of this?" she asked instead as she and Calatin followed Lok back through the camp.

"I think that if we cannot have Lewy, we have a fine choice to replace him," replied the philosophical druid. "Lok is fat and past the prime of youth and not so quick on his feet as the younger warriors, yet he is a seasoned fighter . . . the first such to try Cuculain. The others were arrogant champions looking for quick fame. Beyond that, next to Fergus himself, the power and strength of Lok are known to be irresistible. Last summer, at the Feast of Lunosa, he broke the skull of an ox with a blow of his fist."

"You make a good argument," said Meave, "but it sounds much like another tale told by drunken warriors."

"Ah, does it?" said Calatin. "Look ahead."

Meave looked at the warrior moving ahead of her and knew what the druid meant. The man's sheer height and bulk were evidence of how much truth was in the tales.

"Yet, even with such strength," she said, "there is no certainty he can win. You, yourself, said that only those who trained with Cuculain could defeat him."

"No, my Queen," he corrected. "I said there might be others, if we could find them. This one is a volunteer and a powerful warrior. We've nothing to lose by letting him fight, and we might have a great deal to gain."

Calatin spoke in assured tones, now, for his agile mind had been at work. He knew other means could be found to help insure the success of Lok MacFavish.

Chapter Seventeen
LOK MACFAVASH

Calatin parted from Meave and went to the tent of Lok. He found the giant man, attended by several servants, readying himself for battle, and stood within the tent doors watching the preparations.

A heavy, leather coat was fastened about the chieftain, and over that a light, bronze chest plate. His sword and mace were buckled about his thick waist and his cloak thrown over his shoulders and fastened at his throat with a gold pin. Finally he was fitted with a helmet topped with a tall, iron point and extended at the back with a broad, leather neck piece. Through the entire process of this fitting out, the chieftain checked over each piece carefully and muttered beneath his breath vague threats against the youth who had insulted him.

"Most effective, Lok," Calatin observed dryly. "Do you feel you'll have need of this armament to defeat one, lightly armed young man?"

MacFavash was hard at his work and paid little attention.

"What do you mean, Enchanter?"

Calatin shrugged. "I only wonder if you don't fear Cuculain, a bit, anyway."

"Fear?" Lok repeated. "No animal of this world doesn't fear the thought of death. But, death with glory . . . that overrides the fear."

"Perhaps I can help you with your glory, and insure your survival as well," the druid suggested.

Lok had been examining his shield, a heavy, round device of oxhide, seven layers in thickness, stretched on a brass circle with an outer rim of solid metal the width of three fingers. Now he looked up toward Calatin, suspicion in his eyes.

"What's the meaning of this 'insure'?"

"Ah, well, I could make it . . . difficult for Cuculain to concentrate on his fighting. I could make him hesitate at key moments."

"You could, could you, Calatin!" Lok exclaimed with seeming amazement. "And it's through your magic that this would all be done?"

"It could be so."

The giant's broad visage turned dark in rage. "Then a crawling horror of the fields you are and cursed by every real warrior of Eire. No champion born would use your methods in a fight. Even knowing this boasting whelp could kill me at his ease wouldn't bring me to take help from the likes of you. Be away from me, you treacherous necromancer, and let me not be seeing you about me again this day!"

The druid betrayed no anger at these words. Though he could little understand the logic of the warrior, he had expected such a response from Lok.

"As you wish," he told the chieftain. "And, may you live to see the day after this."

Calatin left the warrior's tent and made his way back to his own, brows knitted in a black frown. Once within the security of his own walls, he called about him his sons, now all returned from their work in the north.

"That great fool, MacFavish, goes to fight Cuculain very soon," he told them. "He might destroy the Hound, but he might as easily lose. I offered my help to see he succeeded, but he refused it. I would let the ox go to his slaughter, but I cannot. Some way we must rid ourselves of this Cuculain, and I'll no longer assume that these warriors can accomplish that task for us. We've no need of Lok's agreement in any case. Though it is dangerous with the army close about, this time we'll cast up a spell here that he and they will not know about. Some of you build the fire, bring the chest. The rest of you circle me and begin the chant, but quietly. Draw no notice to us."

Two sons brought wood and fed the central fire to create a small but fiercely burning blaze. Two others brought to the druid a heavy chest of bog-oak, polished black and harder than iron. The rest of the pale, twisted clan formed in a circle about the fire and began an incantation, their voices soft as they repeated the strange and ancient phrases.

Calatin knelt close to the blaze and opened the black chest. From its depths he lifted vials of the elements whose properties only he understood. Selecting with care, he mixed several together in a bowl of silver. Then, standing up before the leaping flames, he cast the mixture on them all at once.

The fire began to smoke in billows of a greenish-yellow hue that drifted up in a thick column to disappear through the roof hole. A foul smell of decay pervaded the tent, so strongly that even some of Calatin's sons moved back, unable to stay so close to its source.

But the ard-druid was unmoved. He stood facing the smoke and spoke out clearly as if addressing some presence there.

"Now, I want a spirit of the air, a dismal spirit, horrible and cold, to be created here. Take life you putrid smoke and form for me."

At once the rising fumes began to undulate, to writhe as if tortured by spiraling winds. It curled upon itself and then took shape like a sketch made by an artist's hand, first outlined, then filled out with mass and weight. Little-by-little the abominable shape appeared, drawn out of the surrounding smoke as a nightmare shape looms forward from the darkness of childhood's fears. All lights and shadows it was, without a solid line or a clear edge, but only the more menacing for that.

At last the artist who had created this unnatural work stepped back and smiled in satisfaction. He raised his hands upward and the chanting stopped. Even the specter ceased to move and looked toward him with the deep, black caverns of its eyes.

"Your task is a simple one," Calatin told the form. "Go and accompany the giant Lok. Spread yourself upon the air until the time is right, until the Hound is most vulnerable. Then form yourself and appear to him alone! Fly in his face, hamper his movements, scream loudly in his ear. Now, be off. Find MacFavash and follow him to the fight!"

The shape dissolved and floated up to disappear through the roof hole. Calatin walked to the tent door and looked up the avenue of the camp toward Lok's tent. The chieftain appeared there and paused a moment to adjust his armor one final time. As he did, the druid saw the specter, a faint, dusty patch obscuring the blue sky, appear above his head. Calatin smiled again. It was enough. When Lok MacFavash started to the ford, a wraith invisible to the eyes of all floated over him as would the Morrigu, that great, black bird of violence.

Like a moving tower the warrior advanced to the Oun Dia on legs thick as the trunks of trees, broad shield uplifted before him, spears clutched as if twigs in his giant hand. Behind him swarmed the whole army of Meave this time. Anxious to see a real fight, they lined the banks many deep and as far as there was view of the ford, climbing onto horses, chariots, and the shoulders of one another for a vantage point. Gay and chattering they were as if at a fair day, ready to see the champion Lok battle the Hound of Ulster.

MacFavash strode across the islands of sand and through the shallow places, stopping at the midpoint of the river to plant his legs firmly and wait. Greatly different he was from the slim, untried youth who had come that morning and now lay in his tent cursing his own foolishness.

Then, from the other side, the Hound came down to the ford.

Though himself a strong, powerfully built man, even Cuculain seemed little more than a boy in contrast to the massive Lok. More, he was unarmored, clad only in his white linen tunic and crimson bratta, sword at his side, light spear and shield in his hands. Still he advanced without hesitation, his face set in lines of certainty, apparently unaffected by his morning's wounds.

This last was feigned in him. He had been hurt, and fatigue pulled at him, but he fought down these afflic-

tions. Resigned to face the giant he was, knowing how
important was his need to remain a figure of near superhuman strength to Meave's army.

As he came into the ford, one of his light spears was
lifted at once, for he meant to end this battle quickly and
rest. But as the spearhead came up to point at Lok's
chest, the nebulous mist above his head took form and
solidity. Suddenly Cuculain looked into the face of the
horrid ghoul that rested its bearded chin upon its bony
knuckles, met his gaze with the black sockets of its eyes,
and smiled upon him with its lipless mouth.

Stricken with surprise and terror, Cuculain hesitated
and his spear dropped. In that moment Lok aimed and
cast his own war-spear toward Cuculain's unprotected
breast.

The spear was badly aimed and missed its target, but it
struck the Hound's shield, passing through it at the upper
rim and cutting his arm deeply with the point.

It was the second wound in his shield-arm that day,
and the pain of it saved Cuculain, for it took his mind
from the vision before him. As Lok drew in on the thong
that held the spear, hoping to pull the young warrior
off-balance, Cuculain dug his heels into the sand and
braced himself. By that effort he stayed upon his feet, but
the spearhead was stuck fast in his shield and slowly,
slowly, the immense power of Lok began to drag Cuculain forward, stumbling and staggering in the shallow
water.

At this sign of victory the men of Meave raised a great
shout. Like an object of the air it rose into the sky. There
it would have died, but strange breezes caught it and sent
it north where, in far Emain Macha, Laeg, the driver of
Cuculain, still drowsed in his half-sleep. He drowsed until
the shouts bore to him on the wind reached his ear and,
with them, a faint, high voice that cried: "Wake now . . .
for Cuculain contends at the Oun Dia ford alone against
the four provinces of Eire!"

Laeg shook his head and the lethargy which had held
him for so long fell away. He realized some peculiar
madness had been upon him. He remembered the desperate plea of Sualtim and was aghast to realize that had

been days before. Without further hesitation, he rushed to the fortress armories to ready his master's chariot and weapons, fearing it was already too late.

It was not yet too late, but the time was running very short for Cuculain at the ford. As Lok MacFavash dragged him relentlessly through the river, he laughed hugely at the joke.

"Men of Eire," he called to those lining the banks, "never have I had such sport in fishing. I've caught many a giant one in the sea below Luminech, but never a one of them played so well as this. I'll be needing to quiet him as I do them; with a stroking down from my little stick."

As he said this he released the spear's thong with his right hand and drew his war mace, the brass head of it as large as his own and studded with short spikes.

When the constant pull was eased, Cuculain was allowed a brief moment to act. He dug in deeply and, with a swift move, drew his sword and slashed down on Lok's spear, just in front of his shield, cutting through the thick tree with the single stroke.

Before Lok could recover, Cuculain jumped away, sheathing his sword and once more pulling up his spear to cast at the massive target.

But again the fine cloud congealed above MacFavash's head and, again, Cuculain faced the specter, more hellish than before and so close he felt the icy breath of it upon him, though it remained invisible to all others.

This time the young warrior had no fear of it, so much had anger taken him. Instead of hesitating, he only shifted aim and hurled his long-spear at the form, running it through a hollow eye-socket.

His spear-thong was snapped as the weapon vanished into the black void. At once Cuculain was near-deafened by a horrid cry that seemed to fill all the air around. The thing's mouth opened in a scream and it crumpled in upon itself. The young warrior shuddered and moved back as if pushed by a powerful wind and, as he did, he saw the now formless mass drop heavily into the water of the Oun Dia and disappear.

The specter was gone, but Cuculain had lost his second chance at Lok. Before he could pull his sword again to fight, the giant had moved against him like a chariot-of-war at full attack and began to beat him back through the ford using both shield and club.

Cuculain moved and dodged to avoid the heavy blows, having only his light shield to protect him, but twice the ponderous mace struck home, shattering all the middle of the bronze circle.

The Hound edged around Lok, gaining some distance from him and a chance to draw out his sword. Then he turned back upon his opponent as a mastiff at bay, shifting and twisting quickly to get within the slower man's guard and make one, careful, deadly thrust. But, as he approached, black coils were thrown up in the shallow water between. They rolled and looped and threatened to entangle him, and he stopped in wonder at this new danger. Then rose a serpent's flat head from the river, its eyes glinting with the cold of ice, and he knew he faced the fallen specter in a new form.

Cuculain kept his courage, telling himself this was but a shade without real power to do him harm. He strode into it, swinging his sword before him and, like a cloud of smoke fanned by the palm, the serpent dissolved. The specter was finally destroyed.

Still, it had done its work. While Cuculain's attention was taken by it, Lok struck out at him with the mace. The young warrior brought up his shield, but the blow crushed the middle further and broke it out altogether. A second blow Cuculain caught on its border, but he only succeeded in turning it, and the mace struck him a slanting blow across the chest, tearing him with the jagged spikes.

The man of Ulster was badly staggered, and a loud cheer went up again from the watching host when they knew he had been hurt. Even so, he managed to swing his sword down in a savage cut.

It was only more disaster for the young warrior. Lok caught the descending blade on his shield boss where the brass was thickest, and Cuculain's sword snapped off above the hilts.

Cheering was continuous from Meave's army now. From their view of the fighting, Cuculain's efforts had been clumsy and ineffectual, and the giant champion had

only played with him. Now the end would come quickly,
for Cuculain was unarmed and near defeat already.

Fergus, despairing for his foster son, looked toward
Meave and Calatin. There, in the Enchanter's face, he
saw the coming victory clearly mirrored. He was not
surprised. He knew Cuculain would not fight so badly
without some unnatural hindrance and had suspected
Calatin's hand in it. Now the suspicion became a certainty and Fergus swore an oath within himself that, if Cuculain died today, he would seek satisfaction for it in the
blood of the grinning druid.

In the river, Cuculain, now almost without protection,
awaited the advance of Lok who came at him again with
mace upraised. As the blow fell, Cuculain raised the bent
rim of his shield to deflect it. He managed to do so, but
only in part, for he was thrown sideways to fall heavily in
the shallow water of the ford. He felt his elbows and side
scrape against a large, submerged rock as he fell, and
used it to pull himself to his knees as the giant came
toward him once more.

Cuculain made no more move to fight. He stayed upon
his knees and looked up a moment to the wide sky and
bright sun, for it was now a blazing noon. Those on the
bank saw his lips move silently, and told themselves he
had given up his life and prayed his last to his gods.

Relentlessly, like some great beast fixed on its wounded
prey and oblivious to all around it, Lok strode toward
Cuculain, the mace rising for its final blow. Closer and
closer he came, until the raised weapon threw a deep
shadow of its deadly shape upon the crouching form.

Then, with a swiftness born of a final, desperate surge
of strength, Cuculain dropped forward with both hands
into the rushing water. For an instant the muscles of his
arms and back stretched taut as he threw a tremendous
strain on them. Then the hands came out of the water and
the boulder on which he had fallen, half the size of the
hero himself, appeared as he swung it upward toward his
attacker.

So sudden had the move been, so unexpected from a
beaten foe, that Lok stood unmoving as the missile was
released. It struck home in the center of his enormous
shield, driving it into his breast and stomach, knocking

him backward off his feet and landing atop him to force him down beneath the rushing water.

Dazed and broken, his chest crushed and his lungs damaged by the massive blow, the giant lay there, breathing the water that flowed over his face until his breath stopped forever.

Still wary, Cuculain watched the downed man until certain he would not move again. Then, with an effort, he pulled himself erect. He picked up the thick wooden tree of Lok's severed spear which eddied in a pool nearby, lifted his broken shield, and slung it on his back. Without a word to the crowd, now stunned to silence, he raised the tree to carry across his shoulder as casually as a boy would a fishing pole, walked out of the ford, and disappeared back into the trees.

In disbelief the men of Eire watched him go, most with rage, some few with joy. None could believe his sudden and total victory over such an enemy, and none knew that once he reached the shelter of the trees he brought the pole down to keep himself from falling.

Using the spear-tree as a cane, Cuculain moved a little farther into the forest, but he grew weaker and more faint with each step. The wounds of the morning bled again with his exertions, and the new wounds on arms and chest were far more serious, staining all his white tunic red with their heavy flow.

Finally his strength failed him. He slid down the pole to his knees and then fell softly forward to lie amid nettles and nightshade in a deep and deathlike swoon.

Chapter Eighteen
FARDIA

Through the afternoon Calatin raged at his defeats. Too many times had the Hound of Ulster thwarted his carefully made plans. Somehow he had escaped the cloud sent across all Ulster and had destroyed the specter. Somehow he had countered the plots against him and had continued to irritatingly survive. Calatin knew now that he had badly underestimated this youth, but he would do so no longer. From this point on Cuculain would be to him more an enemy than the whole of the Red Branch.

"But, still, he is just a man," he said aloud. "For all his will and strength, he has the handicap all the rest of them have: he is saddled with the foolish codes of honor and the proud loyalties of a warrior. He can be killed."

"You say that," Meave replied, "and yet I've not seen it happen, for all your assurances to me."

They were alone in her quarters again, and had been since the death of Lok, for Meave had wished to discuss with her druid the failure of their plans.

"Now we've lost our chance to have Lewy fight," she went on in a complaining tone, "and we've no more champions fit to go against Cuculain. Our other veteran warriors refuse to challenge him, now that MacFavash has been defeated so handily."

"There are always other ways to achieve the necessary end." Calatin smiled with assurance once more as a new scheme formed itself clearly in his mind. "You are forgetting that there is another in the camp who can still destroy Cuculain, and even more surely than Lewy for, as MacRogh has said, he may truly be the greatest warrior in all Eire."

"What, Fardia?" She spoke with weariness. "Will you not give this up?"

"No!" he answered fiercely. "Not until this Hound is killed and our way clear."

Meave shook her head, her flaming hair flickering in the light of the afternoon sun flooding through her tent door.

"Calatin, it's tired I am of your plottings, and there's none of my heart goes with them. We've tried devious means more than once, and even compromised the honor of our friends who mean only to be honest with everyone."

"Aye, Queen, and that's just it . . . don't you see?" The ard-druid moved close to her, and his voice was hushed as if he meant to reveal some black secret of his magic power. "My methods will work because these simple warriors do not understand them. Think what control that gives us over them. They work for us and fulfill our ends and do not even know it. Is that not the essence of a ruler's task?"

She looked at him with uncertainty. "A ruler? Perhaps. A ruler does what is for the people's good."

"Something which they often do not know. Here and now their good is to cross the Oun Dia. That fact has not changed. Meave, you agreed that it was right to force Lewy to do what he ought to have done out of his loyalty to you. How can you balk at making Fardia do the same? Remember, too, that he is a Firbolg, a chieftain of a conquered race. He cannot dispute your order."

Meave grew indignant at that suggestion. "I'd not think to use such means to make him fight. And, if you tried, I know you'd never succeed. Fardia is a man of full intelligence, not the doltish sheep you seem to think him. I would have thought you'd know of him yourself. He's won a great renown in your own homeland of Espan."

"No, my Queen," he answered with disdain. "I've paid little note to any achievement a Firbolg might attain. I only know his fighting ability might be sufficient for our purposes."

"He is more than a warrior, Calatin. He's shown me talents worthy of my praise and could be capable of leading his people to a greater freedom . . . with my help. Even so, he'll not blindly take orders from me."

"My Queen, why argue this?" Calatin asked her reasonably. "We've no other choice of men who could fight Cuculain successfully. We must look to Fardia."

She was not yet convinced. Another problem presented itself to her.

"What of our other chieftains? You heard their voices at our last meeting. They'll not be liking a Firbolg made the champion of all Eire!"

"They've no more choice than we, my Queen," he told her patiently. "Why do you struggle so against such an obvious necessity?"

She did not know. Perhaps it was her liking for the young chieftain that made her hesitate. In some way this path they must take disturbed her more deeply than the one followed with Lewy MacNeesh. But she could not deny the logic of her druid.

"All right, then," she conceded at last. "We can ask for his help. Yet, what could make such a man accept?"

Calatin smiled. "You gave the answer to that yourself. He wants greater freedom and power for his people."

"Could even such desires bring him to dishonor his loyalty to a friend?"

"Perhaps," said Calatin reflectively. "If we could bring him here to dine and talk with us alone, I think he might be made to see this as we do."

Something in his tones struck an odd chord in her and brought back a reluctance to act, but he met her eyes as he spoke, and she could not find will to challenge him again.

The quadrant of the Firbolgs' camp was some distance from the rest of the army, for their primitive manner of dress and custom and the servile nature of their status made them unacceptable to most of the Milesian race. An ironic circumstance that was for a people who had once held sway over all the lands of Eire.

When Calatin entered their camp area alone, he came under immediate scrutiny by every warrior about. This he totally ignored and made his way along to the tent of

Fardia, outside of which he found several warriors, drinking and amusing themselves by casting stones the size of a man's head for distance. Huge men they were, and solid of muscle, but coarse and ill-proportioned in comparison with the other men of Eire, with great, curling masses of uncombed hair and long, matted beards.

Calatin made no hesitation at the sight of them, but walked up boldly to the group and addressed them with a cool preeminence.

"I wish to see Fardia, chieftain of the Firbolgs."

The men had stopped their game and looked over the druid with seeming awe, for he had donned his finest colored robes of office to make his authority clear even to the meanest intelligence.

"Ah," said one of the warriors, "it speaks! What is this colored thing that wishes our chief . . . some type of bird?"

His fellows laughed at this, but Calatin seemed unruffled, and his voice remained calm and touched with arrogance.

"With such rudeness of manner and crudeness of pastime, it is no surprise that you are kept separate from the other men of Eire. Now stop your foolish talk and tell me where your chieftain is, for I bring him a command from the High-Queen!"

Anger clouded the faces of the warriors then, for they felt the fame of their leader greater than that implied by Calatin.

"It's not for the queen of your smooth and fragile people to command the Firbolgs," one replied. "But Fardia can answer that himself. It's restin' he is, behind the tent on a fine, grassy mound. A warning, though: he'll not be likin' much to be bothered while he rests." He looked to his fellows and smiled broadly. "A great lover of nature is Fardia."

Without a word of thanks Calatin walked around the tent, closely followed by the group of interested men. He found the low hill and, on it, the form of the young chief who was resting easily on one side. Fardia's attention was fixed intently on the scene before him, for many of the families which traveled with the army were camped below and the Firbolg, with a young man's interest, was watching the young women at work and play about their tents.

Calatin, unmindful of this pleasurable but absorbing occupation, walked to the chieftain and poked him roughly with the staff he carried, as one might rouse a great hound from his place by the fire.

"The queen wishes to see you," he said.

In a swift move, Fardia rolled and came to his feet, grasping the staff and tearing it from the Enchanter's grip.

"You've used that manner on me in the wrong place, my old friend," the chieftain said, waving the wooden rod threateningly. "We are on my ground now, and we both know well enough what you are."

The rough warriors laughed heartily at this, but Calatin's look revealed no dismay at the Firbolg's sudden and harsh response.

"I was not aware that Firbolgs had any ground that they might call their own," he said, calmly.

Enraged by that, Fardia swung the staff to strike the arrogant druid. But the blow never fell. Calatin's hand swept up to seize the descending staff and, with a seeming ease, he wrested it back out of the young chieftain's hands.

Surprised by the unexpected show of strength, Fardia and his warriors looked in wonder at the druid who stood relaxed, a slight smile pulling at the corners of his mouth.

"I hope that now your simple amusements are ended," Calatin said. "I've not come here to talk of our own past. The queen sent me to ask you to come to her."

"You know my answer to that," Fardia replied. "I'll not be going to the queen, for what she's thinking is clear enough to me. Lewy has warned me, and with him I stand. I'll have no part in any battle with Cuculain. Now be out of here, and next time speak more softly to a Firbolg."

Calatin did not move, refusing to be ordered by anyone against his will. Impatient with him, Fardia looked to the group of warriors.

"Take this fool and jester beyond our lines," he ordered. "See that he doesn't come again among the Firbolgs with his tricks. And mind him closely! I know his nature well from other times."

Two towering warriors stepped forward as if to seize the druid, but the look he shot toward them so chilled them that they both stepped back a pace.

With great dignity the druid turned and walked back through the camp, the two bewildered warriors shepherding him until he passed out of the Firbolg quadrant. He arrived at Meave's tent even more determined to bring the young chieftain to a fight. He had no love for the Firbolgs or the ambitious Fardia. If he and Cuculain were both killed it would only remove two nuisances to him.

"What's happened, Calatin?" Meave asked in concern.

"Too proud are your Firbolgs," he answered shortly. "You judged rightly when you said Fardia would be against facing his friend."

She understood. "Well, then, is that another way that we'll be giving up?"

"No, no," he assured her smoothly. "It only means we'll need to approach him in another way, and you must be the one to do it."

"I?" She was surprised. She wanted no hand in this enterprise her druid had begun. "You were the one who was to bring him here."

"He'll not see me again," he said, looking at his staff with a faint smile. "He trusts few Milesians, but he has a trust in you."

"I'll not lie to him to gain his help," she asserted with some force.

"You've no need to," he promised, his voice cajoling now, pitched in low and comforting tones. "You've only got to bring him here, tonight, and that I'll tell you how to do."

Greatly surprised was Fardia to find the queen, herself, at the door of his tent, yet more surprised to find she was alone. She had refused attendants for this visit, to show her trust to Fardia, and no warriors, not even the fierce Firbolgs, held any terror for her.

Awed as the young man was by this honor, he kept himself courteous but cool, inviting her in and bringing her a crude bench on which she might sit.

"Our comforts are few and our life simple," he told her, "but I'd not expect to see a high-queen visit our humble quarters."

"I had to come, Fardia," she said. "I had to speak with you . . ."

"Wait, Meave!" Fardia held up a restraining hand. "Don't be demeaning yourself with pleas to me. I know well why you've come and I can save effort on both our parts. Not for all the Plains of Ai, not for the treasure of Connacht and Maugh Turiedh together would I look in anger on Cuculain, or dishonor or slay him. Better it would be for you not to tempt me, Queen, for I've no mind to be discourteous to you, and such tempting would receive no gentle answer. We've lost all our sovereignty and lands and honors, yet I'll not further disgrace my bonds of loyalty at your pleasure."

"A fine speech, Fardia," Meave commented placidly. "It demonstrates what new strength lies in the Firbolgs and what new power they may attain under your leadership. But, it is not because of the troubles with Cuculain that I've come to you, though I'll not say I wouldn't take your help. No, today I come out of a sense of the wrongness of things."

Fardia remained suspicious. "What's your meaning in that?"

"I mean, my friend, that for too many years has the Firbolg power been denied by the Milesians. Today that fact was brought again to me by the callous attitude of Calatin toward you. So outraged was I when I heard of it, I came myself to make apologies to you. And now, as I come into the midst of your nation's warriors, knowing it is in your duns we live, and the riches of your territories, reclaimed by you from the forest, that we enjoy, I feel the shame of what we have done to you."

These gracious words could not but touch the heart of the Firbolg, calloused though it was by the hard years of hatred and prejudice. He knew well that he had no reason to believe a Milesian, but she had aided him and shown friendship for him before, and he felt a trust in her. He told himself he had little enough to lose by leading her ahead a bit.

"And what is it you would do, my Queen, to heal these great, old wounds of ours?"

"That I cannot say for certain, and I'll not lie to you and say I can. But, I've ideas that might be of interest to you, and I think we should talk. For that I've come to ask you to feast with me tonight at my pavilion."

Fardia considered this a time, impressed in spite of his suspicions. He was ready to use any honorable means to better the position of his people.

"And Cuculain?" he asked. "Will our talk be including him?"

"You know him better than most others, and I'll not say his name will not be mentioned. But, wait . . ." she added quickly as she saw his coming protest, "before you speak, remember we will only talk tonight."

He saw the fairness in that.

"All right. I will come. And to bind the invitation, let's drink together now, as equals."

"As we were when we raced together on the Plains of Ai," she reminded him.

"We were children that day," he answered grimly, his face drawn deep with lines that added painful years onto his age. "Now we are wise and old and our barters will be for more than a team of horses."

He called for an attendant to bring some meteglin, feeling that fermented honey drink would be more to the queen's taste than their own, crude ale. The serving-man poured out cups of the heavy, golden liquid, and the two rulers drank of it together.

"A good drink, that," said Meave, setting down her cup. "Much like the mead we make at Dun Cruchane. Thank you for it, Fardia, and come tonight to receive my hospitality in return."

"I will be there," he assured her.

When she left to begin her walk back to her pavilion, Fardia assigned a battalion of his own spearmen to attend her, against her protests. As they passed through the camp, they could not help but to attract attention, and Cormac Conlingas, noting them, felt uneasy to think what Meave might want in the Firbolg camp.

* * *

At the hour appointed for dining, Fardia appeared at the door of his tent, ready to meet his appointment.

He looked a different man than the rough, simply dressed warrior Meave had seen before. Feeling he should present a civilized appearance if he were to discuss his nation's betterment, he had gone to some lengths, and pains, to improve his image.

He had called for a bath, an unusual thing for a Firbolg while on march, though not for him, for he had learned habits of cleanliness in his travels. Knowing their chieftain was peculiar in this way, Fardia's attendants carried in the water and filled his wooden bath, and he rinsed himself over many times with the clear, cold water of the Oun Dia. After that he dressed carefully, bringing out fine clothes brought from many parts of Eire and of the world. These he had not worn for many months, preferring the common warriors clothes during a campaign.

He put on a clean, soft, linen shirt that fell to his knees, and over it a linen jacket decorated with gold thread and lined with white leather. It was fastened with heavy gold pins and belted at the waist with a band of silver rings. Finally he put on his ceremonial weapons—a gold-handled sword and short sword—fastened his bratta of crimson silk about his shoulders, and went out of his tent.

He caused some consternation among his men at their first sight of him. Many did not know whether to be awestruck or to smile at this changed likeness of their chief.

"By my fathers," exclaimed one brash young warrior, "I almost did not know you, Fardia, for you seemed to us a fairy prince of the Sidhe, emerging all dewy and bright from a sacred dell."

Though this drew laughter from the others, Fardia met it with a frown.

"And what is there wrong in that, Aed Shievra," he replied soberly, "when it was we who ruled Eire long before they?"

He stared the young man coldly up and down, and Shievra, totally abashed, lost all his mirth. But then the Firbolg chieftain laughed himself.

"Ah, it's only sport I'm having with you, Aed. You're right in what you say, and it is a little foolish I feel, all done up in this finery. But it's for a good reason, as I'm going to the queen, at her invitation, and to the good of all the Firbolg race."

"Then we wish you fortune," said Shievra. "But let not that woman or her sorcerers do you ill while you're in their power."

"I'm going in good faith, but with vigilance," he told his comrade, clasping his shoulder reassuringly. "I'll visit her, but she's no true friend to us until she has proven it."

He made his farewell and started through the Firbolg camp with the cheers of his men about him. Accompanied by a small retinue of guards, he moved up the broad avenues of the camp toward the royal pavilion. But, as he passed the quarter occupied by the Exile troops, a voice spoke from the shadowed space between the tents.

"Where is it you're going in this splendor, Fardia? To a slaughter?"

Fardia stopped and turned to find Cormac Conlingas close by, watching him with seriousness.

"What is your meaning, Cormac?"

"It may mean that the simple sheep goes to be taken in by a she-wolf."

"We have been friends, Milesian, and you have been loyal to Cuculain. Because of that I'll answer your insult with words instead of iron. I know what may be wanted of me, but I am no fool. Look to yourself."

With that Fardia left him and strode on. Cormac looked after him a moment in concern, then turned and swiftly made his way to the tent of Fergus MacRogh. There the commander was taking reports from his captains on the provisions for the army, but Cormac, interrupting, pulled Fergus to one side.

"What is it, Cormac?" he asked impatiently. "I've many more reports to hear tonight. This long encampment has drained our supplies and the foragers must ride further every day."

"Fergus," Cormac said with intensity, "that's of little matter. I've seen Fardia, dressed as for a royal wake, going to the tent of the queen!"

Fergus only eyed him quizzically. "And what of that? She knows him well enough. They may have important business to discuss."

"They've only one business of any worth here and now," Cormac retorted. "Can't you see it, Fergus? First it was Lewy, now it is Fardia."

"That's not to do with the queen," Fergus answered him. "It was the Enchanter behind those plottings. The queen would never use dishonest means."

"Fergus, is it blind you are?" Cormac grasped the other's arm with a desperate grip. "It was Meave talked to Fireaba. It is for Meave that the druid does his work. We can't let Fardia go to her alone. Fine a chieftain though he is, he's no match for the kind of power she can bring to bear!"

Fergus shook off his friend's hand angrily. "Don't be telling me of the queen. I know her better than you. The Firbolg is safe enough with her tonight."

At a table set before her central fire, Meave sat and watched the Firbolg enter with an uncertain mixture of emotions. She did not like the task she had to do, and she was still puzzled as to how she was to make this hard, assured young man change his mind. If she was aware of Calatin at a table behind her, preparing the wine for serving at the meal, she made little note of it. Her attention was fixed solely on Fardia's approach.

She greeted the young chieftain graciously and directed him to a seat beside her.

"Thank you again for this invitation, my Queen," he told her as he sat down.

"It is only as you deserve," she replied. She lifted a hand to signal the score of servants who waited about them.

"No, wait," he said. "Meave, I have heard words which again raise the same fear that I myself once felt. It must be got out of the way."

She shrugged. "Do so, then, if it eases your mind. Mine is already clear."

"It is a simple thing. I want you to know once more that I cannot be made to fight Cuculain."

"I understand. But our talk tonight will be on the good

of our people together, and on strengthening the Firbolg empire."

"Fair enough that is," he said, smiling at her for the first time. "I'm content."

"Then, would you care for a drink to seal that content?" she asked.

"Aye," Fardia replied with satisfaction. "I'll drink with you as you did with me."

On the room's far side, Calatin handed pitchers to two attendants who moved at once to fill the cups of Meave and Fardia to the brim. The druid watched with a satisfaction of his own as Fardia lifted his wine in salute to Meave and then drank deeply of the dark, red spirits.

Chapter Nineteen
NIGHTMARE

It was dark and becoming chill with damp when Cuculain awoke from his swoon. His limbs were stiff and their muscles protested sharply as he moved to loosen them. He got to his feet and began to make his way toward his tiny camp, driven by his need for food and warmth.

As he passed along through the woods, his head still heavy from the sleep and the exhaustion, he came upon an aged woman who milked a black and bony-looking cow, her back to him, the cowl of her dark cloak over her head. He was surprised to see her, for he had long since assumed that all those in the country nearby had fled.

Curious and overcome with a vicious thirst that threatened to close his throat, he approached her.

"Good woman, it is surprised I am to see you here, but I'll not question your presence. I'm faint and thirsty, and I'd welcome a drink of your fine milk, if you'd make offer of it to me."

The cowl moved slightly. "I will not," said a creaking voice, "unless you give me your blessing first."

He smiled then, in spite of his weariness, and laying a hand on the woman's shoulder, blessed her with the fortune of the gods.

At that the woman whirled around, and the face in the hood was revealed. With a cry of horror Cuculain staggered back, for the face thrust up close to his own was of a thing long dead, the face of the thing at the ford.

As it saw his fear, it screamed a foul noise of victory and vanished, leaving him again alone in the black woods.

Shaking with terror and with a sickness that twisted deep in his stomach, he stumbled on through the dark forest, not looking behind him or around, not stopping until he reached his hidden clearing.

He built the embers of his fire up to a roaring height and stayed close by it, trying to rest. But all night his mind was clouded and disturbed. His own province had conspired against him, he was sure, and left him here abandoned and alone. He knew, now, that he would die here, for he could not flee, and he had no thought of surrendering to Meave.

His body burned with its own heat, and he felt his wounds throb with the beating of his heart. As the bright moon set, leaving only blackness in the forest around, he saw faces that moved amongst the trees mocking him; and horrid things, formless and cold, came from the places man can never go. There was laughter and there were wordless cries about him that echoed in the hollow forest depths. Again the spirit that had followed Lok MacFavash came and floated over him, smiling and beckoning, and the water serpent came up from the grass beneath and wrapped about his feet. All the ordered structures in his mind, all the images of peace, of Emer and Dun Dalgan seemed torn and broken, burned and wasted like the devastation left in an invading army's wake.

The horses were distressed by his fevered movements. They jerked at their tethers madly as he cried out and thrashed about. They pulled loose and, when he finally sank back in exhaustion, they moved close to him. They lowered their heads to him and he felt their warm breath and their great, soft noses nuzzling him.

Loyal and loving to him were the horses of Emer, and their real presence seemed to force back the horrors and give some sanity to him again. Grasping their manes and halters, he pulled himself erect and stood between them, an arm about the neck of each to support him. For a time he stood this way, weak and trembling, but after a while the heat and strength of them seemed to flow into him and bring him comfort. His mind became clearer and his madness soothed. He told himself that all his chances were not lost. Ulster would still come, and his friends in the camp of Meave would help him to hold her army until it did.

As the sun rose over the forest, Cuculain shook off the last feelings of weakness. He even felt hungry again, and he took from the chariot the rest of his provisions, cooking the small piece of venison and draining the last of his ale. It was little, but it helped warm his blood and restore his energy.

He stood and stretched his aching muscles, walking around the clearing to be certain he was not hampered in his movements. Then he looked to his weapons.

His shield was shattered, and he tore away the iron-work from his chariot, filling in the broken center and upper rim with the metal, strapping it in with sections cut from his reins.

His only remaining weapon was the clog, the short, heavy ax he had brought for cutting wood. But it wasn't enough. He needed something more . . . something with reach.

With the ax he cut away the roughly broken end of Lok's massive spear-tree. He pulled the steel peak from the chariot-pole, a pointed spike two hands long and the thickness of a closed fist. He sank its haft deeply into the spear-tree and bound it firmly to the wood with leather thongs. He hefted the weapon and nodded with satisfaction. It was heavy and cumbersome, but the balance was fair enough.

He had done all he could. It was time to go to the river once again.

He lifted his weapons and left the clearing, moving through the woods with a determined stride. As he approached the ford, he wondered which of the champions of Meave would go against him now. When he reached the open ground beside the ford, he saw the whole countryside beyond filled with the men of Eire, and he did not identify, at once, who was the chosen warrior. He had advanced to the water's edge and stopped before he saw Meave's champion, standing forward from the rest.

He looked into the face of Fardia, son of Daman, chief of the Firbolgs.

Chapter Twenty
THE TWO FRIENDS

The same dawn sun that had warmed Cuculain was a painful brightness to Fardia as he awakened.

"Here, my Chief, drink this," said Aed Shievra who stood beside him with a cup.

Uncertainly, Fardia took it and drank. It was spring water, cold with frost, and it drove the last fingers of inebriation from his mind.

He sat up, memory flooding back. Drunken he had been on the wine of Meave. He had been plied with promises, with glittering futures for his people. He had seen their greatness and independence returned and he had promised to do whatever needed to be done to obtain them.

He had only to do one thing, they had told him. Only one thing, and it was such a simple thing, such an easy thing, and he would be a traitor to his people to deny it. He had only to kill Cuculain.

And to that he had agreed.

"No!" The word screamed in his head. It had all been a nightmare. But then his hand, lifted to his thudding heart, encountered something hard and cold and, looking down, he saw the golden brooch of Meave, given him to seal the bond.

He remembered the rest. How Meave had called in the chiefs of all her tuaths and had them pledge their help to the drunken, laughing youth who, in turn, had agreed to his own part of the contract. How Calatin had then come forth from some shadowed place and ratified the whole with the invocation of the sacred names of Buan and Morann and Coirpry Kinkaeth.

"Now, take this brooch," the queen had said, bending over him to fix the golden trinket upon him, "and let it be the sign of our two words. For, little as I like what you'll be made to do, I promise you'll have the gain of it, for you and all Firbolgs."

He dropped his head into his hands, sick with his despair.

"All the gods protect me, Aed," he grated hoarsely. "I've made a bond with Meave to kill my friend."

Aed showed no surprise. "We have heard you will fight Cuculain for our good, my Chief. That news is already known throughout the camp."

Fardia nodded with resignation. "Aye, it would be. Calatin would not miss such a chance to insure I kept my bond."

"But it makes no difference," Aed assured him, kneeling by the sorrowing man. "Not one of us would willingly take gains won by such means. Don't be thinking of us if you've no heart in this."

Fardia raised his head to look on the anxious youth. He smiled without joy and laid a hand upon Aed's shoulder.

"It's a fine thing you say, and I'd expect nothing else. Yet, I've no choice in this. The Enchanter finally has me properly, and it's my own, foolish trust that's brought me to it. I should have listened to Cormac's warning!"

"Oh, Fardia!" Aed exclaimed, getting quickly to his feet. "That name's reminded me. Cormac, Fergus, and Lewy MacNeesh are on our quadrant's edge, desiring to see you."

"No, Aed," Fardia shook his head. "I'll not see them. There's nothing they can do. It's dawn and too late for any schemes. And, even if it weren't, I'd have no will for them. I've pledged myself before the kings of Eire, and they'll not believe it was not of my own choice. To break my pledge now would bring dishonor on the Firbolg race, and my poor loyalty to Cu is very little put against that. So keep Fergus and the others away from here, for I've sorrow enough."

He arose and bathed himself in the icy water to bring a full clearness to his mind. Without further hesitation he put on his armor, took up his weapons, and started for the ford. Behind him thronged the warriors of the Firbolg tribes, grim and angry at their chieftain's plight.

At the margins of their camp Lewy appeared, pushing close to Fardia through the circling men.

"Fardia, how did this happen?" he asked, his disbelief at these swift events still bewildering him.

"I'm sorry, Lewy," Fardia replied. "I've not your cleverness or your strength of mind."

"It's of no matter. Cuculain is our friend. End this madness now!"

"It is too late."

"Then delay . . . delay," Lewy cried. "Give me time to think!"

"And how will I delay with all of Eire behind me to watch?"

Lewy grasped the Firbolg's arm in desperation. "Fardia . . . you cannot do this."

At that Fardia stopped and faced his friend.

"Lewy, there's nothing that can be done for me. Fardia will be dishonored if he lives or dies, while Cuculain will live or die a hero. I've only one thing now: that my people will have some profit if I win. So, win I will, and accept all the rest. Good-bye, my old friend."

For once the thoughtful Lewy was left with no reply. He could only stand and watch as his comrade went purposefully on and was swallowed by the crowd.

When Fardia reached the Oun Dia, it was already lined with many of the army who filled the banks and turned the country to a sea of faces for some distance back. He noted Meave there with Calatin and Fergus by her side, but refused to meet the eye of any of them, marching past to stand removed, on a point of sand which jutted into the river. There he waited, looking intently toward the opposite side.

Then, unexpectedly, a voice spoke beside him.

"Ah, he's coming now," it said quietly.

Startled, Fardia turned his head to see a slender woman near him on the strand; a pale woman clad in a long robe of shining gray. She went on speaking to him in a voice soft, rippling with brightness like the river flowing at their feet.

"Yes, I hear him coming from the woods. The Hound

is coming. A hawk is coming who will not be slow in the fight. A pity it will be for the one who waits here."

"Who are you to be speaking so?" he asked, confused.

"I am one who saw long ago that you would meet a Hound of battle and be rent by his claws. Now I hear him. I hear him coming to you."

"A soothsayer are you? Well, who has paid you to make such praise of him? I am his match. The foretelling of Meave is that I will win. Your foretelling may be false."

"And have you known the prophets of the Sidhe to lie?"

Surprised by that, he looked at her again. He saw the truth of what she was glowing deeply in the dark wells of her eyes and, for a moment, he was afraid. But then his will grew strong once more, and he met her searching gaze levelly.

"The Sidhe tell what they know, but they do not know all. You've no full power to see what will be and, had you seen my death, you'd have said so. No, you're only wishing to frighten me from this."

"And if that's true," she countered, "will you not think again? There's more to this than you understand."

"All that's of little matter anymore. You'll not turn my mind. It is too close."

"Only think, Fardia." Her voice was pleading now. "Forsake this foolish bond. He is coming now, not slowly but quick as the wind, or as water from a high cliff, or like swift thunder."

Fardia looked across the ford into the trees, but Cuculain was not yet visible there.

"He's not come," he said. "I'll not be frightened. You owe him something to give him such great praise, and . . ."

He looked toward her again and found that she was no longer beside him.

Startled, he gazed about him to see where she had gone, but she had simply disappeared as if never there.

"What is it, Fardia?" called Fergus, who had noted the Firbolg's strange actions. "What is it you're looking for?"

The young man shook his head. "No matter," he murmured. "It was nothing at all."

A great shout swept through the army of Eire then, and Fardia turned his attention back to the far bank.

Cuculain had appeared from the trees.

Meave's host watched in wonder as the Hound of Culain moved down through the knee-high grasses to the river's edge. Gone was the buoyant youth they had seen only the day before. Now a worn and a wounded man came toward them, his linen tunic soiled and stained with blood, his long hair matted and tangled. But his heart was made cold iron in him and, for all his wounds, he seemed stronger and more terrible than before as he strode forward to meet his friend and his most dangerous opponent yet.

Fergus looked toward Fardia where he stood tensely watching. The commander wondered if any new uncertainty arose in the young warrior's mind as he saw his comrade so torn and hollow-eyed.

But if there was doubt in Fardia's mind, he did not show it. Without hesitation he started forward, entering the shallow water when Cuculain did. The two warriors splashed toward one another, stopping a spear's throw apart with a low isle of sand between.

They held each other's gaze in silence for a time. Then, finally, Cuculain spoke, his voice toneless and hoarse.

"And so you come to meet me, Fardia, armored and armed and seeking to slay me too."

Fardia did not reply to that. "Go back, Cuculain," he said instead. "Go away from here, back to your people. Go to your Dun Dalgan on the sea and cease this barring of our way and no harm will come to you or your land . . . that I will guarantee."

"And if I'll not go?"

"Then I will kill you in this ford and Ulster will lie open to us anyway."

Cuculain did not answer at once. He looked at Fardia and at the crowd of men lining the banks behind him. He shook his head and, when he spoke, his voice had softened with his disbelief.

"And of all that army of brave men that comes against

me here . . . of all the men of Eire grouped there beneath their bright standards . . . they have sent you." He looked into Fardia's eyes and his tones became almost pleading. "Could no champion be found in this great host that fills the river banks and the green hills beyond? O, son of Daman, retire from me now and it's three men I'll meet here from this day on."

Fardia shook his head and lifted a hand to the gold symbol on his breast.

"This brooch of Meave answers why I cannot. My life is pledged to her, and no man's honor would withstand the breaking of that bond."

"So to keep it you must dishonor me? There's poor sense to that, Fardia. Strange and twisted loyalties there are here to make two friends, parted last with mutual gifts and tears, thirst after one another's blood. We'd never have come to this before. What horrible power can make this wrong be?"

Fardia's gaze dropped and he shifted uneasily.

"I only know it has happened and cannot be changed."

"I can't believe you, Fardia. We slept together beneath the same rug, feasted together, fought side by side, each guarding the other more than himself."

Beneath Fardia's lowered eyes, tears started at these words. He gripped his spears tightly and answered in a voice stern and tightly controlled, but still not hiding the sorrow that threatened, like a flaw in a glass vessel, to shatter the whole at a touch.

"Go back now, Cu, and live. The Red Branch has forsaken you and left you to be destroyed. Dark and empty is the grave, my Hound. Save yourself."

"I'll not go back," he answered, now in a voice as cold as death itself. "Every man comes in the end to the sod where his last grave will be. Forsaken I am, but no power can dissolve my bond with Ulster. Defend yourself or turn away, for I will not!"

On his last word Cuculain moved forward. At that same moment Fardia lifted his javelins in either hand and threw them both at once.

Cuculain dropped the crude spear he had fashioned and raised his shield, warding off the weapons, but behind them came Fardia, pulling his sword as he made his attack. Cuculain jumped back and drew the clog from his belt and set himself to meet the charge.

It was a fierce and wild battle that joined there in the Oun Dia. The two moved about on the sand and into the shallows of the river, throwing up a spray that half-hid the moving bodies. In the spraying water and the flashing of light on their weapons as they rose and fell, the fighters seemed the joining of two lightning storms. The savagery of the combat told those on the banks that each was trying to end it quickly, for such expenditure of strength as was seen now could not go on for long.

Three times Cuculain closed, trying to get within Fardia's broad shield, but each time he was thrown off, and each time the Firbolg's sword left its mark in his unarmored flesh.

Nearing exhaustion now, reddened all over with his wounds, the young Hound tried to stand away from his opponent. But Fardia gave him no space to rest, raising his sword and charging in again. Slashing with heavy strokes, he drove Cuculain back. The Ulsterman could only defend himself against the vicious onslaught as he retreated and, on the river's banks, the men of Meave cheered Fardia's advance.

Cuculain's patched shield was beginning to break apart under the pounding. Soon, he knew, it would be worthless. Then, as he stepped back another pace, he saw nearby the heavy spear he had dropped in the sand. In a desperate move he threw his ax at Fardia to force him away, dropped the battered shield, and snatched up the spear in both hands.

Fardia knocked down the ax with ease, but as he moved in again he was met by a furious counterassault. With his last reserve of strength, brought up not from muscle and bone but from spirit itself, Cuculain took the advantage. Using both ends of the weapon as clubs, he beat at both sides of Fardia, driving him back through the ford and toward the farther bank.

In the assembled army a groan went up and the Firbolgs, fearing for their champion, started forward as one man.

Fergus had foreseen this happening. When he saw them

begin to move, he sprang onto the edge of the river bank before the mob, pulling his sword, and raising his shield before him.

"Stop!" he commanded, but one giant Firbolg tried to push past him. With a single, easy move the Exile swung his sword flat against the man's head, knocking him senseless to the ground. The others hesitated.

"Go back, all of you," Fergus shouted. "The next man and all others who try to interfere I will surely kill!"

As he spoke, others of the Exiles formed behind him, making a bristling wall of swords along the bank. It was enough to turn the Firbolgs back.

In the ford, Fardia labored to recover the advantage he had lost. Seeing no choice but to leave the protection of his shield and strike at Cuculain, he took a blow of the Hound's spear on the right edge of his shield and pushed the weapon up and to the left. At the same time he thrust forward, plunging his sword point into Cuculain's side.

It was a bad wound but, in giving it, Fardia had lifted his shield high, exposing his body. Even in his agony Cuculain saw the opening. He stepped back and pulled himself off the sword. Then, in a powerful return backed by his total weight, he brought his spear up under the shield's rim and drove it toward Fardia's breast.

The Firbolg's shield came down, but too late. The deadly spike went home, burying itself deeply in his chest. He stopped, shuddered, and looked down in amazement at the spear, then up to Cuculain's agonized face.

"That is enough," he choked out. "My heart . . . is turned to blood!"

He staggered and fell backward to the strand. His hand released the longsword and he was still.

With an effort Cuculain wrenched the spear from his friend, almost falling with his weakness. But he forced the dizziness away, for he had yet one purpose he had to fulfill. He leaned over Fardia, savagely pulled the golden brooch from his tunic and threw it far away from him into the stream.

Only then did he let the weakness conquer him. He sat down and bowed his head between his hands and vomited blood into the flowing water.

On the far shore the army of Meave watched him,

silent with its expectation. For a long time he sat unmoving, and no one could tell if he still lived. Then, slowly, he rose to his feet and, using his spear to steady him, walked back toward the other bank.

He staggered badly as he went, and every one of that host watched him as a hunter watches a wounded deer, waiting to see if he would fall.

He did not fall. Finally he reached the bank, climbed it, and disappeared into the trees.

That night there was not a man in Meave's army who did not believe Cuculain had received his own death wound and lay in some lair, like a dying wolf, breathing his final, labored breaths.

At dawn they gathered on the river bank to see if the great Hound would miraculously appear again. They waited through the morning and until the sun was high, but no one came.

Exultant, Meave gave orders for the army to move forward.

"Today we cross the Oun Dia into Ulster," she cried. "The Hound is finally dead!"

Book Four

PATH OF
DESTRUCTION

Chapter Twenty-One
THE CHARIOTEER

South from Emain Macha sped the chariot of Cuculain, his comrade Laeg at its reins and his team of great war-steeds pulling the vehicle tirelessly along.

Through one night and the following day they drove, Laeg forcing the animals to a halt only for short rests and water. All around him as he drove there arose a metallic din from the battle armor and weapons of Cuculain that Laeg hoped to bring in time to his beleaguered master. Beneath him the iron wheels hummed and clattered upon the block-paved roads, and in his ear that dimly heard cry which had awakened him two days earlier echoed constantly, pulling him on toward the Oun Dia ford.

Where the land was rich and there were homesteads, the roads were well-paved and wide. But often he traversed broad plains where there were no chariot-tracks or sign posts, only herds of cattle watched by lonely servants who looked in wonder as the chariot passed, rattling and clanking like a wagonful of iron borne along a bumpy road.

By evening of the second day, Laeg saw that Shanglan was laboring as he went, his black coat flecked with white foam. The mighty Gray of Macha, stronger of the two, still went on untired, but Laeg feared for him as well. He found a small but fresh-flowing stream with fair pasture nearby and stopped them for a full night's rest.

He made a camp and tried to rest himself beside a tiny fire, but in the darkness of the night he was awakened from a fitful sleep.

Weary but cautious, the charioteer rose and looked toward the sound. At once alarm brought him fully awake. Far off to his east a giant force was moving from south to north. It was the rumbling of their many chariot wheels he heard, and he could see the flickering of uncountable tiny points like distant fireflies as the moonlight struck its sparks from the shifting weapons.

Hurriedly he smothered his fire, hoping it had not been already seen. He harnessed the horses again and they rode out toward the west. He went slowly at first, hoping to avoid any wandering patrols but, once the army had been left some distance away, he felt it safe to turn back toward the south and pick up his speed.

He pressed the horses ever harder now, hoping they had rested enough. A great fear was on him for, if the men of Eire had crossed the river, what had become of his master?

When the first light of dawn came slanting across the green fields, it revealed, ahead of him, a glittering line of light whose breadth told Laeg he had reached the Oun Dia.

He oriented himself by the lay of the hills around him and then turned eastward, following the river to the ford. He went with great caution now, watching for any sign of an enemy, but seeing no one.

When he finally reached the ford, he found much evidence of the passage of a large force, but the country around was deserted of men. Seeing nothing more on this side of the river, he drove the chariot boldly to the ford and the horses splashed across. Some way out onto the plain beyond, he saw a broad area torn and littered by much debris. He approached it and found it was the remains of a large camp, now abandoned but for mounds of rubbish which gave evidence that a host had stayed there for several days.

Laeg turned back toward the ford, his concern growing. If the force that had come against Ulster had, indeed, gone on, it seemed ever more certain that he had come too late, for he knew that only the young warrior's death would have allowed their passage.

As he neared the ford again, he became aware of a figure moving some way up the bank. It was the first living being he had seen and he went toward it, hoping for some news. He pulled up by it and found it was a woman, pale of hair and skin, who keened over a freshly made grave.

"Who is it who lies there?" he asked, in dread of the answer.

She looked up at him without surprise, her gaze level and calm. Her voice when she spoke was soft and comforting.

"It is not the one you're seeking who lies here, but the one he fought. It is Fardia, son of Daman, who now lies here, alone."

"Fardia!" Laeg repeated in disbelief. "By all the gods, what's happened here? And, what do you know of Cuculain?"

"For many days that Hound held this ford without help, and many of the men of Eire died trying to defeat him. He waited and hoped for the coming of Ulster to help end this foolish war, but it did not come."

Laeg could not look into her accusing eyes.

"I can give no excuse for my people. Some strange confusion was on them, but their senses were returning when I came away."

"Too late it may be," she responded, looking down at the grave. "Already too many have died uselessly. And good men they were, who would not have died but for the twisted powers at work here."

"I know little of that, or why all Eire bands against Ulster. Only one thing do I know: that Ulster will fight. Men have only begun to die in this."

"And all Eire will surely become a ruined place with only the weak surviving to be ruled by the sly," she told him. "But it may still be stopped. You must find Cuculain, and you must hurry, for he'll not survive another day with his wounds."

"Then he still lives!" he cried with relief. "Where, my lady . . . where can I find him?"

"Go into the woods beyond the river," she answered, lifting a slender arm to point. "Ride upward. You will be led to him."

"And you? Will you stay here alone?"

"I'll be all right here. Go now."

As if the horses understood her command themselves, the gray and black started forward, bearing Laeg away toward the ford with great speed. He looked back toward the woman to wave a farewell, but found the pale figure had gone, leaving the plain empty save for the lonely grave.

Once across the ford again, the steeds turned aside from the track of the army's line of march and, ignoring Laeg's attempts to guide them, wound their way through the labyrinth of the woods. After a time they stopped and Shanglan whinnied loudly. In a moment there came a response somewhere deeper into the dark forest, and the horses turned toward it. A distance farther on, they came against a solid line of brush, and there the horses stopped and the black whinnied again.

An answer came this time from close ahead, and Laeg jumped down from the chariot and pushed through the wall of foliage.

Beyond, he entered a clearing. In it he found the light chariot of Emer that he himself had readied for Cuculain only days before. Nearby, the two horses stood, their heads bent down over a still form lying on the bare earth.

Fearing what he would find, Laeg ran to it, calling the name of Sentanta. He knelt by the quiet figure and lifted the head of the man he had served so long. There was no sound from Cuculain and no movement, and at first Laeg feared he was too late. But a close examination of the young warrior showed him that the heart still beat, if faintly, and an uneven breath still moved past the lips.

Working swiftly, then, Laeg brought in the chariot-of-war and unhitched its horses. He fetched water and made a fire and spread thick rugs to lay Cuculain on. Carefully he washed the warrior's wounds and bound them up with clean linen torn from his own shirt.

He tried to rouse Cuculain enough to feed him some warm food and give him needed strength to heal, but his master was too weak and, in despair, Laeg left him to sleep.

The charioteer seated himself across the fire with a heap of wood beside him to keep up its flames all night. He felt defeated in his mind, for there seemed no will left in the badly wounded man who lay pale and deathlike on the rugs. Laeg felt alone and powerless, removed from the help and comfort of anyone.

But as the night progressed, Laeg began to feel they were not alone in the blackness. He sensed strange presences around the son of Sualtim.

A swift word had been passed across all of Eire, borne on the breezes from the sea, and from every rath and glen and sacred hill the great Sidhe came forth. From the Shannon, from Cruchane and Tara, from Brugh na Boyne and Tailteen the riders of the ancient race gathered, and the sound of their hosting rose like a high wind in the trees as they came to comfort Cuculain.

Throughout that night the Sidhe came, and Cuculain saw them plainly, face to face, while they, with soothing hands and words, eased much of the young man's pain.

Laeg saw nothing of them, himself, but he heard the roaring of them in the treetops about and he felt their awful presence. It struck a terror in the fearless man, but still he stayed crouched near his master and fed the fire and wet Cuculain's hot brow with dampened rags while the stricken Hound called out strange names and thrashed wildly about. And as Laeg worked, he kept his eyes bent down to the ground to keep from looking at the Sidhe he felt were clustered all about, afraid he would be blinded or destroyed by the seeing of them.

When finally the dawn came, the stalwart driver found his friend and master sleeping a peaceful sleep. His crisis had passed and the color of health had much returned to his face.

Laeg knew then that he would live.

Chapter Twenty-Two
VICTIMS OF THE STORM

For three days Cuculain lay in his weakness while Laeg attended him. Not again, after that first night, did the young warrior's life seem in jeopardy, but by the end of this time they began to run out of supplies, and Laeg again grew concerned. Cuculain was growing stronger, but he needed better attention, more comfortable surroundings, and much warm food. For those things he had to be gotten out of this sheougy forest and to some proper shelter.

With that fixed in his mind, Laeg set about preparations for departure. There was little he could do about Emer's chariot and horses. The vehicle itself would have to be abandoned and he could only hope that, with good fortune, the steeds might find their own way home again.

"You have been faithful to Cuculain, as Emer would have wished," he told them. "Go back to Dun Dalgan now, and to your mistress."

With much regret he turned them out of the hidden clearing and sent them trotting toward the seacoast with fond pats of farewell. He watched them out of sight in the trees, then turned himself to loading the war chariot, spreading all the rugs on the small floor of its car, and laying the warrior upon them. But Cuculain was awakened by the movement and looked up at his friend with a smile.

"It's hard enough you've worked, Laeg. I can stand now. I've rested too long already."

Laeg disagreed. "Not long enough, I'd say. Just lie quiet."

He tried to gently push his comrade back, but Cuculain rebelled at that and pulled away his friend's restraining arm.

"I'll not be carried as a load in my own chariot," he said with force. "I'll ride with you as I should."

So it was that when the two set out, Cuculain stood upright in the vehicle beside his charioteer. And, though Laeg worried about him, he knew from past experience that once the youthful Hound had determined something, no further argument would be entertained.

They drove slowly to the north, Laeg ignoring the demands of Cuculain to pick up their pace. He refused to chance a harder, jogging gait, fearing it might open again the barely closed wounds.

All the country beyond the ford was desolate, for everyone had fled before the invading army. It was not until the afternoon of their second day of travel that they saw their first sign of other human life.

"Hold," Cuculain commanded his driver suddenly and, when Laeg obeyed, he leaned forward to peer across an open meadow which they were skirting. "Look there," he pointed. "It's a chariot with a single rider."

Laeg saw it, then, careening across the broad meadow at right angles to them, its horses at full gallop.

"They fly as if all Eire pursued them," he observed, "but I see no one behind. The driver seems unable to check them."

"I'm thinking he's hurt," Cuculain said. "Turn across the field here. We can cross his path and stop him."

"I'll not do that," Laeg protested but, when the warrior grabbed impatiently for the reins, he quickly assented with a vexed growl. Turning the horses skillfully, he urged them ahead at a full run.

The horses of the other chariot moved at breakneck speed, but the great war horses of Cuculain were more than their match. They overtook the racing vehicle and drew up next to it. While Laeg maintained position alongside, the young warrior, disregarding the pain of his wounds, leaned across the car's bulwark to seize the harness of the runaway team. Together, the chariots were finally slowed to a stop.

Cuculain climbed down and approached the tall man who stood within the other vehicle, his lower body tightly pressed against its front.

"My good warrior," Cuculain addressed him. "What's happened? Where is your driver?"

The other man stirred and lifted his head, but as he tried to turn, his strength failed him. He dropped backward and rolled out of the chariot onto the ground at Cuculain's feet.

"By the gods," Laeg exclaimed. "It is the chieftain Cethern."

"He's sorely wounded," Cuculain said, kneeling by the man to examine him. "He's taken a long cut across the stomach that might have spilled his inner parts, but pressing against the chariot's bulwark kept them in. That's why he lives, but where did he come from?"

"Those horses have run far," Laeg answered, looking over the foam-flecked beasts. "There's little way of knowing where he received the wound. There's more wonder in his being unarmed and unarmored. He's not so much as a spear in the chariot with him!"

"I've no understanding of what madness has come over the men of Ulster." Perplexity was strong in Cuculain's voice. "My last words of him was from my father. He told me Cethern and his warriors ran naked and wild through the fields of his tuath and slaughtered his cattle."

"It was no cow did this to him," Laeg replied without humor. "Can he be saved?"

"It may be he can. But we must get him help. Are we not now close to his dun?"

"Close enough. Now, let me care for him. I'll not let you wear yourself again, for I've little mind to carry two invalids with me."

Seeing the truth in this, Cuculain acquiesced, and Laeg took charge, binding the man's wound tightly to hold the exposed organs back within the body.

"If nothing of importance inside him has been damaged, he may live," the driver judged, "but if we meet any more wounded on our way, I'll have no more linen to bind them from my one, poor shirt."

He hoped to amuse the solemn Cuculain with this jest, but the young man did not respond to it lightly, as he once might have. Instead it seemed to deepen the lines of sorrow in his face.

"Not all the linen in Eire will be enough to bind its wounds once Ulster meets the Four Provinces," he said.

The black despair in that reply disturbed Laeg more deeply than had his master's wounds. They told him that something elemental in the spirit of Cuculain had been damaged, too.

The charioteer was uncertain how he would handle his new charge, but Cuculain insisted that he was well enough to help. He took the reins of his own chariot while Laeg drove Cethern's, with that chieftain laid as comfortably as possible on its floor.

They set a very slow pace, but they had not far to go. They came in sight of the dun before nightfall, drawing up before its wooden ramparts and hailing those within. In moments a woman appeared atop the watchtower by the central gate.

"What are you wishing here?" she said. "Go on. We've nothing for you."

"Cuculain it is who comes here," Laeg called in return. "We're needing aid for two warriors of Ulster's own Red Branch."

"That's but a trick to get within our walls," the lady replied. "Cuculain's dead at the Oun Dia ford and the army of Meave ravages Ulster. Now, be away with you."

She turned to leave the palisade, but Cuculain called up to her:

"My lady, wait! I'm not dead certainly or I'd not be in so much pain. Nor would your husband, who we bring with us."

His words stopped the woman and she turned back to him, anxiety now in her speech.

"My husband? Are you speaking the truth to me?"

"Look closely, Iondan, for I know you are Cethern's wife, and you know me as I've dined with you here more than once. Believe me and let us in, for your husband is sorely wounded and we must help him quickly."

She looked more closely then and, in shock, recognized Cethern's chariot and the still form within it.

"You do have him!" she cried. "Wait. We will open the gates."

As the gates were lowered to bridge the foss, the chariots rumbled over it and into the fortress. They stopped in the yard before the dun's main hall and looked about them in surprise, as not a single warrior met them. Instead they saw nothing but women, old men and boys who manned the gate pulleys or watched them apprehensively from the walls and buildings around.

The lady had descended from the tower and rushed at once to the wounded men.

"Tell me how my husband is," she said.

"He is alive," Cuculain replied. "There's little more to say. We found him by pure chance. What's happened here? Where are your men?"

"It is my fault," she said in sorrow, lowering her head over her husband. "A madness came upon them and we hid their weapons that they might do no harm. Still they left us and did not return, and now they've come to grief with nothing to defend them."

That much Cuculain had heard from his father, and he reassured her soothingly. "It was not your doing brought on this." He looked around him. "And there is no blame on you for not trusting us, with no one here to defend the dun but yourselves. Come, let's get your husband inside where he can be made comfortable."

He and Laeg lifted the still form from the chariot and carried it into the hall, laying the wounded chieftain on the bed in his own sleeping room. Cuculain sat down by him, white-faced after his exertion, and Iondan noted for the first time the marks of wounds and the great bloodstains upon his ragged tunic.

"You're hurt yourself," she stated with concern. "I should have known, after hearing of your death, that you'd not escaped without harm. I'll make provisions for you, also."

"There's time enough," he answered. "First bring a physician for your husband."

She sent directly for her healers and her druids, and they labored upon the stricken warrior while she stood by. Darkness had fallen before she felt she could leave his side to visit the quarters given over to Cuculain. She found him still awake, sitting with Laeg, waiting for some word.

"How is he?" Cuculain asked.

Her answer came with little cheer in it. "They do not know. My healers are working, but they've not the skill of the physicians who care for those wounded in battle. They will do what they can . . . then we must wait."

Cuculain did not like to see this good lady so disheartened. To take her mind from it, he turned to other questions which still plagued him and his friend.

"Tell us what is happening about us, Iondan. Where is Ulster? What word have you of Meave's army?"

"Of Ulster I've heard nothing. Some refugees fleeing before the advance of Meave have told me she raids the country only a few miles from us. I've no knowledge of what's caused this disaster. Only days ago we welcomed a fair and peaceful spring. Now it seems the winter has come on us again. The whole country is torn apart."

Guilt filled Cuculain at these words. He'd meant to draw her mind from sorrow and, instead, he had pushed it deeper in.

"You've great courage in you," he said. "Keep it alive. Ulster will come and your husband will live."

"Thank you for that," she told him, smiling with affection on the young man. "But you must rest yourself. I'll send my healers to look after your wounds when they have finished with Cethern."

Cuculain saw her out and turned to find his driver lost in thought. Cuculain eyed him curiously.

"What strange images are filling your head, my friend?"

The warrior's word seemed to shake Laeg from his reverie.

"It's nothing," he answered quickly. "I've only been pondering on our troubles."

That seemed to satisfy Cuculain, and Laeg was glad. He could not tell his friend his real mind, for he knew the young warrior would not be dissuaded from helping him.

But what he had in his mind to do, he could do best alone.

If Meave's army was, indeed, close by, he might yet find some proper help for the wounded chieftain.

Chapter Twenty-Three
THE PHYSICIAN

Deep into the night it was that a sound awakened Cuculain. Instinctively, ignoring the pain of his wounds, he rolled from the couch with his sword already in his hand. He crept out of the room into the main hall and waited, looking about into the darkness beyond the faint glow of the central fire.

Then the shadows moved and two dim figures appeared near the entrance of the hall. Standing ready, his sword lifted, Cuculain voiced a quiet but firm challenge.

"Wait there! Who is it?"

"Laeg it is," the familiar voice replied.

"By the Dagda," Cuculain said with surprise and relief mixed in him. "What is it you're doing creeping about in the night . . . and who is that with you?" He peered into the darkness to make out the second figure.

"I've brought someone," the charioteer replied, moving forward into the small circle of light thrown by the fire.

Behind him a short, powerfully built man came forward also, looking about him in perplexity. He wore a long, white shirt that appeared to be streaked with brown, and a heavy, dark cloak was fastened about his shoulders. He was unarmed, but carried a square object in his hands.

"Where are we now?" the man asked uncertainly. "Where are the tents of the camp?"

"We've work here, sir," Laeg told him. "A great warrior, badly wounded, needs your help. Could you come with me?"

The man shrugged. "I work where I can, as long as I have sufficient light and fresh water. Where is he?"

"This way," Laeg directed, and led the way across the hall.

The short man moved to follow, then paused to look more closely at the young man who faced him with a naked sword.

"I know you, sir, do I not?" he asked.

"We've never met," Cuculain told him quietly. He thought he understood now who this man was, and he wished to say no more.

"Perhaps," the other replied without conviction, then hurried after Laeg.

Cuculain also followed, some way behind, as they crossed the hall to the quarters occupied by the stricken chieftain. Inside they found Cethern lying quiet in a heavy slumber, his wife seated beside him. She looked up in surprise as Laeg and the short man entered.

"This is a surgeon of the army, Lady," Laeg explained with such simple ambiguity that Cuculain almost laughed. "He will look to your husband."

"A surgeon?" she repeated in astonishment. For a moment she was confused by this sudden appearance, but then her urgent need recalled her senses to her. "I am grateful," she said. "What can I do?"

"Bring tapers, many of them," the physician commanded, becoming assured and direct now that he was in his own domain. "Light this room as the day." He set his strange box on a table, opened its top and removed several shining instruments which he laid out carefully. "Bring me hot water and much clean linen."

Iondan went out of the room, Laeg and Cuculain behind her. Outside she paused a moment to speak with them.

"I do not ask how this miracle was done," she said. "I only thank you. I'll get the servants now."

As she moved away, Laeg was forced to face his master, and met Cuculain's penetrating stare with reluctance.

"She may not ask, but I certainly will," the warrior said. "Where is it you obtained this surgeon so late?"

Laeg smiled broadly, unable to suppress his feelings of triumph. "It was not difficult. I found the train of

Meave's army still moving after dark, for they'd been left behind by the warriors' swift advance and were trying to reach the camp of the main force. I simply told this surgeon that he was needed quickly and he came most willingly. No one thought me other than a messenger of the queen."

"Most clever. But why was it I was not told of this dangerous quest of yours?"

"Your rest was important," Laeg replied with simple honesty.

Cuculain could not be angry with the courage of his friend. He only lifted a hand and clasped the other's shoulder a moment, smiling his congratulation. Laeg understood.

When the arrangements the physician had requested were made, that man went to work while warrior and charioteer looked on from the doorway in fascination. He was careful and skilled. He unbound and examined the wound critically, then cleansed it out and bound it up again. As he worked, the hurt man stirred and groaned quietly, but did not struggle. When the physician had finished, he leaned down to Cethern and spoke in slow, clear words.

"I fear there is no hope for you," he told the chieftain, to the horror of the watchers. "I tell you this now so that you may begin preparing for your death."

There was a moment of silence, and then Cethern exploded. Suddenly he lifted from the couch like a ferocious hound roused carelessly from sleep. Fiercely he seized the physician in a grip that seemed none diminished in strength by his wound, and pulled the man's face down close to his own.

"You misbegotten bloodletter," he grated savagely. "Not all the swords in Eire or all your clan of scavengers can kill Cethern of the Red Branch."

His grip tightened and the physician would have suffered harm, but Cuculain stepped quickly forward and, gently but firmly, pulled the hands of Cethern from the man.

"If you'd be making truth of what you say, you'd best sleep now," the warrior reasoned.

The chieftain seemed to understand the sense in this, for he relaxed and lay back, but his dark eyes still glittered with a dangerous fire.

Cuculain led the doctor from the room while Iondan went to her husband. Outside, the man rubbed at red marks where the powerful fingers had gripped his throat and grimaced with the pain.

"Thanks for your rescue," he told Cuculain, again looking curiously at the young man.

"It was a foolish thing to say to such a man," Cuculain pointed out.

"Foolish it may have been, but it was necessary."

"Necessary?" Cuculain repeated without understanding.

"The wound was serious, but not deadly in itself. None of the internal organs were penetrated. Still, he was a dying man. There was no struggle left in him. I believe I know why. I think it was terribly beaten from him."

"I'm not yet certain what you mean," Cuculain said carefully.

"I mean that I believe I know this man," the physician answered, meeting the young warrior's eye thoughtfully. "I saw him at a distance, two days ago, after we crossed the Oun Dia." He paused there and eyed Cuculain closely, as if seeking a reaction. The warrior's face remained impassive and he went on. "I'm certain it is he, for his size and proud spirit are clear in my mind. Like some pack of beasts he and many others came down upon our army as we moved north into Ulster. Unarmed they were, and unarmored, their only weapons clubs and implements of farming. Still they attacked without hesitation and fought strongly through the morning and carried bloody carnage deep into our ranks. Ah, it was many dreadful wounds I treated that day. But, finally, they fell from the overwhelming strength in our numbers. Most of them died, some few were driven off and that one in there I saw, deeply cut, borne away by his frightened steeds. It was a sorrowful sight to watch those men so defenseless, so outnumbered, yet still fighting for their land."

His voice faltered on the last words and he fell silent, grieving over the carnage he had witnessed.

Cuculain raised his eyes to the darkness above them.

"Eire, Eire!" he cried with tears of frustration and pain welling in his eyes. "Why is this senseless war?"

He recalled himself, then, and looked down to find the physician regarding him with a calm perceptiveness.

"I'm sorry," Cuculain told him soberly. "You know that what you've said tells me you've realized you're not among your own people now."

"Aye, that I do," he answered simply, still undisturbed. "I knew that when I walked within this dun."

That surprised the warrior. "You knew? And yet you treated a warrior . . . a chieftain . . . of your enemies?"

"He's no enemy of mine, no more than any wounded man." He smiled shrewdly. "I was brought to treat someone, and that I've done."

"We owe you many thanks, sir. My friend will see to your safe return."

Laeg raised an arm to point the way and the physician turned to go, but then hesitated. He looked back toward the tall, gaunt warrior who seemed so old and grave for one of so few years.

"I said the will to fight for life had all but left your friend," he said. "I see the same thing very near in you. You are oppressed by more than your wounds, which seem much healed already. Some weariness lies very deep in you. Please, rest yourself."

"My weariness is beyond what rest may help, healer, but I thank you again for your consideration."

"Good fortune to you," the man said and then, with Laeg, departed from the hall.

In the days that followed, Cethern improved greatly. The deathly pallor left him and his tremendous strength returned. But for Cuculain the rest seemed not to help, and Laeg worried. Indeed, the days of inactivity seemed more to reduce the spirits of his friend.

Each day refugees, fleeing the devastation wrought by Meave's army, brought fresh stories to them. All the south of Ulster was under the queen's sword. Its fields were plundered, its cattle herded away, its homes and duns destroyed.

The tale of one old man named Feogh brought great sorrow to the listeners, for it told of the capture of great Dun Cuailgne. Its warriors had abandoned it to go north to Emain Macha. But King Dary had refused to leave the bull who was his trust and had stayed behind to fight. Donning his battle-armor, he had stood alone before the gates of his home, to face the host of Meave and pile up the dead about his feet.

There he had made his end, pinned against the timbers of his gate by an enemy spear, arms hanging at his sides, head fallen forward against the wooden tree as if to caress the weapon of his death. He had not lived to see the black bull, whose ownership had been the first cause for his end, driven away to join the captive herds of Meave.

Through all of these reports Cuculain chafed; restless, angry at his inactivity. He argued constantly with Laeg, attempting to convince the driver they must leave, but Laeg was stern, only replying that until Cuculain's wounds had healed, he would be of little help in the fighting.

Laeg's argument was not a completely truthful one. He saw, as he changed his master's bandages, that the wounds had healed with astonishing speed. It was this very fact which caused his worry for, though Cuculain's physical health had all but returned, his spirits remained those of a badly wounded man. Laeg had overheard the physician's remarks to the young warrior and realized they echoed his own feelings. He feared to let the Hound go out to battle with such a humor upon him, for it could be more lethal than any sword.

But at last a day came when Laeg knew he could argue no longer. A messenger, sent out from Emain Macha, brought word that the army of Meave had turned and left Ulster, recrossing the Oun Dia to the south. More, he told them that the Red Branch, finally free of the madness which had confused and scattered it, had gathered itself and started in pursuit.

"At last they come," said Cuculain.

They were in the main hall of the dun to receive the messenger, Cuculain and his driver flanking the couch on which Cethern was laid.

"King Conchobar presses our army hard in pursuit," the messenger went on. "Already they have passed south of here. If you mean to join them, you'd be best to intercept them at the Oun Dia ford."

"I know the place," Cuculain told him dryly and turned to Laeg. "We'll wait no longer while the Red Branch goes to war. Ready our chariot. We'll be leaving at once."

Laeg knew there was no choice now but to obey. Without a word, he went to do as he had been commanded.

"I will be going too," Cethern announced, struggling to rise.

"No, Cethern," Cuculain told him. "You're too weak, yet. Gather more strength and join us later."

The pain that flared in Cethern's stomach muscles as he tried to rise told him Cuculain was right.

"Aye, Cu," he agreed. "Then, all fortune with you. Help to avenge the wrong done on Ulster."

"Avenge?" said Cuculain, his voice curiously empty of emotion. "Yes, I suppose that is what will come now. And no more sense will it have than the rest of this."

He made his farewells and left the tec to join Laeg who had brought the war-chariot into the enclosure yard. Without waiting for the command, the young driver urged the steeds out through the gates of the dun and turned them south, back toward the Oun Dia.

Chapter Twenty-Four
THE BANQUET

A day's march south of the Oun Dia lay the broad and softly rolling plain called Fremain. A sacred place it was, never farmed or grazed by herds. Its grasses grew unbroken and its sod went unplowed, for in the past its only use was as a place of meeting.

But this night the host of Meave, fed full by its plundering and bloated almost beyond limit by its captive herds and people, lay sprawled across the torn, trampled meadows.

Like a sated beast of prey the army had staggered away from the carcass of southern Ulster and started a slow return toward its own lands, stopping at Fremain for its first camp. Now that camp was the scene of wild celebration.

Fergus MacRogh had argued against such an activity so close to Ulster's border, but the chieftains and the queen had forced him to agree to allow it. The day was Beltinne, the first of summer, and a traditional time of celebration for those of Eire. Fergus saw that the warriors would not let that be passed, especially when there was such reason to exalt. So, throughout the far-spread camp, the men of Eire celebrated with great din, the joyous and intoxicated roar going up from all the host as warriors ate and drank and recounted the great feats of the campaign.

It was only the warriors who rejoiced around their campfires, however. Their chieftains were not with them. All had been bidden to the pavilion of Meave to feast with her, and they now filled long tables in the vast room.

Around them on the plank and timber walls were hung

the shields of the many clans. Those of the sons of Maga and of Munster were there, and those of Clan Derga and the men of Leinster. With them, too, now hung the shields of the Firbolg tribes for, since the death of Fardia, guilt and the might of the queen had brought the Milesian overlords to recognize and honor the subject race.

The banquet was a merry one, lit with candles and a blazing fire, filled with laughter and the songs of the bards. But Fergus MacRogh had no joy in it. From his champion's seat at Aileel's right hand, he looked darkly out upon the bright gathering. He took no part in the feasting or the drinking which followed, but sat like some great rock defying the raging sea, silent and unmoving.

Meave watched her captain with deep concern. Blacker and blacker had his mood become since the raids in Ulster were begun. She knew the cause of that and did not deny him deep feelings at commanding the devastation of his own homeland. Still, she could not understand why his mood had not been changed since their withdrawal from Ulster.

They might have taken advantage of the light resistance to drive to the gates of Emain Macha, itself. But the spring season was at an end. Once their initial objective, the bull of Cuailgne, had been achieved, the warriors had felt a need to return home, for summer was a season of rains and lush grasses and they needed to tend their own herds once again. Anxious though Meave was to go on, she could not argue the logic of her men and had ordered a withdrawal. But even this decision had not brightened the mood of her commander.

"Fergus seems unhappy," she said to Aileel, leaning close to him. "Perhaps some entertainment would cheer him."

"Well enough," the old king agreed and lifted his staff to strike a silver gong above them. It rang sharply through the room and silenced all talk, leaving only the dim background hum of the army camped about the pavilion.

Then, from the lower tables in the room, a lad who wore the badge of a bardic novice arose and approached the royal couches. From a table by the platform, he removed a gray leather package and carefully unwrapped

it. The layers of fur-lined sheathing dropped back to
reveal a golden harp, richly decorated and carved in the
sinuous lines of Milesian ornament. The novice lifted it
carefully and presented it, kneeling, to a man at a table
just below the queen.

The man who took the harp was Bricne, son of Cairbre
and ard-ollaf of Connacht. Proudly he lifted the instrument and tuned its strings with a gentle, practiced hand.

He paused a moment, eyes closed, head back, arranging the proper order of the lay in his mind. Then his hand
touched the harp strings and his voice lifted in song and
his music captured the minds of the warriors.

He sang of the events of the war just passed in beautiful terms, both musical and poetic, for the high-bards did
not carelessly improvise, but composed perfect works that
would be passed by memory from bard to bard and live
past the ages of all. For hundreds of years had the bardic
orders worked to perfect this skill, and this young ollaf
represented their success, for he rivaled even Calatin in
his position in the court.

But, though Bricne's voice was pleasing and his rhymes
flawless, Meave was angered when she found that he
seemed always to turn his words to Cuculain, to recount
the Hound's efforts, alone, against the whole of Eire.

To many others in the hall, such a tale seemed a fitting
thing. The friends of Cuculain openly mourned for him,
none less than Lewy MacNeesh, who felt the loss of both
of his close friends. Only Fergus MacRogh neither wept
nor spoke but sat upright, unmoving on his couch, staring
out before him with eyes of iron.

Even seeing that the song was approved of by her
warriors could not keep Meave's own discomfort from
continuing to grow. The memory of the bloodied young
Hound was one she wished to be rid of, along with that of
the part she had played in his destruction. The constant
praise of him grated more and more upon her, and she
cast a scornful gaze at this bard whose composition
seemed to have no end. Finally she could stand no more
of it.

"Stop, enough!" she cried.

The voices of harp and bard ceased. The eyes of

Bricne and Aileel and all the gathering turned toward her in surprise.

"There is enough said about Cuculain . . . our enemy," she announced with emphasis. "He died with valor, but he . . . did . . . die! We are the victors here."

There were murmurs of agreement about the hall, but Bricne seemed confused.

"My Queen, it is customary to extol the virtues of our enemies. If we cannot be gracious in victory . . ."

"It's more than gracious you have been already," she told him firmly. "Cuculain has been praised. If you wish to praise a noble enemy, praise Cethern who came against us naked and unarmed."

"I must sing the lay as I have written it, my Queen," Bricne protested with indignation. He was of a noble class and not a servant to be commanded rudely by the queen.

But Meave would not relent. "Then cease to sing it at all."

This raised some grumblings among the assembled chieftains, but not enough. Bricne saw that their mood had changed and would no longer support him. He chose against arguing further and sat down, silent and crimson-faced.

"My chieftains," Meave called, rising to address the crowd, "ourselves it is that we should praise today."

At these words Fergus rose from his seat, still word-less, still like a great rock in the sea, but now like one that seems to rise up massively as the tide sinks down around it. The assembly looked to him and held itself waiting as he glared about him, for they expected him to make some defense of the Hound who had once been his foster son. Meave waited, also, daring him to speak.

He did not. Instead he stepped from the dais and strode out of the pavilion, followed by his Exiles. Only Cormac Conlingas stayed behind, for that young chieftain felt it might be amusing to watch the men of Eire congratulate themselves.

He was not disappointed in this. Once the oppressive presence of Fergus had been removed, many spirits suddenly became bold and many voices grew loud in lauding their own victory.

"Indeed, chieftains," Meave cried, "it is right for you to cheer. No modesty in this, for the once invincible Ulster has trembled before us."

She looked down toward Calatin who sat with his many sons at a near table and noted that the druid, like Fergus, did not seemed cheered by this celebration. He, too, had been in a dark mood since the withdrawal from Ulster, for he had argued hotly against it and had been deeply angered when the will of Fergus and the other chieftains had prevailed. But Meave did not care about that. She refused to have both her chief supporters so melancholy at this, her greatest victory.

"Calatin," she called to him, "have you no wish to rejoice in what we have done?"

"Rejoice?" he said in a voice soft but so cold that the single word cut through the cheering and brought the warriors to silence. "I could rejoice if these brave warriors had shown the courage to continue. All Ulster lay open to our taking, yet they retreated because of some selfish lesser ends. They gave up the rule of Ulster . . . for the sake of some cows!"

Surprisingly it was Bras MacFirb, the timid one, now emboldened by much wine, who replied with overbearing pride to the druid.

"And just who are you, now, to speak to the flower of Eire that way? You're no warrior. You've not bled in the fighting. We had no need of your poor magic to overcome Ulster. Our own strength was enough to cause all to flee before us and keep the Red Branch hiding in its duns."

"You did not need my powers?" Calatin replied, rising in anger. "It was I who was the salvation of this host!"

A roar of laughter went up from all the hall at that. Every warrior despised the druid and all were quick to show their disdain for his boasts.

"It's a fine jest you make, Calatin," Bras said, smugly, "but there's no one who can doubt that the victory was of these fighting men of Eire."

"These fighting men?" Calatin echoed in a fury. He turned his gaze upon the ranks and they fell silent on the instant, stricken to their hearts by the hot rage flaring in his eyes.

"Now that you are drunk with victory and ale, you

deny my help," he continued. "You fools who know no more than the shaking of spears and the waving of swords, what chance had you? It was I who clouded the minds of Ulster so they would not fight. It was I who found the means to destroy Cuculain when your 'champions' could only die at his hands. You think it was your honor and might won for you? Well, I say you've fooled no one but yourselves. I am Calatin, and your victory is mine!"

As he spoke, he changed in the eyes of the assembly. His stature seemed to grow and power blazed out from him suddenly, as when the sun abruptly emerges through a rent in a gray, concealing mist. Those in the room felt no amusement now. For that moment the druid had revealed himself and the dark forces behind him, and the warriors who looked upon him felt terror.

Only Cormac Conlingas seemed unaffected by the druid.

"Ah, Calatin," he said with quiet amusement, "once indeed I thought Cuculain was a hero and a noble man, but, on hearing you, I'm surely disenchanted. Now he seems like a raging wolf while you and your matchless progeny are clearly the true ideal of manly beauty."

Cormac's words directed every eye to the table where sat the sons of Calatin. The pale and twisted bodies of his misbegotten clan could not be hidden, and the humor in the Exile's words could not be ignored. The image of great power the ard-druid had created melted away as, once again, the warriors saw only a sly and alien meddler.

Calatin might have responded harshly to Cormac but he, too, had been recalled by the ironic words. The image of the Enchanter—the strange being who was shunned by every warrior—had served him well in his dealings, and he meant to make further use of it for a time. Only his anger at the disregard of him had brought him so close to exposing the true extent of his power and influence.

So, with these thoughts, the druid only smiled sardonically and bowed slightly to Cormac, saying:

"It's thanks I give you, Conlingas, for reminding me of my place. I only serve the queen and her warriors. Since that is my proper station, I will keep it."

He looked toward Meave with an expression now completely mild and nodded to her as if to acknowledge her leadership.

Meave met and held his eyes for a brief time, trying to fathom her advisor's changing moods. She knew how much truth lay in his angry words, but his savage outburst had alarmed her, for she began to wonder what other unknown forces still lay hidden in him.

Something in the deep recesses of her mind urged her to take more note of this, but she had no chance. The controversy Calatin and MacFirb had begun was raised by a few others in the hall, and a full-scale storm of argument threatened to burst. She pushed away her thoughts of Calatin as she was forced to seize control again.

"This continued argument over Ulster's fate will be decided now," she said commandingly, drawing attention back to her. "Both Calatin and the chieftains are right in what they say, but it is Aileel and I who will decide."

When no one seemed willing to dispute that, Meave was soothed somewhat and continued in more gentle, reasonable words.

"Now, I've listened to the separate views in this, and it seems clear what can be done. Our decision has been made to leave Ulster for a time, and it has been made with good reasons!" Here she cast a threatening eye at her ard-druid, but he continued to play the humble servant role. "And so, I'll use the Beltinne celebration fittingly, by announcing the dispersion of our army. Tomorrow will the plunder be divided and we may go our different ways back to our own provinces and duns."

A roar of acclamation greeted Meave at this announcement, but she raised her hands to silence it. She had something else to say:

"Yet, remember, my chieftains, that you owe a victory to me! When the summer is past and the fall season comes, I will summon you again to Dun Cruchane. Ulster is defeated now. We'll have but to return to sack its fortresses, fill its defensive ditches, and impose our tribute upon it. I mean to subdue the Red Branch for all time. Will you come?"

Again the cries of assent arose, this time in a wave of

sound that engulfed the queen. Many climbed upon the tables and brandished their swords as they cried out.

This, at last, became too much for Conlingas. He rose and pushed his way through the confused throng toward the doors. On his way he met Lewy MacNeesh, whose own heavy spirit made him unable to participate in such a celebration. Together the two slipped from the tent, unnoticed by everyone but Meave, who watched their going with a thoughtful eye.

Once the tumult died, the queen made her excuses and left Aileel and the chieftains to their drink and talk. She well knew it would continue through the night and felt a need for solitude. She left the pavilion and walked alone to her own tent, but stopped in surprise as a giant figure appeared in the avenue before it.

"I hoped I might see you again tonight," she said with pleasure.

"Aye, and well you might," Fergus answered tersely.

She smiled. "Well, well, another surprise. It seemed for a while that you might never speak again."

"There's little humor in this," he said impatiently. "Why did you announce the dispersion of the army and say nothing to me? The time and place of such a move should have been mine to make."

This seemed to stun her. "Is that what's brought you here? I'd . . . I'd hoped it would be something else. I hadn't even thought that this minor thing would so upset you . . ."

"But why?" he interrupted. "Why announce it so suddenly?"

She shrugged. "It was the celebration. It seemed a natural time for such good news." She looked at him in puzzlement. "Why this distress? I'd have more easily understood if my announced intention to re-enter Ulster in the spring had aroused your wrath."

"Ulster?" Now Fergus reacted with surprise. "I've no care for your future plans." He met her eyes levelly and saw the real bewilderment there. "Can it be you don't yet see? Meave, understand me: I've never feared the destruction of Ulster, only our own!"

"Our own? What do you mean?"

"Ulster is no province of defeated men. They will come against us surely, now." He walked about the space before her tent restlessly as he talked, casting his eyes down in thought. "I'd never really understood why the Red Branch did not come before. It seemed madness that they only fled from us or stayed within their duns and refused to fight. But now there's sense to it. A madness was put on them somehow . . . by your ard-druid. Cormac told me what he said tonight, and I've no doubt of its truth, though it seems to have been overlooked by you."

"Calatin? How could he . . . ."

"Who knows what he can do? He's surely capable of such a thing. And he has powers no one understands. You know that as well as I." He stopped his pacing and faced her squarely. "Think what it means, Meave. It was not fear that kept the Red Branch in its duns. They are not beaten and they will yet come." He stepped close to her and spoke with slow intensity. "They can easily catch us, hindered as we are by captives and herds. And the army of Connacht alone, separated from the other provinces of Eire, will have no chance."

"My province army is, itself, as large as the army of Ulster," she countered, still undisturbed. "And with your Exiles . . ."

He shook his head impatiently. "Of all your force of warriors, I'd say there's not but a few score I'd put against a Red Branch warrior. My Exiles cannot save you. Remember, Meave, it was with ease that we were expelled from Ulster when we rebelled. It was not children or weak men who did that to us."

"I've listened to the tales of Ulster before," she said, irritated by his persistence, "and I've yet to see a sign of truth in it. It's no matter to us in any case. There's been no sign so far that they are in pursuit. We'll be across the Shannon River into Connacht before they can even call a hosting!"

"I'll simply not make you listen, will I?" he asked her angrily. "It's only pride that's speaking in you now. You can't believe your own words so completely. You're saying them because you haven't any other choice except to agree with me, and that would be too great a blow to your damnable arrogance!"

"My arrogance?" The cruelty of his words stunned her. At first she had no way to deal with this attack. "Fergus, what have I done?"

"You have killed Cuculain and Fardia with some treachery. You have broken my bond to further your own ends."

"It had to be done," she tried to explain. "For Eire . . ."

"For your power!" he broke in. "You need to command too much. It has made you destroy my friends. It has led you to make this rash promise tonight."

"And, what of us?" she asked.

"There is no us. There is only you . . . the Queen of Connacht. Your need to command destroys everything else."

Her sureness faltered a moment and she dropped her eyes from him in pain and confusion. But almost at once she met his gaze again with a look of fire as her own strength of will came up to match his.

"Once you were a wandering Exile," she said, "cast out of your own land. I received you into my province. I made you a noble in my realm and a commander of my armies. I gave you my trust and my love. And yet, for all that, you've been the only man ever to answer me with such daring words. Well, I'll have no more of it. We'll not argue further. See to your command, MacRogh!"

She turned away from him to enter her tent, but stopped abruptly, startled by a figure that slid forward from the darkness to block her way.

It was a tattered warrior she faced, bleeding from many wounds. His face was dimly seen in the shadows and, for an instant, Meave saw in him a specter come to haunt her. She felt a fear of him but stood her ground and addressed him:

"What spirit are you coming to me with your shattered shield and bloody spear?" she demanded, her voice trembling with strain. "What evil tidings do you have to cast on me your hollow look and hold out to me your bloody hands?"

"Easy, lady," said Fergus, coming up beside her. "He is just a man."

He had recognized the warrior at once as belonging to

the Munster battalions, and he signed the man to come forward. As the warrior obeyed, the light fully revealed his youthful face, aged now by deep lines of pain. Yet it was a stranger's face, and that fact seemed to make Meave's fear vanish.

"My Queen," the warrior began, breathless with his effort to remain erect, "no bloodier are my hands than are the waters of the Boyne River. Our rear guard was crossing there at dusk, herding cattle and moving slowly. From the darkness men appeared . . . hundreds of them . . . led by two giant warriors. We fought, but we had no chance. Only some few of us escaped across the river."

"Two warriors?" Fergus said with excitement. "How did they look?"

"Look?" The man was near the end of his strength, but he struggled to think clearly for his commander. "One . . . one was bearded, with blue eyes that seemed to flash like the metal of his sword. The likeness of a woman was painted on his shield. The other wore a black cloak with . . . with a large iron pin for a brooch."

Fergus struck his sword hilts angrily and turned to Meave. "I know them. The one is Kelkar, son of Uther. The other . . . my Queen . . . the other is Conchobar Mac-Nessa, King of all Ulster. The Red Branch has found us at last!"

Chapter Twenty-Five
HOSPITAL

The young warrior staggered and would have fallen had Fergus not caught him.

"I am all right," the youth protested, struggling to stand by himself. But the commander kept a supporting arm firmly around his shoulders.

"You need attention," he said, then looked to Meave. "I'll take him to hospital. Then we must make some decision in this."

"My decision has been already made, Fergus," she told him firmly, her control fully returned to her. "This does not change it."

"What are you saying, woman?" Fergus cried in disbelief. "This is the host of Ulster he has seen."

Meave shook her head. "Your thoughts are too obsessed with your old comrades. You see every started hare as a gray wolf. This might have been little more than a harassing raid on our unguarded rear by a few scores of men."

"Even if that is so, can we ignore it?" he countered.

"All right, Fergus," she conceded with reluctance. "We'll talk of it further."

"I'll be returning shortly, then," he said. "Come on, lad."

"Wait, sir," the warrior said, holding back. "I've got to be seeing to my other men."

Fergus smiled with affection on this young officer who, while himself badly hurt, yet gave his first thoughts to his fellows.

"Where are they?" he asked.

"I sent the lesser hurt along to be tended, but there are some, worse hurt still, on the camp's edge."

"Then come along. I've help close by."

They moved away from Meave's tent and turned into the main avenue that ran through the camp. There they encountered Cormac and Lewy who had waited to see what word Fergus would bring from his meeting with the queen. They were astonished when he appeared supporting the wounded youth.

"What's happened?" said Cormac.

"An attack was made on our straggling rear," Fergus replied. "I've got to take this lad to hospital, but there are others on the camp's edge who must have help to be taken there."

"I'll fetch some warriors and bring them along," Lewy volunteered. "Where are they, friend?"

"On the west edge, just by the Leinster quadrant."

Lewy left at once to fetch aid. Cormac and Fergus each took an arm of the officer and helped him along toward the hospital.

"It's strange that the return of wounded men would raise no alarm in the camp," Cormac commented.

"There's no surprise in that," Fergus replied. "Look about."

As they moved along the camp's main avenue, the sounds of revelry went on unabated all around them. No one took any notice as they passed. All seemed unaware of the disaster which had befallen their comrades. It was with grimness that Cormac noted the contrast between the torn and bloodied warrior and the bright celebration throughout the host.

"Now do you see why no alarm was raised?" said Fergus. "We've gotten careless to a deadly point. They're all so certain they are safe."

Hospital was set up on the camp's western edge. It was a facility carefully arranged and managed, for Meave and Fergus, concerned for the welfare of their warriors, saw to it that the ancient Brehon Laws were always strictly followed in its functioning.

As a result, the hospital tent was a square-built structure, with doors opening to the four winds so that the air inside might always be fresh. And through the tent flowed

the waters of a small, swift stream, to carry away waste
and keep the hospital as clean as possible.

Even at the late hour of the night, this tent was brightly
lit with many candles and Sohl, chief leech and bone-
setter, was already at work helping the first wounded who
had come in.

When Fergus and Cormac entered, they found the
physician at work on a warrior's foot that had been
damaged by the weight of a chariot wheel run over it in
the confusion of the fight. The injured man sat upon his
cloak at the stream's edge with the foot in the water. Sohl
stood in the stream, examining the wound carefully while
a student waited near by in readiness, a tray of instruments
in one hand and waxen taper in the other.

The two chieftains made the wounded lad easy. Soon
Lewy arrived with the rest of the hurt men and joined his
two friends to wait patiently for Sohl to finish. Finally the
physician came erect and waved the instruments held out
to him away.

"No, no. We'll not be needing those. Just clean and
bind it. There's nothing broken there, just some deep cuts
from the shoe buckle being pressed into the skin."

As the student moved to obey his master, Sohl stepped
from the stream and took first note of the three chieftains.

"Fergus!" he exclaimed. "What is it that's happening
here? And who are these you're bringing to me?"

"We've had a skirmish, Sohl. These are the worst
wounded, and they'll allow you little rest tonight. One of
them brought me word at great pain. Could you look to
him now?"

"Of course," Sohl agreed, and approached the young
warrior Fergus indicated. But as he knelt by the man to
examine him, the officer tried to turn away the help.

"Others here are needing your arts more than myself,"
he told the physician. "I am content to wait while the
deadlier wounds are cared for."

The doctor ignored the plea. "You could have such a
wound yourself for all the blood on you," he said, beginning his examination. "I will never come to understand
the foolish courage that fills your heads. I saw another lad
not many days ago who should have rested long by the
look of him, but refused to."

Fergus and his comrades listened with amusement to the idle talk, for they knew it was the good physician's way to prattle on and on as he worked, to take minds of wounded men off their pain.

"Curious it was," Sohl went on. "It was another warrior I was taken to help, and an Ulsterman, too."

"Ulster?" said Cormac with curiosity. "Now, how did that come to happen?"

"I was taken by trickery to tend a wounded man, and I did," he answered simply. "I did not know or care at the time who it was."

"Did the Ulstermen harm you?" Cormac asked.

"They made no threats. One of them helped me, to speak the truth. When the wounded man became violent, I might have been hurt if that young man had not come to my aid."

"What young man would that be?" asked Cormac, now becoming more intrigued by the strange story.

"The one I mentioned before. A fine-looking lad, but with a pallor of death on him. More like one of the Sidhe he was, coming out of the dark. But, still, there was a great strength in him, for the man I tended had me in a grip like a sparrow in a hawk's talons. I thought not even the gods could save me, until this boy came in and shook us apart with one hand."

"Who was this warrior?" Cormac said with seriousness this time, for something in the story disturbed him. "What did he look like?"

"I cannot really say. I thought I knew him, or had seen him, but later on I realized who it was I had recalled." He smiled. "If I believed in the strength of spirits, I would believe it was the spirit of the Hound who I saw that night."

With that he stood up from the warrior, his examination complete.

"Well, young man, you've many a small wound, but only one of note, there on your thigh. Nasty and deep it is, but it missed cutting your great artery or you'd be bled white, now. Who was it bandaged it so tightly?"

"I did it myself as I drove back here in my chariot," the warrior replied.

"Well, you may have saved your own life. Honors to yourself. Rest now and we'll have it properly bound."

Sohl turned, then, to the chieftains. He saw thoughtful expressions on the three of them and interpreted them as worry for the youth.

"Be happy! This fellow will survive," he said. But then he thought back on his words and realized their sorrow was for someone else. "Ah, it's a fool I am to ramble on and speak so of Cuculain. I had forgotten you all were once his friends."

"It is no matter doctor," said Fergus gruffly.

Cormac said nothing, for something more than sorrow seemed to occupy his mind.

"Well, this lad will survive," Sohl told them, "and thanks to you for bringing him in. Leave him now and I will see him back to his company."

"I've none left," said the youth, "save for those men here."

"He'll serve in my own guard," Fergus decided and, to the wounded officer, said, "Report to me when you are able. In the meantime, rest well. You are a courageous man. With wisdom you may live to be an old one."

Once outside the tent, Lewy stopped and faced his friends.

"Fergus, what of this attack? Will Meave do anything?"

Fergus shrugged. "She has announced her plans to all the chieftains. She may not change them."

"But she cannot pretend that Ulster will not come!"

"She can if pride is greater than fear in her. She has already argued that this was but a small raiding party."

"You don't believe that any more than I."

Fergus met Lewy's eyes for a moment, then shook his head. "No. Ulster will come."

To that Cormac responded with harshness. "And that madwoman will divide the host and see us all destroyed."

"No more of that," said Fergus, his voice low with warning. "She is our queen."

"Aye, and you her loyal commander," Cormac replied. "And so, what will you do?"

"I will organize as well as I can. If Ulster's main force

is still distant, we may divide and be across the Shannon far ahead of them."

"Fergus, if they come upon us at once the other provinces have gone, we'll have no chance." This came from Lewy who, as usual with him, had been reflecting upon the situation. "It's only together that we might hold our own."

"Pray, then, that Ulster comes before the fall of night tomorrow. Come on, let's get about establishing a sound defense. We'll shake these celebrating fools out of their mugs of ale."

He started forward at a fast pace and his two allies fell in beside him.

"At least the Hound will not be among our attackers," Cormac said, but in such a strange tone that Fergus looked at him with puzzlement.

"There seems to be some doubt in you. Did the healer's story of ghosts disturb your ease?"

"I'm not certain. Fergus, is there no chance he might have survived?"

"I could almost wish he had," Fergus replied.

Chapter Twenty-Six
EINEY

The chariot of Cuculain raced toward the south. Many miles passed under its iron-rimmed wheels that day but, as the afternoon came on, Laeg noted with concern that his master seemed to be tiring. Still, Cuculain commanded Laeg to press on in an attempt to catch the army of Ulster. They kept up the murderous pace until nightfall, and only when the track they followed had become almost invisible did Cuculain agree that they might stop.

They planned to make their camp in the open, but as they surveyed the countryside for a clear space they noted a light flickering amongst the trees some way ahead.

They went on toward it. As they drew nearer, they realized they were in territory somehow unplundered by Meave's army, for around them in the dark they heard the occasional low of cattle grazing in the fields. Finally the track they followed widened and entered a broad area of lawn edged by great trees. Across it the two men found themselves facing a large, timber liss.

"It is unfortified, and no royal seat," Laeg observed, for by law only the residence of a king was ramparted and fossed, giving it the nature of a dun, while a noble's home, called a liss, was undefended. "Still, by the size of this tec I'd say someone of high position holds it. It will make a fit place for your rest."

He could not hide the relief in his voice as he said this. He knew his master still had need of more comfort than hard ground and open sky could provide.

He pulled the chariot up in the yard. Cuculain alighted, but Laeg drove on around the house to the stable buildings he had noted there. His first duty was to feed and put up the horses, and there was no question in his mind that he could freely do this. No noble would refuse a warrior a place to rest, and especially one of Cuculain's fame.

As Laeg went on, Cuculain walked up to the doorway of the liss and beat upon its timber. His knock was answered by a tall, round-shouldered man whose long nose and thin, gray-thatched head gave him the look of a starving horse.

The warrior greeted him pleasantly. "Good evening, sir. Is the master of the liss about?"

"No sir, he's not. I'm house steward here."

That much Cuculain had surmised. The man had that overwhelming arrogance of manner, that unnatural dignity that he had come to expect in his own chief servants. It was a trait of the position, he supposed. The result of a servant assuming the power delegated him. Normally Cuculain found it amusing, but now he feared it was going to cause him difficulty.

"What is it you're wanting here?" the austere individual asked him, looking the young warrior up and down as if he were a common herder.

Cuculain struggled to keep his humor. "My man, it's certain I am that my usually impressive appearance has suffered a bit, but even so, you must see I'm no base wight. I'm asking only for a place to rest and shelter for this night. I'm on my way to join with Ulster's army."

"And you wish to stay here?" the man asked, his disbelief growing ever greater. Once more he looked the young man up and down. "Why would you be going to help the Red Branch? They've many better men than you."

Cuculain felt anger rising in him. "Now, you should know that I'm a weary man," he said slowly, "and getting wearier of you as each moment more passes."

He considered the eminent satisfaction he would receive by knocking down this overbearing fool, and then noted his own feeling with surprise. The man's misplaced authority had overcome the strange lethargy that had seized him in these past days.

The two stood at impasse, eyeing one another warily. But it was not for long. The door was suddenly pulled farther open and a young girl appeared at the steward's side.

She was a fair child, not more than ten years of age, her face round and cheerful and full of color, her long hair plaited loosely as if to keep it out of her active way.

"Angus, do not keep him outside," she said reprovingly. "No warrior of Ulster should be refused here."

She smiled at Cuculain but, when she saw him clearly, her smile faltered as she took in his alarming thinness and his hollow cheeks and the livid scars which marked his pale flesh.

The warrior flushed with embarrassment at her shock. For the first time he saw the sorry figure he had become openly mirrored in someone else. It made him feel deep anguish at his weakness and at the impression it made. And that feeling only added more weight to his already laden spirit.

But then she smiled again, more brightly than before, and threw wide the door.

"Come in and welcome to our house. Follow me. Angus, go on with your own work."

The steward's dislike at being dismissed by a child was evident in his face, but he went, turning off through a passage toward the back of the house.

Cuculain, a little bewildered by the sudden change in his welcome, followed the girl into the central chamber of the tec.

It was a large room, warmed by a peat fire in its central hearth, brilliantly lit by candles in the many wall sconces. Its timber walls were hung around with exquisitely dyed tapestries, ornamented with antlers and weapons of the chase, and its earthen floor was strewn thickly with rushes freshly cut, still fragrant with the scent of green meadows. A pleasant, comfortable room it was, and Cuculain at once felt cheered by it.

Nor was his cheer diminished by the woman who rose from a seat beside the fire to greet them as they entered. He had no doubt she was the lady of the liss, for her manner was gracious and her bearing proud. Yet also visible in her was a warmth and friendliness that he recognized as closely akin to that of the girl beside him.

"My daughter has rescued you from Angus, I see," she said, smiling. "I welcome you here."

She showed no fear of this strange, ragged warrior. She had seen his youth, noted his bearing and demeanor and determined he was one to trust. She had noted, too, that some great hardship had taken much from him.

She asked him to sit on a couch before the fire. As he did so, the girl moved around the fire and sat on a stool to stare across at him in fascination.

"I'm sorry for my steward," the lady said, "but my husband and sons have gone with the king, and Angus feels the need to be protector of us."

"Our visitor goes to join the army, too," the girl put in with much enthusiasm.

"Oh?" the woman responded, guardedly, and he felt her appraising him with doubt in her eyes. He knew she, like her daughter, questioned his ability to fight.

He laughed to cover his abashment. "Your Angus might bring down more wrath on you than he turns away, my Lady. But I thank you for offering me your home. I've another with me too. You don't mind that?"

"Ah, no. We're well provided here. When he joins us, I'll have some food served for you both and have a sleeping chamber done up for you, besides."

At that moment Laeg entered the hall from the back of the liss, the steward on his heels. A tall, strong and imposing figure, burdened now with armor and arms unloaded from the chariot, the driver had totally cowed Angus, so much like some great champion he seemed. Cuculain almost laughed aloud to see the arrogant servant so completely fooled. Then he noted that the lady, too, was deceived by Laeg, for she rose to welcome him as if he were a warrior of note.

The young man could not find fault with her for deeming Laeg the greater. He knew that in comparison the driver now looked the more noble of the two of them. The thought amused him further and he said nothing. There was no pride in him that might have caused him to assert his proper station.

Still, though in words and actions the lady gave the great son of Riangowra first place, she yet treated Cuculain with gentle care. The war-worn, weary Hound drew her compassion and roused her thoughts of her own sons, now far away.

After she had seen the two men fed, Laeg arose and bowed to her graciously.

"My lady, I thank you for a meal the like of which I've not tasted these past days. Now I must go and see to the proper cleaning of the armor and weapons."

"As you wish. I'll have chambers prepared for you both."

"One room is enough," Leag assured her grandly. He had noted that his master had done nothing to dispel the lady's view of him as the superior of them both. He knew that Cuculain was content to let him play this part, so play it he did. "My comrade and I have become used to sleeping near one another. We've been so long in dangers that we're used to watching each other's back, you see."

"Very well," she agreed, smiling, but her expression changed to a quizzical one as she watched Laeg go out.

"A strange, casual manner has your friend for a warrior," she said to Cuculain. "But I find him more to my liking than many I've met who put on their bold airs."

"I find him so myself," said Cuculain wryly. "There is a simple honesty in him more like a working man than a great and noble warrior."

As he spoke, he wondered if this all was an insult to Laeg. He knew the man was proud of his own position as a champion driver in Eire and deemed it a greater talent than that of mere warrior. Most likely he'd consider this a drop in rank.

Of a sudden a cold seemed to run through Cuculain's body and he shivered. The lady saw it and realized some fever must still plague the wounded man.

"Here," she said, "you are tired. Why don't you rest by the fire?" She moved a couch close to the hearth and laid a thick coverlet on it as a cushion.

"I dislike troubling you," Cuculain said, but his weariness made his protest a weak one. He moved to the couch, smiling faintly and thanking her.

"Sleep if you like," the lady said. "We'll not disturb you . . ." she looked across the fire to her daughter ". . . will we, Einey?"

"Oh, no, Mother," the girl replied sincerely.

"Well, I've some household duties now. I'll have your chamber prepared."

The lady went out and Cuculain settled himself more comfortably, propping his chin upon one knee. But as soon as her mother had gone, Einey moved her own stool around the fire, moving quietly not to disturb him, and sat down close to watch him.

Cuculain tried to stay awake, feeling foolish because of his unaccountable and irritating weariness, but he found himself nodding off and caught himself as his head rolled forward. Angrily he shook his head to clear it and found the girl watching him, her gray-green eyes intent.

"Hello," he said. "I think I've been asleep and revealed my sloth to a pretty maid. And what have you been doing?"

She was embarrassed by his address. Still she spoke up without any fear.

"I've been watching you. You've a noble head and great strength, even wounded and tired as you are."

"Thank you for that," he said. "I've had cause to doubt my charms lately. But, have you never seen warriors of the Red Branch before?"

"My father and my brothers," she answered, shrugging as if they did not count. "But they fought only when there was need. They are not warriors who fight for their profession as you do. Such as you do not come here. Our liss is far from the main ways, and if warriors pass through our tuath, they are entertained by the king at his great dun."

"Then doubly ashamed I am to make so unheroic an impression by falling asleep."

"I did not wake you?" she asked, alarmed by the thought.

"No. It was by my own thoughts I was awakened."

"Glad I am," she said, relieved, "for beyond my mother's warning I would never wish to break a gesa of yours."

Cuculain was taken aback by this simple statement, for it was a gesa, a bond, on him that bad fortune befell if he were awakened from sleep.

"It's a certain thing that you have never seen me

before, and I've not said my name. How is it you can describe my gesa?"

She smiled with pleasure at that. "Well enough I know you," she said. "Mother was fooled, but she knows even less of warriors than I. You are that same Cuculain who they say was killed on the banks of the Oun Dia."

"And how long have you known this?"

"As I sat watching you tonight and saw the true face masked beneath the weariness and pain. I wept many a night when it was heard you were slain."

"Sorry it makes me ever to have brought sorrow to one such as you," he said gravely. "How do you know so much of me if you have never seen any of the Ard-Rie's champions?"

"We have many a wandering bard here, from Emain Macha and from Dun Dalgan as well. Since I was old enough to stay up and listen, I have heard many of them sing their lays of you. Many questions I've asked about you, and much I know. I even know you are said not to be Sualtim's son but that of Lu Lamfada of the Sidhe."

At that Cuculain shuddered again and she stopped in deep distress.

"My speech has run away from me in my excitement," she said dolefully. "I did not mean to speak of things which are no business of mine."

He could not stand to see her downcast. He smiled at her.

"No, do not worry. But do not believe all the bards sing. Their work is to tell a lively story, even if they must add to it a bit."

"Then what I've heard isn't true?"

He considered. "My pride forces me to say that it may be partly true and partly false. You can see yourself that even a hero may be hurt."

At that she smiled, too, and they were easy together again. After a time she brought to him a small tympan of polished boxwood with a silver comb upon it. She explained that it had been a gift from her father, bought at the great Tailteen fair.

"Would you like to hear me play upon it?"

So timid yet so hopeful did she sound that Cuculain

could not refuse, though he knew he would have difficulty forcing himself to remain awake through it. But he had no need to try. She tuned the little instrument skillfully and sang a lay in a fine, clear voice that delighted him.

When she had finished her song, she did not wait for him to praise her.

"Do not thank me," she said. "Instead, tell me what your life is really like."

Cuculain laughed ruefully. "My life? Why would you be wanting to know of that? Hard it has been, and violent."

"And yet it is your chosen way. Why would you do it if you had no pride, no liking in it?"

He became grim and silent at that, and Einey feared she had again touched on something far beyond her understanding. But soon he raised his head and regarded her.

"Strange it is to speak to a child of this, but you see much more than your years have given you. You have said something I had never questioned myself until these last few days. I do not know whether I have felt pride or honor or any other reason behind my actions. I may have once, but things have become confused. I only know that, since I was little older than you, fighting was to me as playing at hurley was to other boys. I fought against men older, harder, better trained than I and never lost. The why of it never seemed important. But now I've been brought to asking why. What good is my skill if I am to be nothing more than a slaughterer of men, a killer of friends as well as enemies?"

"You held the army of Eire at the Oun Dia," she reminded him.

"To what end? I hoped to stop the war, but it came anyway. I've stopped no killing, only added to it. No, that's not enough. The whole thing has been senseless from the start. It rushes on and I am drawn with it and see no purpose."

He stopped again and was silent. He looked about the room, still warmed by the fire, made fragrant with the rushes and the smell of peat, lighted mellowly by the many candles.

"It would be nice to stay here," he said, "resting like

this. Never have I thought of it before, but why can I not live for myself, in happiness and comfort? I've my own life. Why can I not live it?"

"Because you would never know," she told him quietly. "Like the cattle in the field a man may live out his life grazing and enjoying the warmth of the sun. But cattle are beasts which we herd about for our own ends. Man is something else. There is more to the way of things for us, and we must know what it is. That is why you would not stay here. You will never stay."

He considered this and then he had to smile. "You're like myself the day that I took arms, declaring I'd be content to live only a day if my fame lived on after me. Your spirit has given me back some of that determined boy and driven out a little of the careworn ancient that's crept upon me. I thank you for that."

He laid his broad palm out and she unhesitatingly laid her own slender one upon it.

"You are now a lady under my protection," he said, "and I am your champion. You may call upon me from anywhere and I will come."

"And you may come to me if ever you have fears," she told him with great solemnity.

While the two talked quietly in the main room of the liss, Laeg held a court of his own in the kitchen.

He had carried the armor there to clean it and had found the servants and some local tenants gathered for their evening talk. Amidst them sat the steward, playing the lord-of-the-liss in a grand way. But when the charioteer entered, the man's glory was instantly eclipsed.

Laeg asked two servants to bring a table near the kitchen hearth where he might work with light and warmth. About him the rest scurried to clear a place at the main work table to give him more room. As he laid out the equipment there, the armor and weapons and harness with its silver ornament, the people left the steward and gathered around him until Angus was left sitting alone.

The bolder ones began to question Laeg and, finding him both friendly and willing, a general talk began, largely on the devastation wrought by Meave's army. Only

Angus refused to join in, sitting stone-faced in his chair across the room, glowering at them.

While he talked, Laeg examined each piece of equipment for rust or tarnish, wiping each down carefully until it shone and glittered in the fire's light. With harness and body-armor finished, he turned to the weapons, pulling first the shield of his master from a thick, leather sheath.

At the sight of the warlike piece with its brightly painted device, the crowd about Laeg gasped and moved back, suddenly reminded that this was no mere servant they were now with. Only Angus, glimpsing the sign upon the shield, rose and advanced, for he saw a chance to regain his position with his fellows.

He stepped close to the table and examined carefully the painted head with its fiery eyes and gleaming tusks.

"All Red Branch warriors have their own symbols," he observed, "and it is said this wild boar's head is that of Cuculain. It is unlawful and dishonorable for any lesser warrior to wear the device."

The implication was clear and Laeg, angered by it, quickly replied.

"This is Cuculain's shield. It is he who is now beneath this roof."

The steward laughed scornfully. "Be takin' your story elsewhere if you want it believed. You've been given the hospitality of the liss, but don't be abusin' of it. I know a warrior when one comes before my eye. I don't want to be detracting from a poor, wounded man, now, but you'll not persuade me that this lad or you are the Hound of Ulster and match for a whole army."

Laeg was enraged beyond words. In a sudden move he seized the steward by the throat and forced him to his knees. The steward, weak as he was thin, struggled none at all.

"You wretched churl," Laeg growled at him. "By Cuculain's sword and spear I will kill you now myself if you don't withdraw this lie."

"What is happening here?" a voice asked with alarm, and Laeg looked up to where the lady of the liss stood on the gallery above the kitchens.

"You'll pardon me a little violence, my Lady," said Laeg, his tones becoming gracious, though he still retained his grip on the hapless steward. "But your man here called me a liar for saying my master was Cuculain and now beneath this roof."

The lady gasped, realizing who the young man was. "And you?"

"I am Laeg, Lady," he said proudly, assaying to bow grandly while his hands were occupied. "Champion driver of Eire and happy to be servant to the Hound of Cuculain."

"You've done it now, Laeg," said that very warrior who, drawn by the commotion, had appeared with Einey at the lower door to the kitchen. "Now will this lady be greatly embarrassed and the whole liss be turned inside out for us, because you could not curb your pride."

Laeg looked toward his master, confused for a moment. He released the steward who sank down, grateful for his life and swearing to his gods that he would from that day take care to mind his overbearing ways.

But Cuculain could not keep his grave look for long. The steward had deserved his punishment and their own deception had been unfair. He smiled broadly, then laughed. Einey and Laeg joined with him and, finally, the lady herself forgot her embarrassment and laughed too.

That night Cuculain and Laeg slept in comfort. They arose at first sun but, even so, they found Einey already up and preparing a fine breakfast for them. Afterward the two men took a warm farewell of the girl and her mother and departed, riding away from the peaceful home that seemed the only shelter from the storm upon Ulster.

Einey stood in the doorway of the liss and watched until they disappeared from sight.

Book Five

THE COMING OF ULSTER

Chapter Twenty-Seven
THE RED BRANCH

When the sunrise that saw Cuculain and Laeg on their way lit the host of Meave, it revealed it already in great activity. About the margins of the camp, where the herds and the prisoners were held, much shifting and dividing was in progress while, in the center of the camp, about Meave's pavilion, a large crowd was gathering.

Throughout the night the queen had considered the portent of Ulster's coming, but Fergus had correctly judged what her final decision would be. For good or ill her promise to divide the force had been made, and the men of Eire were anxious to return to their own homes. So, when the balance of the night brought no further alarms, she called for the division to begin, showing no outward sign that she was troubled.

Meave had a platform set up before the royal pavilion. There she sat with Aileel and several of her druids most skilled in the science of computing numbers. As chieftains of all the army's forces waited patiently, the queen set about the delicate task of determining how much of the plundered wealth of Ulster would go to each tribe of the four provinces of Eire.

This sharing of the plunder went rapidly, for the men of Eire trusted the queen's judgment in its being fairly done, and many were not concerned with the spoils of such a war, only wanting to be finished with it and begin the journey back to their own duns.

But no man, no matter how disinterested, could deny they had done proudly by themselves in what they had brought away. The plain about the camp was black with herds of cattle and sheep numbering in the thousands. As their numbers were told out amongst the various clans and tuaths, many fires were lit and many men worked to mark with heated brands the signs of their separate ownerships.

The whole task of division was a giant and a complex one for the queen. As she struggled with it, she felt her impatience grow. She wanted this finished, too, but it never seemed to come any nearer to that. With the passing time her attention strayed more and more. She found herself making frequent errors in her additions and starting when any messenger or herald appeared from the flying squadrons of chariots which scoured the open country east and north for any sign of Ulster.

Suddenly, at midmorning, in the midst of orders she was giving, she became aware of a strangeness. She paused and realized that a vast stillness had enveloped all of them, as if a bell of glass had dropped over the entire camp. No bellowing cow was heard, no shouting man. For a moment all the world seemed to have halted and held its breath.

"What is this peculiar stillness hung about us like a shroud thrown on the dead?" she cried out, her voice echoing back to her shrilly in the vast silence. Then she cocked her head to listen. "Aileel, do you heard someone speaking?" she asked her husband.

The old king shook his head. "I hear nothing."

"But a woman spoke," she insisted. "She said: 'They are no longer under fear. Bloodshed comes.'" Meave lifted her voice to call out: "Faythleen, is it you speaking to me?"

She heard no reply.

Then, just as suddenly, the silence was lifted. A horn blast sounded through the camp and the harsh noise of moving warriors and clashing armaments rose like a cawing flock of great blackbirds all around the pavilion. Fergus appeared at the edge of the gathering before the dais and his voice boomed across the area.

"Chieftains, return to your battalions. Prepare your men!"

No one questioned the commander's order and, in the confusion of warriors rushing back to their units in quick obedience, Meave had no chance to make her own protest. She had to wait with anger burning in her until her commander approached her.

"What are you doing now, Fergus?" she said accusingly. "We've made our decisions. Why do you issue orders without my knowing of them?"

Without comment Fergus climbed to the platform beside her and pointed toward the east. The queen's tent, like the tec of a dun, was on the highest ground, and the platform provided a commanding view of the broad plain all about.

"Look," he said. "What do you see?"

She peered in the direction he indicated for some moments, but there was little to be seen. Birds in great numbers were flying up from the ground and trees. Behind them a swelling cloud of gray-brown mist rose up in soft, delicate billows like the purest wool, suspended against a deep-blue wall of sky.

She shrugged and looked at Fergus. "I see that a storm is rising there, blowing toward us from the sea."

"A storm?" he said, and smiled without humor. "It may be so. But, is it certain of that you are?"

Puzzled by his manner, Meave looked again. Now, on the ground beneath the cloud, she could detect faint, twinkling spots of light that seemed to shift constantly within the mist and grow more numerous as the storm approached.

"Listen, now!" said Fergus in a hushed voice. "What do you hear?"

She listened, and there was something in the air, faintly heard above the din of the host around her. A droning it seemed to her, as of bees in a hive or the constant roll of surf.

"By the Dagda, Fergus!" she exclaimed, meeting his knowing gaze with sudden comprehension.

"Aye, my Queen. A coming storm it is, but of men. Ulster has arrived. The cloud you see is the steam breath of men and horses running anxiously to join us in the cool, morning damp, mingled with the dust thrown up by the many feet and hooves. And those twinkling lights are the weapons and chariots and armor, throwing from their metal surfaces the sun's light!"

"Then the roar . . ." she said with awe ". . . the roar is

the sound of thousands of chariot wheels, their iron rims humming against the ground. But, Fergus, such a vast army they seem. How can that be from one province?"

"It's more than the standing battalions we'll face here," he said. "Our wrong to Ulster is greater than any suffered by her before. I'd judge that every man of that country old enough to cast a spear and young enough to march is with that host. And, whether babe or ancient, there will not be one of them unwilling to fight as a madman to repay us."

"Can we withstand them?"

He looked at her with incredulity.

"Now that they have come and you see I have not made too little of their might . . . now you ask me that?"

"Fergus, there's no point to argue it. I'll own that you were right. What shall we do?"

"We'll fight. By fortune our army was not yet dispersed. I've made provision to deploy our force."

"What of Ulster? How will they come against us?"

"First they'll deploy, but they'll waste little time with that. Ulster is never slow to enter the fight."

Once more she looked toward the army of Ulster, which was pouring onto the far edge of the plain and clearly visible now. Their columns moved right and left to form a broad line. It rippled with the movement of close-packed men as does a swiftly moving stream; and it glinted with a steam's brightness, too, from the sunlight flashing on the trappings of war.

"All right then, Fergus," she said. "See to our battle lines. It's for the best they've come upon us now. At last we'll see who is the power in Eire."

"Aye, Queen, for what that's worth," he replied and left her to take command of his warriors.

"What's happening now?" demanded Aileel, who sat on his couch, peering ahead, desperate to see this coming battle and angry because he could not.

"My King, forgive my thoughtlessness," she said, going to him. "The lines of Ulster have been formed opposite us. They have begun to move boldly forward in a solid mass, infantry to the front, squadrons of chariots behind, ready to make lightning moves into any gap opened in our lines. And, in front of the first ranks of marching

men, the younger warriors, their blood fired by their first
chance at war, ride in their chariots wildly, wheeling back
and forth and raising their arms in mocking salutes to our
fighting men."

"Have your pleasure in the thrill of war while you
may," Aileel muttered, as if addressing these exuberant
young lads. "Soon enough you'll be feeling the real truth
of it today."

Night fell on the plain of battle, and its darkness drew
a concealing blanket over a scene of destruction and
despair.

The broad, virgin meadows of Fremain, so long un-
touched by plows, had in one day grown a crop both rich
and barren. All the plain was filled with dead and dying
men, with overturned and broken chariots and with the
mangled bodies of horses, some horribly alive and struggling to rise, only to fall back again upon the already
splintered ruins of their war-cars. The night echoed with
the constant sounds of pain as men and animals cried out
their agony.

The armies had separated after their bloody labor of
the day and lay at either side of this harvest they had
reaped at such great cost. Now men of both their camps
went forth under signs of truce and walked and searched
among the heaps of men to separate the living from the
dead. All over the plain the red flares of their torches
moved as they, with patience, sought out the wounded
and carried them back to the hospitals and the hard-
pressed men who labored fiercely to save their lives. The
physicians' work, like that of the searchers, was a sorrowful one, for the weapons of war—spear and sword and
scythe—were brutal and ugly in their effect. They left few
small, easily treated wounds, and more hurt men died
under the healers' hands than were saved.

But though the dead and wounded were heavy on both
sides, the men of Eire treated theirs with less difficulty.
For it was the host of Ulster who had suffered most in
that fight. Of all the grand army come so gallantly from
the north, there were more dead and wounded men than
whole ones by nightfall. And while the host of Meave
celebrated in a camp lit as the day with blazing fires, alive

with songs and laughter, the tents of Ulster's camp were dark and silent.

In the pavilion of King Conchobar, few candles burned to expel the dimness and a mourning silence covered all who were gathered there. All through the vast chamber the proud champions of Ulster crouched or stood or lay outstretched or leaned heavily against the walls, motionless and soundless. About them moved the servants of the king to attend them, but they too went wordlessly and on tiptoe, like priests moving in the darkened, hushed aisles of a temple to pass between glowering statues of the gods. They brought food and drink to the men, but few of the warriors moved to touch it, so weary and spiritless were they.

Three times that day these men had thrown their full might against the men of Eire. And three times they had crashed like waves against a marble cliff and been broken by the solid strength of Meave's army. With enormous loss had they been repulsed and, now, this remnant of the great champions who had led the rest knew for the first time what defeat could be.

At the chamber's upper end, seated at a table lit by a single taper, sat Conchobar MacNessa, king of the Red Branch. At dawn he had been a figure of royal command, splendid in his dress and armor. Now his fine cloak hung ragged, torn, and spotted with blood. His hair and beard were black with the dust of battle while the shadows created by the single candle revealed a face sharply etched by sorrow and made black caverns of eyes hollowed by fatigue. But, in those caverns, the eyes glowed with his burning hatred.

He looked about the room at his battle-worn chiefs and the fire blazed up even more brightly in him. Determinedly he levered his long body up from the couch to stand and lifted his arms, both spotted to the elbows with brown blood. He held his longsword tightly grasped in a hand stained solid with the gore, as if he had wielded that blade so long he could not now release it.

"Three times today we entered Eire's camp," he said savagely. "We swept them before us. We walked in their own streets. And now, like beaten dogs, we lie here and keen for our own defeat. How can that be?"

To one side of him a pale, dark-eyed youth raised his head and spoke:

"There were too many, my King. By midday our men had all been tried while half of theirs were fresh. Then did the Clan Derga come from some hidden place and strike us unaware . . ."

"I'll not accept that, MacConud. Ulster is a match for any army of Eire."

"But not for all Eire," MacConud added stolidly.

"Laegaire is right," another said. "Three times our number did we face today, and Fergus MacRogh and the Exiles among them."

"Yes, Fergus, and my own son," Conchobar growled, the hot light in his eyes flaring again. "Of all that host, those two are the ones I most wish destroyed."

As if in ironic reply, the sound of distant merriment came to them, borne on some idle wind from the opposing camp. It gave harsh reminder of the hollowness of the king's words.

"It's only ourselves will get our end in this," a chieftain said. "Our only cause for celebration is in our living now. Even so we've an unbidden guest stalkin' amongst us with the name of Death."

The grim truth in these words struck through to the enraged king. Suddenly weary he sank back in his chair and silence once again filled all the tent.

But then a young warrior sitting near the tent's mouth raised his head to listen.

Above the cries of wounded and the sounds of revelry from Meave's camp, he heard another noise. At first he was not certain what it was, but it grew swiftly in volume until he realized it was the voices of their own men, raised in a joyful shout!

The others in the tent had not yet noted it, but the young man did not hesitate, springing to his feet with a cry.

"Quickly everyone, outside. Someone is coming!"

Moments before a chariot had entered the camp of Ulster.

It drove along the streets, its two riders looking about with horror at the chaos of defeated and bewildered men.

The ways were choked with warriors seeking attention for wounds or trying to locate their clans and companies. But many units of the army had been shattered that day, and many of those who now sought their fellows would find their units had ceased to exist.

The chariot continued for some way, the self-absorbed men in the avenues paying it little note, when the warrior within the car spied a figure in chieftain's dress directing a company of men in the setting up of a defense. The warrior thought he knew the chief, but he told himself his weary mind and eyes only played pranks with him. This man who stood so proudly and gave commands with such bold authority was not like the one he knew so well.

Yet, at that moment the chieftain turned his head and the light from a torch held by the lieutenant at his side revealed his features clearly.

"Sualtim!" the man in the chariot shouted with astonishment and placed a hand upon his driver's reins to stop the car.

The chieftain whirled at hearing that voice. At first his face showed only disbelief, as if he could not credit what he had heard. Yet when his searching eyes found the warrior, he came alive, running forward with an exultant cry.

"Sentanta! It is alive you are!"

"Alive, Father," Cuculain said happily, some of his weariness swept away by this joyous reunion. He leaned over the bulwark of the car to greet the older man as he reached it. The two clasped hands and beamed at one another, neither able to find words that would express their elation at finding one another still alive. But there was some urgent news that was needed by the Hound, and his first questions were directed to it.

"Father, tell me quickly: have you been home? How is Emer? I've been afraid to think of her these past days."

"She's well . . . very well," Sualtim assured him. "Dun Dalgan was not touched. Don't be worried about that fine lady, now. She has courage in her that the Red Branch could use today. She never feared for you, even when all of Ulster did. When we heard rumors you were killed, when your horses came back to her alone, everyone believed you were dead. Everyone but Emer. She said the keening of the Sidhe would tell her when you died, and only that."

Cuculain smiled. He felt the warm closeness of her within his heart and mind. Even so far from Emer, her faith and her support strengthened him.

"She may have felt no fears," Sualtim went on, "but to me it's still a miracle that you found Laeg and came to join us here."

"A miracle is to find you leading men, and with such sureness in you as I never thought to see again," the warrior replied. "How do you come to be here yourself?"

"I returned to Dun Dalgan as the madness was leaving the men of Ulster. Hearing that the Red Branch was hosting, I brought our household companies to join with Conchobar. We've fared badly today, as you can see, but perhaps with your support we'll rally yet."

"Rally?" said Cuculain. He looked about him at the dismal camp and the fatigue weighed down on him once more like an iron cloak dropped about his shoulders. "Father, I've my doubts about that. It may be I've done you little favor in coming. I'm weary and I've been so for some days. It's a strange weariness that has grown on me more and more as I approached the army. If the Red Branch is as badly broken as it looks, to rally around me might only cause more deaths to little gain."

But even as he spoke, this dilemma was being taken from him. First his own troops of Dun Dalgan, then other warriors in the avenues recognized him. His name was quickly passed from man to man and finally it was raised in a shout.

"Cuculain! Cuculain is here!" they cried and, from all the avenues, men began to crowd toward the chariot. The Hound and his charioteer were trapped by them, unable to drive on, and Cuculain felt he had to make a show of strength to them, standing upright and trying to force the irritating weakness back.

At last the shouting of the men brought Conchobar and his other chieftains. They shouldered through the cheering mass of warriors to greet Cuculain with a tremendous show of happiness and relief.

None was more grateful to see him than the king

himself, for that hard and ruthless man saw in Cuculain one more chance to save this disaster and yet take his vengeance on the men of Eire. At once he climbed into the chariot to clasp Cuculain close to him in friendship and welcome, raising an even greater cheer in the assembled men.

"Ah, there's spirit in them still," he said with satisfaction. "Drive ahead, toward my pavilion," he ordered Laeg. "Let all the warriors see their greatest champion is returned."

Obediently the crowd parted for them, and Laeg drove along an avenue lined with men, wounded as well as whole, who cheered themselves to hoarseness as they greeted Cuculain. The chariot reached the pavilion of the king and its three riders all dismounted there. Before the royal structure Conchobar stopped and raised his voice to address the throng.

"Warriors of Ulster, hear me now!"

The men fell quickly silent and the king had only to wait for a brief moment before he was certain he would be clearly heard. Then he went on:

"Before you here you see your own great Hound, come back to us from the dead, returned from the bloody beak of that goddess of slaughter, the black Morrigu herself!"

Another cheer went up, but he raised his arms to silence it.

"Wait, friends, there is more than his return to cheer. For, if Cuculain can come safely away from that carrion-eating crow, can the Red Branch do any less?"

"No, no!" came back the answer to his challenge, shouted by a thousand warriors, none so weary or so badly hurt that they were not now fired again to blazing life. Nowhere was there evident to Laeg or his master the bewilderment and defeat that had been so evident when they had first entered the camp. Conchobar, for all his arrogance and pride, was yet a master in taking hold of the spirits of men.

"Ah, I knew it would be so," the king told his warriors with satisfaction. "Then be about preparing a strong defense. Tomorrow we'll be going against all Eire with the Hound of Culain at our head!"

Throughout the king's harangue, Cuculain had stood

quietly by his side, his calm demeanor masking the tremendous effort he put forth to fight off the weakness that assailed him. But, as the crowd dispersed and Conchobar led him within the royal tent, his will to struggle more failed him and he sagged against a table.

Only Laeg's quick move to catch him saved him from falling, and Conchobar looked to him with amazement, as if taking first note of the young warrior's condition.

"By the gods," the king exclaimed. "What is it that's ailing him?"

"He's badly worn, can't you see it?" Laeg asked coldly.

Conchobar examined Cuculain and shrugged. "He seems fully healed. He'll be all right with some rest. Put him on my own bed. With the preparations to be made, I'll not be needing it this night."

Laeg eased Cuculain down onto the king's rugs and the young chieftain lay back gratefully on the soft pile, sinking at once into a heavy sleep.

"See that he rests well," Conchobar admonished the charioteer. "He's all that's keeping Ulster from defeat."

"You may have put too many hopes on him, my King," said Laeg boldly, unable to hide his irritation at Conchobar's callousness. "If this was lost before we came, there's no certainty he can change it. Is there no way we could settle this foolish war without risking destruction for us all?"

"So long as Ulster has the will to fight, we'll not let the damage done us go unavenged. He's given us the will again, and I mean to make use of him."

"But he's been badly hurt, in body and in will," the charioteer argued doggedly. "He is only a man, not some cold iron weapon you can wield to your own ends."

The king's face darkened at that and he strode forward to stand over the kneeling Laeg, a towering figure, tense with his rage.

"My ends?" the king repeated wrathfully. "My ends are Ulster's. Better she die with pride at this place than live under the shadow of Eire from here on. Cuculain, himself, would not say anything different than that. We've little choice in this but to go ahead. So be taking good care of your master, Laeg. Tomorrow we will fight."

"And if he cannot?" Laeg asked.

"Tell no one that," Conchobar warned. "Let no one know about his weakness. He has returned the spirit to our host. As long as they believe that he will join the fight, they will not fail me. They will strike Eire to its bloody heart."

While the host of Eire celebrated, Cormac Conlingas walked the perimeter of its camp.

He wanted no part of the victory revels taking place in Meave's pavilion. His mind was troubled by the defeat he had helped to put upon Ulster.

He had stopped at an outer guard post and was looking across toward Ulster's camp when the first cries went up from it. They began at one edge of the opposing host and rolled across it like a wave, sweeping up the whole in one, great, loud cheer that lasted for long moments.

"Do you hear that?" he asked a guard beside him.

"Aye, that I did," the man answered. "I'd thought we'd beaten them fairly today, but there's not the sound of beaten men in that."

"It might be they're received new reason to rejoice," said Cormac thoughtfully.

The guard shook his head. "It would take a score of battalions to bring them back to strength after today."

"Perhaps," Cormac replied. "Or perhaps a single man."

"A single man?" the guard said in disbelief, but then he grinned. "Ah, sir, you're jestin' with me now. What man could bring such cheer to them?"

"A dead one," Cormac told him, and there was no sound of jesting in his voice.

Chapter Twenty-Eight
DISPUTE

Unsettled by his thoughts, Cormac wandered the avenues of the camp. He found himself, at last, near the tent of Fergus MacRogh. There was a need in him to talk with his comrade and, after a moment's hesitation, he entered.

He found the commander was not alone there, but sat in quiet talk with several of the Exile chieftains. The same oppression that lay heavily upon Cormac's spirit seemed to lie on them, too, for the gathering lacked the cheer that the rest of the army evidenced.

Fergus greeted his friend and asked him to join with them. The young chieftain was at first reluctant, having meant to speak with the commander alone. But seeing that the others were all comrades and fellow Exiles, he determined to make his feelings known to all of them.

He sat down at a long table, at the far end from Fergus, and accepted a mug, filling it from a pitcher they passed to him. He listened for a while to the aimless conversation, no one seeming anxious to speak about the day's events. That only made him hesitate again. The thoughts which plagued him were complex and sensitive ones, not easily put into words. For once his clever wit was useless to him.

It was his long quiet and his dark mood, both so unusual in him, that finally drew Fergus to address him.

"Cormac, what is it that's weighing down on you tonight?"

"I . . . I'm thinking that we must talk about Ulster," he began awkwardly.

His comment stilled the other conversations and drew all eyes to him. But he had no chance to continue, for another voice, a loud and a boisterous voice, spoke in reply to him:

"Talk about Ulster? And what will we talk of? How badly its warriors die?"

The speaker lifted himself from his bench. His name was Duvac Dael Ulla, commander of three hundred of the Exiles. His shining, slate-black hair and dark eyes were startling in contrast to his pale skin. The Black Chieftain he was called by many, and his pride in the name was clear in the black cloak and tunic that he wore. He leaned forward on the table to look up its length to Cormac, and his grin was like that of a wolf over its crippled prey.

"Come on, now," he prompted Cormac again. "I'll talk of Ulster. All evening I've waited to revel in her destruction, but those here do not seem interested."

The man's obvious joy in Ulster's plight made things more difficult for Cormac. He looked to Fergus, but the commander sat stone-faced and seemingly unconcerned. Cormac understood at once that MacRogh would make no reply to Duvac's open display of hatred. It determined him to make some response himself.

"Does your rage with Ulster go so deep in you that you find pleasure in the deaths of men?"

"Aye, right enough," Duvac replied with satisfaction. "You know, I had a vision that we chased the bloody Red Branch back across the Oun Dia and cleaned our swords on the last man's cloak."

"And did you see yourself, Duvac, like a great, black thundercloud, blotting out the stars of their champions?" Cormac asked him without the smile which normally would have accompanied such bantering words.

"My dress is black, and I'll not deny liking it that way, but it makes me no slower in the battle." The chieftain laughed and took a great draught of his ale. "I've seen those northern braggarts have their punishment, and I've gloried in it. Cormac, do you remember how they chased us across the border and went on slaughtering our shattered rear through Westmeath, and sent insults after us like pellets from a sling as we fled across the Shannon to Connacht? By all the gods, that's burned within me ever since!"

"It was a long while ago," Cormac said quietly.

Duvac had lifted his cup again to his lips, but at these words he stopped there, holding it without drinking while his eyes rose to meet the other's in astonishment. Then, slowly, he lowered the cup back.

"What does that mean? You think we can forget what has been done?"

"Ulster has been bloodied enough today. How much slaughter would you call enough?"

Duvac looked skyward, as if calling the gods to witness this blasphemous utterance. Then he looked back to young Conlingas.

"How can you be saying that, Cormac? I'd think that next to Fergus you would most want to tear out Ulster's bowels."

Cormac could think of nothing in reply. The Black Chieftain looked a moment into his doleful face, then swept his gaze around the table at the others as if seeing them for the first time.

"Not one of you speaks up with me," he said. "You turn your heads or look down into your ale. You're all in pity of Ulster. All of you! I'd marked your strange, dark manner since I came, but couldn't understand its cause. Now that it's clear to me, I understand why I did not see before. What Exile would believe that any heart among us would bleed for the one who wounded it!"

Cormac grew angry at this attack and rose to reply to the other chief:

"You rant and boast in your great pride, Duvac, about the wrongs done you. But what is it you were in Ulster? A second light at best, as I was. Now you wear your grand clothes and rule among the chieftains of Connacht. Can you not be content with the broad lands you hold and with the price we've made Ulster pay?"

"No! No!" the Black Chief shouted. "My dreams are haunted with the sights of Ulster, and I awake in emptiness, knowing I am in exile, cast out of my own land by your father with his cold heart. Only when that heart ceases to beat will my dreams end also."

"I had such dreams," another at the table said, his voice soft in contrast with Duvac's harsh outcries. He was a young chieftain and had been still a lad when the expulsion had come. "Often I saw the hosting plain at Emain Macha, and the trees on the lawn where we practiced the art of fighting as boys. But a few days ago, seeing Ulster again, I realized that all the beauties meant little to me, now. My dreams had made them brighter, more beautiful than they were. I knew then that the true beauty lay in what had become my home: Lough Derg and splendid Cruchane."

"You are too young to remember the disgrace," said Duvac angrily. "I'll not see the Red Branch survive."

"This all seems a waste of argument," said Fiecha MacFir-Phoebe. "Ulster is beaten now. Why speak of it?"

"It's to speak of it that I came here," Cormac said. "I've fears that Ulster will not give up this fight."

"How can that be?" asked young Fiecha. "They were thrown back when they came at us in their full strength. Now, ravaged as they are, they'll have less chance."

"There's no denying that," Cormac agreed. "But I heard cheering in the Ulster camp as if . . . as if some new cause for hope had come to them." He exchanged a look with the still silent Fergus and saw that his friend understood what he implied.

"You think they might yet come against us?" Fiecha asked.

"They might," said Cormac. "And what, then, will we do?"

"Do?" said Duvac. "Why, we fight again, as we did today."

Cormac shook his head. "I say we've done enough slaughter for Meave on our own cousins. Tomorrow let her armies do the warring."

Several heads nodded in agreement to this and only Duvac showed his disbelief at this proposal.

"I'll not listen to the madness here. How can we refuse to fight?"

"Meave cannot force us to the fight if we are all agreed," Cormac reasoned. "What do you all think? If Ulster comes out again, will we hold back?"

"No!" a quiet voice said, drawing all eyes to the table's head, and to the giant, red-haired man who had listened patiently to all of this.

"Fergus?" said Cormac in surprise. "What are you meaning? You've not wanted this war from the start."

"But it's still come upon us. We owe Meave far too much to go against her now. My loyalty is with her and I've no good reason to be changing that. Remember, the cause of this war was in Ulster's insult to us, and this battle was joined by them. I'll not break my oath to Meave for sorrow over my homeland."

"Your oath," said Cormac bitterly. "It's the only thing you value. Will nothing give you the right to break it? Think, Fergus. Oaths killed Fardia and made Cuculain fight an unequal contest. There's deception and treachery all through this. When will you see?"

"Only when I know what you say is true, without any doubt," Fergus told him. "Until then we will fulfill our bond."

"And do more bloody slaughter to that end," Cormac added.

"No more, now," said Fergus warningly. He looked up toward the doorway of the tent. "Some faint light is growing in the sky. This argument has kept us through the night. You must go to your battalions and call them up, for dawn will be fully upon us soon. We'll see then what Ulster does."

The chieftains dispersed to call their warriors into position along the camp's eastern edge. Fergus left his Exiles and walked to the queen's pavilion, for from the commanding ground there he could see the disposition of Ulster most completely.

He found Meave and Aileel on the high platform before the tent with their ollavs and druids. About them were drawn up the companies of their household troops.

"Ah, Fergus," the queen greeted him. "Is all in readiness for another victory?"

"If those of Ulster will fight again," the commander returned.

"That we'll be seeing. Soon there will be enough light."

Together they waited, peering into the grayness that separated the armies as the sun, weakened by a heavy overcast, rose higher in its attempt to light the day.

"I'll wager they've pulled out in the night," Calatin chortled.

"Is that so?" Fergus replied, remembering Cormac's words. He pointed across the plain, now bright enough to be clearly seen. "Well, what of that!"

There, from north to south in an unbroken line, rose a high rampart of earth, thrown up by desperate workers during the night. It curved out toward them in its middle like a great bow, its ends resting against the forest behind. The front was pierced by a score of gates, and a great double one, five chariots in width and closed by rough-hewn timbers, pierced the middle of the fortification nearest the camp of Meave.

"Ulster will fight," said Fergus, and his words rang with an unhidden pride, for the slighting words of Calatin reminded him that his own blood was that of Ulster, and his own strength of will had come from it.

"Then Ulster will be destroyed, and this settled at last," the druid answered. "Now we'll quench that arrogant torch of theirs and not be bothered with their pride again to the time's end."

"You'd wish them all destroyed, wouldn't you?" Fergus asked. "Not just made subject to the will of Eire."

"And why not? Your hatred is as mine, Fergus. In that one thing we are alike."

Inwardly Fergus was revulsed by this comparison. To have his act against Ulster made one with Calatin's only heightened the horror of it to him.

"Would you be speaking so boldly if Ulster's numbers were not less than a quarter of ours?" he asked.

Calatin laughed. "I'd count ten-to-one as not unfair against those fools with their suicidal bravery."

"Listen, a clarion call," said Meave.

They looked across the plain and saw the gates in the earthworks open. Then, from within, the battalions of the Red Branch began to emerge.

Chapter Twenty-Nine
THE EXILES

The army of Ulster streamed through the gateways and formed itself in battle lines as it came onto the plain.

As it spread itself, Fergus saw clearly how painfully thin its lines were. Outnumbered from the start, Ulster was now but a remnant of its former strength. If ever he wanted his revenge against them, this would be his time for it. The Exiles alone were nearly a match in numbers for the shattered battalions of the Red Branch.

As Ulster began its advance, Fergus issued his orders, sending messengers to the forces of the four provinces. Soon the men of Eire began their own advance, the warriors of Connacht at the center and those of the other provinces at either side. Only the Exiles remained in line on the camp's edge.

"Why are your troops left behind?" asked Meave.

"I mean them as a reinforcement," Fergus explained, "to break through should a weak point appear."

"And why your own men, not some others?" Calatin asked suspiciously.

"My men are the most experienced of the army," Fergus reasoned patiently. "It's best they be reserved for a death blow."

That satisfied the queen and was, in truth, MacRogh's purpose. But as he boldly stated it aloud, the grimness of its meaning came home to him.

From their point of vantage on the royal dais, the company about Meave watched as the battle joined. The men of Eire expected to push back the battered Ulstermen at once, but quickly realized they faced a force determined not to give ground.

With a spirit that more than equaled their lack of numbers, the Red Branch drove into the men of Meave. For a time the savage fighting equalized, neither side gaining, but then the center of the host of Eire began to give way, and it withdrew to save its integrity.

"What's happening?" cried Aileel, hearing the battle shouts but unable to see.

"It's brave men the Red Branch has," Meave conceded grudgingly. "Our ranks give back before them, and the Clan Derga has been badly bloodied."

The old king clenched his twisted hands in frustration. "Ah, I wish I had the limbs that once were mine, to swing the sword again."

"My good King, it's champions such as you we've need of today," Meave told him comfortingly.

"What gives Ulster this power?" Aileel asked his wife. "Have they new forces with them?"

"None I can see," said the queen, scanning the Red Branch lines. "I can find no reason for their renewed strength."

Fergus could see none either. If anyone had come, as Cormac suspected, and given Ulster new hope, they were not in the battle now.

"The Clan Derga is barely able to hold its own," Calatin cried. "Fergus, why do you save your men? You must commit them."

Fergus turned to face the others on the platform, a new determination formed in him. As he had watched the battle he had become convinced that it was the last, desperate strength of Ulster which had carried it this far. He knew that for his men to join the fight would only speed the destruction of the Red Branch, which would come soon enough in any case.

"I'll not commit my men," he stated flatly.

Meave was aghast. "Fergus, we need them now!"

"You've had your use of them all along, and they've done as you asked. But not this."

"How can you refuse?"

"My Queen, we've helped invade our homeland, ravaged duns where we were born and lived, watched while men and women we once knew were enslaved or killed. Yesterday we helped throw back and slaughter men who were once our friends. We will not insure their final end. That must be up to you. Your strength is more than enough to defeat them in this."

"Do you then defy me and withdraw your Exiles from my host?" she demanded.

"No. We will remain and, should your host be threatened, we will fight. But in return you'll not ask us to finish this unequal battle. If those terms are not acceptable, then we will withdraw and you'll be no better off."

She knew that he was right. She could not hold the independent Exiles to her, but she could less afford to drive them off for fear it would cause division in her entire host. In frustration she looked to Calatin, but her ard-druid seemed strangely passive, glancing away as if to indicate he wished no part in this contest.

After a moment Meave turned back toward her commander and spoke to him in measured tones that barely concealed her torment.

"Fergus, you once told me that if you gave me cause to question your loyalties or doubt your motives for action your use to me as leader would be ended. Surely you must see that you're forcing me to that decision now! Are you saying you will give up your command?"

"If there is no other way," Fergus agreed. "And I'll not say that saddens me. But, believe this, Meave: it's loyal as before I am to you, and I'll stay so until I'm given cause to know my bond with you is falsely made."

He held her eyes as he spoke and she could feel the simple honesty in him that once she had accepted. He was appealing to her to respond in kind. For that moment their minds touched once again and she felt the pain and sorrow his command had given him. She understood.

"All right," she conceded. "I'll not press you more. Yet . . ." She struggled for something else to say, wishing to keep this fragile contact, but the moment was too short, events were moving too quickly.

"I'll be going to my own men, then," Fergus said. "The battle is yours, Meave. All your skill in war, all your ability to command will be needed here. You have always wished to lead this host yourself. Now it will be."

As he turned away, she realized the enormity of her

loss. It threatened to overwhelm her and she raised a hand as if she would restrain him. But then she caught herself and let the arm drop back to her side. She was alone now, and so it had to be. With the acceptance of that, her own instinct for command rose in her again. With new determination she turned her eyes back to assess the battle raging on the plain.

No one in Eire in many scores of years had seen such fighting on such a scale. The plain seemed crowded with contending men, ranks muddled, order confused, swirling in a chaotic jumble of colors and flashing weapons, until individual units were lost.

Generally she was aware that her center was giving way before a furious onslaught of Ulstermen. She could see the great curve of the hard-pressed line bowing ever farther back toward her camp, ready to break under the weight of Red Branch infantry who tirelessly hewed their way into the Connacht ranks with madmen's strength. And behind the Ulster lines moved battalions of their heavy war-chariots, circling, circling, as would bright birds of prey above a harried foe, sun glinting on their outstretched metal wings. She knew they waited for the line to crack, to open even a narrow fissure, for they would drive into it, a broad wedge forced into the thin break, ripping it open, tearing apart the host like a steer carcass split from throat to belly to spill its vitals out.

"I must bring wing battalions back to support the sagging middle of our line," she said.

This first decision by her was without solid conviction, and Aileel was quick to come to her support.

"Aye, Meave," he agreed. "Pull out those behind both flanks where they've not been hard pressed."

"I'll pull out every third squadron of chariots and form a flying battalion behind our lines to rush in should any break appear," she added with growing confidence.

"A good plan, Meave," Aileel said, "but it will take more than that to keep the Ulstermen from breaking through!"

"Then I will go myself! I'll take our household troops and every other man still in the camp. I'll see the Red Branch driven back."

"There is an easier way, my Queen," Calatin said.

"Be out of this, Enchanter," Aileel grated. "We've no time now for your plotting."

"Wait, Aileel," Meave said. "Calatin has knowledge in war. Tell me your thoughts, but do it quickly."

"Of course, my Queen. Your tactics might retain our line, but they'll not win this day. Only the Exiles can insure that."

"The Exiles!" Aileel said in disbelief. "They'll not fight. Were you not listening, man?"

"They can be made to fight. I can convince them." The druid stepped closer to Meave. "It is the only way."

"No, Meave," said Aileel warningly. "Fergus will never listen to him . . ."

"It is the only way," Calatin repeated in a soft and reassuring voice. "Fergus will listen."

"The Enchanter plots some trickery," Aileel cried.

"My Queen, I can convince them," Calatin said again, insistently.

"All right, Calatin," she decided. "I must act now to use our men to good advantage. You try to deal with Fergus, but do it swiftly. We've very little time."

"I will," he promised and strode away. But he did not go directly to the Exiles. He made his way first to his own tent.

While Meave and Calatin went about their work, the Exiles sat impassively and watched the battle raging on the Plain of Fremain. Fergus MacRogh, now mounted in his chariot of war, took position before his men, the chariots of his chieftains at his sides. All were satisfied with his decision to hold back unless the host was threatened with destruction. All, that is, save Duvac Dael Ulla who rode back and forth madly before his battalion, raging loudly at being thus restrained.

Cormac eyed the emotionless commander for a time in puzzlement. Then he leaned toward Fergus over his chariot bulwark to speak in confidence to him.

"Fergus, tell me, why did you change your mind?"

"Our ard-druid it was who helped me decide," Fergus told his friend, smiling with the irony of it, "though he'd choke with rage to know it. He said we were alike in hating Ulster. When I heard that from him, I knew it was not so."

"Look there!" a warrior beside them cried then, lifting an arm to point.

The chieftains turned to look and saw a new contingent of men moving out from their camp toward the hard-pressed center of the line.

"The queen is leading them herself!" said Cormac. "Fergus, do you think she can defeat the Red Branch?"

"She can if she uses her own skills. She is as trained to command as any one of us. I hope she is not acting on that Enchanter's advice. I wonder what's become of him in this? He's not with Meave."

"You'll not have to wonder long," Cormac observed dryly, looking back toward the camp. "I see your great comrade is coming now, and his pet horrors with him."

"But, what is it they've got with them?" Fergus asked as he watched Calatin and his clan approach, for each of the sons carried a tremendous urn, so large that some of the weakling lads could barely manage to bear the load.

"MacRogh," the druid hailed as he drew near. "You've not yet seen fit to commit your men."

His tones were almost hearty, and the suspicions of Fergus and Cormac were aroused at once.

"Our actions are nothing to you, Enchanter," Cormac replied. "Be off with you now, and take your questionable offspring with you. The sight of them disturbs our horses."

Unruffled by this insult, Calatin smiled serenely.

"Ah, but it's wrong you are, Conlingas. Your actions are everything to me. I'm advisor to the queen and wish her success, yet she'll not gain it while her best force sits idle, watching the rest be torn apart."

"You're far from her protection now, my friend," Fergus pointed out quite casually. "I'd think to watch my words."

"I've little fear of you and your mindless herd of bulls," the druid replied, still with a softness of tone and a graciousness of smile that were in peculiar contrast to his words.

"But, still, you've come to beg our mindless aid,"

Cormac noted. "Perhaps so you'll look more a hero to the queen?"

"We'll say I've come to ask you again to fight."

"And if we refuse?" asked Fergus.

"Then I'll be free to use other means to weaken Ulster's attack."

That angered Cormac. "Such methods are a coward's way!"

"You're wrong, Cormac," Calatin reasoned calmly. "Any means are legitimate ones when you champions refuse to fight."

"And what are these great vessels your sons have?" Fergus asked with curiosity. He looked along the line of sons which had formed across the front of his Exiles' ranks. "Have you brought something be bribe us with?"

"Oh, these?" Calatin said nonchalantly, waving his hand vaguely over them. "Why, yes, to be putting it in your own, crude terms. I brought them in hopes of leading you to change your minds."

"Well, you've made your error then, druid," Fergus told him. "We'll not fight as long as Meave can hold her own. And that she'll do if you'll keep from hampering her."

"I see," Calatin said, apparently amused. "I thought it would be so. But, let us at least show your men what we've brought. They might determine to change their minds in spite of what you say!"

At these words the clan began to pull the leather coverings from each of their urns.

"Don't be wasting their time or ours," Fergus protested, but the sons finished their work, revealing a dark, shiny substance within the vessels.

"What is that, now?" asked Cormac with surprise, for he had expected to see the gleam of metal riches there.

"This is a liquor, more powerful and more precious than any gold. It's made by me with seeds of the earth and fire. Here, look!" He lifted an urn toward the two chieftains while his sons moved through the ranks carrying the other vessels as if to display the liquid to all the men.

"It has a pungent smell," said Cormac, noting that the vessels all exuded the aroma strongly, filling the air about.

Suddenly Fergus knew that some dark treachery lay hidden in this. Without warning he swung his arm and knocked the vessel from Calatin's hands to the ground. It smashed, spreading the liquid in a wide pool that sent up its aroma even more strongly.

"You're seeking to make my men drunk and then lead them to the fight," Fergus cried, pulling his sword.

"Oh, no, Fergus," Calatin assured him airily. "The inhaling of my liquor is more than enough. And you'll not be led. You'll wish to fight. Does not that very desire rise in you now?"

Fergus saw the Enchanter's face laughing up at him and leaned forward to strike out at it with his sword. But the face suddenly grew dim and was replaced by confused images.

"See, now?" the druid's voice came to him with the soft confidence of a parent soothing a bewildered child. "You've no desire to use that sword on the likes of me. No, it's Ulster that's your enemy. Think, Fergus! Think what Ulster has done to you!"

At those words the memories flooded back to him. The images became clear. Once more he watched Conchobar break the guarantee of safety made by him, destroying innocent lads out of treachery, killing Fergus's own son. Once more he relived the bloody war of rebellion against the king and the ignominious expulsion from Ulster. And, with him, all of the Exiles relived the shame and sorrow of their casting out. The beauties of the Ulster they had lost grew bright to them, and they ached for their homeland. Cries of rage and anguish went up from many and weapons were drawn and brandished throughout the battalions.

"Now is your time!" Calatin shouted to them. "Now Ulster is before you. Your chance is come at last. Your unforgiving sword is in your hand and your heart is iron in your breast. Go and destroy the Red Branch. Let none of them survive!"

Sped by their anger, the Exiles surged forward. Mindless with rage they struck against the right wing of Ulster's line, their infantry slashing savagely into the flank. The resistance there was weak, for the better warriors had been drawn off to feed the assault on Eire's center, and the Exiles quickly broke through Ulster's astonished ranks. At once Fergus ordered in his flying squadrons of chariots to tear open the gap, with himself leading them.

"All scythes out!" he cried to the wedge of chariots behind him. "Attack!"

The gleaming blades were almost touching side to side as the machines swept into the broken line of Ulster infantry, cutting down all in their path. In confusion born of blind terror, the warriors turned and ran. In moments Fergus and his men found themselves behind the Ulster ranks with no one to challenge them.

"To the gateway in the ramparts," he commanded. "Cut off Ulster's retreat and we'll have them all!"

As the Exiles moved to obey, King Conchobar of the Red Branch, fighting in the center of his lines, saw what was happening. Like Fergus he understood at once that his army might now be easily trapped. The gates were poorly defended, for most of the able warriors fought on the plains. Should the Exiles manage to seize and hold those gates, the Red Branch would have no avenue of retreat.

Giving orders for the whole host to begin a slow withdrawal, King Conchobar quickly gathered a company of good men and rushed to the wide, central gates of the rampart, determined to hold them open for his men. He reached them simultaneously with the first of the Exile forces, and there a vicious and a desperate battle ensued, each side knowing that here lay the key to victory or loss.

Though outnumbered, Conchobar held back the attackers. At first his driver skillfully guided the chariot against those of the Exiles while the king, with tireless precision, struck down the warriors within. But soon the pressure of men grew so great that the vehicles had no room to maneuver. Both sides dismounted and fought on foot, the battle now becoming a melee of men and flashing weapons.

Fergus, directing the assault elsewhere, soon took notice of this knot of men before the central gates who so successfully held his own at bay. His rage increased and, heedless of the danger, he ordered his own chariot in at attack speed.

He drew back the scythes to keep from cutting down his own men, then climbed onto the pole, walking out to stand between the steeds' heads, sword ready. As they drove into the throng, he called a warning and his warriors moved back out of the chariot's path.

The force of Red Branch warriors cried out in victory, thinking the Exiles had withdrawn. They started forward until, in that opened avenue, they saw the figure of their once-sworn friend laying death about him as his vehicle swept down upon them.

Deep into their ranks it drove, and Fergus leaped from the chariot-pole, swinging his sword in a great circle with such heavy strokes that soon a space was opened on all sides. He moved ahead, the bloodlust on him now, crying his revenge on Ulster.

Then before him appeared a figure who did not move back at his dreadful coming, but stood and faced him squarely.

He stopped and peered at it. His rage and the streaming sweat from his labors had half-blinded him so that the tall warrior who faced him was only a dim shape.

"Who are you to stand before me now when all your warriors have run away?" he demanded. "Are you some madman to challenge me?"

And then he heard a voice answer him, calm and cold and too familiar to his ears.

"The man you face is the same man who took from you your sovereignty, who slew the sons of Usna and your own son, who seized your lands, and cast you out of Ulster like a wolf."

"Conchobar," grated Fergus.

"Aye, MacRogh. I made you an exile and a woman's servant, and today I will kill you."

"I know you to your treacherous heart," Fergus thundered, "and I've wanted nothing but to have you in my reach. Raise your shield, son of Nessa, or I'll kill you where you stand."

The two rushed together, while around them all the other fighting stopped. Ulsterman and Exile alike saw that here their own part of this war had found its center. For them the battle on the plain had little meaning now.

Beneath the dirt embankment of the fortification, in the broad, flat gap before the gates, the two men fought. No greater hatreds had yet motivated the combatants in all this war so far. Madness of a kind lay on both men, and a desire for nothing but to be rid of this one enemy for all time. No thoughts of country or tribe were in their minds here. Just a personal need.

Thus they fought with a strange abandon and fearlessness, striking blindly, giving and taking massive, cutting blows that only seemed to enrage them further.

For long the battle wavered back and forth, neither gaining any advantage. But before Fergus MacRogh there hung the constant image of Conchobar's treachery and that seemed to fuel him to greater efforts while the strain began to tell upon the king.

Conchobar begun to fight desperately, knowing his strength was failing him. On the defensive, he tried to back away, but Fergus was relentless, striking wildly and continuously as he advanced, and Conchobar reeled before his wrath.

A blow sent the Ard-Rie of Ulster staggering and another knocked his sword from his hands. He tried to defend himself with his shield, but the swiftly flashing blade of Fergus beat him to his knees and lifted to make its fatal stroke.

"Fergus!" a voice cried from above.

The cry seemed to reach through his madness to his real mind and he hesitated.

"Fergus," it cried again and, this time, he lifted his eyes to find the source of it.

Above him, on the wall beside the gates, Cuculain stood.

Chapter Thirty
LUGH OF THE LONG ARM

Since his arrival in Ulster's camp, Cuculain had rested alone.

At dawn, when the Red Branch formed to fight again, Laeg went to the tent assigned his master to help him prepare. He found Cuculain awake but in a staring, motionless state from which it seemed nothing could stir him.

The charioteer, deeply concerned, left his master to rest on and watched the Ulstermen go forth to battle without the very champion who had given them new will. Laeg himself hoped that the odd, trancelike repose came only from the great fatigue on Cuculain and would soon pass. Yet as the sun rose higher in the iron-gray sky, his hopes turned into fears.

Impatiently he strode the avenue before his master's tent and watched the battle raging on the plain. He had no way of knowing what to do, and that frustration brought him close to ranting at the peculiar fates now binding them. He thought of Cuculain's words to Sualtim—that their return might only help destroy an already beaten host—and despair came upon him more and more.

He noted, then, that Ulster seemed to hold its own. Indeed, it was driving in the center of the host of Meave. He rejoiced, thinking that the need for his weakened master might not come.

But his cheer was short-lived for, from the right, a new force struck the Ulster lines. A powerful and ferocious attack it was, rending and scattering the Red Branch

warriors like a pack of wolves would a herd of grazing
sheep. They drove right through the ranks in moments
and sped their chariots onward to Ulster's very ramparts.

In helpless rage Laeg watched them come, and then an
even greater shock came to him as he saw that these were
the exiled men of Ulster, and led by Fergus MacRogh
himself.

He ran to Cuculain's tent and pushed inside. The
resting man still lay face up and unmoving on the rugs,
only his even breathing showing that he lived. Laeg shook
the warrior and leaned close to speak into his ear.

"Cuculain, rise! The Exiles are come to make revenge
on Ulster and all our army is in confusion. Eire will seize
the gates and have the Red Branch trapped, and only you
and I are here to stop them."

The warrior stirred. His staring eyes shifted to fix
blankly on Laeg, and his lips moved.

"No, no . . ." he protested feebly. "I'll not fight them
alone . . . no . . . not alone! Find someone else to bleed.
Kill someone else's friends . . ."

These vague ramblings were unclear to Laeg. He shook
Cuculain again, but his friend did not rouse further.

"Cuculain, you must get up," the charioteer cried out
in despair. "Here, I will get your chariot and your armor.
Please, try to get up!"

Hoping that the sight of his equipment of war might
bring a fighting spirit back to his master, Laeg rushed
from the tent, leaving Cuculain alone.

The young warrior watched him go with little care or
understanding of what happened now. He was too tired,
his strength gone, his mind clouded with strange
thoughts. Images whirled there; of Einey and Laeg, of
Fardia and all the other men he had killed. There were
many dead faces. He did not know the names of most and
it disturbed him that he did not. Why had they died? Why
had he survived?

Einey had told him that he had to do that which he
did. But, what made it so? He wanted no more of it. No
more blood. No more dead faces in his mind.

"That cannot be," a voice said to him.

Startled by an answer to his thoughts, Cuculain lifted

himself on his arms and looked across the tent. Just inside
its doors a figure stood; a familiar figure in a shimmering
gray cloak, pale face glowing as the moon.

"Faythleen," he breathed. "What is it you want here?"

"It's time for you to fight, Sentanta. You've come to
this place for that very thing. Why do you hesitate now?"

"I've no more will to fight, Faythleen. In these past
days I've done too many things that have brought me
pain."

"You have," she agreed, her voice caressing with its
sympathy. "But your fair strength has healed all your
wounds."

"It's healed my body . . . not my mind and heart. There
I have pain that throbs and tightens on itself like a knot
drawn always tauter. The things I've done, the many men
I've killed have given me these wounds, and I've seen my
labors come to no purpose. The war goes on and on.
Well, it can end itself without me now. I've enough of
it!"

Faythleen seemed puzzled, and it was a strange emotion to see clouding the face of one of the powerful
Sidhe.

"I've no understanding of you in this," she said. "Your
purpose has always been to fight. It's why you've been in
it since the beginning."

"Since the beginning?" he repeated with surprise, but
then he nodded wearily with comprehension. "Aye, now I
see. It was for this you made your appointment with me
at Tara. You meant it as a way of bringing me before the
host of Meave. And why me?"

"There was only you with power enough to act that
could escape the madness laid across all Ulster."

"And why did you not tell me that in the beginning?"

"Would you have come, knowing a force would invade
Ulster, knowing what things you might have to do? No.
You would have gone to Emain Macha to raise the Red
Branch and been trapped there as were the rest."

"Perhaps," he conceded, but then an anger seized him
and his voice hardened. "But you've done nothing here
except to tell me that what I've suspected is true. This
was not my own doing. I was directed here by you. How

much of my whole life has been the same; killing men for some purpose I don't understand?"

"You are a warrior."

"I am a man, with my own will!"

"You are more than a man, Cuculain," said another voice, and a man stepped into the tent door to stand beside Faythleen.

She seemed relieved to see him, and it was clear that he was one of the Sidhe, like herself.

He was a tall, lean man, clad simply in a white tunic and a gray-green cloak that glistened with lights like dew upon a meadow. His face spoke of years of life without a sign of age, his light gray eyes were sure with knowledge, his bearing was erect and casually proud with uncounted years of carried authority.

"Who are you?" asked Cuculain, not certain if he wished the answer or not. "You are a stranger to me, yet I feel I know you."

"I am Lugh of the Long Arm."

Cuculain's face clouded with concern. "Is it the truth you tell me now?"

"It is, and you do know me . . . in your heart."

"No! I do not!" Cuculain's denial was vehement. "I've nothing to do with you."

"You do," the man insisted in a gentle way. "It is a part of us you are. Our blood flows in your body."

"It cannot be." Cuculain hid his face in his hands, unable to think clearly. "Rumors they are. I know my mother, and my father."

"Sualtim is a good man," Lugh replied sincerely, "but he knew the truth well enough. It almost destroyed his mind . . . until you helped him. But he knew the truth, and you know it too, young Hound."

Cuculain lifted his head and looked to the man, tears filling his gray eyes. There was great anguish revealed in that youthful face, but now belief was revealed there, too.

"And, if your blood does run in my poor veins?" he asked. "Does that, then, mean my soul belongs to you? Is that why I was conceived . . . to be a tool for your own ends?"

The Champion of the Sidhe shook his head sadly. "My son, we've never meant to give you pain. We have only good intentions for mankind. Your mortals are a noble race with much potential. You are the proper inheritors of this land. It's for that reason we withdrew into our secret places. But, still, we wish to help you when we can. And, though there is little we can do to act openly in your affairs, we can direct, advise, or warn. That's why you are so valuable a man, both to us and to your mortals. Through you, we can have an instrument; a link with the events of the world and a means of influencing them."

"And what of Cuculain?" the young warrior asked ruefully. "Does he just act as he is led, like the very hound whose name he bears, led on a leash?" He laughed scornfully. "A fit name . . . 'Cuculain.' Was it you who led me to have that, too? And, my skill . . . was it your power that gave me my doubtful virtue of being the foremost killer of men?"

"Those questions have no simple answer, my son. The Sidhe control no man, not even you. Our blood is in you, and from that your power is increased. Our thoughts and our actions direct you at times, but only to the good of all."

"Ah, what fine excuses you make! You did not think that my own will, my own mind might rebel?"

At this Lugh laughed grimly.

"Better it might have been if your mind had not developed as did your strength and skill. We did not think of it, but we should have. You are much Sidhe in all ways."

"Except in my knowledge. Your purposes are still all unknown to me. As I can see there is no earthly reason for what happens here. I'll not fight more without my own cause."

Lugh met his eyes a moment and saw the determination in them. He nodded.

"Would it help you, then, to know there is a purpose in all of this? A great and a deadly purpose?"

"Not if it is not my own. A senseless war between the provinces is no longer enough."

"It is far more than that!" Lugh assured him. "Something dangerous is at work here. Something that cares not

who wins or loses your war but threatens all of Eire. No
warrior of Meave or Ulster is your enemy."

"I don't understand. Who is it, then?"

"There is a separate force. You know it is abroad.
You've felt it yourself, have you not?"

He had. How often had he wondered what twisted
spirit was at work. How often had he felt the cold horror
of some presence moving against him.

"I see by your dark looks that you do know," Lugh
went on. "You know I am speaking the truth. You know
how great a power it is we face."

"I do," he admitted reluctantly. "But, what does it
mean?"

"It means you must fight now. Your conscience is
hard. It stopped you from fighting in a senseless war. But
can the same conscience let you stay idle while Eire and
your own way of life are destroyed?"

Cuculain's hands clasped tightly together as he fought
a silent battle in his mind. Finally he looked up, his face
expressionless.

"I will go, but against my will and without any happiness in what I do."

"No one has asked you to be happy in this, and your
own will must be satisfied in your own way. But, remember: we only wish to stop this war and have tried to do so
from the start. Our hope has been that you would help us
end it, but the choice to do so can only come from within
yourself. We cannot force you to it."

"And what is it I must do?"

"You must stop the fighting. Find the real enemy."

"I will," Cuculain said. He got to his feet and lifted his
cloak to fasten about his shoulders, then turned back
toward the two. "And who is the real enemy in . . ." he
began, but stopped.

Faythleen and Lugh Lamfada were now gone.

Cuculain moved to the doors and looked out. The
camp avenues were deserted save for Laeg who had
drawn up the chariot-of-war and had unloaded his master's armor.

"You are up!" the charioteer said with rejoicing.

"Aye. Did you see them leaving?"

"I saw no one," Laeg replied with puzzlement. "All are at the battle. What did you want?"

"One final answer," his master said, then shrugged. "Well, we must move swiftly now. Bring in my armor."

Is short moments Cuculain and Laeg raced their chariot toward the main gateways. Much of the strange fatigue was gone from the young warrior, and what remained, throbbing within him like a dull knot of pain, he forced his mind to ignore.

They reached the gates and he dismounted, sword in hand. He climbed the earthen rampart overlooking the gateway to gauge the progress of the battle below. In shock he saw Fergus MacRogh, seemingly mad with rage, raise his weapon above a kneeling Conchobar to deliver a killing blow.

In desperation Cuculain called to his old friend and the man's eyes, clouded with anger and bewilderment, rose to him.

Chapter Thirty-One
CONFRONTATION

"Fergus, stop!" Cuculain cried. "That man before you is not your enemy in this!"

The voice was familiar to Fergus, and he stared up at the figure on the rampart above him. He could not see it clearly in the bloody haze that hung before his eyes, but something about it seemed to make no sense to him. Those men he attacked here were his enemies, but the voice was that of a friend. He hesitated and his sword dropped as his mind struggled to understand the conflicting impressions. He shook his great head angrily, and it helped to dissipate the haze, for the figure above came suddenly clear to him.

"Cuculain!" he shouted in astonishment. "You are not dead?"

The young Hound realized that he had to be careful. The uncontrolled rage which filled his old friend's eyes told him that something had taken the reason of Fergus from him. Cuculain knew he had to find a way to bring the Exile back to his full sense.

"I am alive, Fergus. I've come to stop this war."

"This war?" the Exile bellowed angrily as the blind hatred tried to win back full control of him again. "Nothing can stop it until all Ulster is destroyed."

"Think what you're saying, Fergus," Cuculain implored. "Are those the words of the same man who told me that he, too, would see this bloodshed end? Is the man who plotted with me at the Oun Dia to keep Meave from Ulster the same one who now leads his men to threaten our gates and insure our total annihilation?"

267

Confused by these words, Fergus looked about him as if seeing his surroundings for the first time. He realized he stood before the ramparts of Ulster. He saw the piled dead and the bloody sword in his hand. Finally his eyes rested upon the man who knelt before him, returning his gaze with stony resignation.

As he looked at Conchobar, the rage in the Exile began to fade, to be replaced by a deeper uncertainty. He felt he had good cause to hate this man, to kill him, but the mad impulse to do so had now gone. The painful memories that had led him there faded and only the bewilderment remained.

Once more he looked upward. Now fully recognizing Cuculain, he seized upon him as the only source of solid reality in the whirling cloud of tangled images that buffeted him like a physical wind.

"Cu, what has happened?" he asked. "What are we doing here?"

Cuculain felt immense relief. The man who spoke now was the one he knew.

"Ah, Fergus, it's glad I am to hear those words. No sane man would have acted as you did. Your men came against us here as if possessed. What power could drive you to this?"

At that the confusion in Fergus was dispelled as the madness had been. His full senses returned to him once again and, with them, the memory of what had happened: the urns, the strange liquid, and the druid's face grinning up at him.

"Cuculain," he said grimly, "I thank the gods myself that you are alive. You saved us from something that was not of our will!" He looked down upon the kneeling Conchobar. "Rise, Ard-Rie. I'll not be killing you this day."

Suspicion in his black eyes, the king arose and faced his old captain.

"And have you had such a change of heart, my friend?"

Fergus laughed in scorn. "No, 'my friend.' Someday you and I will be finishing this. But when we do it will be by my own choice, and for my own reasons."

"No one could wish to hear that more than I," Conchobar replied, smiling himself now. "Such an appointment with you I'll gladly keep."

Fergus turned to his men. They too had felt the battle madness fade in them, leaving only emptiness behind. They stared about them blankly at their cousins with whom they had been engaged in savage combat only moments before and searched their memories to find how they had come to be there.

"Exiles, we will withdraw," Fergus commanded. "This is not our fight."

None of them argued with him, for their will for further combat had drained from them along with their madness. Even the blazing fury of Duvac Dael Ulla seemed much banked, and he meekly turned his chariot and joined the others as they rode back toward the camp of Meave.

"Thank you, Cuculain," Fergus called to his young friend. "We'll take part no longer in this battle. I know now it was Calatin's will, not ours. Good fortune ride with you!"

The name "Calatin" echoed strangely in Cuculain's mind. He wished to know more and shouted after the Exile:

"Wait, Fergus, who is this Calatin?"

But Fergus did not hear. He was already too far away, mounting into his chariot and turning it to follow after his men.

Cuculain entered his own vehicle and directed Laeg to drive out through the gates. There he joined Conchobar, who was still perplexed by Fergus's strange behavior and stood staring after the retreating men.

"The Fool-of-the-Forth has touched them all," he exclaimed. "They had us all but trapped, and now he draws them back. Why did they not take their revenge? I would have done so."

Cuculain looked coldly at his king. "Perhaps Fergus is a different man than you."

This seemed lost on Conchobar. He only laughed derisively and said: "Then a fool he is for certain. Look there, the whole host of Meave is thrown aback by him."

Conchobar was right. The sudden withdrawal of the Exiles on the brink of victory had confused the army of Eire. Certain that some powerful force must have attacked the Exiles to so quickly drive them off, many of the warriors took fear. Other officers ordered their units to join in the retreat until, suddenly, the entire army was breaking off the fight and pulling back to re-form near their camp's edge.

The ravaged force of Ulster, so unexpectedly left alone, was too weakened to do anything but stand amazed, looking after its attackers and thanking the gods for its life.

"I've no understanding of this," said Conchobar, "but we've been saved at the end of our strength. Come, Cuculain. We must organize our battalions while we have the chance."

King and champion rode then into the shattered ranks, gathering officers, issuing orders, and drawing the men back to re-form before their earthen ramparts.

Finally, the parted forces of grim and battered warriors faced one another across the bloody plain. Both sides were exhausted and uncertain now, and both waited silently to see what would happen next. Neither side was anxious to renew the costly struggle quickly. Indeed, many men hoped deep within their hearts that it was near an end.

From his high platform before the royal tent, Aileel had listened intently to the battle's progress as described to him by a young bard. The camp about them was deserted, all others having followed Meave into the desperate fight. Only one other man was there: the ard-druid. He paced the ground before the dais as he kept his own scrutinizing eye upon the fight.

"The Exiles battle with savagery and recklessness," the young fili reported to the king. "They've won all the ground to the gates of Ulster's ramparts."

Then, without a warning, the Exiles turned away and began their retreat. The druid, who had watched with satisfaction until this sudden change, stopped and noted the unforeseen reversal with disbelief.

"Fergus has pulled them back," he cried venomously.

"His mighty Exiles lack the courage to finish their own, worst enemy."

"Their worst enemy is below me now, I think," said Aileel.

"What do you mean, old man?" Calatin asked him callously for, alone as they were now, the druid left off all pretense of homage to the king.

"They had chosen not to fight and there is little in this world that would make their minds change," the king judged shrewdly. "It must have been your black arts that drove them to fight with such madness."

"And if that is so?" Calatin challenged. "They were traitors to Eire. I did what needed to be done. The methods I used are of no matter."

"But they are, Enchanter. The actions of Fergus were honorable, even if they were not to our ends. Your actions were an attempt to have him compromise that honor. It's once too often you've used such trickery. I'll have no more of it."

Calatin had been but half-listening to this point, absorbed still with the actions on the plain. But these last words brought him around to look up at the king with mild astonishmest.

"You'll have no more of it?" he repeated, then laughed aloud. "Don't you know how hollow those words are? If you've no awareness of it yet, I'll tell you now: you have no power in this. It's Meave who rules, with my help, and only my influence carries weight with her."

"Do you say so?" Aileel pulled himself up proudly. His bent shoulders lifted and he came erect, displaying that breadth of frame that had made him a giant warrior once.

"It may be you've put your hold upon her," he continued, "and managed to cut her off from all others. But I am still her husband and the king. I'll tell her of your devious ways. She'll listen, and she'll not condone them. Fergus and I will wrest her trust from you."

"Fergus!" Calatin spat out the word like an oath. "You still defend the honor of that man. He's no friend to you. He's brought dishonor into your own dun and made a fool of you. He's tried to usurp your power for himself along with the love of your own wife!"

If the druid thought to hurt the king with this cruel revelation, he failed. Aileel only looked in pity on the man and spoke in words made heavy with disgust.

"It's you who are the fool, you poor, sly sorcerer. I know what there has been between Meave and Fergus. I've known of it since its start and been well pleased. I am a dying man and Meave is young. No better partner could I have picked for her. Never has she caused me any pain, nor has either of them thought to dishonor me. Only you would try that with your filthy tricks. But you've accomplished nothing except to prove how honorless a man you are." Aileel smiled with self-assurance. "Well, you'll not be using your ways again. When Meave returns, she'll know what you've tried."

"So, the old gray-feathered crow still has some flight left in his battered wings," Calatin said thoughtfully. "Still, I'd not count on your words influencing Meave."

"You'll not prevent me, Enchanter," Aileel told the druid confidently.

But had the dimness not laid upon the king's eyes, he would have realized that Calatin was beginning to move purposefully toward the royal dais, grim lines hardening his face.

It was thus that neither of these men noted a chariot-of-war entering the camp below them. It had returned directly from the fight ahead of all the others bearing Fergus MacRogh with but a single purpose in his mind: to find the ard-druid.

For all the battle-madness that had been upon the Exile in the conflict just past, none who had faced him would have denied that now his aspect was yet more terrible. Many ills had that proud man suffered in his life, but no one had ever forced him to act against his will. For such a violation of his spirit, the accounting could not be too swiftly made.

As his vehicle rumbled up the deserted avenues of the camp, the chieftain's gaze swept balefully about him, seeking the Enchanter. Finally he glimpsed the figures of Aileel and Calatin before the royal pavilion. He commanded his charioteer to drive toward them and the man urged the horses ahead in a full run. As they charged into the open space in front of the dais, Fergus leapt from the rolling car before the driver could bring the straining team to a full halt. With his longsword swinging in his hand he stalked toward the druid, head down, body tense, eyes fixed upon the object of his hatred.

Calatin had whirled as the first sound of the chariot had reached him. Initially he had been startled by this unexpected intrusion, for he had assumed all were still engaged in ordering the tangle on the plain. But that expression gave way to one of calm command as he recognized that it was Fergus who approached.

"You failed, MacRogh," he said accusingly.

Stunned by this extraordinary statement, the chieftain stopped as abruptly as a charging bull colliding with a high, stone wall.

"I failed?" he said. "It was your trickery failed, Enchanter. You've no longer any hold upon my men."

The druid showed no dismay at these words. Though puzzled by the failure of his spell and faced now with two accusing enemies, he only met Fergus's eyes levelly and replied to him as if he did not comprehend.

"What are you saying, Fergus? You had the men of Ulster. You could have destroyed them and had your revenge. I gave that chance to you and you denied it."

"A chance was it?" the Exile bellowed. "A command it was! There was nothing of our revenge in it. All of that came from you. Your bloody sorcery drove us into it. Well no more. You hear me? No more!"

He stepped close to the druid and his sword rose to threaten, but Calatin did not move.

"We pledged to conquer Ulster," he reminded Fergus with a quiet voice. "I kept that pledge. You did not. I was only doing what I had to do."

"It was far more than that you did!" the Exile said. "I should have seen your part in this long since. I should have suspected it when you were boasting of the madness you'd put on Ulster. But your throwing a like madness on me was the proof. You've been making use of us from the start!"

"I've no understanding of what it is you mean, Mac-Rogh," Calatin told him.

"I think you do, Enchanter. Seeing the way my men and I were tricked so easily gave me answers to many things I'd never understood, like our expulsion from Cuailgne and Dary's challenge to Meave. Those were your doing too."

"And what makes you so certain of it?" the druid countered.

"Why the whole thing smells of you," Fergus grated, looking Calatin up and down with distaste as if some vileness wafted from him now. "It was you who first brought the bull of Ulster to Meave's notice. It was you who suggested the bargain be made. But you planned then that it should go awry."

"How might I have done that?" Calatin asked, apparently intrigued by Fergus's deductions.

The Exile eyed his adversary speculatively a moment, then began a restless pacing as he went over his thoughts.

"It would not have been difficult for you. No wonder that you asked to go after the bull alone. You could easily enough have begun some argument with Dary. Simpler yet; you might have never gone to Dun Cuailgne and then reported to Meave that he had challenged her." He stopped and looked at the druid, smiling grimly. "How angry you must have been when I was chosen to go to Cuailgne too. It forced you to act in some other way. Still, it worked out better than you could have hoped. How was it done, Enchanter? What spell did you put on that honorable king?"

Calatin smiled slightly in return. He seemed to find amusement in this game.

"Your reasoning impresses me, MacRogh, but you underestimate me. I needed no spells for such as Dary. His own pride worked against him, as pride always does. A foolish old man was easily brought to believe my words; a man who Dary had no cause to doubt."

At this a forgotten image returned to Fergus's mind. It was the image of an ancient, trusted servant of Dary's house whom he had seen speaking with Calatin in the empty hall of Dun Cuailgne.

"Feogh!" he cried. "You used him to make Dary believe we meant him some harm. At every move we have been betrayed!"

"Betrayed do you call it?" the druid responded, not with anger but only with the tones of a man deeply

offended. "And do you call the defense of Eire betrayal?
It's refusing to fight for her that's a traitor's act, Mac-
Rogh. Each means I've used was used for Eire's good."

"Her good?" Fergus pointed his brown-stained blade
toward the plain below. "Look there, man! How can that
carnage be for her good?"

"Who was it did not want this war?" Calatin asked in
turn. "Who was it argued against it? No one! All of them
welcomed an excuse to war upon Ulster. What I've done
was wished by all of Eire!"

A small uncertainty surfaced in the Exile's mind,
throwing a ripple of disquiet across the whole of it like a
rising fish might in a quiet pond. Was there truth in the
Enchanter's words? But how could the acts that he had
judged so evil seem suddenly to have some sense to
them?

"The best ends of Eire mean little to you," he accused,
trying to freshen his assault and shake off this feeling of
perplexity. "It's power only that you're after."

The druid's response was a reasonable one, made in a
soft but an insistent voice.

"No, MacRogh. It may seem I've wanted power, but I
want none of it for myself. It's the glory of Eire I wish
realized."

As he listened to this, Fergus felt a sudden conviction
that the druid was speaking from his most honest self. He
was drawn to listen more, to understand what thoughts
lay hidden behind Calatin's calculating front.

"You see, I seek a different Eire than this one," the
quiet voice rolled on. "Mine is a place at peace, a place of
wealth and ease for everyone. Law and justice embrace
all tuaths and duns in one, spreading government. Men of
law administer contracts, arbitrate disputes, see to the
rights of everyone, not just a few. No more do champions
and battles decide the right. No more does property
belong to the strongest arm and the sharpest sword. Wars
are reduced and your warriors replaced by craftsmen of
all kinds."

This speech held Fergus's attention fully. Now he was
certain that the druid revealed his true motives, and he
looked in wonder at the world Calatin had created with
his words. The vision of it glowed there before him within

the Enchanter's eyes. It seemed to light his own mind like sparks leaping to kindle a new fire.

Calatin moved closer to him then, his eyes still fixed upon the Exile, his voice convincing, assuring.

"Fergus, I've been in many places in the world. I've seen powerful civilizations rising, but I have never seen one with the potential for greatness that Eire has. She could rise, if she could be united. But until her people act for a single end, that greatness will be denied!"

Fergus listened and found some truth in this. It was fine to think of an Eire that challenged all the world with its united strength. He had himself once hoped for such an end. Still, something in the image troubled him.

"Then, this war on Ulster was meant by you to bring them to submission to the will of the rest of Eire?"

"Certainly, Fergus," the druid said. "All those others who joined with this host see the need of that. Ulster, aloof and arrogant, stands in the way of Eire's unity. As long as she defies us, we will be divided. Her foolish pride must be quenched forever, and only you stand in the way of it."

"I?" Fergus said with deep concern.

"Only you have hindered our ends. We fight for our future, yet you chastize me for using my means to bring this war to a swift end, even when it's you who have delayed that end again and again. Think of the sense in that, MacRogh. Ulster is your greatest enemy, yet your pride and your loyalties have prolonged a bloody war. Tell me then: who is the villain here?"

Fergus was confounded. He had been so certain of the druid's treachery. Yet somehow Calatin's reasoning had twisted the meanings until now it seemed that treachery was his.

"Cease to fight me, Fergus," the druid cajoled. "We're on the same side in this. Help me defeat the Red Branch and there will be no further need for war. Eire will be one!"

Now was Fergus nearly drawn fully within the cloud of seeming logic which Calatin had skillfully wrapped around him. He saw nothing but the clear vision of a united land that needed only his help to be realized. But then that image was overlaid by another. It was the image of a thin, weary young man, standing defiantly upon a rampart alone. Fergus remembered that same youth bloodied, abandoned, fighting friends and enemies sent against him. Again, as at the rampart, the reality of what Cuculain had done helped Fergus to see the real truth.

"You are a sorcerer who makes day of the night," he told the druid. "But you'll not be deceiving me again, not with your spells or your beguiling tongue. Your glowing vision hides a black reality. You spin dreams of peace and justice, yet your every act has been to crush our will. You've no way to disguise the evil in your acts, and I'll not become a part of them. Better Ulster free and Eire divided than to have your ways used again."

At these words the druid's manner was transformed with the swiftness of a late autumn day when the soft warmth is swept away by the chill bite of a winter wind. His eyes narrowed and glittered with a new, hard light.

"Then, fool, you will perish with the rest." He looked with arrogance upon the Exile. "I knew you would never understand. You are as dangerous and as much a hindrance to me as Ulster, or any of your odious kind. But I will see the end of brutal, mindless heroes. Their breed will vanish utterly before the sane power of my new order. As were the Fomeroh destroyed by the Tuatha, so will the proud warriors, so restless and so barren as the clouds, perish before the might of ollavs and druids. In my Eire the people will see that rule by the sword is savagery. They will know you as you are: mindless devastators."

"And once we are destroyed," Fergus asked, "what then? What is it you'll have left to people your new world? Nothing but soulless beings without courage, doing what they are told and afraid to lift their eyes to see the stars burning so separate and so bright. A land without pride or honor that would surely be!"

"Honor?" the druid echoed savagely. "That's your excuse for irresponsibility. It is a symbol of the independence and simplicity of the warrior. It represents the overweaning pride that is so dangerous, that keeps Eire a land of warring clans. Honor is a chain that tangles and confounds. Look at yourself, MacRogh. All your life you've tried to satisfy it and been caught between conflicting loyalties each time. Honor destroys. It killed your friends and even your son. It can be used against you. Look at this war. I only needed to provide the spark for it. I knew your own honor would feed the blaze that would consume you all in time. And when it does, Eire will only be the greater."

"Honor is the greatness of Eire," Fergus responded with deep intensity. "You'll not see that you mean to destroy what gives our strength to us. We are a people whose wills are our own, and that is where the spirit of this land lies. If I've no choice but between your Eire or mine, I'll be the starving wolf hunting the broad forest alone before I'll become a tended cow grazing the meadows in a herd."

"Then you will not survive," Calatin grated harshly. "And you will find there's little you can do to save yourself."

"That's bold talk to be coming from you now, Enchanter."

"What, do you intend to simply kill me here?" Calatin asked, looking pointedly at the Exile's sword.

Fergus glanced down at the weapon he still held, forgotten in the argument. He looked back to meet the other's eyes and shook his head.

"No, Calatin. I'll kill no unarmed man, no matter what the cause. That is a part of the honor which you see as barbaric."

Calatin shook his head and smiled disdainfully.

"You've not learned anything, have you, MacRogh? Once more you prove the foolishness of your own belief. If you see your way as right, you should kill me without another thought, knowing it is best for all of Eire. But your own private sense of honor keeps you from it. As long as you never see the absurdity of that, it will destroy you at the last."

"I've no need to kill you," Fergus said. "I'll reveal you to Meave. I know now that her ends cannot be as yours. You've made an error in telling me of them. She'll not accept your help once she understands."

Calatin merely shrugged his shoulders. "Knowing my purpose will give you little you can use against me."

"Can you tell me you're not bothered by my threat?"

Fergus asked, perplexed by the druid's continued self-assurance.

"I've said before that there's nothing you can do, so long as your honor protects me."

"Your visions and your arrogance have made you a madman, then," Fergus cried. "You will be finished now."

"It may be so," the Enchanter replied. "Your chance to find out is at hand. The queen is coming!"

Chapter Thirty-Two
DECISION

The queen's chariot raced from the camp's main avenue into the open area, sliding to a stop before the royal dais. Behind the driver stood Meave, glaring down upon the druid and Fergus. Her anger was magnified by her appearance, for her cloak was torn, her tunic and weapons covered in blood, her fair, white arms splattered elbow-high in still gleaming crimson.

Standing thus, in the throes of her battle-rage, flushed with her exertions, she was like some personification of Eire itself; both beautiful and terrible at once.

"What is this here?" she demanded of the confronting men.

"MacRogh blames me for his defeat," Calatin said before the Exile could speak. "He came here to kill me in revenge."

Meave looked at the drawn sword in Fergus's hand, then lifted her spear in a swift move to point at the Exile's breast.

"Put up your sword, MacRogh. You've given me just cause already to strike you down."

"No, my Queen!" Fergus protested. taken off his guard by the druid's unexpected ploy. "I'm not the one who is your enemy."

"Strange words from someone who retreated for no cause and lost a certain victory over Ulster. I thought that at least I had your loyalty still. Now I see I was wrong."

"Meave, it is the very reason why we fought which made me withdraw. I've discovered that the reason for this war is false. The Enchanter has brought us into it by the same means he used today to trick my men into the fighting. It is all against our will!"

Calatin laughed. "You think that Meave will believe such a tale; that I could influence you, of all men?"

"He lies, Meave," Fergus said in desperation. "He's betraying us at every turn!"

"Fergus, put up your weapon now," Meave ordered wrathfully. "For, of you two, the proof of your actions supports the loyalty of only one."

Resigned to defeat, Fergus shook his great head sadly and returned his sword to its sheath.

"I'll put up my blade," he said, "and I'll not pull it again in this war. It is over, Meave. If you take his part and will not listen to me, then any bond I had with you is ended."

"What do you mean?" she asked.

"My men and I will be leaving you. Fight this war yourself if you wish, but don't be thinking it will be easy to win."

"Ulster is beaten now," she said. "The withdrawal of your Exiles has given them only a temporary reprieve. More than half of their forces are bloodied."

"But they've a new spirit," he told her. "They have something that will give them more power than all their warriors made whole again. Look. Look, both of you!"

Queen and advisor looked across the plain to the lines of Ulster. Before the ranks of waiting men they saw a warrior riding, restlessly, back and forth while he watched the host of the men of Eire.

"Who is that bold warrior?" Meave asked, not able to see him clearly at that distance. But Calatin knew at once who it was, and a faint uneasiness flickered in him for the first time.

"It is the Hound," he said tonelessly, knowing now what had broken the spell put upon the Exiles. "I should have guessed it."

"Aye, Cuculain," Fergus said. "He's no dead man. But his return here, like some black spirit of revenge, will do more to frighten your men than twice the army of Ulster at its best. Good fortune to you, Meave. You are a fool if you go on."

At that he turned and mounted again into his chariot, ordering it back to join his men.

In shock and dismay Meave looked from the departing Exile to the hero who rode back and forth impatiently before his host.

"How can he be alive?" she cried. "How can that charmed Hound be still alive?"

"He is a man of powers I could wish to understand," murmured Calatin. "He is more dangerous than any other man."

Meave looked after her commander again. "Fergus broke off the fight because of his old friendship to this Hound. That's clear enough to me now. He means to abandon us for Ulster."

"He means no such thing," a voice interjected from the dais behind them.

Meave and Calatin turned to see the figure of the king, who had sat unnoticed through the heated exchanges below him. He had not spoken up during the revelations made by the druid, for Fergus had expressed his own determination to expose Calatin to Meave once she returned. But the swiftness of events had prevented that, and it was left to Aileel to warn his wife.

"Meave, Fergus is needed now more than ever," he said. "If you force him to leave, others will go with him, believing you have lost the strength to rule."

She saw the truth in that. The careful alliance was already in confusion, and that would deepen as the fear of Cuculain returned. It was largely the strength of Fergus and his continued loyalty to her that had kept unity in the four provinces this far. If he should now depart, the whole alliance would be shattered, as might a nest of eggs, in one, sharp blow.

"But I cannot trust him now," Meave reasoned, climbing from her chariot. "Even if he wished to stay, I could not trust him now."

She mounted to the royal platform, Calatin following close behind.

"Fergus is more loyal than any man you have," Aileel argued.

"How can any man of honor truthfully say that after what has taken place?" countered the druid.

"Meave, I heard what happened here before you came," Aileel insisted. "Fergus means you only good."

"Those are the ramblings of an age-weakened mind," Calatin said. "Meave, Fergus is a traitor. You've only my help left to you."

"No!" Aileel thundered. He had arisen, and the swiftness of his move and the threatening aspect he now displayed were like those of a dark sea storm suddenly risen on the horizon of a cloudless day.

"No, Meave," he cried again. "There is another you must beware who seeks only to . . ."

Then, and for only an instant, Calatin turned his eyes away from Meave and threw his gaze toward Aileel with the force and savagery of a hard-cast spear. A vast and an unchecked fury filled that look.

"Quiet, old man!" he said in a voice that for that same, single moment became a hard, striking edge.

The words and the look cut into Aileel's aging body like frozen iron. He was thrust back into his seat by the sudden spasm of his clenching muscles and his fragile strength was driven from him. He sagged down on the couch, unable to speak further.

Calatin turned his gaze back upon Meave and found her reaction one of anger.

"Who are you to be speaking so to my king? What is it you've done to him?"

"I've only silenced him," Calatin assured her, but with no apology in his tones. "We've no time for his misdirected intentions and loyalties. We alone know where this war stands now. Its outcome is for us to decide, and without delay."

"And what can we decide?" she asked him wearily. "Little except whether to try to fight Ulster or come to terms with her."

"There is one other thing," he told her with such presumption that it astonished her. "Only one thing needs to be accomplished to win this victory for us. . . . with no one's help!"

"One thing?" His words were so absurd that, even with the grimness of her plight, she felt like laughing. "In this chaos of contending wills only you could ever dare to make such a claim."

"My Queen, think! A single man now holds Ulster together. It is the same man who has blocked us all along. I can destroy him. I can remove Eire's fear of him and put fear upon the Red Branch instead. Without Cuculain they can be defeated by the army of Connacht alone, and led by you! All Eire will then be forced to see how strong Meave's dominion is."

"You draw a worthy image, Calatin," Meave said musingly. But then she looked upon her advisor with a doubt in her eyes. "Yet, it's more than once before you've promised me Cuculain's head. He still wears it."

"This time, my Queen, I'll take it myself. My own power will be balanced against his, and then we will see how long this Hound survives!"

"But, if you mean to use some trickery," Meave said, "what honor will our victory have?"

"My Queen, what honor will there be in the failure of your host? You must do what is best for the rest of Eire. They will never know what means you've used to win. They will only know what benefits they've gained, and who secured them. Meave, you have only my one, final chance to save this, or never more dream to be more than a tuath queen . . . if your chieftains will allow you even to keep that!"

She felt a twisting pain deep within her at those words. He had touched an elemental part of her and, as she examined it, she realized it was the only thing that was truly herself. Fergus had been right to say she could have nothing else within her. Too many years of care and labor had been spent nurturing her subtle mind and vigorous spirit to create a force no man might challenge. She would not see it go so easily, and her certainty in that drove out all other thoughts and fears from her.

"Your chance is granted you, Calatin," she said. "But, mark this: if you fail, we will be done. If I survive, I will be forced to come to terms with Ulster. And if I die, it's your head that will be sitting a spike by the side of mine."

"My Queen, there is little fear of that!" he said, smiling. "I'll be about making my preparations at once. You'd best see to your king, now. The activities of the day seem to have wearied him."

As Calatin moved away, Meave went to Aileel who sat still slumped on his royal couch, too weakened to move, yet glaring after the druid with dim eyes lit by a flame of hate.

"He will destroy us surely, Meave," he told his wife. "He brings the chill of death into my bones."

Meave took his hand and held it tightly in both of hers.

"Heavy clouds are drawn upon the sun today," she said to comfort him. "There is a chill upon all of us."

Fergus MacRogh had rejoined his warriors at once and ordered their withdrawal from the host. Now he paced among them impatiently, watching as the Exiles struck their tents and gathered their equipment.

They were well along with this process when Lewy MacNeesh appeared, a look of bewilderment clouding his young face.

"Fergus, what are you meaning here? You're not intending to quit the fight?"

"I am, Lewy," he answered uncompromisingly.

"But, you're sworn to Meave, as we all are. Your Exiles are looked to by all of us."

"I'm sworn to a hosting meant to war on Ulster for injury done by her. That purpose is a false one contrived by the Enchanter to serve his own ends."

"What?" cried Lewy, only the more bewildered by this. "Tell me what you've found!"

Fergus did that, relating everything the ard-druid had said and what had created the war with Ulster.

"If we continue the battle now," he concluded, "we'll only be serving Calatin's purposes. If we destroy Ulster, then he'll seek to control all Eire through Meave. If all of us are destroyed, it will leave him and his own power ascendant."

"How can we stop him if all of that is true?" asked Lewy.

"Only one way now. Meave will not listen to me. We'll have to end this war ourselves and leave the druid no way to act. The four provinces are badly bloodied and afraid. Their hard pressed unity is near its breaking point. If we decide to leave, others will follow. The host of Meave will scatter to the ends of Eire like a flock of blackbirds startled by a thunderclap."

Lewy listened and grew suddenly very tired. He looked down at his sword and thought of all the courageous lives it had taken that day.

"And all of this was for a worthless cause," he murmured, then looked up to Fergus with cold determination in his heart. "Well, no more of it will I or my warriors take part in. If your Exiles withdraw, mine will follow. And after us the rest will surely disband."

"Leaving our druid with no one to bend to his will or play his tricks upon," Fergus added.

"By all the gods! Look there!" a voice cried out, and the two chieftains turned at once to see what might have brought such a note of fear into its tones.

They saw at once what it was. From within the camp itself a great cloud had appeared; a heavy cloud, dark as if a hundred violent storms had concentrated all their force in it.

It had been stationary when the warriors first saw it looming above the tents, but now it began to move slowly forward through the camp. As it approached the ranks of the host of Eire, the men pressed back from it in a terror which increased as the cloud passed. For, while a storm, however violent, brings fresh winds and life-giving rain, this black cloud exuded only a foul and clinging odor like that of things long dead and well decayed.

It passed the ranks of the men of Eire and rolled onto the plain, and all the warriors watched it motionless, frozen with an icy fear of it.

Across the plain, before the ranks of his men, Cuculain still rode aimlessly, uncertain of what he must do next. The war seemed deadlocked now, and he could not find any sign to indicate who was the real enemy he had to face.

Then he saw the darkness moving forward out of the host of Eire.

Like a mist it appeared to him, but so solid and black that it blocked out any sign of earth or sky and seemed to swallow all light. Yet in its depth flickered a strange illumination of its own, throwing distorted shadows of nameless things that shifted about within.

So real was its illusion of weight and mass that, as it ponderously advanced, it became like some vast machine of war that would bear down and crush anything which came into its path.

Transfixed stood the warriors of Ulster, stricken deeply with fear by this unknown force. Their ordered ranks were turned to a tangled confusion as their chariot horses, mad with panic, fought to move away. Cuculain, too, felt terror rise in him as the shapes within this thing recalled to him the specters which had come to plague him at the Oun Dia.

Still, the young warrior knew that here, at last, was the thing that he must face.

"We must attack that, Laeg," he told the charioteer in a toneless voice.

That faithful man looked to him as if his master had gone mad himself.

"What, attack that? Why, it's big enough to swallow the whole of Emain Macha. What might we do to it?"

"I've no more idea than you," Cuculain said with resignation, his grim look fixed upon the advancing cloud. "We'll know that better once we've entered it."

"I had an idea you might be suggesting that," Laeg said unhappily. "Well, let's be at it, then."

Laeg was taut with his fear of the thing, but his trust in his master overcame his unreasoning need to fly. He lifted the reins and urged the horses toward the clouds. The fearless beasts, the Gray of Macha and Black Shanglan, went ahead without hesitation, but as they neared the moving darkness, Cuculain ordered Laeg to rein them in.

Now, from the depths of it, voices could be clearly heard. The moaning of tortured men, the screams of the insane, the cries of children in agony were blended there, as if the homeless spirits of the earth were gathered, waiting to claim another for their own.

"Enter . . . enter," they whispered together in a single voice that rose and fell from shriek to rumbling in a continuously changing tone. "We will take you away to be lost . . . forever. No Tir-na-nog . . . no everlasting life . . . no glory for you then. Only an everlasting death . . . to be forgotten . . . to be lost . . ."

Cuculain hesitated before the evil there, before the overwhelming sense of death that pervaded the darkness in its sights and odors and sounds. But then a clean wind arose about him, blowing back the stench of decay, and a woman's bright voice, filled with the promise of life, spoke close to his ear. It was a voice that he knew well, come to bring him assurance once again.

"Sentanta, you must strengthen yourself. You know now that your enemy is here. It and its evil brood are hidden in those black clouds, and only you can see it as it truly is. You must fight, not for yourself or the Red Branch but for all of Eire. If you lose today, then this land will no longer see heroes and peaceful meadows. It will become a land of marsh and fen where there live things monstrous and foul, and those men who survive will be few and base and never more free. Go, and the Riders of the Sidhe will go with you, to dispel the evil cloud and help you find what lies within."

Cuculain listened to these words and was invigorated by the cool, brisk wind upon his face. He pulled his sword from its sheath and slung his shield upon his arm.

"I must go in alone," he said to Laeg. "I'll not risk you or my brave steeds in this."

"No, Cuculain," Laeg protested, though it took his whole will to overcome his own fear and to bring himself to speak. "It may be this infernal storm will swallow two with the ease of one, but I'll not let you go without my help."

Cuculain smiled at his charioteer with deep affection, for he knew what courage it had taken to say that. But then he shook his head.

"I'd like to have you beside me, Laeg, I'll not deny it. Even so, I'm not giving you any choice in this. That cloud may hide some real force, but its power of illusion is greater yet. It might confuse your mind and make you more a hindrance than a help. I'm sorry, my friend, but you must stay here."

Without waiting for further argument, the Hound climbed from the chariot and marched boldly toward the cloud. That vast darkness now had stopped its own advance and seemed to wait before him, the black fog churning and boiling madly as if in restless anticipation of his coming.

As he reached the edge of the cloud, fingers of it reached out to clutch greedily at him and draw him in to be engulfed by it. He felt he had entered a charnel house piled with new dead, haunted by spirits newly ripped from their mortal selves. The strong smell of putrid flesh enveloped him and the images of the dead gibbered at him from the roiling blackness while their dying cries echoed about him in a continuous, eerie din.

Cuculain took a final step forward and vanished from the sight of all those who watched, terror-stricken, from the ranks of the facing hosts.

Chapter Thirty-Three
THE DARKNESS

When Cuculain entered the mist, he was attacked at once by a host of warriors who came at him out of the concealing blackness. He had expected to find some unnatural force within, and what he faced was indeed as dreadful as what he had anticipated.

Dead men these warriors seemed; whole battlefields of dead torn from the corrupting earth. Their faces were set rigidly in the agonized lines of their death throes and the cold horror of the nameless grave gleamed in their staring, empty eyes. In rank after rank they came upon the Hound, seeking to overwhelm him with their mass.

Cuculain moved against them, but he made little progress. Though he fought desperately to cut his way through them, he found these beings almost impossible to stop. Blows that would have killed a mortal man had little effect on them. Again and again his blade sank home in their decaying bodies and they reeled away, only to come back again, clawing at him, trying to drag him down. Cuculain literally hacked the beings apart, and still they moved against him, their gaping wounds exuding the slime of their corruption to make worse the stench of death in the air about.

Soon the young Hound was covered with the filth of them, surrounded by the odor of decay. It sickened him, nearly gagging him. His revulsion and his growing weariness began to have their effect upon his thoughts. He felt abandoned, alone, left to be overwhelmed by this terrible host.

Fear of the dead edged forward from the deepest

shadows in Cuculain's mind. His nightmares of the past days came alive once more, and he found himself searching the ranks of attackers as he fought, looking for the faces of men he had killed. He wondered when the Nearas would appear, holding their blackened, leering heads before them. He asked himself when young Eiderkool would come, his proud dress tattered, his fine looks rotted to formless clay. He shouted for the towering Lok MacFavash to challenge him from amongst the other walking horrors. He expected all of them to come against him now.

"Ah, Faythleen," he cried in anguish toward a sky hidden in swirling mists, "where is your comfort when I've such need of it?"

Then a thrust spear grazed past him and he realized his wild imaginings had made him careless in his guard. He took a firmer hold upon his thoughts and told himself these beings were part of some illusion whose sole purpose was to confound his mind. He recognized that same cleverness at work which he had sensed before, that same use of trickery to gain an advantage upon him. It was the very danger that the Sidhe had warned him of, and he had to destroy it somehow.

He pushed ahead more rapidly through the mass of living-dead, his battle consciousness fixed wholly on the destruction of the darkness. He seemed to move more easily, and the Riders of the Sidhe, as a fresh wind, were better able to dissipate some of the pall of death.

Finally he reached the center of the darkness. The cloud swirled all about him there. The specters swept against him from all sides, forcing him to turn and turn constantly, swinging his blade about him in wide, gleaming arcs. Around his head the winds of the Sidhe circled, too, fighting to counteract the mist.

All the malevolent power of that mist was directed against him then. All of the forces it contained, real or not, were turned inward on the center where he stood. Above him streams of energy, like lightning bolts, tried to reach down to him, only to burst on the protecting canopy created by the Sidhe. About him the army of the dead moved faster, closer, spinning around him in a constant flow that blended the grotesque faces into one surrounding menace and made him dizzy with his own constant turning as he fought to keep them all at bay. To his disoriented mind it seemed the ending of the world he witnessed there. The screams of its people, its wakened dead, the explosion of the stars, and the madness of the winds. It rose to a great peak in one, total effort to crush this single men who defied its power.

For long moments Fergus MacRogh had stood with the rest of the warriors, frozen with shock, staring at the darkness on the plain. But then Cuculain had advanced to challenge the vast thing alone and the Exile had been moved to action himself.

He leaped into a driverless chariot that stood nearby, lifted the reins and urged the horses toward the ominous mists. The fearful animals were reluctant to move but, with threats and cracks of the reins, the chieftain drove them on across the meadows. As he drove he cursed his foolishness in thinking that the druid could be so easily thwarted. Now it was due to him that this Enchanter's darkness threatened Ulster, and he could not let Cuculain face Calatin's trickery without help, even if it saw them both destroyed.

He was still some distance from the brooding cloud when he noted a changing in the look of it. The flickering lights had intensified until they were like lightning flaring continuously within a towering thunderhead. And the cloud was moving faster than before, coiling on itself as if crosswinds whipped it in opposing directions at once. A struggle was in progress there. A struggle between forces vaster than any hosts man had yet produced. It was the storms of two great seas met in collision, the spirits of the earth and air contending for dominance. The violent rending of the atmosphere spawned gales and cyclones that battered at the approaching Exile.

Then it ended.

In an explosion soundless save for the howling of the winds, the darkness was torn apart. Some force within seemed to blow the cloud outward in all directions, ripping it to streaming tatters that dispersed at once. The winds died, leaving a stillness that lay upon the empty plain, a silence that was oppressive in its contrast to the violence just past.

The horses of Fergus lost their fear and he could turn them directly toward where the darkness had lain. He pushed them to a hard run, desperate to discover what the chaotic storm had left in its wake.

Far ahead of the Exile on the plain, Cuculain stood where the heart of the darkness had seethed moments before. But the power that had held together the giant illusion had faltered and failed and the fair winds had destroyed the clouds. Suddenly the scene had become clear to him. He saw his adversaries strewn about him on the trampled meadows and looked for the first time upon the true form of the treacherous enemies who had peopled the evil mist.

He stood in the center of a circle of strange dead whose thin, twisted forms and sprawled attitudes in death made them seem more like dry twigs snapped and thrown carelessly upon the ground. Yet, for all their frailty, he realized that they had created the deadly illusions in the mist, and there was no pity in his heart for them.

Then he saw that one of them still lived. One figure stood before him on the field, its back to him, its body enshrouded in a long cloak of many hues, like some great bird huddled upon the ground.

Immensely weary, but resigned to make an end to his loathsome task, Cuculain started toward the figure, sword and shield raised to ward off any attack. But as he approached, the man turned and revealed a face that smiled on the Hound with gentleness and warmth.

"Fardia!" Cuculain cried in astonishment. He stopped, looking in amazement at the image of his friend.

His reason, still muddled by the deluding mists, told him there was something terribly wrong in this. He had expected to see the faces of those he had slain in the mist, and now one had appeared. Yet, it was no decaying corpse that stood before him. This man was real, alive, flushed with health and beaming with pleasure as at a bright spring day.

"Fardia, is it alive you are?" he asked. "Are you meaning to challenge me or give me help? Tell me, Fardia. Tell me as my friend."

The young Firbolg's image only smiled. His arms lifted in what seemed to Cuculain was a welcoming gesture and he started forward.

Cuculain knew he must make no mistakes now, but his troubled mind left him in uncertainty. He stood unmoving, his eyes fixed on his friend's face while he relived again all of the tortures of the past days, all of the agony at Fardia's death. And, while he stood thus, captured by his thoughts, the form of Fardia, smiling, always smiling, moved closer to him.

But Fergus MacRogh, racing toward the two figures in his chariot, did not see the form of Fardia. Instead he saw Calatin advancing grimly on a strangely passive Cuculain with a spear upraised in one hand to strike.

"Cuculain, watch yourself!" the Exile cried.

The young Hound turned his head to see the war-car charging toward him, guided by the giant MacRogh who seemed like some ancient, avenging god, his mane of fiery hair billowing about his face to make a blazing halo of battle light.

Fergus pulled out his sword as he came in, ready to strike at the druid as he passed by. But Calatin acted more swiftly. He jumped aside from the plunging vehicle and, as it passed, thrust his thick spear-tree through the wheel spokes. It locked the wheel at once, throwing the car over. The chariot-pole broke, releasing the horses and leaving a tangled, splintered wreck of wood and iron, with Fergus MacRogh half-buried beneath its weight.

Stunned by the swiftness of these events, Cuculain took an instinctive step toward the chariot to help. Then he stopped, bewildered, looking from the struggling figure of MacRogh to the figure of Fardia. What madness was it that had seized them all?

The struggling Exile felt he was unhurt, but he could not free his legs. He pulled himself up on his arms and shouted a desperate warning to the Hound.

"Beward that man! He means to kill you."

"Beware him?" Cuculain repeated vaguely, looking at the still smiling face whose eyes had once more returned to meet his own. "But . . . he is Fardia."

"No!" the Exile cried. "He is Calatin!"

The name brought all of it home to Cuculain. It blew

away the concealing mist laid on his mind as the winds of the Sidhe had driven away the darkness. He looked into the black eyes, finally seeing what they really held within. For the first time in days his mind was fully clear, his uncertainties gone. He understood, and he was again a man of his own will.

"It's not Fardia you are," he said. "Fardia is surely dead, his heart split by my spear. Yet, I could have believed he was still alive, for I wish it so much. But now I see that it wasn't myself who killed him. You confuse men. You make them believe what isn't real. You use their own emotions and honor against them. It was you and your illusions killed my friend. It was your illusions that have been haunting me all along. But no more, Calatin. I know who you are and what you are now. Your powers will not be fooling me any longer. There's nothing more that you can use against me!"

As Cuculain spoke, the image of Fardia before him shimmered and fell away like a shed skin, leaving the Enchanter revealed.

It was no defeated man that Cuculain faced.

The Hound had expected to see another thin and frail sorcerer, like those he had destroyed, hidden beneath this disguise. Instead he faced a large and solid man who showed no sign of fear. Indeed, the Enchanter smiled with a strange satisfaction and threw back the many-colored cloak which draped him. Beneath it were the trappings of a warrior: armor and harness and jeweled sword hilts.

"You are a gracious lad," Calatin snarled, "to give me the role of beaten when your rescuer lies helpless and you face me alone. I don't know what magic you've used to counter mine, but I am tired and irritated by your continued survival. I've no need of enchantments. I have a method more direct!"

He whipped the bright cloak from his shoulders and flung it aside. Purposefully he drew his sword and short-sword from their scabbards and dropped into a fighting position, the weapons balanced easily in his large hands.

"It will be my own pleasure to destroy you and be finished with you both at last!" he said.

Cuculain eyed him appraisingly. His experience told him that it was no untrained warrior faced him now, but a combat veteran, larger and fresher than himself. Calatin's carriage and address were those of a fighting man, and his well-conditioned body was as hard and smoothly muscled as those of the finest warriors Cuculain had faced. Warily, the Hound lifted his sword and shield and moved in.

As the two closed, Fergus MacRogh, hopelessly pinned beneath his broken chariot, could only look on in frustration.

It was a long and a brutal fight. The determined adversaries moved constantly about the field, slashing and beating at one another as each struggled to seize the offensive. But slowly the larger man began to gain the upper hand against the Hound. For all Cuculain's strength and skill, he could not match the calculated onslaught of the Enchanter, who was now fighting solely for his own ends. Never had Cuculain felt such force directed against him and, though he was filled with hatred for this vile deceiver, he could not help but experience awe at the determination with which his opponent was trying his last.

Realizing he could not win by direct assault, Cuculain began to analyze Calatin's style of combat. He gauged Calatin's strokes and felt for his weak spots, seeking an opening while saving his own strength for the point when Calatin's would falter.

Fergus watched Cuculain's hesitant work and saw with horror that his friend had been forced to the defensive. Desperately he tried to drag himself from beneath the wreckage, but his legs were solidly pinned. His sword had been lost in the crash, but as he shifted himself he found that he could reach the double-bladed ax at his belt. He pulled it free, hoping to cut himself from the shattered car.

Calatin noted the Exile's movements then, and realized MacRogh might free himself. He knew he had to finish Cuculain quickly or possibly be faced with two opponents. He redoubled his effort, throwing in all his power, striking out with both swords to knock Cuculain down. The young warrior let himself be pushed back and only parried the attack. Then the Hound's shield dropped, exposing his neck and shoulder. Calatin saw the opening at once and swung his longsword in a vicious cut at the vulnerable point.

But the move had been a feint on Cuculain's part, calculated with an end in mind. As the Enchanter's blade swept in, the Hound stepped sideways from its path and lifted his shield high. The descending longsword hissed harmlessly past the young Ulsterman. Backed by Calatin's savage power it struck the ground, sinking its point deeply into the sod. At that same instant Cuculain made his planned reply.

Parrying Calatin's shortsword with his own, he slammed his shield down upon the buried weapon. He'd meant to trap the druid close to him and drive home a lethal thrust before the other could pull away. But the brass rim of his thick shield snapped Calatin's blade close to the hilts.

Armed only with the shortsword now, Calatin staggered back from his opponent. He crouched and eyed Cuculain a long moment as if calculating his chances. Then, suddenly, he came erect and threw his remaining weapon down upon the ground.

Cuculain was surprised by this action but he remained wary. He stood waiting, weapons uplifted to counter any fresh assault.

"What trickery is it you're about?" he asked.

"No trickery," the druid replied, calm as if he had not just been engaged in a taxing fight. "I simply yield to you."

"You yield?"

"Of course. I said I'd try whatever means I could. This one has failed. I cannot beat you and my death would gain me nothing. Or . . ." he eyed the Hound quizzically, "will you kill me anyway?"

Cuculain was left at a loss. "How can I kill a man who will not fight?"

Calatin smiled in satisfaction. "I knew it would be so. None of you will learn. You'll yet be destroyed."

"Destroyed?" Cuculain looked suspiciously around, expecting to find some strange, new threat descending upon him.

"Ah, not now, my Hound," Calatin assured him. "But when the time is right for me, I'll yet find the proper means."

Cuculain shook his head. "I do not understand."

"You never will!" Calatin said, then he began to laugh. He laughed uproariously, throwing back his head. He laughed at this fool before him . . . at all these fools.

Then he stiffened. The sound of laughter stopped abruptly, replaced by a sharp intake of breath. His lifted head snapped back and he fell forward against Cuculain. Startled by this, the warrior stepped away and Calatin toppled heavily to the trampled grass of the broad meadow. From his back protruded the heavy ax which had struck him down.

Cuculain looked from the weapon to the face of Fergus MacRogh who still lay trapped beneath his chariot. The gazes of the two men locked. There was no need to speak. Cuculain saw in the Exile's eyes the anguish at what he had done and understood the sacrifice that had been made to do it. He knew that Fergus had seen the danger more than he and had acted when he could not.

"Thank you, Fergus," he said simply.

The pain in the other's eyes faded at that and a faint smile appeared at the corners of his lips. Then the Exile spoke in a brisk, impatient voice.

"Well, then, how long will you stand there staring at me? Are you too fatigued by your little exercise to give your old teacher some help in getting from under this pile?"

Cuculain grinned and ran to the wrecked car. With the effort of both men the chariot was shifted and Fergus pulled himself free. He rose, but found his legs numbed from the weight that had laid on them. Cuculain gave him a supporting arm and, together, they walked to the body of the druid. For a moment they stood silent, looking down on the still form. It seemed very small and unimportant in the center of that vast expanse of ravaged plain.

"He meant a strange fate for us all," Fergus said at last. "He might have succeeded, too."

"He was a powerful man, Fergus," said Cuculain. "Powerful in ways we may never know."

"He is nothing but another dead warrior now," Fergus replied quietly. "Another man killed in a senseless war." He looked about him at the littered battlefield and the bloodied hosts. "All of this was his doing. Its purpose is finished with his life."

"Is it finished?" Cuculain asked.

The Exile nodded. "Aye, it is. Meave will have to make terms with Ulster now. None of the other province chieftains will trust or support her after this. For that I'm sorry."

For a moment the regret showed in his face. Then Fergus looked down upon the druid once more, and the memory of the suffering Calatin had caused drove the sorrow from him.

"I'm sorry for Meave," he said coldly, "but I'm not sorry this Enchanter's influence is ended. Let's be rid of him and his black sorcery for good. We'll burn his body and those of his sons on a fire of their own druidical wood and scatter their ashes to the winds."

"Cast them to the sea," Cuculain advised. "He was never of our soil."

"The wind and waves of the sea have a way of returning such drifting elements to us," Fergus said.

Cuculain smiled grimly. "No matter. His part in this is ended."

The wind, which had been still since the destruction of the darkness, lifted about them again. It seemed to fly away from them in all directions at once, fanning the grasses of the plain, dying away finally, and for good.

"It is all ended," Cuculain added softly. "The hosting of the Sidhe is disbanded now. Their riders have gone home."

NOTES

This story is a fiction, a tale of adventure and fantasy. Yet, though its central characters and events are drawn from legends, the culture in which it is set truly existed in Eire.

Over two thousand years ago, and for millennia before, the Celtic peoples held undisputed sway in Ireland and in much of what we now call the Western world. They were a strong and a proud culture with a highly developed appreciation for learning and the arts. The branches of their tribes on the continent were destroyed, buried by the Romans who became the recognized heart of Western civilization. But in Eire the Celtic race survived and preserved a remnant of this separate world intact.

Still, for a time, even that was almost lost to us. The Irish, beaten and dominated for too many years by an outside force, had to suppress their own origins to a great extent. Studies of Western civilization and its arts included the Classic and the Christian contributions, but ignored the Celts.

Ironic fact, since the legends provided by those same Celts served as a basis for so much that most of us in the Western world have known with affection since our childhoods. For King Arthur and Robin Hood find their roots there, as well as the tales of faerie that Spenser and Shakespeare and Barrie found so fascinating. And when the Irish found their freedom again and created a Renaissance early in our century, it was in these ancient legends that Yeats and Synge found an expression of Ireland's unique soul. Even the sword-and-sorcery fiction which flourishes today owes its spirit of magic and heroism to these ancient tales.

A great many legends came from the Celtic race. They traced the history of the island called Eire from its first invaders to the coming of Christianity; an event which marked the final decline of this extraordinary people. The story of the war between Ulster and the rest of Eire is, itself, only part of a much larger collection of tales revolving around the Red Branch and its great hero Cuculain. For those interested in the legendary events that provide the motive for the story told here, the following outline will, hopefully, suffice.

We are dealing with a time about that of the birth of Christ, although the flood that tiny ripple produced would not reach Eire for several hundred years. In that far western island it was the high-tide of the Celtic world.

Ireland had long since been divided into four provinces—Connacht, Leinster, Munster and Ulster—each ruled by an Ard-Rie who held sway over a loose confederation of highly individual clans. A supreme High-King of Eire, chosen and empowered by the joint agreement of the province kings, administered to them all from his seat at Tara na Rie, a great dun located northwest of where Dublin is today.

This, then, was the normal state of affairs. But Ireland is a place where the normal is often in abeyance, where clouds can fill a sunny sky in moments. At the point in time that our story begins, two major events had already caused ominous thunderheads of hatred and mistrust to sweep across the seemingly peaceful land.

The first event was the death of Conaire Mor, Ard-Rie of all Eire. This fine king had controlled Eire wisely for some years, settling its disputes, bringing it greater prosperity. Then he had been treacherously slain by outlaws. The kings of Eire had been unable to agree on a suitable successor and the throne had been left vacant. A power struggle had ensued, a struggle which had seen Connacht, under Queen Meave, begin to fill the power vacuum. Slowly she had drawn her authority over the provinces of Eire, save for one: Ulster.

No one had ever dominated Ulster against its will. Under Conchobar MacNessa it had reached a pinnacle of independence and strength. And, as its power had grown, its age-old rivalry with the rest of Eire had grown as well. So, even in these early times Ulster evidenced that separateness and hardness of spirit which were to mark it through the years. But the high passions, internal struggles and unforgiving hearts which were to be its sorrow to the present day were also a part of these ancient tales. Indeed, it was these latter aspects of Ulster's nature, coupled with the pride and ruthlessness of its king, which were to cause the second of our two events.

Some years before our tale's start, the betrothed of Conchobar had fallen in love with one of the three sons of Usna. She had left Eire, accompanying the sons to Alban, leaving the king in raging jealousy. He had sworn to destroy the sons and, to get them within his reach again, had sent his Commander, Fergus MacRogh, to ask them to return with his forgiveness. The always trusting Fergus had fulfilled his mission, giving the sons his bond of protection. But once they had re-entered Eire, Conchobar had broken that bond. He'd lured Fergus away and attacked the sons, destroying them and the son of Fergus who had remained with them.

The treachery of Conchobar and the slaying of his son had driven Fergus to revolt. He had gone to war against his king, joined by his clan and other sympathetic clans in Ulster. But they had been too few. Defeated, expelled from their lands, they had entered Connacht. There Queen Meave, seeing the potential in this hard band of Exiles, had given them a home and earned their loyalty.

Thus were the conditions set, the threatening clouds all gathered, the atmosphere still but charged with energy, awaiting only some single catalyst to begin the storm which, once begun, would have to follow out its path.

While I have made use of historical facts and legendary events and characters of Celtic Eire, I have used them only as a basis for this work. *A Storm Upon Ulster* has been developed freely according to what I felt provided the most readable story in terms of contemporary, popular interests. I make no apologies for that fact. I have not intended this as a scholarly work of history or literary criticism. My primary purpose has been to provide a story that would be as entertaining to a modern reader as the ancient tales were to those who sat about the fires of the duns and heard them recited by the bards. If I have also stimulated a greater interest in this neglected part of Irish culture I will consider that a welcome bonus.

Finally, though readers have expressed little difficulty in interpreting most of the cultural elements included, some have noted a problem with certain terms and pronunciations

I therefore provide here a brief glossary of such problem words. Items for which both pronunciation and definition must be given will be found only in the second of the two lists.

GLOSSARY

Several translations of the Celtic legends were used in the research for this work. Since Celtic spellings vary widely in different translations, we have chosen those spellings which most clearly convey English pronunciation to the reader. For words which may still cause some difficulty we provide approximate pronunciations here:

Cethern	Kethern
Conchobar	Conachoor
Connacht	Con-äct
Cruchane	Croo-can
Cuailgne	Coo-alney
Cuculain	Cu-cullin or Cuhoolin ("Hound of the Smith")
Emain Macha	Avvin Maha
Lok	Lōk
Lough	Lokh (as Scottish Loch)
Maugh Turiedh	Moytirra
Meave	Meeve (trans. "She who intoxicates")
Muirthemne	Mŭr-hĕv-na
Sualtim	Sooltim

The following are terms which readers may feel require some identification for full understanding.

Alban—An island to the east of Eire now known as Britain. In Celtic time the two countries were closely related.

Ard-Rie—High-King in Eire. The word "ard" itself means "high" and can be applied to other chief positions such as bards (ard-ollaf) and advisors (ard-druid). In this case it refers to the sovereign of an entire province or the ruler of all Eire.

Beltinne—One of four major festivals that marked the four parts of the Celtic year. Celebrated on May 1, its aim was to promote the growth of cattle and crops. One ritual involved the driving of cattle between two fires for purification. Other festivals were those of Lughnasal (August 1), celebrating the harvest and the god Lugh; Imbolc (February 1), celebrating the goddess Bridget; and Samain (November 1), the Celtic new year festival.

Brehon Laws—Irish law tracts dating far back into the Iron Age. A repository of information as to the organization of Celtic society. These laws were elaborately worked out and provided a solid system of government. Some historians feel that if the Celts had followed these laws in everyday life, they might have become a strong political force. Outside pressure and internal strife might not have had such disastrous effects. Perhaps it was this fact which Calatin, as a scholar, understood more fully than the warriors of Eire.

Cathbad—Ard-Druid of Ulster under Conchobar MacNessa. As a good advisor, a teacher, an intellectual, he provides a more realistic example of the druid in Celtic society than does Calatin. Cathbad was teacher to Cuculain during the Hound's days in Emain Macha. His prophecy prompted Cuculain to take arms as a young boy that his name might be greater than any name in Ireland, though his life would be short.

Cromlich—(Cromlik) A giant burial structure largely composed of two upright stones crowned by another flat stone. Many exist today in Eire. One of the most famous is Poulnabrone, located in the Burren area of western Eire.

Dagda—Chief god of the Celts. The "Good God" of Ireland, the divine ancestor god. A powerful being and mate to the Morrigu.

Druid—A member of a class of intellectuals with broad knowledge of both the natural and supernatural realms. Though now largely associated with a pagan religion, the druids actually functioned as political advisors and scholars. Their training was long and arduous as was that of the Bardic class with which they were interrelated. They held a high position in Celtic society,

the ard-druid nearly equal to the high-king in rank.
Though they could utilize tremendous forces, few
abused this ability as Calatin did. Most, like Cathbad,
were more than content in their well-respected roles and
sought wisdom rather than power.

Espan—A land now known as Spain. The Milesians (Celts)
were said to have first come from there.

Firbolgs—An ancient race, once closely related to the Sidhe.
A division of the two caused rivalry and saw the Firbolg tribes devastated at the first battle of Maugh
Turiedh some fifteen hundred years before Cuculain's
birth. The invading Milesians found the scattered Firbolg tribes and quickly made them a subject race.

Fomeroh—In legends they were one of the earliest races to
inhabit Eire, approximately 200 B.C. They were a race
of grotesque giants and forced tribute from all other
invaders of Eire until the Sidhe destroyed them at the
second battle of Maugh Turiedh.

Fool-of-the-Forth—Thought by the Irish to be a supernatural
being capable of turning mortals mad by merely "touching" them. Possibly related to the concept of mad people as touched by the gods and somehow special.

Gesa (Ges-ä)—A concept of taboo considered important in
the Celtic society. It was the notion that some things
must be done in a certain way and that others must be
avoided altogether. (Fergus, for example, had a gesa that
he must not leave a feast in progress.) Violation of a
gesa would inevitably lead to trouble; loss of honor or
even death.

Lugh Lamfada (Loo)—Called Lugh of the Long Arm in
English. It was Lugh who led the Riders of the Sidhe
in the defeat of the Fomeroh which made the Sidhe
ascendant in Eire. Legend says that Lugh is also the
true father of Cuculain.

Milesians—Another name for the Celts. The Clan Milith is
said to have come to Eire from Spain (Espan) about
1500 B.C. The Sidhe, recognizing them as the proper inheritors of the island, retired before them into their hills
and sacred places.

Morrigu—Chief goddess of battle who could take on the crow or raven shape at will. In altered form she appears later in literature as Morgan La Fey in the Arthurian legends. Like Meave the Morrigu is both a good friend and a ruthless enemy; a fit representative of the dual nature of Eire.

Ollaf—A member of the poet class in the Celtic hierarchy of learning. The bards held an exaulted position in society as chroniclers and composers of lays, but the class of fili, of which the ollaf was the highest rank, were scholars and had some druidic abilities as well. Trained in schools, they studied twelve years to learn their craft which in part consisted of the memorization of the culture's oral literature. The ollaf was equal in rank to the lesser kings and could travel freely anywhere in the land.

Rath and Cathir—Mounds and circles of earth or stone marking ancient sites of homes and forts. They are thought to be places now occupied by the hidden Sidhe. Many of them dot the countryside of Ireland today.

Sheoguy—A place felt to be haunted. A place where one feels strongly the many mystical forces present in Eire. Many of these places also exist in Ireland today.

Sidhe (Shee)—Also referred to as the Tuatha de Dannan. A race of beings with long lives and great magical powers. They once held sway in Eire but withdrew to their hidden places when the Milesians appeared. Although they take no direct role in the affairs of man, they watch over him with interest and help (or hinder) him when the need arises. The Banshee and the Leprechaun are degenerated forms of the Sidhe.

Tailteen Fair—A great triennial fair held at the dun of Tara. People traveled from all parts of Eire and beyond to attend this event.

Tec Meadcuarta (Chok Meed-carta)—Tec is the Gaelic word for house. The Tec Meadcuarta is the central house or great hall of the dun, a place of gathering for the dun's population.

Tir-na-nog—Land of Eternal Youth. The Celtic afterlife. It is believed to be a great island in the western sea. The concept is related to that of Avalon seen in the Arthurian legends.

Tuath (Too-a)—A subdivision of a province ruled over by a lesser king or a tribal chieftain.

ABOUT THE AUTHOR

KENNETH C. FLINT is a graduate of the University of Nebraska with a Masters Degree in English Literature. For several years he taught in the Department of Humanities at the University of Nebraska at Omaha. Presently he is Chairman of English for the Plattsmouth Community Schools (a system in a suburban community of Omaha).

In addition to teaching, he has worked as a freelance writer. He has produced articles and short stories for various markets and has written screenplays for some Omaha-based film companies.

Mr. Flint became interested in Celtic mythology in graduate school, where he saw a great source of material in this long neglected area of western literature. Since then he has spent much time researching in England and Ireland and developing works of fantasy that would interest modern readers.

He is the author of two previous novels, A STORM UPON ULSTER and RIDERS OF THE SIDHE. His next novel, MASTER OF THE SIDHE, will be published by Bantam in 1985.